Lover In Stone

The Darkest Kynd Series #1

S. C. Dane

Published by
Melange Books, LLC
White Bear Lake, MN 55110
www.melange-books.com

This is for you guys—
J, H, and A.
My little pack who is everything to me.

Also, a thank you to my writers' group. We may
forget pens and paper, but we never forget
talent still needs to be honed into craftsmanship.

And finally to my editors
Sherri Good and Erin Elliot
who turned this beaut into a beauty.

Thank you, all—
You've proven there is
a We in Writer.

Once, the Kynd existed under God's grace, bearing witness to all things passing. Until the Schism, when God and Lucifer clashed and the Archangel was flung from the Heavens. Refusing to choose sides, the Kynd were damned, too. Forced to take part in the darkest realms without the touch and comfort of another, their honorable name disintegrated into the dust of history. Now they are remembered merely as gargoyles and chimerae, and in their deaths, they become monsters of stone: Grotesques. Their Chosen Ones can save them. But after enduring centuries of solitary madness, who could love something so doomed?

Chapter One

The pose didn't suit her. Although far be it from Angelia Delacroix to notice she formed the perfect imitation of a long-legged grasshopper. Not when her attention was riveted to the skin-bound book spread open in front of her.

She felt like the member of the bomb squad holding the wire snips: her breath locked in her lungs. And not because the pages of the book were fragile, either. Given its age, the darn thing had defied the ravages of time.

What worried her, and kept her from breathing, was the aura of magic surrounding the thing.

The relic sitting in front of her was volatile as a real bomb. All it would take would be one wrong move, one offensive stumble from her, and the book could do *anything.*

So, she couldn't screw up.

As it was, the only reason she sat in the same room with the ancient tome was because she was the only being it allowed to read its pages.

Like the Scriptum had an inkling of its own.

Which made it one scary so and so.

Because, let's face it, she wasn't anyone special. Not in this world of faery, vampires, shifters, and ghouls.

And Grotesques.

She would never forget to add the gargoyles and chimerae to her list of supernatural wonders. When she was younger, she used to fantasize about them, spending countless nights conjuring tales of derring-do for her Grotesque heroes.

Which was fine when you were a little kid. Playing make-believe was as normal as snot dripping from your nose. Even as a teenager, she could be excused when she'd gripped tight to her fascination, practically wallpapering her bedroom with pictures of chimerae.

Except she never outgrew her fascination.

Which made her a loser on all counts. She was a mere human, living in a realm populated by creatures with innate talents that left her wanting.

And feeling pathetically inadequate.

Ugh. Yeah. She'd polish that nugget of loveliness later. Right then, she was preoccupied with sliding her silver reading blade along the pages she was translating. She had come to the running end of an unfinished sentence about her favorite subject: gargoyles and chimerae.

So to her, the Scriptum read like a *New York Times* best-selling novel: a real page-turner. Hastening to devour more, she flicked the blade to roll the page. Only to slice her finger on the vellum—even though she'd been using her knife.

"Ooh, crap!" She jabbed her bleeding finger into her mouth, her eyes dancing like frantic maids to find something, *anything*, to dab the blood off the ancient page.

"Oh, God, oh God, how could I be so stupid?" Mortified, she jumped to her feet, tipping her stool so it clattered to the floor behind her.

The droplet of blood spread in a widening circle into the page. Like an atomic cloud.

And just as flipping devastating.

She'd marred the ancient Scriptum. With her stupid human ineptitude, she'd scarred a relic which had remained in near pristine condition for centuries.

Stumbling back, she couldn't peel her helpless stare from her blunder.

Fear snatched her breath as droplets of sweat stung her armpits and prickled the small of her back. Aro, her vampire boss, would be…enraged.

See? Pathetic. Aro would never lay a fang on her. Not when her father was Vampyre, one of the ruling Triumvirate.

Okay, so he wasn't her real father. But she'd been raised since infancy as Anton's own, and it was no secret to the vampire realm. Inept human she might be, but Angelia moved freely within her father's world.

No vampire in their right mind dared touch her.

Including Aro.

Right. Taking a deep breath to calm her panic, she bent to put her stool back onto its three feet. Then bolted upright, her hand clutched to her heart like a clichéd heroine wrapped tight in her corset and long skirts.

Singing expanded inside her head.

"Holy rum raisin ice cream." The Scriptum hummed. The voices stuck to her pulse, pulling and twisting along her veins as they sang. They magnified inside the amphitheater of her skull to the point she thought the bone would fissure and sound would blast forth like footlights—to illuminate the ceiling over her head.

Her knees buckled, as if she knelt in supplication to the concerto. Tears tumbled down her cheeks. Trembling, she reached forth, as though Jesus himself stood in glowing magnificence in front of her, and she sought the privilege of touching his modest robes.

The voices flew ever higher, and Angelia's heart strained to devour every truth, every glorious exultation…until the pounding lump of muscle stuttered, fluttered, and fibrillated.

As her vision tunneled, the Scriptum shrank into a tiny pinprick before disappearing, just like scenes in old movies ended.

Angelia cashed out like an empty register, her body folding to the flagstone floor.

* * * *

Like a gift, the Scriptum lay open upon the table above the unconscious woman. A single lamp spilled buttery light on both, assigning the rest of the narrow room to shadows where the intruder

3

lurked a few moments longer, waiting. Watching, despite the fact most of his attention was on the book, which looked no different from any other relic he'd stolen during his life.

Old. Valuable not because it was made of anything precious, but because its worth lay in what he was going to get out of it.

Power. Unlike anything he'd ever experienced.

In exchange for this book—if he could get it into the right hands.

But the man understood greed as a supreme motivator, and he would deliver the Scriptum into the right hands.

Come hell or high water.

Well, the hell would come. But not the high water.

The soulless man let his lips twist into a smile he felt nowhere within himself; an odd reflex to something sublime he couldn't emotionally fathom.

He nudged the unconscious woman's wrist with the toe of his black moccasin.

She was not beautiful.

Plain.

Definitely not vampire, or fae.

Which explained why it was she he was stealing this book from in the first place.

The man suspected enough about the Scriptum to know that few would most likely be able to touch it, let alone decipher its mystery.

But this brown paper bag of a female?

Indecent.

If he didn't have this matter of stealing the book pressing upon him, he would do her justice.

The man uncurled his fingers from the bowie blade riding his hip.

He would not cut her as he so desired to do. Yet, how remarkable she would be if only he could slide his sharp knife from one cheekbone to the other. Give her a puppet smile that would permanently grace her unexceptional face.

Only the anticipation of the payment awaiting him stayed his hand, and he stepped back from his inborn urge to carve beauty where it was lacking. He turned his attentions to the relic, to the object that, should he succeed at delivering it into the guts of Hell, would gift him an eternity of joyful sculpting.

He bothered not with wondering why the woman had been studying blank pages. That wasn't where his interest lay. The soulless man stepped over the woman to reach her worktable and closed his gloved hands over the Scriptum.

He was surprised by its heft.

For such a small, unassuming object, it seemed as though weighted with the things not written upon its blank pages.

The man yanked and lifted the tome, then slid it into a silk bag, which he then placed inside his backpack.

As he stepped back over the unconscious woman, his hand once again drifted to his hip, to his bowie knife.

Just one quick sweep of his blade.

And yet.

He would not. He could not.

His hand reluctantly slid from the cool steel of his blade.

With a stealthy tweak of the doorknob, the man slid into the dimly lit hallway. Skulking along the rows upon rows of dusty manuscripts, he made his way to one of the many dark recesses of the vaulted library, his ropes hanging as quiet and unnoticed as jungle snakes.

With practiced ease, the soulless man pulled himself upward toward the vent at the height of the thirty-foot wall. He disappeared into it as silently as he had emerged, like a spider born from one of the hundreds of billowing webs stretching like banners across the ceiling.

Bound for Hell, with the Scriptum riding safe upon his back.

* * * *

Sometimes it's a blessing to remain unconscious. At least, to Angelia's way of thinking anyway. Once she'd come to after having fainted like a wuss, she'd had to endure Aro's wrath. Which came in the form of silence. He had picked her off the floor with a grip shying just short of breaking her arm, and had her escorted to a "room" at the Triumvirate's holdings.

For her safety.

Bah!

She knew exactly why Aro had sent her here. She was to await her punishment for ruining the Scriptum. She sat on a stool in the middle of a ten-foot square cell, thinking the only thing missing from this interrogation scene was the bare bulb overhead.

Running her palms up and down her arms did nothing for her shivering as she remembered her last botched job. The details of which dug their sharp nails into her fragile ego.

She'd been in a similar predicament before, when she'd first joined the Literati.

Well, okay, it was similar only in the sense she'd effed that job up, too.

The Recovery Team wasn't even out the door before she'd inadvertently bungled the protection magic the Mage had painstakingly conjured to keep them safe. To this day, she didn't know how she'd done it, but she could remember the faces glaring at her. Each one was covered in soot, like the spell had blown up, turning the faces of her teammates into cartoon characters.

Which was kind of funny. Except no one laughed with her.

Aro had yanked her off the team faster than she could say *whoops.*

And figuratively chained her to a desk for the next ten years. Until the Scriptum had been unearthed and remained stubbornly shut for six months, even for the Demon Decipherer.

Angelia had again proven how inept she was when she'd gone into the room to ask Aro and the Decipherer a question. Somehow, she'd managed to trip on the flat stone floor and brush her fingers along the Scriptum's sealed cover as she'd thrown her hand out to catch herself.

Aro and the Demon Decipherer had watched in helpless horror as the great tome teetered precariously upon its binding.

The vampire had a flaming curse on his lips when the book split wide open to finally reveal its secrets.

Well, not quite.

The text on the immaculate vellum promptly disappeared the moment Aro ordered Angelia's clumsy ass out of the room. Which was the only reason she had been assigned to translate it.

Because the writing didn't remain for any eyes but hers.

And now those pristine pages were forever marred with a blotch of her pathetic human blood.

Angelia's insecurities assailed her as she sat on the stool in the cell. As if their weight was too much to bear, she turned in on herself, curling her body around the growing hole of humiliation, the shame that had taken up permanent residence in her gut years ago.

God, Aro was going to fry her for this.

The clank of the heavy steel door had her hopping to her feet, like she was going to kick butt. *Or run.* A more likely outcome given the strength of her spine.

The same vampire who had escorted her here came into the cell. "They are ready for you, Miss Delacroix." He bowed his blonde head as if he felt bad about her situation, offering his arm like an usher at a formal wedding.

Angelia took it, even if it was just to hold onto something to keep her hands from shaking. She felt hard muscle under the shirt sleeve and shut her eyes as she sucked up a little comfort from the solidity of it.

"Where are we going?" She peered up at a strong, tight jaw.

Her escort kept his eyes straight ahead. "The Triumvirate wishes to see you."

The Triumvirate?

Holy Moses, she was in bigger trouble than she thought. Was Aro demanding they give permission for him to release her from the contract?

Her father would be flipping cartwheels while he sang *Yes!* So, Aro would get at least one vote in the affirmative. Angelia gripped a little tighter to the young vampire leading her down the stone paneled corridor, her stomach churning as her feet turned to slippery clay.

She would be stripped of her duties. Severed from the one thing making her feel a little special in this world of super beings. Cold, familiar fingers of inadequacy clamped around her guts, just as her escort halted in front of a thick wooden door. He leaned forward to open it, revealing the stone gallery where the Triumvirate conducted their interviews.

Oh, man, this is so not good. Angelia stepped into the room, yet no one acknowledged her presence. Not a good sign at all considering the occupants of the room were hypersensitive vampires. They continued arguing as if she wasn't there at all.

7

S. C. Dane

Aro paced, his violet eyes snapping, his fangs barely sheathed.

On the dais abutting the far wall sat two of the Vampyres of the Triumvirate, Godrick and Kristov, who watched him march with bemused expressions on their faces.

The third Vampyre of the Triumvirate, her dear father Anton, remained on Aro's level. Leaning against the stone buttress nearest the dais, he rested his blonde head on his arm. The lesser vampire ignored Anton, preferring to address the Vampyres on the raised platform.

"She is a sworn member to the Literati, do not forget," Aro fumed, barely veiling his threat to the ancient members of the Triumvirate. He shook with his insubordination, yet couldn't seem to help himself. "She has pledged her oath," he seethed, his fangs lengthening.

"She is merely human!" Anton raged, slicing across the room with his claws unsheathed. The Vampyre veered from his assault at the last second, his control tamped. "She will never survive this mission." His demeanor deflated as if his body wasn't like iron.

Angelia barely tracked her father's averted assault on her boss it happened so fast.

"She is my daughter." He groaned, not caring to shield the torment of his dilemma from the others in the room. Or from Angelia, whose heart strangled in her breast to see him so defeated.

Angelia clapped her jaw shut and went straight to her father to comfort him.

She had to. He was extremely upset. She could see it in his silver eyes, the centuries weighing heavy in them when usually they sparkled bright.

The sight of them turned her blood to freezing slush.

This meeting was about her and her blunder with the Scriptum. They were convening to decide an appropriate punishment. So, what mission were they talking about?

Anton's fingers curled around her hand, and for an instant Angelia didn't know if she felt trapped or comforted. But she held her ground. Whatever retribution was due her, she'd face it. Even if she was glad her stomach was empty so she wouldn't vomit. *Much.*

Puking wasn't exactly a hallmark of bravery, so she took the tight smile her father gave her and let him lead her to a wooden chair situated

8

a little off-center of the room.

To sit? *Oh, heck, no.* She wanted to bolt.

But that would make her a coward, and she already had a long list of inadequacies chalked up against her. Angelia took the seat her father offered then watched him trudge to the dais like a man heading for the gallows. She gulped past the knot gripping her throat.

Okay, she could do this. She had signed on with the Literati knowing full well what was expected of her. Of course, her father had been beyond livid when she'd done it. He'd threatened to kill Aro as soon as he'd found out she'd daubed her blood to the contract. He'd accused the vampire of treachery and deceit. Even went so far as to say the only reason Aro would want his daughter was because she was human.

A lovely revelation that had stung like a slap. Yet, she'd refused to cry over it. So what if that was the only reason Aro and the Literati wanted her. For once in her life, being human had some merit. And Anton's fears that she'd be traipsing all over the world, going into places where only her kind could go, remained unfounded.

Angelia hadn't left her desk for ten years. No Indiana Jones adventures for her. Since her debacle with the Recovery Team, she got the drudgery, the research where the only excitement came from getting off her stool to stretch her back.

The Scriptum had been the first and only assignment where being human was an asset. And that was only because Aro and the other Literati's greedy little fingers couldn't pry the cover open.

And I've bumbled my one chance to prove my worth.

Her shame and guilt overrode her initial fear like a three-hundred-pound jockey.

"Aro, sit," Godrick commanded quietly. But then, his authority wasn't to be breached, so he didn't have to raise his voice. The chairman of the Literati plunked his butt at the long table, his alabaster fingers drumming on his briefcase.

Angelia cringed inwardly. Inside that briefcase would be her contract, with her stamp of blood on it.

"Angelia Delacroix." This time the voice that spoke carried a soft undertone. Kristov had always been kind to her.

"Yes?" She sat up straighter, facing the Triumvirate. Her poor father had paled beyond pale, throwing wide the door to her fear so it crept back in subtle as an elephant.

"We are sorry for having kept you in the dark while we weighed our decision."

Angelia decided to study her boots rather than watch Anton suffer. If she was going to face her punishment with any dignity, she couldn't look at him. Not if she wanted to keep her backbone, spindly as it was. Because he was her Papa. She'd cave like the weak little girl she was, and he would happily bundle her up in his arms to comfort the both of them.

She knew that. Anton adored her.

Even after his son had been born, Angelia still resided in the same cherished place of his heart.

"Is there anything you can tell us about the disappearance of the Scriptum, Miss Delacroix?"

Huh? Angelia dragged her gaze off her shit-kickers to gawp up at the Triumvirate. *The disappearance of the Scriptum?*

"She doesn't know a blasted thing," Aro griped from behind her.

Angelia turned to her boss, still too stupefied to play catch up.

"She was completely unconscious. And we did a mind sweep." Aro swept his hand out, indicating the two Literati ghouls who sat like well-preserved, sagacious corpses at the long table with him. "She knows nothing of the theft."

"The theft?" Angelia's jaw finally worked just enough for her to say something, but it fell back open as she stared at her boss. This meeting wasn't about her punishment? She felt the one-two punch of relief and panic. "The Scriptum has been stolen?"

She didn't need a verbal answer. Anton's distress hadn't been about the punishment she was going to receive; it was about this mission. And—ding, ding, ding—she was being assigned to retrieve the Scriptum. Hence, the mission Anton had referred to.

"Miss Delacroix, it is our understanding you are the only one capable of retrieving this artifact. Is this so?"

Angelia turned her attention to Kristov. *The only one?* "Yeah, I guess. I mean, I'm the only one who can read it." Which didn't exactly mean she was the only one who could retrieve it. Did it? Excitement revved in her belly, tingling her skin.

Was this finally it? Was this her chance to prove her worth, to show everyone she wasn't entirely useless and clumsy? She'd waited a decade for her Indiana Jones crusade and now it seemed as if it was finally going to happen.

She bowed her head so no one would see the flush of anticipation coloring her cheeks.

"You will not be expected to endure this treacherous journey alone, Miss Delacroix, if you should accept the terms of your contract."

Blah, blah, blah…*treacherous journey?*

Okay. She needed to get focused here. Indiana Jones and his stunts were fictional—she was about to embark on the real deal.

"You will be escorted through Hell by Merrick the chimera, the Guardian to Hell's Archway. Is that acceptable to you?"

Angelia didn't know whether to collapse into her chair from fright or shriek like a teenager at a rock concert.

A chimera.

Taking her straight to Hell. The real Hell. Not the figurative one.

Okay. Right. She could do this. She had been waiting ten years for such a chance and had always known that the places she could pass— where Aro and the rest of the Literati couldn't—wouldn't be pleasant.

Hell as a destination had traipsed across her imagination more than once.

But a chimera to guide her? She'd be safer than a glass of holy water at a Literati Convention.

Wait, Kristov had asked her something. She glanced up, not hiding her confusion, or her embarrassment. "I'm sorry. Could you repeat the question?"

"We asked whether your escort would be acceptable to you," Godrick repeated, his patience a trifle thin. She couldn't blame him. As much as he respected Anton, he had always wondered how the Vampyre could be so smitten with a dull-witted human.

"Ah, yes. Yes, it's acceptable to me. I mean, yes. *He* is acceptable."

Chapter Two

As he stood outside the thick double doors of the Triumvirate's gallery, Merrick the chimera wanted nothing more than to give himself a swift kick in his leather-clad ass. He was the Guardian to Hell's Archway, for Christ's sake, and he'd let the soulless thief slip right on through. On his watch.

So, now he felt obligated to answer this frigging summons from the Triumvirate and the Literati. As if he needed another reason for his rage to swell like the flood waters behind a crumbling levee.

Standing alone in the corridor, he felt the push of his claws against his fingertips, his mane thickening behind his ears. He shrugged his gargoyle shoulders, adjusting his leather coat, which helped to bind his wings safely beneath his skin so his full chimera didn't surface.

For this, too, he let his anger simmer. Merrick would never forget the day he and his Kynd had been cast from Heaven, along with the Archangel Lucifer.

The Kynd, as Witnesses, had not taken sides when Lucifer had pushed for his power play, nor when Heaven had spewed its traitors to damnation.

Yet, God had relegated them to Middle Ground, an intentionally ironic punishment underscoring where the Kynd had preferred to stand during the colossal struggle.

Condemned by God to be Hell's gatekeeper for the past two millennia, Merrick had witnessed a lot.

And he'd had enough.

His guts were swimming in the filth of Hell's madness, its terror.

His skin was getting thick, growing rough as stone—the telltale sign of what his Kynd were fated to become.

Grotesques.

He was inevitably turning to stone as thousands of his brethren already had, succumbing to the wretched isolation of his post at Hell's Archway.

Little wonder he wasn't in a rosy mood when he stepped into the gallery. And into an ephemeral wall of honey and lavender, the twin scents stopping him as if that wall were solid.

Instantly, his full chimera seethed to be let loose from its singular gargoyle form, as if his whole self needed to bask in it. Merrick pushed aside an unfamiliar fluttering in his gut to concentrate on the source of that wicked scent.

Anton's daughter.

He stifled a derisive grunt. She wasn't exactly the Vampyre's and his life-mate's daughter. She was human. Raised on milk and solid food, not blood. Quite the sacrifice for a pair of leeches, considering the babe would have made a delicate meal.

A smear of blood on Anton's pallid cheek had him eyeing the ancient one a little more carefully.

The Vampyre wept.

Merrick had seen many things in his long life, but never that. Maybe he felt a little sorry for the guy.

Just a little, though. He wasn't about to go overboard with the sympathy.

"Merrick, you've come. We thank you." Godrick's voice chimed like a crystal bell, arresting everyone's attention, including that of Anton's daughter. She lifted her gaze to Godrick, and Merrick caught a flash of worry in those dark blue eyes.

What fine, dark eyes they are. The irises were nearly black, with just enough blue to make him think of iridescent ink, reflecting the reds and golds from the flames of the wall sconces.

A man could get mired in those liquid pools.

If one were just a man.

Merrick again rolled his shoulders beneath the heavy weight of his leather coat and returned his attention to Godrick.

13

"You summoned. I answered."

The woman had settled herself off to the side of the Literati, and Merrick thought her a flowering apple tree in an orchard of shriveled trunks. She wasn't tall, but she had soft curves that caressed his sharp eyes. Her scent wafted toward him like nectar, tightening his ball sac with an urgency he'd never known.

Rather than think on that gripping conundrum and gnash his teeth into powder, he dragged his eyes off Anton's daughter to pay attention to the Triumvirate and the mission they'd hired him for.

Yet his tongue slid across the bottom of his sharp teeth as he thought about what he'd like to do to that woman's skin, which seemed creamy as, well—*cream*. A lustful twinge gripped his balls anew, forcing him to adjust his stance to ease the crush of his stiffening erection in his leather pants.

Christ.

Godrick blabbered on about something. Merrick tilted his head to focus on anything other than the bulge growing behind his buttons.

"You have agreed to descend the Circles of Hell to retrieve the Scriptum?"

"I have," he growled, biting down on the *Your Excellency* part. The Vampyres weren't his and they sure as hell weren't excellent.

"Good. Then you and the human woman Angelia will depart as soon as you collect the supplies we have prepared for you. We expect you to return to the surface within seven days' time."

The room bloomed red before his eyes, his strident erection forgotten.

"What?" The Triumvirate and Literati expected him to tote a living human through Hell? Were they daft? Such a risky undertaking had only been done three times before, and two had been under God's protection. Well, Virgil's safeguarding more precisely, but Dante's guide had been acting with permission from the Big Man Himself. The third brain-fart had just been one lucky son of a bitch.

And these morons expected him to lug around a human female as he navigated the Circles?

"You're out of your blood starved minds."

Two members of the Triumvirate stiffened and Anton drew his palm across his eyes, his distress evident. But it was Aro, the scrawny head of the Literati who whined in his ear.

"Our like cannot touch the Scriptum. It will only allow itself to be handled by humans. You will need her, *gargoyle*," he sneered. His contempt for the Kynd advertised like a red button begging Merrick to punch it.

Which gave Merrick just the little push his rage needed to resurface. He flashed his fangs, his sheer size cowering the bloodsucker as he lunged, halting a paper's thickness from Aro's stricken face. "You take that tone again when you say *gargoyle,* leech, and you won't have eyes to read your precious Scriptum." His words were barely audible within his guttural threat.

Aro cringed from Merrick's crushing weight, bending backward on one supporting leg, cutting a fabulous imitation of a café table.

It was all Merrick could do not to twist Aro's anemic neck in his hands. They itched to do it, too, his claws emerging to better hold the skinny straw in his grasp. Wresting control from God only knew where, he turned his attention back to the three on the dais, forcing his seething fury back into its cage.

"With all due respect," he snarled, not caring that he patronized the ruling Triumvirate. He barely respected the ancient Vampyres. He was as old, if not older than those three who presumed authority over him.

Merrick only answered their call out of concern for his Kynd. Because if the Scriptum held the secrets rumored to be etched upon its pages then they had as much, if not more right to it than the Literati. He would return it to that order of haggard crones only after his brethren had their chance to study it.

Maybe not even then.

"I can't drag a human through Hell," he argued.

Even if she smells as good as she does. "It will be dangerous enough without having to keep something—" Merrick ground his teeth and cleared his throat, his derision clear. "I mean *someone* else alive while I'm doing it."

He didn't look at the woman. He needed to keep his gaze drilled on the ancient trio seated in front of him. The clothing he wore had grown tight enough as it was. He didn't need it cinching his crotch. Nor did he need to dwell on why he'd thickened in that region in the first place.

"The Scriptum, it seems, won't come back in your hands."

Oh, but damn. Her voice stroked like warm silk across his skin, making his chin tilt to better indulge the caress of her tone. He ground his jaw the second he realized what he was doing.

He was acting like a dog who loved the scratch of his furry ears.

"I'll bring it back," he growled, and instantly regretted the alarm flaring in those blue-black eyes. Merrick took an unpracticed step back. "What I meant was—"

"Of course you will, Mr. Merrick," she assured him, as if she'd never flinched. "But I'm afraid that's not the issue."

Mr. Merrick. Like he wore a business suit and wasn't part gargoyle.

"Only *she* can bring it back. The Scriptum wanted her to touch it. She has to be the one to bring it back." Aro's needling grated on Merrick's one nerve as his claws pierced into his fisted palms.

Ignore him. Ignore her. Concentrate on the Triumvirate.

No better advice had ever been given. With a practiced eye, he watched the trio's every subtle movement. His sharp hearing trained on the slender thrumming of their pulses, on Anton's heartbeat.

The Vampyre suffered, yet did not speak against his daughter's participation, or Aro's assumption.

"If you don't trust me…" Merrick dangled the bait, his sly gaze holding to the three in front of him.

"It is not a matter of trust, Merrick." Anton rose, pushing his knuckles into the highly polished tabletop. "It is a matter of my daughter's safety. She must go in, but she cannot go in alone. We need you, chimera, to escort her, to keep her safe. That is all we ask." He spread his hands, as if defenseless.

Because he was. This daughter meant a lot to the Vampyre. "And the Scriptum?" Merrick challenged.

Anton hesitated less than a heartbeat, yet Merrick couldn't have missed it. He wasn't just gargoyle. His blood was an elixir of three formidable creatures, and Merrick knew the Vampyre could smell the subtle potency of the combination.

Even without being the one to escort Anton's daughter through Hell, the Vampyre would deem it necessary to respect him. It would be perilous to do otherwise.

Resignation softened Anton's expression. "I wish I could say it meant nothing. But I, too, have my duty to my kind. We will all benefit from the teachings of the Scriptum, its secrets. We cannot leave it in the hands of those who have stolen it away to Hell.

"My daughter is the one to retrieve it for us," he admitted, his breath vacating his lungs on a long exhale. Anton's silver eyes held Merrick's, and hid nothing of his fear for his adopted daughter.

Merrick locked his gaze where it was while he chewed on his predicament.

The seconds limped by.

Keep not one but two, precious items from getting destroyed? A nearly impossible feat given where he and the woman were expected to go.

"It will cost you," he finally conceded, as forthright as the Vampyre who stood at the dais.

"Anything, chimera." The deal steeped down to the two players, as if the others in the room evaporated like non-essential vapor.

Well, not all of the others. Merrick never lost the trace of the human woman's scent, of her watching him. She watched her father, too. He couldn't have missed a single gesture of hers if he tried.

Anton and the Triumvirate would pay for that, too. Why not? "When I bring your daughter back with this book, you will owe the Kynd a building in their honor. One engineered with their *retirement* in mind."

He couldn't bring himself to say their deaths. The Kynd didn't truly die. At first, anyway. They spent centuries encased in stone, perched on eroding ledges. They witnessed ceaselessly, watching the living below them until their bodies crumbled under the incessant ravages of time and weather.

Christ on the cross. Where was the deliverance from that torture? Oh, right. There wasn't one. The Kynd got the nosebleed seats to the eternal game of life. Perennial passes for every season.

"It will be done, chimera." Anton's acceptance rained on Merrick's pity party, but his attention snapped back to the fore, like a pitbull scenting blood.

Just like that? This woman meant an awful lot to the Vampyre, and he cursed that he might fathom why. Merrick risked an appraising glance toward the woman who had cost the Vampyre so much, surreptitiously observing her dark eyes pool with tears, her fingers press to her lips before they formed the words *Papa* in a dreadful sigh.

Dear God. He wanted to hold her. Not just feel her small body enclosed in his arms but to rub that honey-lavender scent all over himself.

By thunder, Anton would pay. The chimera would not rescind this deal, not when this human woman confounded him, made his body ache to do things it had never done before.

Merrick nodded his agreement then turned his attention to the rest of the Triumvirate. "You mentioned packs for the journey. We'll leave before this hour is up." He didn't wait for their reply but stalked from the stone room that had begun to press on him like a cave.

He hated the underground. But more than that, he hated that he felt as if he'd just bargained for more than what was on the table.

* * * *

That man makes walking look like a sport. The kind of sport performed by Greek athletes back in the days when the Olympics were played in stone constructed coliseums. She wouldn't sigh, gall-darn it. She peeled her eyes off the gargoyle's tight butt to watch Aro's departure, instead.

Which was like switching TV channels from Skin-emax to PBS.

She refused to think about the smug victory on the vampire's face as he hastened from the gallery. He parted with no words of gratitude, dispensed no advice, not a single word of warning for her.

Secretly? She'd enjoyed watching the guy bend over *backward,* as the chimera threatened him.

Shame on her. Aro was her boss. He had offered her a place within the Literati, albeit more for selfish reasons than for her skills as a researcher. But hey, beggars couldn't be choosers.

Besides, what words of wisdom could Aro have imparted? Her education with the Literati was supposed to have prepared her for such an eventuality as a trip into Hell.

Even if she could have never prepared for her guide.

Sure, as the only human member of the Literati she'd be expected to enter into dangerous situations by herself, and she had readied herself for it. She had trained, honed her fighting skills and her body so both would be up to any challenges she might face.

Studying her butt off, she'd learned everything she could about the beings she'd grown up with and the creatures she'd heard about while growing up with her Vampyre parents.

Just in case Aro forgave her for her first blunder.

But for all her lifelong fantasizing and wishing, she had never met a gargoyle before. Not just a gargoyle either, but a chimera, a being made up of two other creatures he kept hidden away from the rest of them.

Merrick had her just as nervous as her impending excursion into Hell.

Well, there's a fine line for you.

Not much separated Hell and the chimera. Except she didn't think Hell would have such a fine ass if it wore leather pants, nor would its long, muscular thighs flex suggestively, like they ached to be stroked by her personally.

Oh yes, if she kept thinking along those lines she'd prove *again* she wasn't worthy of the Literati. She had to stop thinking about how sexy Merrick was and start concentrating on the danger oozing out of him. She hadn't missed the undercurrent of rage swelling into the room as he'd stood on the threshold.

The chimera was menacing, and she'd agreed to walk straight into Hell beside him.

Had she been born without a brain?

Moot point now. She and Merrick would start their descent into Hell soon, and it wasn't going to be an easy trip. Peril surrounded her within and without. She'd need every scrap of her fortitude and intelligence, if she was going to resurface with the Scriptum in her arms.

And only that book in her arms. Nothing else, she swore, even if there wasn't a stack of Bibles on hand. There would be no sexy chimera in her embrace. Wasn't. Going. To. Happen.

She locked down on those thoughts like the doors on a submarine lest someone, especially Merrick, should read them. It was bad enough she felt the burn of embarrassment on her cheeks.

"Angelia."

Nothing like a father's voice to throw gasoline on the fire of her cheeks. Anton spread his arms wide for her, a faint smile of inevitability playing upon his lips.

"I'm sorry for this, Papa. Really, I am." Of course, she meant the Literati thing, not her carnal thoughts. Of which, the Vampyre would pick right up on if she didn't flush said thoughts straight into the gutter where they belonged.

Anton closed his arms around her. "Hush, now. I know. You're a grown woman, my Angelia. It is time for a father to let his little chick go."

Eek. He doesn't suspect, does he?

He rubbed his cheek to her crown, as if savoring the scent of his little girl.

No. "But the price—"

"You never mind about that. From what I understand of fathers and daughters, it is a small price to pay to make my princess happy. Besides, I never paid a cent toward college tuition. Think of it as that, hmm?"

She nodded before her head went deer in the headlights as Merrick's shadow filled her personal space.

Surprise, surprise. That looming shadow didn't chill her or shroud her with a sense of foreboding, despite the vibration of his simmering rage. She peered over her father's shoulder to watch Merrick stride near, a leather backpack in each strong knuckled fist, his lips pressed firm on a locked and square jaw.

Forbidding as all get out but wicked fine.

Dragging her gaze from the bracing sight of Merrick closing in on her, she smiled bravely for her father. "I don't have time to say anything to Mom."

"She will be all right. Do not worry, chickie." Her father dabbed her nose as he winked. "Or should I stop calling you that, now you're all grown up and flying the nest?"

She loved that he smiled, showing her his luminous Vampyre teeth. She thought his smile one of his best features of so many great ones.

Angelia blushed. "I'll always be your chickie, Papa. You know that."

Anton placed a chaste kiss upon her forehead at the same time she felt Merrick's heat closing over her.

* * * *

Saps.

Yet, Merrick felt the weight of his longing, the sharp bite of its teeth, and suppressed the growl brewing in his thick chest. He'd been without the comfort of another being for more than two thousand years; this familial scene *would not* bother him. He couldn't let it. Remembering how it used to be among his Kynd, the way they once touched to give solace to each other, would only puncture holes in an already faulty dam barely keeping his rage from spewing outward.

Merrick squeezed his eyes shut and gave a sharp shake to his head. Setting it straight. His lot was what it was, and he wouldn't let this blatant display of affection rattle him. The two doing the lovey-dovey thing weren't even Kynd, for Christ's sake.

"Hate to break up the sloppy good-byes, but if you're going…" He held Angelia's pack out for her then let it drop just as she was reaching for it. Her father snagged it before it touched the stone floor, lancing a wrathful, silver-eyed glare at him.

Promises, promises. Merrick smirked, welcoming the stab of his antagonism as it buffeted his leaky defenses. "You won't be there to catch her when she's too slow, Vampyre. Better she learn right off she'll be no *chickie* on this trip."

He intentionally goaded them; he couldn't help it. Not when his insides betrayed him with odd feelings of seeing her so vulnerable in her father's arms. She should be looking at him like that, not some other man.

Aw, Jesus. If only he could slip out of his gargoyle body. It acted funny around the woman, made his chest ache as if there wasn't enough air in the room. He needed to get moving, to get his mind on something else besides this human.

Although he knew that wasn't going to happen any time soon. He was stuck with her for the next seven days, at least. He wasn't heading to Hell—he was already there. "Grab your pack, and let's go."

Sticking around to catch her reaction was a bad idea. It was torture enough to have the smell of her curling around him, as if it was some kind of magical serpent taunting his stiffening cock.

Christ Almighty. Merrick almost cupped his balls in a bid to make more room. Instead, he forced his hands to stay busy shouldering the bag he'd picked up for the trip. He did not look back to see if Angelia followed. He didn't have to—he could feel the warmth of her soul swirling across his back.

As if his skin wasn't thick at all.

* * * *

"Wait, I'm coming." Getting breathless, Angelia turned back around to give her father a quick hug. "I've got to go." She nudged her chin toward an impatient Merrick bounding toward the stairs.

"I could speed you there so you arrived before he did," Anton lifted a dark brow accenting the mischief swirling in his silver eyes.

"No." She grinned, unable to resist his stoic charm. "He's right. I'll catch up."

"It's goodbye then, chickie. Be careful."

"I will, Papa. And hold Mom tight, give her my kisses."

"Of course."

Angelia spun on her heels and ran for the staircase.

Of course. Her father would most assuredly hold her mother to him, he was going to have to. Marguerite was going to go berserker.

She felt bad for leaving her father with her mess to clean up, but she had no choice. Merrick was right about needing to leave as soon as possible. Enough time had been wasted. The Scriptum could already be within the Second Circle and spiraling farther downward by the minute.

As she ran, she shuffled the pack to her back, cinching the belts across her chest and waist to keep it from bouncing. Her heart thumped too hard but no telling if it was because of the daunting prospect of her mission, or the exhilaration of going on an adventure with a real chimera.

She couldn't separate the two things, not when her feet drew her closer to Merrick. Slowing as she neared him, she sized him up until she was standing so close she could smell the smooth leather of the clothes he was folding into the pack at his bare feet. Some other scent teased her senses, too, something crystalline and very male.

Merrick turned when she approached, and Angelia ripped her eyes from his broad, naked chest with its flat nipples to look up into a tight face. Slate gray eyes hit her so hard she took a physical step backward. Away from him.

"That's right, chickie. Not too close." His sneer revealed one long, thick, and very sharp canine. "You wouldn't want the big, bad chimera to eat you."

"If that's to intimidate me, you'd better try harder. I was raised with vampires." She was a braggart, an empty windbag in the cruel face of his taunting.

"If you're not scared, human, then you're a bigger idiot than I pegged you for."

Her retort never left her lips. Merrick abruptly yanked her snug against his taut, naked body, and exploded around her with a snap and flutter so thunderous she'd have cowered if he hadn't been holding her so tight.

She understood then, in one terrifying blur of black feathers that swallowed her body whole, that she was indeed an idiot. And so very beyond her realm as the chimera engulfed her in his wings and rocketed her toward Hell.

Chapter Three

They stopped at the Archway, where for the past two thousand years, Merrick had perched as Guardian to those passing into Hell. He felt the grass on his bare soles as he alighted, his bones registering the solidity of the earth beneath him.

Yet, his skin and muscles felt so much more as he basked in the warmth of the body he pressed to his. The human woman's heart pumped fast, priming her blood so it raced beneath her skin. Her unique blend of honey and lavender puffed under his nose.

He wasn't sorry for the fragrance of her, he was chagrined to have caused her fear. He'd done it on purpose, like a lout, in a fit of temper. Because she unnerved him. The confusing part? She did so even in his distilled form.

The human woman wielded a power over him that shouldn't be possible. He'd gloried in the contrasting silk of her cheek against the thicker skin of his torso, the heat of her breath, the clinging of her delicate, yet strong arms around his waist as he'd vaulted them into the sky.

So help him, he fought not to dig his lion's claws into her, resisting the urge to press her tighter with his padded palms. God in Heaven, but the ancient Vampyre Anton and his wife had named their foundling correctly.

This human seemed like an angel.

And strike him dead if he harmed her. As it was, he danced on the edge of suffering his demise. Because he was holding her too tight, even with both sets of their feet solidly planted on the ground. He should release her, not stand there gripping onto her like a stricken imbecile.

He was Kynd, damn it, he didn't do the mating thing. He was not a performer in the carnal arts of creation.

Folding his wings with a powerful ruffle, he slid the rest of the chimera beneath his bare skin. In his shift, he kept the human woman trapped upright in his changing arms, lest she wobble and teeter to the dirt.

He gazed down at her when he was finished, to register her alarm, her vertigo.

Well, his night just brimmed with surprises. The woman seemed barely fazed, just a little flushed, gazing up at him with those dark blue eyes shining with the thrill of her ride.

Merrick released her as if her skin caught fire and would burn him.

* * * *

Swaying like a lone two by four standing vertical, Angelia glanced straight up into the fierce glint of granite eyes, and clamped her jaw shut. Which did wonders for her balance. Good thing, too, since Merrick scraped her nerves until they sang for him. She didn't need him knowing it.

But their passage through the sky?

Sheer terrifying exultation, unlike anything she'd ever experienced. The chimera had gifted her with something wondrous.

Flight.

Scary, yes, but she'd felt incongruously safe in Merrick's grasp. She'd forgotten all about his tenuously tamped rage as the air ripped over them, across the surface of his feathers, filling her ears with a sound she could only liken to the strains of a choir. A sound that resonated to the core of her, as though it was a deeply buried memory she couldn't excavate.

She'd dig later. Right then, she'd rather think about being wrapped snug in those singing wings. She'd felt none of the frigid night sky, only the chimera's strength, his heat, the rough skin of his chest against her face, as if he was encased within a film of stone.

Immediately, she thought of his eyes, so like slate. She stole another glance up at him, steeling herself against the vision.

He moved before her as naked as Adam. Well-built, powerful, his muscles dragging on bone, flexing as he bent over his pack to retrieve his clothing. As he reached into the sack, his spine curved and his ribcage expanded masterfully.

Two symmetrical scars lined his back. Where he kept his wings?

Transfixed, Angelia ogled.

The chimera had secreted his full self from view, maintaining just the gargoyle part for her to see. He seemed innocently unaware of his physique, like he had no inkling to the irresistible draw of it.

Angelia remembered to close her gawping, fly-catching mouth lest she embarrass herself. She was on a very serious, life-threatening mission. Any minute now, she was going to be passing through the gates of Hell, nothing proverbial about it.

Turning her attention elsewhere, she noticed bones scattered and half-concealed in the trampled, tufting grass. Like they were the stripped shells of cars at an abandoned junkyard.

Ookaay. So, he wasn't the Guardian in the sense that he took your ticket and let you in. The thrill from her flight drained south, abandoning her like rats from a sinking ship. What she needed was a life raft named ADOS, as in Attention Deficit-Ooh, Shiny!

Look at something else, idiot. Like that sign etched into the keystone of the Archway.

Huh. It didn't exactly say what she thought it was supposed to. "Why doesn't the inscription read *Lasciate ogne speranza, voi ch'intrate?*" *Abandon all faith, ye who enter here.*

Merrick pulled the leather of his pants up over his hips before turning to answer her.

"Because Dante got it wrong, and the world accepted it as truth," he spit out, his anger over the mistake evident, and apparently too fresh, despite the centuries that had passed.

She felt an inkling of it herself. "So, there *is* hope after all? Why hasn't anyone amended this?" Angelia knew she sounded a bit shrill, but she couldn't help it. Dante's error was colossal, and she couldn't slow the wild threading of her pulse, the hammering of her heart as realization dawned. "There are people down there who can repent." Not a question.

"Angelia," Merrick warned, his tone a mere octave above a growl.

She gripped her pack like maybe it could defend her. "Yeah?"

Merrick softened. A little. If she hadn't been sucking up every gorgeous detail of him, she'd have never noticed. "Turn back."

Quick as a spark, regret flashed in his granite eyes then disappeared.

Well, well, well. Merrick wasn't all stone. Her father had seen it, too, or he wouldn't have agreed with the Triumvirate to let her go. Anton trusted Merrick and so would she.

"I appreciate your concern—*I do*. But, I've got to do this. The Scriptum holds too many secrets to fall into the wrong hands." She didn't say she needed the boost to her self-esteem.

Merrick's thick muscles stiffened as a growl boiled from the bottom of his lungs.

She'd have to be a block of wood not to feel the charge crackling through the air or that growl rubbing across her flesh. Merrick thought she didn't trust him with the Scriptum.

His anger was justified. The Scriptum was about the Kynd, after all. About *him*. But, Angelia didn't trust anyone with such an important relic, not even the members of the Literati. The book had revealed its secrets to *her*, even if she was fuzzy about the details.

She felt wholly responsible for it because it had entrusted her with its encrypted knowledge, and it had been stolen during her entire damsel-in-distress routine. If she hadn't fainted, it wouldn't have been taken.

He needed to understand how responsible she felt about that, how compelled she was to right her wrong. "What I—"

Merrick spun around so all she could see was the length of his broad back tapering to his narrow hips. Which, *sigh,* were hugged in rich, brown leather. A nice view, but she'd been trying to explain something a little important.

"Hey, I was trying—"

Merrick glared over his shoulder. "Shut it, chickie. We've got company."

Angelia clapped her jaw shut for the umpteenth time already that day.

27

S. C. Dane

Another gargoyle maybe? Or something more dangerous?

She would not look at the bleached out bones scattered around her. *Heck, no.* Like squirrels gunning it for the nearest tree, her feet scurried her closer to her guide and protector. Feeling safer, she peered around Merrick's side and tried to catch a glimpse of who, or what, he was waiting for.

* * * *

The woman's touch went straight to his groin.

What in God's name is she to rile me like this?

Without turning around, he curled his fingers around her hand to remove its temptation. He didn't need the distraction or the pain of his thickening flesh in his pants. Not when he was going to be greeting an old friend.

Merrick left Angelia with her excuses on the tip of her tongue and her electric hands empty. "Darken, my old friend. I was afraid you hadn't heard my call."

He pulled the other gargoyle close for a hard hug. Darken's strong arms enveloped more than just Merrick's body. They were a balm to his raging heart. Savoring it, he held his friend for several long moments, enjoying the rare touch of another Kynd.

At one time, the Kynd were unabashedly open in their affections for each other. But since the Schism, when they'd been cast from Heaven, many didn't have the opportunity to indulge their natural geniality.

God had seen fit to scatter them to the winds, where it was impossible for them to share in each other's company for longer than a few stolen moments. As a result of this forced isolation, they were turning into the Grotesques the humans thought them to be.

"Anything for a change of scene, Merrick, you know that." Darken pulled back to reveal a smile loaded with a beastly row of sharp teeth. Yet, his gray eyes glowed warm. An uncommon sight, given the gargoyle had little to be happy for. Darken lifted his chin. "Who's the human?"

Merrick turned, as if surprised to find such an anomaly standing behind them. "She's my charge. She's going in with me." He ignored the squeezing of his chest.

Darken whistled appreciatively. "No! Such a wisp of a thing, too. What's she done to deserve her turn in the Circles?"

"Nothing. She's the Vampyre Anton's daughter. Under direction of the Literati, we're going in together and coming out the same way. I'm her guide."

Darken choked, incredulous. "Her guide?" He looked around Merrick, addressing her. "You do know there are lovely vacation destinations right here on the surface, don't you?"

Angelia nodded and pointed two fingers to her brow, acknowledging the gargoyle's playfulness with a salute.

"She's a little daft, Darken, pay her no mind." Merrick grinned, and a rusted laugh scraped up his throat, sounding more like an angry caw than any effortless bubbling.

Thank God it was Darken he shared it with, his dearest friend. As a Kynd himself, Darken knew all too well the weariness borne by those of their station. He understood, too, Merrick's particular hardship, that he never observed joy, or love, nor any of the finer emotions that made creatures beautiful.

"Aye, well, Merrick," Darken's good humor faded as he slipped an arm around his comrade's shoulders. "If they can bring a spark of happiness, it's worth the gamble, eh?"

"You're a bloody philosopher, brother." Merrick clasped the gargoyle's hand. "You'll watch for me, won't you? They've given us seven days. If we're not out—"

"Aye. I'll not let you surrender so easily, you Nancy. It's only been two thousand years and some change, you can't quit on us already."

His gratitude swamping him, Merrick clutched Darken to his breast.

After a couple of claps to his back, the other gargoyle nodded, indicating the woman behind them. "Besides, you've got company this trip. And by the looks of her, you'll be too preoccupied to dwell on your inner demons."

Merrick turned again to gaze at Angelia, who had perched on a boulder to better watch the reunion. She was braiding her long, blonde hair into a golden plait.

"She'll keep me on my toes, for sure." Merrick shrugged to settle his wings even though they were tucked and hidden.

Maybe he should be the one to turn back, let the Triumvirate find someone else to guide the human in her search for the Scriptum. Because now, as he prepared to set foot beyond the Archway, his doubts walked in on cold fingers, gripping his heart with a chilling fist.

He hadn't been kidding about reminding Darken to come looking for them after seven days.

Two thousand years of observing the torment of millions of tainted souls, of destroying creatures trying to sneak through the gate to raise...hell, and Merrick wasn't far from pitching his own lot in with Lucifer's.

At least then he would no longer be Witness and Guardian, would no longer have to endure the endless burden of his Kynd.

In Hell, the chimera could let his rage have its due. He could give in to the violence steeping inside him like a fetid brine. Better that than to poise on a building's ledge, his fury still shackled to him. He would be unable to vent its poison as he perched helpless, entirely consumed in stone.

Merrick stole another glance toward Angelia. The woman was standing now, moving toward their packs. "I guess it's time to go." He winked at Darken, masking the fear that crept in with his doubts.

"I'd say. She looks like she'd go without you. Who's guiding who, anyway?"

Merrick shoved his fist against the thick muscle of Darken's shoulder. "Funny. You're a regular comedian. I'll come back just to catch your show."

The other gargoyle nodded, his smile slipping as he grew serious. "No, but you will come back. See you soon, old friend." Clapping a rough palm to Merrick's back, he pushed the chimera away from him. "Now get going, you're wasting my time."

Without looking back, Merrick left Darken, although his thoughts remained behind on his brotherkynd.

They had been cast from Heaven together, along with all the other gargoyles and chimerae. Merrick might have plucked the short straw when he'd been assigned to watch over the Gates of Hell, but Darken's lot wasn't any better. The gargoyle was shackled to Death, and it didn't take much imagination to figure out how that particular duty ate away at a Kynd's soul.

Darken knew full well the agony of too many centuries lurking within the rim of shadows, when such a fate ran counter to the true hearts of the Kynd. Not that anyone bothered to know. Gargoyles and chimerae had been vilified, and there they would remain, eternally maligned.

Merrick shrugged his shoulders again, this time to slough off his gloom, and walked toward Angelia, who held his pack out to him. For a brief moment, he thought she'd pay him back for his ill manners back at the Triumvirate's gallery and he tensed, ready to snag his supplies before she could drop them on the ground as he reached for them.

* * * *

Angelia stood with Merrick's pack in her outstretched hand, watching the chimera sift through his emotions, seeing his mistrust shift to resentment as he reached toward her. She felt a pang of sadness for him, especially after having seen how affectionate and unguarded he'd been with his fellow gargoyle only moments before.

The greeting had been a private moment, one not many on the outside ever had the chance to see. That Merrick would let her witness it? A squirming twinge played in her belly, expunging the sadness, as she recalled the easy smile on his handsome face.

Like Darken's eyes, Merrick's had glowed warm, reminding Angelia of smooth-worn rocks on a sun kissed beach. He had looked back at her without masking his joy at seeing his friend and her heart had stuttered at the sight of him.

If only she could elicit such affection from him.

Okay, so for now she'd be content with the bone he'd thrown her by not hiding his affectionate side, and ignore the tormented rage he exuded the closer he got to her. She was brave, darn it. She'd give him a bone, too.

"We should be going. The longer we take getting started, the—"

"Farther down we'll have to go," he snapped, snatching at his bag. She didn't let it go, and they both stood holding the bundle between them, united for an electric moment.

Was she feeling the heat of Hell, because it was getting awfully warm under her clothes.

Merrick's smooth jaw ticked, his nostrils flaring like he was smelling something.

Dear God.

Angelia released her grip and stepped off to preoccupy herself with adjusting the straps on her own backpack, making sure the chimera couldn't see the flush on her cheeks. She was sure it was there, if the burning of her face meant anything.

She didn't dare look at him but started off, too self-conscious to look back. Each step that led her closer to Hell made her heart flutter and tingled her skin, as if she was nearing her destiny. Which she felt certain was somehow entwined with that of the Scriptum.

And with the chimera. Who was nothing like she imagined him to be.

Aside from her inexplicable fascination with the Kynd, Angelia knew she was just as prejudiced in her thinking as the rest of the world. She thought the chimera chosen to guide her would look as hideous as those fashioned by the hands of man and mounted onto old buildings and churches.

Surprise, surprise. She hadn't expected him to have a gargoyle form, or to have a physique like he posed for GQ in his spare time, or to have eyes that left his soul wide open when he let his guard down.

Not that she'd meant to, but she had seen the depths of his anger as she'd gazed into the slate of those eyes, and had felt like a trespasser. Never mind she'd yearned to drop the bundle she was holding to kiss those tortures out of him.

Well, she couldn't overlook that part, actually—her cheeks still burned hot enough to remind her. So, she trucked along, oblivious to her surroundings while images of the chimera and his leonine grace dominated her thoughts.

* * * *

Merrick didn't immediately follow Angelia. He stood as if planted while he waited for his heart to slog back to its natural rhythm. Which it wouldn't do so long as he kept thinking about the woman's kind gesture and utter lack of retaliation. If she'd have just plunked his bag at his feet, he'd have understood. He would have bitten out some sarcastic comment and dragged her delicate ass down the path after that damned book.

Instead, she'd been *nice* and that scraped at his rage without feeding it, confusing him. Ergo, his rapping heart.

Angelia's backside grew incrementally smaller while he stood grounded like an idiot.

Finally taking off after her, he lied to himself that he didn't want the view of that round ass a lot closer to him than it was.

He was merely concerned she was getting too far ahead of him for her own safety. They weren't yet in Hell but the rim around it contained its own dangers. For being one of the Literati she seemed awfully blasé about stepping across the threshold into the Vestibule.

Surely she wasn't ignorant about what resided in the antechamber to Hell. It didn't matter that all around them, stretching as far as the eye could see, was nothing but vast prairies of trampled grass and an unattainable horizon, charred blood red.

The grass beneath their feet wasn't merely crushed, it was macerated, the dents and crescent prints of unshod hooves and bare feet tattooed into the pulverized sod.

Yet, still the human walked on. Undaunted or unaware? Merrick wasn't sure, but his mane thickened, the ends of it curling along the collar of his leather jacket. He wanted her safe.

For the deal I've made with Anton.

Yes, of course, that was the reason why. It had nothing to do with the way his eyes kept drifting downward to watch her wiggling ass. Nothing whatsoever.

The woman swatted at bothersome flies, slapping one of the biting insects at her neck, which piqued that unfamiliar urge to protect her and made his chest too tight.

Scanning the plain they traveled across with renewed wariness, Merrick ignored his body's reaction and loped to catch up with her even though he hadn't a clue what he would say once he closed the distance.

He didn't do small talk. He had spent too many centuries by himself to have mastered the art of chatting. Yet, the second the smell of lavender drifted into his nostrils, his tongue loosened like a flapping sail in a stiff wind. "So, how does a human find herself as one of the Literati, anyhow? You're no withered husk."

Though her spine stiffened like his words lashed her, she kept walking.

But she isn't. Even if he did argue with himself, he obviously liked the shape of her. Not that he knew why. Kynd didn't take mates, *or lovers*, as humans called them. He shouldn't be feeling these strange sensations as he watched her hiking in front of him.

No, she wasn't hiking. She was marching now, and he found himself lengthening his stride to keep close to her.

"What I meant," he cleared his throat, "was that members of the Literati seem to have made a bad bargain with Knowledge. They look, well, you know what I mean."

Merrick held his breath, waiting for the woman to say something, anything, before his mouth opened again to spew God knew what out of it. He was a chimera, for the Lord's sake, accustomed to endless years of saying little to nothing.

He thought maybe the last thing he might have spoken was "Hey, I'm going to tear your legs off, vampire, if you take one more step toward that threshold." Or something like it. Yet, here he was dribbling nonsense off his tongue like a yenta.

Angelia slapped at another fly. "I know what you mean."

His skin tightened instantly. He didn't like the surrender of her tone, as if she agreed she was trading her life for something that maybe cost more than she wanted to pay. He didn't want to look close at his reaction to that, either.

She flapped her hands over her head, whisking away the cloud of tiny gnats hovering there. "So, how long will it take before we see the Acheron?"

"You know where you are, then?"

The woman bristled under her pack, her spine stiffening again as she trudged doggedly forward, and Merrick silently cursed his traitorous tongue. He'd insulted her worse than telling her she was a withered husk. Couldn't he just keep his mouth shut around her?

"Yes, I know precisely where I am, Mr. Merrick." Angelia spun to face him, her fingers coiled around the shoulder straps of her backpack, her eyes swirling, dark pools.

He almost walked over the top of her, she halted so abruptly.

"Jesus, woman." She was so close he felt the heat of her anger. *And her body.*

"Mr. Merrick, if you—"

"Merrick. Just Merrick. I'm not a—"

"Whatever." Angelia waved her hand as if shooing away his explanation along with the swarming flies. "If you think for one minute I'm not wholly aware of where we are," she brushed a hornet off her arm. "Then we're going—"

Merrick pressed the rough pads of his fingertips to her soft lips as he felt the rumble under his feet and thunder drumming his sensitive ears.

Jesus Christ. Far from it, but he didn't have time to list the differences. Bearing down on them was the one reason he thanked God for not being quite so cruel as He could have been.

The tormented hordes.

Angels unwanted by Lucifer and rejected by God for their indecisiveness, were barreling down on the spot where Merrick and Angelia now stood. The tattered banner the spirits eternally chased loomed so fast Merrick could hear its flapping as it sped closer.

He shucked his coat, not caring where it landed as he crushed Angelia to him and dropped to the ground. His wings exploded from his back, and he folded them around her body to shield her from the flies and hornets that descended in a choking, stinging cloud.

The swarming mass stole the very air they breathed, suffocating them. They bumped against his stone-rough skin, their screeching buzz piercing his eardrums as he strained to listen for the following hordes, the hundreds and thousands of shaded souls on foot and horseback who pursued the banner.

Angelia would be crushed by the charging throng if he couldn't get them off the ground. Yet the insects swarmed too thick, their teeming mass a solid, burning thing that would flay human skin if he removed the protection of his wings to fly them out of harm's way.

35

But he had to do something—their time was running out. He could feel the earth shuddering under his feet, rattling his bones with the sheer force of stampeding feet.

Merrick clutched Angelia tighter, fear for her safety crushing heavy on his chest, tightening like a steel band, making it even harder to breathe.

He didn't pause to ponder why, but used his desperation to get her the hell out of their predicament.

"Hold on," he bellowed into her ear. The instant he felt her fingernails dig into his forearms he unfolded one wing, drew it back, and shoved it forward through the thick swarm of insects as hard as he could, propelling them off-kilter, but at the same time backward, out of the direct path of the rushing hordes.

He staggered with the effort of their tilted getaway but refused to ease his grip on the woman. Merrick curved his battered wing back over her as he surrounded her body, blanketing her from the insects until they, too, receded with the awful tremor of the ground.

Chapter Four

Angelia, curled and protected beneath the chimera, couldn't ignore the slam of Merrick's heart against her back, the fierce hold of his arms, or the heat of their bodies trapped within the canopy of his wings.

Her own heart kicked her breastbone as it ricocheted off the chimera's muscled forearm.

She had nearly gotten them killed with her inattention, with the preoccupation that had consumed her when she'd felt Merrick draw near, as if she had antennae tuned to the frequency of his presence.

Images of him in her head had sharpened the closer he'd gotten. He'd completely dominated her senses so that the landscape around her had diminished to the narrow space under her feet.

But his presence hadn't suppressed the insecurities always hovering around her like an aura.

You're no withered husk. She'd kept walking when she'd heard Merrick's words, blazing her ignorant trail as she'd nursed the sting of his backhanded compliment, his flippant comment cutting too close to the bone.

Of course, she'd known what he'd meant. She had passed enough hours fretting about that very thing. Not that she was vain, she just didn't want—well, she didn't quite know exactly what it was she'd hoped to get from joining the Literati. Adventure, maybe, like Indiana Jones.

That the chimera saw traces of her fading and wasted youth hit her harder than any of her own self-criticisms. It was one thing to blast herself, but to hear her self-conscious fears voiced by a Kynd she harbored a secret enthrallment for?

Angelia had felt like a bug splattered on a car windshield. And just as gross.

Seconds later, she'd almost wound up as exactly that.

If it hadn't been for the chimera's quick thinking and his tremendous strength, they would both be mangled road-kill, and a scrumptious meal for the billions of flies, which had descended in a swarming, stinging mass.

"Angelia?"

She stifled a sob. When Merrick had peeled back one of his wings she had seen the nightmare boring down on them, the tortured, fanatical visages of the hundreds of thousands of souls raging by.

Her thin skin had been pelted by thousands of stinging hornets and chips of dirt flung up by pounding hooves. Thank God she'd had the wherewithal not to open her mouth to scream. As it was, her lips and nose burned as if raw, and she wasn't too sure they weren't stripped clean of skin.

She certainly didn't mind if the chimera had yet to let her go. His arms kept her from freaking out, his hold on her body transferring to a grip on her mental state. It allowed her a few minutes to sort out what she had just seen.

Hell.

She just got her first glimpse of Hell, right up front and horrifyingly personal. Doubt crashed down on her, feeding the sobs mushrooming in her chest, threatening to choke her as the insects had done.

"Angelia?"

She hadn't answered him, and his tone seemed genuinely concerned, which squeezed her traumatized heart.

"I'm okay." Except her bottom lip, raw as it was, trembled as tears pooled to blur her vision. Not that she could see much anyway, only Merrick's knees and his bare arms as he remained hovered over her.

* * * *

Merrick breathed in the honey-lavender of Angelia's hair, grateful she finally answered him. Her bones felt so fragile in his arms he worried that maybe he'd hurt her, that he'd been too strong.

If she'd been harmed? Well, there would be hell to pay for it, ironically.

Merrick shunned the real reason for his alarm and shifted the woman in his arms, releasing her slowly as he'd done when he'd taken to the air with her. As then, he didn't want her tipping onto her lovely behind, which had become all the more beautiful since he'd discovered it might be precious to him.

Yeah, right. Forget it, dumb ass.

He was a lost soul, a hopeless cause. It wasn't going to be long before he abandoned his post at the Archway to Hell and either threw his lot in with Lucifer, or perched his granite-turning butt on the ledge of a building.

Still though, he couldn't stop looking at her. She was terribly shaken, her eyes almost black and shimmering with tears as she unfurled herself from his embrace to stand up. Her face bore the evidence of his preoccupation with her taunting ass, her cheeks and pert nose were dappled with angry stings.

She swiped at her watering eyes and heaved a breath, yanking Merrick's attention to her breasts.

Great Christ Almighty. Her chest lifted and dropped repeatedly, and those beautifully bulbous things seemed to fill before his eyes. Two points projected from her shirt, like buttons wanting to be pinched, and Merrick fisted his hands and locked his elbows.

He would not touch her like he was driven mad to do.

He'd never touched a female in his long life. He'd probably scare her worse than she already was. What did he know of a woman's breasts? It wasn't as if he had instincts in the mating department. It wasn't like he would know what to do that would make her glad he was fondling them.

Did he?

His tongue certainly thought so. It slid across his fangs, which almost itched with the yearning to nip those points. His mouth wanted to suckle them in, like a babe to its mother's teat.

Merrick gave his head a sharp shake, dislodging such notions. He was no babe, and Angelia no mother. So, why did he want to cup...

Merrick shook his head harder.

The woman took a step back, her eyes still huge.

He needed to remember how he'd failed her because of his callous attitude over her being just a human. She wasn't Kynd, or one of the Others, for that matter. She was human, one of the millions who were currently overrunning the earth, who shunned the Grotesques, who forgot to honor them by erecting architectural wonders on which the Kynd could spend their remaining years.

She would shun him as surely as her ilk already did.

God be damned, he shouldn't care. But he did.

"You should go back. Get another guide." He wasn't the one for this mission no matter what the Triumvirate thought. He was too hard, he had been alone too long to interact with something as volatile, and fragile, as a human being. Especially this one, who reminded him too sharply of all that he used to be.

Of all that he now was, and was soon going to be.

* * * *

Angelia shook her own head, denying Merrick's suggestion.

Even denying the hunger she'd seen burning in his slate eyes. Because it hadn't lasted long, and now she wasn't sure it had been there in the first place. Why would he have gazed on her with wanting?

She was mistaken. She was sure of it, especially when now what she saw in his stare reminded her of flagstone—flat and hard.

Dear God, he just saved my life from…

She swung her arm out as if it could possibly encompass the enormity of what had just trampled passed. It was that, or open and close her mouth like a fish while she fought for air.

She was in shock and had merely imagined the chimera's wanting.

But, she couldn't go back. She couldn't look at Aro's disappointed face and admit she wasn't the human he should have pegged his hopes on. Even her guide no longer wanted the responsibility of her. Wasn't that just the icing on her crap cake?

Oh, she was utterly freaking priceless.

Angelia swirled to face the glowing horizon and put one determined foot in front of the other, her jaw clamped tight with determination. If the chimera wanted to wash his hands of her, then she'd make it easy for him. She didn't have much in the dignity department, but she had enough to know when she should cut her losses.

Her dream of working with one of the Kynd being one of them.

Never mind that every step she was taking in the opposite direction from Merrick sluiced so much regret down her throat she couldn't breathe from the pressure of it. She willed her rubbery legs onward. She would retrieve the Scriptum on her own if it killed her.

What a delusional ninny she'd been. Getting all hot and liquid for a creature Michelangelo would have palavered over. As if the chimera would welcome her advances if she gathered the nerve to try.

He was beautiful, mythical, and she was—well, she was nothing special. But she did have one last opportunity to prove her worth. Throwing it away was not an option, not with her future riding on the success of the Scriptum's retrieval.

Okay. She'd be a little more honest with herself.

She felt a personal connection to that book, and she wanted it safe in her arms. The codex sang to her. Its message bypassed her logical brain and speared its truth straight to her heart, which was why she'd come to with Aro's livid face hovering over her.

She remembered how everything had dissolved around her, including herself, as she'd listened to the strains emanating from the open pages.

The Kynd. They were meant to do something, but she couldn't recall what. So was she, but she couldn't remember how she was connected to them or what she was supposed to do about it. She'd passed out. And when she'd fainted, the answers must have dribbled out of her ears and dissolved into the cracks in the stone floor of the study.

I'll get them back. With one determined step forward at a time.

* * * *

Merrick watched the woman's backside grow smaller for the second time in the same day. And just like before, he was struck dumb.

Was that shame he'd seen flash in those blue-black eyes? The chimera had lived a solitary existence for millennia, but he recognized humiliation when he saw it. He witnessed it almost every day, perched atop the Archway with damned souls plodding beneath his paws.

That the human woman Angelia should fall victim to such a

debilitating emotion cut away at the stone of his heart, something she alone seemed to have the knack for doing.

And Merrick wasn't sure how to take that.

He didn't like humans. With God on their side, they were doing a fine job of destroying themselves and the beautiful planet that had been gifted to them. Their egos acknowledged no bounds. Nothing was too great or too low for them to grasp with their greedy, bloodstained hands.

Yet, Angelia seemed different somehow. As clever as she was, there was a naiveté she emanated, an innocence he hadn't encountered since he'd been exiled to the gates of Hell.

Merrick plucked his leather coat off the ground and smacked the dirt and dead insects out of it.

This could have been her.

A rosy thought. One that made him think of how fragile a human being she was. She'd offered him nothing but kindness and fair play, and he'd shoved it back down her throat. It was either that or acknowledge how he reacted to her. The scent of her went straight to his groin, so it thickened and grew painfully heavy.

What was he going to do with that? Mate her?

Not on God's green toy called Earth. Or in Hell, for that matter.

Except he wanted to, which was the problem. He wanted to taste her, he wanted to know what her softness would feel like as she encased the damned thing hardening between his legs. She was the opposite of stone, which was the chimera's fate, and just once, before his body succumbed to its doom, he would like to feel soft flesh yielding for him.

Merrick scoffed, shoving such nonsense out of his head. He would have to be satisfied with something more platonic—curse his infernal erection—if he wanted to savor the presence of the human woman.

He could cram his rage and the fact of his hardening skin away for the next several days. Hell, if he could do that it would give him something nice to think about while he was perched in immutable stone for the next few centuries. Maybe thinking of her would ease some of his rage so he could endure his granite prison.

"Angelia, wait." Merrick trotted after the one thing that shined a little like hope, even if he could never touch her.

* * * *

Her feet halted like the booted traitors they were when the chimera's growling command caressed her eardrums.

Brilliant. So much for her shred of dignity. That was about to get tossed to the curb like the paltry thing it was. Angelia took a fortifying breath and turned to face her anguish head on.

"What, Merrick." Her curt response was all she could muster as she watched him jog toward her. God, he was beautiful. Not pretty in any way, but striking, the way a tiger sliding through the jungle was beautiful. Sublimely powerful, muscles rippling with every self-possessed movement.

Who knew? Maybe one of the animals of his chimera *was* tiger.

Oh yeah, the idea of that just stuffed her with confidence.

"Not *Mr.* Merrick?" He coaxed a chagrined smile to his lips as he pulled up in front of her.

Angelia hadn't been expecting his grin, and the sight of it stabbed straight for her womb, which wrung taut with raw need. She bit down on a gasp, and for one horrifying second she thought she gave herself away.

God, she couldn't even focus on her Indiana Jones adventure without somehow messing it up. Getting moist for her guide would not prove her self-worth. Not to her father or Aro. Least of all to herself.

Merrick lifted his chin as his nostrils widened. He took a step back.

Angelia's cheeks warmed, the stings and bites prickling from the heat rushing to her face. Oh, she must be gorgeous, all reeking with needy sex and mottled like a toad. So attractive, the chimera took a step *backward.*

Angelia stiffened her spine in the face of his revulsion. Then spun on her heel to flee toward the River Acheron with as steady a hiking pace as she could muster. She wouldn't let him see her run. She wasn't a coward, dang it. She was not.

Yes, he weakened her.

But she couldn't deny the soaring of her heart as he fell into a quiet pace behind her.

* * * *

They reached the River Acheron by what would have been nightfall if they hadn't been traveling beyond the Archway. Time simply didn't exist in Hell—the sun didn't rise or set. The sun didn't appear at all. Instead, a red sky reigned above their heads, a constant part of the scenery Merrick paid no attention to.

Because as Angelia walked, he followed her like a dog, trying to steal more of her scent whenever the breezes cooperated. She never looked back at him, so she didn't have a clue what he was doing. Hell, he didn't have any idea what he was doing.

Chasing a scent like an animal.

Yes, he was. He couldn't help himself. The smell of her had him hooked, as it had from the second he'd gotten a whiff of her back at the Triumvirate's gallery. He could follow her scent instinctively, so the rest of the time they walked he turned his mind to the task at hand.

A surprisingly difficult feat given the way he practically salivated as he watched her walking ahead of him. She had a cushy, yet tight ass, one that begged to be squeezed, and long, lithe legs dropping out from the bottom of that tempting bum.

Merrick kept his hands clenched in fists lest he indulge his urges. He had more important decisions to make than whether or not to sandwich his phallus between the cheeks of her ass. Besides, the fact that he wanted to should have been fueling his rage.

Humans were higher up on his list of dislikes than ghouls. So, why wasn't she pissing him off the way others did? Well, he could rub that little nugget, too, while he sat frozen in Grotesque form on a window ledge.

Right then, he had more immediate concerns, like how he was going to convince Kharon the Ferryman that the living soul he escorted should be granted passage across Acheron.

Unless they were all lucky, and Kharon had recognized the Scriptum for what it was and had seized it from the soulless man. Which could be possible. Like Merrick, Kharon was Kynd, and one observant son of a bitch.

The Ferryman, Merrick knew, also nursed resentment toward his lot just like every gargoyle and chimera cast down from Heaven. It would do them both good to see each other. If Kharon had the Scriptum, so much the better. Merrick would squander a bit of their saved time staying close to his brotherkynd.

They could both use the comfort. And maybe between the two of them, they could convince Angelia to read some of what was written in that book.

Rumor was, it contained knowledge of gargoyles and chimerae, and God only knew what else. But Merrick didn't care about the rest. He wanted to know what it revealed about the Kynd.

Too much information in the wrong hands could be devastating for them. If others learned that Kynd truly turned to stone? An involuntary shudder ran up Merrick's spine. The Kynd fought hard enough to maintain their fluid forms as it was, they didn't need enemies ushering them quicker to their demise.

Enemies. Merrick wanted to spit the word into the trodden dirt beneath his feet.

The Kynd had never had enemies before they'd been tossed from Heaven. They hadn't had allies, either, but they hadn't needed them.

Had they?

It was a compelling thought. Maybe if they'd had friends outside of the flock, the Kynd wouldn't be suffering as they now were. Which was water under the bridge, as far as Merrick was concerned. The damage was done.

Besides, they neared the Acheron. Merrick could hear the gentle glide of the water passing along the shore. He lengthened his strides to close the distance between himself and Angelia, who slowed ever so slightly, her back bowing imperceptibly toward him as he drew close to her heels.

Did she even know how her body reacted to him? Probably not. Being Kynd meant he picked up on things most others never did. Even if she did notice, *he was Kynd*. Chimera. Nearly Grotesque. She wouldn't want him touching her more than was necessary to save her pretty neck, no matter what her body craved.

* * * *

Angelia's lips curled into a contented smile when she felt Merrick's warmth on her backside. She knew he only bridged the distance to

45

protect her, to fulfill his obligation to keep her safe, but she treasured the feel of him just the same.

His nearness felt so darned good, like he fortified her somehow, just by being close. And she was bone tired. She'd grown weary with the burden of having to sift through everything that had happened in the past twelve hours. She needed a nap or a good night's rest before crossing the Acheron.

Her puffy sleeping bag, crammed in her pack, beckoned. She'd do well to heed its call. It was going to take every scrap of cunning she could muster to get by Kharon's legendary scrutiny.

"We'll camp here tonight," Merrick announced, twisting his thick shoulders out from under the straps of his bag and letting it slump to the ground.

Never mind his sublime grace, was he a mind reader? "Shouldn't we keep going?" She wasn't being disagreeable. It was just that resisting made her feel like she had a little bit of control over this escapade into Hell.

"No. We're close to Kharon, and I want to be ready for him."

As much as it peeved her, she knew Merrick was right. If the Ferryman didn't grant them passage, then the Scriptum was lost. There was no way of getting into Hell proper without first going through Kharon.

Angelia shrugged out of her own pack, letting it plop down by her feet. She wanted to plunk right down with it and not get up until she'd slept a good thirty-six hours. Swear to God she would have never said, "I don't suppose you happen to have a spare danake or obolus to pay the Ferryman?" if she wasn't so tired.

Oh, and yeah. Why not give herself a reason to look down at Merrick's leather pants, to the bulge that definitely wasn't a coin purse. She shot her gaze back up to his face, utterly thankful for the red tint of the river so she could blame its cast on her blushing cheeks.

The chimera's eyes turned granite hard. He moved away from her to stand at the bank of the river to watch the blood-red water flow by. An excuse to ignore her.

Gads, she was such an ass. Why couldn't Merrick have been the hideous creature she'd imagined gargoyles and chimerae to be?

Oh, no. He had to be Mr. Effing Universe *and* Captain Captivating. Even his hair attracted her. It was just long enough so the ends curled along the tops of his ears and across his forehead. The black of his locks was a startling contrast to the slate gray of his eyes, making them appear much lighter than they were.

He was tall, proportioned well. And for all his surliness, for all the rage emanating off from him like heat waves, she wanted him. Like a living cliché, she was attracted to the dangerous man. She wanted to feel the giddy rapping of her pulse, the strength of the chimera's arms around her.

So much for forbidden passion. Angelia let loose a tremendous yawn, the great suck of air as attractive as the grating hum of a kazoo. Merrick turned back around, his hard eyes piercing as they slid down the length of her. Even then he was every bit the impenetrable stone of the Kynd.

Man, her brain felt thick, like it was swaddled in cobwebs. "I'm sorry." Angelia cupped her palm over her mouth, stifling another yawn, too sleepy to stay embarrassed. "I guess I'm more tired than I thought."

* * * *

Watching Angelia, Merrick felt his heart pinch then decided to ignore it. She was damned beautiful standing there, her lids growing heavy over eyes that reflected the deep maroon of the water rolling by. "As you should be. Get some sleep. I'll wake you when it's time."

"You're not sleeping?"

Merrick suppressed a rueful grin. "No. I'm Kynd, remember? We don't exactly sleep."

Angelia shrugged. "I suppose not. But don't you nap, at least?"

"Yeah, when we need to." Or wanted to, as Merrick did just then. He wanted to slip into Angelia's sleeping bag right along with her, feel the weight of her body pressed to his as she drifted off with her dreams, while he lay with her in his arms, protecting her.

"And, you don't need to," she said, reminding Merrick all too clearly of who and what he was.

"We aren't alone along the river. Souls are gathering for the crossing."

47

"Right. Forgot." Angelia stumbled from the riverbank to her bedroll.

Merrick hoped she'd settle in soon. He could feel her eyes on his back and he thickened with his need for her, the leather of his leggings pulling tight.

Bloody hell.

Just what he needed, another torment to contend with. As it was, he stood mesmerized by the murmuring rustle of voices in the water as it rushed past his boots, beckoning him to follow, to surrender his will and loose his chimera from its singular gargoyle form. His heart strained in his chest, rending him in different directions.

Merrick cursed as he turned to follow the woman. Better he risk her seeing his physical need for her than succumb to the invitation of the voices. He was rewarded by a spontaneous smile when she spotted him. His chest grew tight.

Without undressing or removing her boots, she spread out her sleeping bag and burrowed into it. Merrick leapt onto a large boulder and crouched, facing her. To his sensitive ears, her held breath seemed as loud as the creaking of his leather coat.

The human woman scrutinized him as closely as he did her and the third of Merrick, his lion, wanted to devour her one sensuous lick of his rasp-like tongue at a time.

"Tell me what you know about Kharon," he growled, his voice thick with need.

"What I know about Kharon?" She looked like she was trying to reconcile his expression to his words, her feather-light brows pinching over her sleepy eyes.

Merrick rubbed his palm across his mouth and nodded. He hoped talking would get both their minds back on why they were in this predicament in the first place. Heaven knew, one more minute of watching her watch him and he was going to do something he'd never thought possible of a Kynd. He was going to ask a human woman for the novelty of a kiss.

"Yes. You know he's the Ferryman," he said, leading her, his eyes following the dip and rise of her throat as she swallowed.

"Of course. He escorts dead souls to Hades." Wisps of her blonde hair, tinted by the red of the sky and the river, framed her face, her braid curving like a tail over her shoulder.

Dear God, help him. He wished it was his tail draped there.

Angelia yawned and rubbed her fingers over her eye. She was getting sleepier, falling under the spell of the Acheron as he knew she would.

As it should be.

Merrick turned to stare back out at the river, letting Angelia surrender to the sleep that was fast creeping up on her. He felt the stirrings of unease that he duped her, that she wasn't aware of what was happening to her, and he almost caved, almost blurted out the deception.

He recalled her determination to get the Scriptum, and bit down on his urge to confess. She'd be upset if they were refused entry, and that clinched his resolve.

He'd let her fall into a dreamless slumber, exactly where he needed her to be in order to get by Kharon. Because, no matter how refreshed she'd be from a good night's sleep, she would never be ready for the Ferryman.

She wasn't supposed to be, that wasn't how the crossing worked. Besides, Kharon would know she wasn't destined for the Circles. Angelia, upon her death, would cross a more pleasant plane than this one of fetid, bloodied water and fire.

Which was why Merrick could not give in to his base desires. No matter how bad he wanted to feel and taste every inch of the woman's bare skin, no matter how he longed to slide his hard, stone-rough body into her soft one, he could not. Angelia's destiny was the exact opposite of his. Merrick understood, only too well, what his future held, and it had nothing to do with God and His chosen angels in Heaven.

So he kept to himself while he waited until he was sure Angelia wouldn't stir when he moved her. Then he knelt down to lift her so he could carry her across the river.

Yet, as he lowered himself, the scent of honey-lavender spread through him. He couldn't resist dragging his face along the skin of her slender neck, where the smell of her lingered strong, pooling where the shorter strands of her hair curled along the base of her delicate skull.

So wondrous. He followed his nose along the slender line of her jaw to behind her ear, and it was all he could do not to press his lips to the silk of her skin, to drag his tongue so he could taste her. God in Heaven, he could cast aside his resolve as easily as he could steal a forbidden taste of her. He backed off, biting down on a frustrated snarl.

He wanted her as desperately as he wanted to stay in Hell.

Merrick took a steadying breath then crammed his wanting down into the same abyss where his fury swirled. He gathered their things then gently plucked Angelia off the ground, sleeping bag and all, and started down the path toward the Ferryman.

* * * *

Death trailed the vampire.

Aro could feel it in the throbbing of his veins as he followed his victim.

He was too hungry. He'd waited too long to feed, so his control was a little flimsy at the moment. Putting it off hadn't been his idea, though. Dealing with the Triumvirate had taken more time than it should have.

Fucking Anton.

If Death followed him along this backwater excuse for an alley, then so be it. The specter could belly up and watch. Besides, it wasn't as if the man he was following could serve Aro's business purposes any longer. He could afford to drain the victim's body dry now that the human had played his part in connecting the vampire to the soulless thief.

Just so long as he didn't get caught with the corpse stuck to his fangs.

Aro and his kind weren't allowed to kill their food sources anymore, not since the Triumvirate had wrangled vampires into a tidy community of pansy ass do-gooders. The three Vampyres—older than dust itself— had been more than capable of doing it and, *damn them*, the strength to maintain the edict.

Except Anton, the rotter. Who grew soft because of his affections for the human child.

Letting that old wound fester, Aro turned his ear to the squish of the footsteps ahead of him. The man he pursued was speeding up, as if he knew he was being followed.

Clever.

Aro's own blood slipped fast through his veins as the man broke into a run. Oh, he loved a good chase!

The damned Triumvirate. They'd all but eliminated that thrill from feeding. *Shadow your victims, make sure they remember nothing, heal the wound you leave.* Sniveling diplomats. They took the fun out of being vampire.

Aro might be one of the selected vampires to deal with the Triumvirate on a regular basis, but it didn't mean he was a cowering mutt who did his masters' bidding.

Quite the contrary. Aro had killed too many of his victims to bother counting. Tonight would be just one more body in a sea of blood. And he was going to happily glut himself till he was half drowned.

As if his dull instincts had kicked it up a notch, the human broke into a dead run. Aro could hear his breaths chuffing in the crisp evening air, his footfalls heavy and slapping. Smoke much? The man wasn't accustomed to sprinting. But the plus side? His running enflamed his blood.

How glorious! A warm feast that would shotgun straight down his vampire throat. Aro could hardly wait just thinking of how the blood would spew forth in heated torrents, stuffing his mouth so fast he wouldn't be able to swallow it all.

The promise of it tightened his skin. His fangs stretched long, throbbing hard in his gums.

With the scent of Death in his nose, Aro craved the inevitable, the excess. His vision bloomed red with his lust. Now the slapping footfalls were united with their runner, and in a blur, the vampire snatched the man's collar in his fist. The pungent, old-onion odor of the man's sweat assaulted his senses as Aro tugged him close.

Nose curling, his stomach heaved a slow roll before settling. Always it was thus when he dealt with the filth. Yet a meal was a meal when one was very hungry. Beggars not being choosers and the like.

But first.

"Uh-uh-uh, Mr. Smith. Not so fast." Aro twisted the collar until the fabric cut into the skin of the man's neck. Bulging his carotid artery. "Where are we off to in such a hurry, Mr. Smith? To count your money?"

Mr. Smith shook his head.

"Tsk, tsk."

Mr. Smith nodded.

The fool. Perhaps he'd overestimated the man's intelligence. It was good he felt Death so close.

"You have the key?" Unfolding his empty hand, Aro thrust it under the man's crooked nose. "Hmm?"

The human fumbled at the waist of his jeans, twisting his legs to jam his meaty fists into his linty pockets. He was a big man, by human standards. Strong shouldered, muscled. Stink or no, Aro was going to enjoy this meal.

A skeleton key, pinched between white, shaking fingers, bobbled upward into his line of sight. The rank tang of fear punctured through the old onion, forcing the vampire to fight his own shivers.

Aro plucked the iron key free and disappeared it into his sleeve as if he was a street magician. He tilted his chin so close to the man's ear his cool lips brushed the slippery skin, so intimate he could feel the slush of his victim's banging pulse.

His own blood raced through his veins, nearly distracting him from the reason he stood in a filthy alley in the first place.

Business. Ah, yes, there was that. Along with what it all meant.

"The Guardian of Hell may be permanently removed, thanks to you and your partner, Mr. Smith. You've both done well."

So they had. Because of Laurel and his sidekick Hardy here, the Scriptum was coursing a sweet descent into the bowels of Hell, with the human woman and her chimera escort chasing their merry way after it.

The vampire's plan to remove the Guardian permanently couldn't have gone better. Aro's gamble that the Scriptum would lure the chimera away from the damned Archway was paying off better than even he could have hoped.

He had seen Merrick's distraction with the human woman and was glad he'd decided to sacrifice her. *Finally,* she could be put to some use. Another fortuitous break had been when the Scriptum literally unfolded itself to reveal secrets of the Kynd to her, and therefore to Aro, head of the Literati.

It was as if God Himself aided his plan!

That the Vampyre's daughter was the only one within the Literati able to decipher the text was utterly priceless, and a stroke of luck that carried with it the force of a sledgehammer. Anton despaired, which made him weak.

Angelia could be replaced. But Anton? Never. The Triumvirate would falter.

And now this unexpected cherry on his blood sundae. *Perfection.*

Aro squeezed his long, strong fingers around the front of the man's shirt. Lifting him, he pressed the hulk of his victim tight to the plank fence lining the grass clumped alley. Never mind a preliminary lick of skin where he intended to sink his fangs. It was a meal he wanted, not a dining experience. Still, the popping of punctured skin dragged a moan up Aro's throat, while hot blood slid down it in choking gulps.

The Grim Reaper hovered, waiting. Patient.

Invisible to the living, Darken stood at Death's heels, his huge fists clenched to keep his shrieking silent.

Merrick. The vampire spoke of Merrick.

Death sidled in tight to the human, preparing to extract his soul from his dead body. Darken readjusted his grip on the scythe.

Chapter Five

Angelia stirred as she awakened, snuggling deeper into Merrick's arms, closer to his chest. The sleeping bag she was cocooned in seemed thicker than a pillow, dulling the delicate feel of her body against his.

Which shouldn't matter. Still, he found solace in the wafting of that honey-lavender scent billowing from deep inside the warm nylon of the woman's bedroll. Not once did he put her down, not even during the crossing of the Acheron. Holding her had replaced his instinctive urge to take Kharon in his arms, to crush the other Kynd to him in a desperate hug to assuage his longing for touch.

To make up for his selfishness, he'd pressed close to Kharon, unabashedly sharing himself without having to put Angelia away from him.

Much to his surprise, the Ferryman peered down at the sleeping woman without saying a word. A strange light suffused the Kynd's expression instead, and he reached out to caress a stray lock of her golden hair from her forehead.

Angelia slept like a swaddled babe the whole time.

Even now as they traveled on firm ground, she wasn't fully awake. But he felt her soft gaze on him, and he glanced down to steal a precious glimpse of those twilight eyes, which were hooded with sleep.

The small body he cradled in his arms stiffened under his glancing scrutiny, the woman's senses firing to full alert. He didn't relinquish this stolen chance to hold her, but drew her tighter against his chest to still her.

And his thoughts, which kicked like the hobbled horses they were.

He refused to delve into his reasons for not setting her down, preferring instead to fall back on the excuse of who he was. Kynd needed touch almost as much they needed air to breathe, so of course he stole physical contact where he could.

Liar.

Ignoring that, too, he squeezed out the hint of a smile.

Which she ignored. However, she no longer squirmed to get out of his arms. Now *that* was a gift. He could enjoy the feel of her a little longer, even if she didn't care whether he offered her a rare smile or not.

"Where are we?" Angelia craned her neck to get a better view of their surroundings.

"Nearing the castle of the First Ring." His attention forcibly returned to the path before them, Merrick thought again of the Scriptum and how it had made it through Kharon's scrutiny, even though the Ferryman had seen the soulless man with the relic.

Maybe it does have a mind of its own.

What was it about that damned book that another Kynd would let it slip beyond his grasp? Well, Merrick wasn't going to find out as soon as he'd hoped, which also meant he hadn't been able to indulge in the company of his fellow Kynd beyond the length of the boat ride.

He and Kharon parted with longing hugs and said nothing about Angelia beyond the obvious. Merrick figured Kharon felt bad enough as it was. If the human woman was the only one to retrieve that book, then the Ferryman wasn't going to deny her passage.

"The castle? I missed Kharon?" Angelia's dismay yanked Merrick into the present. "How could I have missed a whole darned trip down a river?"

Merrick had known she'd be disappointed, but he still hated the sight of it. He wasn't too fond of how it clenched like a vise on his heart, either. Exactly where it shouldn't.

"I figured the river would do its thing as it had done with Dante. It knocks humans out, makes them swoon." He shrugged. "Or sleep, as it was in your case." Even with his leather jacket acting as a buffer, he still felt the slide of her sleeping bag in his arms.

"But not you?"

God, he didn't want to see such disheartening failure crowding into

55

those blue-black eyes, but there he was, gazing down again just the same. "No. The river doesn't have the same effect." If only she'd leave it at that, but he knew better. She was a scholar, wasn't she? It was her nature to know, even if she wouldn't like his answers.

"Go on."

Merrick stared straight ahead, concentrating on the path in front of him so he wouldn't stare down at the woman pressed close to his chest. He'd been enjoying his hike with her in his arms. While she'd slept he'd indulged his senses, had even pretended she wasn't human. That she was an angel sent down from Heaven to bestow quiet moments of peace upon him.

Which she had done. For a little while, the fomenting fury that pressed from the inside, toughening his skin, abated, giving his body a break from its inexorable transition into stone. Even now, she didn't fight to get out of his arms, and Merrick savored the feel of her, which unleashed his tongue so it roved like a stray dog.

"The river has a voice—many voices." He risked another peek down over his cheekbones to view the woman he carried. "Its flowing is like breath passing through the voice box, making sounds. The pitch is too high for human ears, so they can't hear what's being said. But on a subconscious level their brains are getting flooded, hypnotized. Which is why you swoon, or pass out." Could he blabber on just a bit more?

"And you hear these voices?"

He nodded, not daring to look down again. Besides, awake, her body was heating up the sleeping bag she was in, as though the speeding up of her pulse warmed her from the inside out. "They're mesmerizing, spellbinding." *Shut up, Merrick.* "They make me want to stay, to enter into Hell and stay here."

"But you can't."

Merrick snorted. "Yeah, well, it's easier than you might think."

At least, it had been easier, until he'd met the woman he now carried in his arms. He set her down, steadying her as she shimmied out of the constricting bedroll. She clutched his arm as she did so, and the grip of it shot a twinge straight to his balls.

God Almighty. He'd have to take her back to Acheron just so she'd pass out again, and he could function normally.

56

"But now that you're away from the river, surely the urge is gone? I mean, you can't want to spend the rest of your life in Hell."

"Why not? It certainly has its advantages."

* * * *

Angelia didn't like the honesty chiming through the words he spoke. Merrick was dead serious, which quieted her all the way to the bone.

"Don't worry. I'll get you back out before I do." The chimera's moment of being unguarded evaporated as if it had never been. He was again the storm cloud passing over the sun.

His snide comment pissed her off, a visceral reaction that rarely happened to her. Usually, she just got sad. But maybe Merrick was right, and being in Hell did have its advantages.

Angelia balled up her sleeping bag and stuffed it into her pack while she indulged in a rare mental tirade.

Did he really believe she was so shallow that the only thing she could be concerned with was her own safety? Did he really think his choice wouldn't bother his friend, Darken, either?

Merrick was the selfish prig, not her, believing that staying in Hell wouldn't bother anyone.

How could he do it? Yeah, she knew he harbored a thick rage he barely concealed, but still, it didn't mean he had to dwell in this ungodly place. She yanked the drawstring of her bag, cinching it taut like a hangman who relished his job.

"Angelia."

Merrick calling her name was just as enthralling as the voices in the river.

At least this voice she heard. Regrettably. Swallowing a deep breath, she cocked a disgruntled hip. "What."

Merrick ran his hand across the top of his head, mussing his black hair. He seemed frustrated with her, like he didn't know what to do with himself. His whole body tensed, his jaw clamping. She saw the slate of his eyes harden as his rage resurfaced.

"What?" She wouldn't gulp, damn it.

The chimera, still in his sexy gargoyle form, drew up to her. He was a full head and shoulders taller than she was and definitely twice as wide.

57

Angelia's head fell back just so she could keep looking at him.

Towering over her, his body electrified hers. They weren't even touching and her hips felt the pull of him, so that she had to fight to keep herself from slinking up against him like some big cat in heat.

Merrick glared down at her, the depths of his rock-like eyes fluctuating, plunging impossibly deep, constricting until they were flat and shallow.

"The castle," he growled, lifting a muscle-roped arm with a clawed hand at the end of it.

Well, hookay. She couldn't see the muscles rippling under his coat, but she sure as dog-crackers was imagining them. Angelia peeled her wanton gaze from Merrick to look where he pointed.

"Full of learned men, from before Christ." His voice scraped thick, menacing.

Yeah, that growling factoid ought to register a little stronger than it did. She should be heeding the message, not the vibration. The castle housed the greatest minds of all time. Aristotle, Ovid, Socrates. Yet, all she could think about was the chimera, who moved to stand behind her. *Very* close behind her.

He felt huge looming back there. She could smell the leather he wore. She could smell *him.*

What were a few dusty, old minds when she stood next to such heat? Such life? She didn't want to meet the revered minds of history, she wanted to get to know this chimera who delivered her to them.

Merrick lowered his head to drag his nose along her nape. Goose bumps erupted over her skin. "Someone might know where the human who stole the Scriptum was headed."

Dear God, she was practically panting. "Good point." And *oh yeah,* it was a lead to follow, even if he'd said it to taunt her. Because they were on an important mission.

Except.

"Merrick?"

"Hmm."

Ooh man, she loved his growl.

"I'd rather learn about you." There. She said it. Looking dead ahead and not at him, but she'd said it. Maybe her little fit of anger had given her the courage. She didn't know, or care, but she would risk his denial.

* * * *

Merrick's heart pinged then swelled, then constricted again like it couldn't figure out what its job was. His whole body went rigid so Angelia's softness, in contrast, seemed like a warmth cushioning the thin space of air between them.

He didn't want to tell her a damned thing. He didn't want to refuse her, either. Not this angel who tautened every nerve within him to singing. She had given him something of herself when he'd carried her across the Acheron, even if she hadn't known it. Christ, she was giving him something now, a thrill in his skin he'd not felt since…

Never.

Merrick had never felt this taut sensation before. It maddened him, drove him wild. It was all he could do to rein in his urges. He could and should give a little something back to this woman, no matter how she tormented him. No matter if she was human, she deserved his consideration.

He wanted to give her more than his *consideration.*

Jesus. What was happening to him? A day ago, he wouldn't have given a rat's ass about hurting any human's feelings. Now? Now, he'd met Angelia, Anton's miraculous, beautiful daughter, and his own emotions had somehow gotten tangled up with hers.

She wanted to know about him. The Vampyre's adopted darling was looking beyond the chimera's thickening skin, past the rage simmering in his very muscles. Merrick knew how volatile he was, yet she was seeing beyond that.

No, she was coaxing him beyond his consuming rage, and it unsettled him. So, for both of their sakes, he would opt to tell her something a little safer, a little easier on his baffled emotions, while he steered them toward the castle.

He dared to brush his knuckles against the small of her back to bump her forward. Even through her clothing, his fingers measured the inward curve of her spine, the bowing out of her wonderful ass. He curled his hand into a fist lest it grope for something more.

"Kharon is Kynd, like me. That's how I got you across the

Acheron."

She spun around so fast he had to lean back or bump into her. "He's Kynd?" Surprise brightened the blue in her dark eyes, her cheeks flushing with it.

And screw him, but he wanted those eyes grazing every inch of his body so his skin could bloom like that.

"Yes, unlucky bastard. My work is a walk in the park compared to his." He smelled her heat rising between them, the tendrils of musk soaked within it. She was a fertile woman, sensual, inadvertently stroking his Kynd soul. He mourned the loss of her ink-like irises as she turned forward to watch where her booted but dainty feet were going.

She took mincing steps, as if she was reluctant to be far from him.
And I crave it.

When she spoke, every cell within him tuned into her. "I believe it, considering all you do is watch souls walk by. You don't have to row," she jested.

Her words were the pulling of the pin on a hand grenade. His body stalled out as his rage exploded, swallowing him whole in its shrapnel cloud.

He knew she joked. He even saw the twitch at the corner of her mouth. She was kidding, God damn it. But he bristled anyway, like she'd snicked the business end of a knife across the meat of his heart.

Instantly, she noticed and stopped, like she was a frigging barometer attuned to him. Beautiful blue eyes blinking upward, she turned into the brunt of his fury. Her breath clogged, and she took three steps backward. Fear washed the earlier blush from her cheeks, and the sight of it ripped at him sharp, like a fist with talons. Merrick shook his head once, hard enough to rattle some sense back into it.

"I'm sorry," he growled, trying to rein in that sudden outward surge of his rage. His muscles trembled with the effort. "I wasn't expecting—" He couldn't breathe enough to form words. Hell, he hadn't been prepared for her comment in any way.

"N-no, I'm sorry, Merrick. I wasn't thinking." Even with the pounding of the blood in his head he heard the stammer in her apology, saw her hand lift like she was going to touch his arm then drop to her side.

He watched that shining confidence leak out of her pretty eyes, and the sight of it hit him low in the gut. He didn't like that her self-assurance could be so easily bruised. Then lost. As if it were a fledgling bird, easily battered by the winds assailing it.

Yet, he couldn't bring himself to coddle her. She stood brave in front of him; he wouldn't take that away from her. What he could do was get a stranglehold on his rage and give her an explanation. One she deserved.

"It's been too long," he hissed like a leaking gas pipe. His knees unhinged as though they were suddenly tired from lugging their burden, and Merrick dropped his ass onto the nearest rock.

Angelia sloughed her pack, too, and sat on that. She kept her head down while she fiddled with a twig, as if acutely interested in the peeling of its bark. Merrick studied her profile, the delicate slope of her nose, the silken wisps of hair kissing her temple and cheek. The sight of her helped him get a grip, helped him to dredge up his confession.

"It's been too long, Angel. I've done too much."

She let out a breath without looking at him. Then, as if he hadn't just alluded to his violent nature, she abandoned her pack to sit *closer* to him. Like it was safe to do so.

Pushing her away for her own welfare wasn't an option. Not when having her close eased him the way being with his Kynd did. Lord knew, he could use the frigging help.

Except with Angelia there was something more than what he shared with his brothers—a resonance. Which he didn't want to look too close at, not when he could barely keep his shit together.

He let go of the breath he'd been holding, drawing in a hint of the honey-lavender sitting at his knees. He fisted his hands so he wouldn't touch, wouldn't stir her scent by dragging his rough fingertips across her soft skin.

No. Better he confessed, so she would keep a healthy distance away from him, no matter how badly he craved and needed her beside him.

Reluctant to cause the wariness he knew he should, Merrick's words barely squeezed out through his clenched jaw. "It's our punishment, Angel. Kynd aren't Witnesses anymore." His damned breath shook as he sucked it in. "We do things. Things we were never meant to do, but

61

must."

"But that would mean—"

"God is a rat bastard?"

The corner of her lip twitched, working miracles on his equilibrium. "Yeah, but I was going to say it would mean you don't just sit on the Archway counting souls."

Merrick didn't answer her; he stared off at the castle. What could he say that wouldn't frighten her more than she already was?

Nothing. No words could lessen the mortification of the butchering he'd done to guard Hell.

She placed her palm on the flat of his thigh. Grounding him. Offering comfort. Picking at the scab protecting his heart from the colossal agony of his loneliness.

He hadn't felt comfort like this for more than two thousand years, and it scared the shit out of him. His entire body went rigid trying to dam two thousand years' worth of pain he shouldn't release. Certainly not onto an unsuspecting human woman who was only offering simple consolation.

Merrick gave a gentle squeeze of her fingers as he removed her hand to stand up.

But he didn't release his grip.

He gazed down at the woman who had chosen to kneel beside him.

Angel.

She was, too, looking up at him with those dark blue eyes as if she trusted him to a certain degree. But she held herself very still, lest one move from her untethered whatever emotions he barely contained.

Pain. A lot of it. Fury. *Confusion.* He felt like a bomb waiting for one hair to detonate him, he was that tense. Hell, he'd already pulled one pin. Hadn't he been sitting on a rock bleeding all over himself from a recent discharge?

The woman was smart to be wary. It was what he'd wanted. Fear draped over her like a cold, damp blanket—he felt it in the icy chill of her fingers.

God damn him for it. He'd wanted her cautious, not terrified.

Merrick shivered, choking a firmer grip on the leash of his rage.

She might be human, but he wouldn't make her his whipping post.

He would hate himself even more if he did. Which he hadn't thought possible, but there it was. He was a violent beast, and had been for the last two millennia, laying waste to too many Others to count.

Ghouls. Demons.

Vampires.

What would she think of him if he told her that? When he confessed to murdering the beings who gave her shelter, who invited her to live amongst them as though she were one of their own.

Thanks to God and His divine punishment, Merrick had been reduced to a base and vile creature. No different from those he was forced to savage.

God bless him, he had become the very thing he'd been condemned to kill.

* * * *

"Merrick?" Angelia's voice quavered like the chicken she was and she silently cursed herself. The chimera needed someone sturdy, not some quaking ninny, so she'd better stiffen her Ramen noodle spine to be strong for him. Even if she had to fake it.

Her lips had not suddenly gone dry, dang it. But the swiping of her tongue to moisten them was like a slap to the face of her denial. Which she chose to ignore and stood up, coiling her sweaty fist tighter with Merrick's hold so he wouldn't let her go.

Because she saw his agony. Heck, she *felt* it.

Whatever he did up on that Archway wasn't good. She'd seen the bony carcasses. Did she really want to know the gruesome details?

Yes. If it meant she could ease some of that drowning grief from his gray eyes. She wanted to comfort him so bad the need to do it quivered inside her, her body demanding she open up and take him into herself.

Acting on instinct, she reached out, pulling Merrick's rough hand around her back and pressing her body to his.

He hissed as his arm drew her in tight. Through the opening of his unbuttoned leather jacket, she could see the hammer-like blows of his heart punching the thick muscles of his chest. She could *smell* him, forcing her to remember there was a reason she'd let herself get squashed this close to Merrick and it wasn't to bask in that crystalline wildness.

She was trying to give him solace.

"You stop souls from entering Hell, don't you?" It wasn't a true question. She'd seen the evidence. But she wanted to come across as accepting, not as some dang coward.

He growled his answer, and Angelia closed her eyes as the scrape of it dragged delectably across her skin, pebbles of goose bumps shivering in its wake.

"Yes."

Ooh, she loved his growl, and needed to dredge up every ounce of self-restraint she had to keep herself on track. She would, for Merrick's sake. "And humans without souls who wish to pass?" She knew such beings existed. They were the stuff of her nightmares from as far back as she could remember. They were the things the gargoyles and chimerae of her dreams protected her from.

They were probably why she idolized the Kynd.

Merrick pressed his forehead to her crown, his uneven breaths caressing her hair. "Angel, no more." When he pulled back to look at her, he somehow plumbed a reassuring grin. The sight of it made her go all gooey inside.

Maybe it was because he seemed to be asking for mercy while his strong teeth reminded her that physically, he wasn't vulnerable at all. "This castle is probably the last beautiful thing you'll see for a few days. You should be paying attention to that instead."

Pfft. She highly doubted it. Merrick was beautiful, what with his black bangs curling in little spikes across his forehead. Like a row of mini scythes, they cupped his smallish ear, dragging her attention so her gaze followed the cords of his neck to the leather of his collar.

And he'd just called her *Angel.* She bet he didn't even realize it.

Besides, when she pulled her mind out of the gutter, she experienced something far more beautiful than architecture or a sinful body. She was aglow from receiving the compassion of a chimera.

Now that she knew how well guarded a secret that was, she felt the privilege of his gift. He was treating her like Kynd. Which made him irresistibly sexy. Even to a virgin.

Her core squirmed again, only this time it pulsed.

The muscles of Merrick's broad shoulders bulged as he lowered his head to take a deep breath.

Dear God, he was sniffing her! He'd sense, too, the heat of her hand, the heat of her thighs, and she had to struggle not to place his hand where she readied for him. She had to resist the flaming urge to pull it between her legs and ride his rough palm.

His fingers gripped hers so hard she thought he might break her bones. She couldn't stop her eyes from wandering low, to watch his manhood thicken and stretch the leather of his pants. Her tongue stole out to caress her lower lip, for different reasons this time.

"Come on, Angel." As Merrick tugged at her to resume their march toward the castle, she caught the glint of thick fangs. Which should have frightened the bee turds out of her. Seriously, what was he going to do with those? Bite her?

Oh, please, yes.

She ought to wash her brain out with soap. She wanted the chimera to bite her? Maybe it was time to stop living with vampires. Kynd didn't drink blood, she knew that much. But she couldn't shake visions of Merrick's sharp teeth pinching her nipples or sucking her breasts in between them.

Gads. She wasn't helping the situation here, not when her nipples went rigid with the promise of what Merrick's mouth could do. Turning her attention to where her feet were going would be far more helpful. Merrick was dragging her toward the castle. She shifted gears to follow willingly, and freed her mind from her breasts to think about the words he'd spoken as he'd pulled her with him.

He'd called her *Angel* again. Merrick might have spoken to her like his teeth were smashed together, but he had called her Angel.

An endearment, not a curse. She knew that because he didn't let go of her hand.

He kept hold of her.

And she took it for the truce it was.

* * * *

Even though Death hovered to claim the vampire's victim, Darken couldn't budge from the edge of the shadows.

Not this time. For too many centuries, he'd obediently performed his task.

Watching death upon violent death was taking its toll on him, just as it was his brotherkynd. Like them, he had no one to ease the terrible burden of watching men pass. Or from watching the women writhe, anguished in the throes of their deaths.

And if Death grew impatient? If the timeline was threatened by a stubborn hanger-on? Then Darken stepped in. His ultimate punishment. To be the wielder of that terrible scythe. The Grim Reaper no longer carried it. The condemned gargoyle did.

Now? Now Darken stood in horror as Aro dragged the human male's blood into his body. To live. While Merrick would not.

Blood trailed like a bird's eye view of a flooding delta, the many fingers pooling and branching off, soiling and soaking Aro's clothes. The vampire, in the throes of his greed, couldn't swallow all that was gurgling from the neck of his victim.

Darken watched, stricken.

The vampire took no notice, so enrapt was he in his feast. He hovered over the prone man like a macabre vulture, a golem leeching life. He didn't slide his fangs from the pallid flesh until Death fanned his long, bony hand across the human's heart to extract the soul.

The opposite of his victim, Aro flushed with life, his violet eyes sparkling.

Glittering just as Merrick's did with every rare greeting to his friend. Every time he and Merrick came together, the chimera's first gaze flashed brilliant, his joy evident, effervescent—spilling over in spite of his thinning soul.

Despite his thickening skin.

The sorrow engulfing him nearly buckled his knees. His skin felt as if it was a suffocating sheet of plastic, shrink-wrapping him so he couldn't breathe.

He and Merrick had been friends for thousands of years. They strove to stay in touch, however briefly, since their expulsion from the Heavens. Merrick's skin against Darken's was as familiar as his own.

At least, it had been.

Despair mushroomed thick as tar in his lungs, smothering him.

His brotherkynd could very well be stone already. Or locked forever in Hell, his magnificent black wings shorn from his back.

Oh God, please no. They were the chimera's pride.

For Merrick to see them severed from himself? Laying broken and useless in the filthy, red dust, would be torture beyond even what Darken could fathom. The bloody stumps protruding from Merrick's wide back would never heal. Connected to the chimera's heart, they would perpetually seep blood.

Tormenting his brother for all eternity.

Darken snarled, the first sound he had made in more than two thousand years while he'd trailed Death's cloak like a good little prisoner.

As if cued by his growl, Death moved to stand silent before him while the freshly claimed soul, upright but broken, waited with resignation beside its reaper.

Behind the specter and its harvested soul, the vampire staggered from the corpse, his entire front soaked with blood. Aro tottered like a drunkard away from the dead man. Death, with its reaped soul, turned to go, its job half completed, as the soul had yet to be delivered for judgment.

Darken could not unmoor his feet from the ground to follow. He ripped his gaze from the vampire to the receding figure of Death, his heart breaking, his breath clogged in his throat.

He could not move in either direction. The specter, with its soul, dimmed into nothingness on one side, while Merrick's murderer disappeared around the opposite corner of the alley.

Darken threw his face to the star spangled sky and roared his anguish toward an uncaring God.

He did not follow Death.

Chapter Six

Angelia stood at the base of the castle gawking up, her hand still folded within Merrick's. "It's even more spectacular close up."

Warmed by her awe, Merrick gave her fingers a gentle squeeze. He feared she would yank her hand away, but instead she shined those inky eyes up at him like she grasped the full extent of his gesture.

He wanted to have this contact with her. Doing so gave him a glimmer of what his life had been before he'd been cast to the gateway to stand vigil. After two thousand years, he was actually touching another being without killing it.

The beauty of the simple gesture resonated through every molecule of him and nearly loosed his true essence. Merrick was a fragmented heartbeat from exploding into full chimera.

A dangerous slip if he did so. One more time and he could kiss his precious wings good-bye. Right along with what was left of his soul, like they were a package deal.

Retaining his hold on his gargoyle form with his wings and tail safely cached, he stole a peek at the human woman standing beside him. He was pleased she found the castle beautiful, it was one of his favorite places.

Here there was none of the fire, blood, and torment of ravaged souls—only pagan magnificence. Clean lines, uncluttered foliage, statuary. Vast and airy galleries of marble and acres of polished granite. Alabaster rooftops spiking toward a scarlet sky. A place where the mind could soar, or rest in easy meditation. A place the great poets called home and never tired.

Angelia was a little breathless. Merrick watched with fascination as her chest lifted and dropped. "So, this is Limbo, huh?"

Peel your eyes from the temptation of her heaving breasts, idiot. So, he did. Reluctantly turning his gaze upward at the scenery in front of them. "Yes. God saw no reason to punish these souls for being born too soon. They knew nothing of His Greatness, and he does not fault them for it."

"Yeah, but he doesn't exactly forgive them either." She clapped her hand to her mouth. "Oh, my God! I'm so sorry." She shot Merrick a wild look, as if lightning was about to flash from the sky and scorch her where she stood.

Faster than any lightning strike, his guts clutched in reflex to her fear, and his rage, never far from the surface, tightened his skin. Yet, he chuckled as he pulled her palm away from her lips, as if it was more important to ease the woman than it was to unleash his fury.

"You're right. He doesn't forgive them, or else he would allow them entrance to Heaven. Intelligent and courageous souls reside in these halls. Every one of them capable of understanding the concept of God, even if they were born before the Son."

Her hand slid back into his. Merrick resisted the urge to squeeze his eyes shut with the joy of it, even as his thoughts railed against the truth that her touch had the power to dampen the rage inside him.

"You know, I don't think we have to enter the castle. I'm pretty sure we can assume where the thief took the Scriptum."

He barely heard her words, the sense of touch swamping his acute hearing. His angel had reached out for him. She sought him.

Damn it.

He didn't want to like her this much. She was human. Born of the very race God and His angel, Lucifer, had fought over. The very reason Merrick and his Kynd were now relegated to an eternity of misery doing that which they were not meant to do.

"Probably," he bit out. "But while you're here you might as well do a little sight-seeing." Merrick released her hand and strode off into the woods, leaving the confounding woman to show herself around the castle.

S. C. Dane

He hated parting from her, but continued his hard, angry pace toward the trees. He wouldn't explain himself. She'd either trust him, or not, and he didn't want her nose in what he was about to do, what he *needed* to do.

She was driving him dangerously mad, and he needed a quiet moment to think about that. Where better than at his favorite spot in these pagan woods, nestled by the little falls. Where the clear water cascaded in a pleasant runnel. If Merrick closed his eyes, he could pretend the warmth he felt on his rough skin was sunlight.

Not the regular sunlight of Earth, either, but the glow of celestial auras in Heaven.

The chimera, for all his rage toward his Creator, missed his home. So, he stole fragments like these when he could and listened to the gurgling of the falls, as if it was the angels' murmuring, in order to heal what was left of his tattered soul.

If he was going to keep Angelia safe, he had to do something to repair what little soul remained within him. Otherwise, they were both doomed and he damn well knew it.

Merrick slumped down on the thatched grass. He loved this hidden place. None of the Shades in Limbo ever came to this spot. Merrick liked to think it was his alone, that maybe God preserved it just for him.

To help him.

He refused to scoff while the music of the waterfall filled his head. It was a rule he held within himself in order to suspend reality. Only happy thoughts. Forget how corny it sounded. After eighteen hundred years of visiting this place without disturbance, Merrick could let all his troubles go.

He stripped out of his leather clothing to spread every inch of his thick skin upon the grass, where the heat from the ground worked into his bones, furthering the illusion of peace.

Here he could think without really thinking. Problems were resolved of their own accord when his rage wasn't interfering.

Except this time, it wasn't just his rage he needed to shed. He needed to shuck this physical urgency to join himself to the human.

To his Angel.

70

Thinking of her as an angel did nothing to enhance the fantasy he was in Heaven.

In Heaven, he had never lusted. He'd never lusted since being condemned, either. Which was why he worried about the Second Circle they were approaching, and meeting Minos, who guarded it.

The Beast wasn't Kynd, and would home in on Merrick's base desires like the infallible Judge he was.

"Shit."

Merrick kept his eyes closed, hoping his daydream of Heaven would wash over him to clear his thoughts. No luck. All he could think about was how nice it would be to have Angelia's warm, naked body curled alongside his while they lay together on the grass. His cock kicked, thickening as he envisioned her tail-like braid tickling him as she straddled—

Christ.

He bolted upright, elbows on his knees as he stared out over the pool.

Fighting Minos for passage into the next Circle was going to be unavoidable. Merrick palmed his erection, surprised by how easy the damned thing swelled to life with a mere thought.

He couldn't shake the human woman out of him any more than he could dislodge his chimera, and that made him uneasy.

No other Kynd, that he was aware of, had ever had this problem. Which meant he'd lost more of his soul than he figured. Merrick rubbed his hands over his face as he sucked in a deep breath, hoping he'd keep the last of his soul, paper thin as it was, long enough to get this woman and the book back to the surface.

A splash launched him onto his bare feet, his wingtips bristling to explode from the scarred creases in his back. Merrick felt the slide of his lion's claws pull upon his fingertips. With a predator's gaze, he followed the rippling vee trail cutting along the surface of the vermilion pool.

Angelia's slick head popped up like a seal, her naked arms stroking clean arcs as she pulled herself through the water.

His breath dropped out of his lungs in a single gush. "Holy Christ."

The woman, who wore only what God had bestowed upon her at birth, skimmed through the water like an otter.

S. C. Dane

Merrick trailed his tongue across his lower lip in anticipation of tasting the woman. He moved like a predator toward the bank, enthralled with the sight of her, how the clean, red-tinted water sluiced across her bare back, how her blonde hair fanned about her in weightless tendrils.

The water encircled his thighs as he stepped into it, and Merrick cut quietly through the pond, his body blessedly light and buoyant. He slipped beneath the surface, his strong limbs propelling him toward his quarry.

When he could feel the currents of her strokes caress his skin, he popped his head above the surface.

* * * *

Angelia, caught off guard, yelped and splashed backward, twisting away from the swimming chimera. She'd thought she was the only one around or she would have never dared to strip out of her clothes for a swim.

"Merrick!" she sputtered, as she folded her arms across her bare breasts, which to her shame bobbed buoyantly, her nipples like rocks in the cool water. Without her arms to tread, she started sinking immediately.

Merrick's strong hands clasped her ribcage, holding her aloft so she wouldn't drown from her virtue. She felt his body glide up close behind her, solid and substantial even in the water, and God help her, but she almost leaned into it.

She turned around to face him instead.

Big mistake.

He suffered no chastity. His shoulder muscles were sleek, his chest powerful. In the red-tinged pool she could see the bold lines of his stomach muscles as his legs stroked to keep them above the surface.

His slate eyes glistened like rubies in the reflection of the pond, yet the quirk of his lips softened the hardness of his gem-like stare.

He was gorgeous. A nymph of the water.

"What are you, chimera?" she blurted on a breath, and her embarrassment reared like a slap to her face. Thank God the pool reflected the colors of burning embers, masking her chagrin.

Merrick held onto her, his thumbs caressing the bulbs of her breasts. "Doomed." He didn't smile, but the corner of his lips twitched to reveal a thick fang.

Angelia swallowed, and her legs, without needing to hold up her body, betrayed her as her thighs lifted to ease the sudden throbbing of her clit. She couldn't drag her eyes off him. "No," she denied. Yet, she didn't know what she was denying. That he was doomed? That he would let go of her?

"What are you doing here, Angel?" Suspicion hardened the line of his jaw. A muscle in Merrick's cheek ticked as she watched him and read the emotions passing across his handsome face. His black hair, curled in wet, scythed spikes, lined his clouded brow.

Angelia felt the stirrings of fear. "I'd been walking around. I found the pool and wanted to swim." Her voice quavered, revealing her to be the coward she was. Even as she yielded to the stroking of his thumbs, her back slightly arching into his palms, her chin lifting.

* * * *

He felt her softening under his palms and knew instantly the moment her body caved, because his hips instinctively canted to reach her. Merrick worked the muscles of his jaw, hoping that grinding his teeth would distract him from this desire engulfing him.

The urge to slide that painfully stiffened part of himself into the woman he held carried too much power over him. He *needed* to join himself to her, *craved* the meshing of their bodies. The compulsion boggled him. And infuriated him.

As Kynd, a physical union wasn't necessary to feel close. But this drive to bind himself to another body scored deeper. The connection with this human woman hinted at something mind-blowing, and he knew it would carve deeper than anything he'd ever known before.

Merrick was developing a healthy dose of sympathy for the motivations of man.

"You were spying on me," he accused.

Her eyes grew wide with her denial. The water around her shoulders rippled with her agitation, swirling those soaked tendrils of her hair like lissome snakes. "No! No, I swear. I swear I didn't know you were here."

73

In her urgency, she grasped his forearms, inadvertently drawing herself closer and releasing her bobbing breasts. Her lips parted as her breaths quickened, the rim of the pond's water, like viscid whiskey, curved round each of her boobs. Merrick's mouth watered to kiss her.

He had never touched a human's lips in his life. But he wanted to taste her, he wanted to slide his tongue along hers, to feel that intimate connection of breaths. He wanted to trust her, because he couldn't trust himself.

She tilted her chin to look up at him. "Merrick."

Just his name, as if she wanted, but didn't know what.

He blinked hard, then backpedaled, dragging her with him until his feet touched the bottom of the pool. "Don't." His voice rasped; he didn't let her go.

She licked her bottom lip, as if to console it.

"God in Heaven, woman, why are you here?" He cursed, breathless, as his eyes followed the trail of her tongue.

"I don't know, Merrick, I swear I don't. All I know is that I saw this trail, the one leading here. I thought I was alone."

He hated how her beautiful eyes widened with fear, that she was scared of him. Because he believed her. She hadn't been following him as he'd first thought. If she had been? He wasn't as upset as he should have been. She'd caught him in an unguarded moment, something reserved for Kynd.

The thought of her watching him cracked open something in his chest he'd thought long dead.

Damn it. He couldn't let her in. "Angel."

She raised her eyes to him, and he saw the hopeful trust in them bloom, as if she sensed the shifting of his thoughts. So help her, she was an innocent, and Merrick bit his sharp teeth down on another curse.

For all his barely tamped rage, she trusted him.

"Come on," Merrick tugged her weightless body to the shallower waters, regretting the one shredded fiber of his decency he had left. Turning away from her to give her some privacy, he made his way to where he'd piled his things on the bank.

Well, he wasn't fully altruistic, now was he? He left her alone to get a grip on his damned traitorous body.

"I'm sorry, Merrick." She followed him, and he didn't need the warbling of her voice to tell him. The honey-lavender scent of her blossomed in the moisture of her skin. As though her singular odor was a tapered finger hooking his chin, he turned to her.

She stood before him dripping, her clothes and pack bundled in her arms to hide her breasts and the soaked knot of curls at the apex of her thighs.

He wanted to touch that so badly, to know if it would be coarse, springy.

He balled his leather pants in his fist to hide his burgeoning erection. "You found your scholars all right?"

She nodded, then turned around to dress, baring her plump, heart shaped ass. Merrick's hips rocked forward, instinctively drawn. Putting on his human clothing seemed like a damned good idea, and not because the leather helped to keep the rest of his chimera locked beneath his gargoyle skin.

"I came up on two of them arguing the merits of beer over wine. Can you believe that?" She shoved her arms into her shirt, her wet skin sliding delectably across her spine. "Two of our world's greatest minds and they're railing like drunks at a pub."

"You expected something a little loftier."

Angelia spun around half dressed. "Yes!" Immediately she reddened, but went to work hiking her pants on over her wet legs. "Yes, I did. I mean, they seemed so normal sitting there. They were as regular as you or me," she confided.

Merrick's lips twitched into an unfamiliar grin. "Angel, we're not very regular."

"You know what I mean."

Not really. She was the most extraordinary creature he'd ever set eyes on, and that was saying something. During his centuries of guarding the Archway, Merrick had seen many a being. Were-animals, demons that defied description, even warlocks. He'd killed them all, which wasn't something he wanted to think about just then, no matter how bad he needed to get his mind off the half-dressed woman in front of him.

Angelia plunked down on her butt to lace up her boots, her hips widening, demarcating her slender thighs. She seemed blissfully unaware of the ways her body moved as if to taunt him. "But it got me to thinking."

Merrick tucked his cock into his leather pants then buttoned them to trap the damned thing. "And?"

His question fetched her up. Her cheeks flushed a warm scarlet, and he realized she was too embarrassed to admit how chancing upon the scholars made her feel. At least, that's what he was going for. She hadn't dropped her gaze as he'd squished himself, so he had his hopes.

Merrick grinned fully, half-adoring the bloom of her skin. She didn't seem to have a clue how she was affecting him beyond his physical needs. Her presence lightened him, kept his rage at bay. For the moment, anyway. "Go on."

"You'll think I'm an idiot." She waved him off as she slung her bag onto her back.

"I won't. I promise." Daring, he took her hand again, to lead them back onto the trail toward the Second Circle. The gentle curling of her fingers around his somehow did the same to his frigging heart. He wouldn't let go, no matter how disconcerting the feel of it was.

Movement unhooked her tongue. "Okay, but don't laugh. Scout's honor?"

"Scout's honor." Whatever that meant. He tightened his fingers over hers.

Nervous expectancy shined in her eyes as she tilted her chin up to look at him. A little stubbornly, too, like she challenged him to poke fun at her. She took a breath and gushed out what she had to say. "I didn't feel so stupid. Like I wasn't as useless as I thought I was."

She shared an intimate fear with him, so he kept to his oath and didn't laugh. Which wasn't hard. He wasn't amused by her admission. A growl crept out of him instead; low and menacing.

Merrick yanked her close. "You're walking into the guts of Hell, lady, to retrieve an important relic. How is that useless?"

"Yeah, it's, ah..."

In a blink, he girded her slender waist, tugging her hard against him, so that she straddled his thigh, her hot core branding him. The tips of her wet hair feathered his forearm, blowing his thoughts apart, scattering them to the winds.

He wanted to say something to her, but what?

Damn. He couldn't think, not with the glorious heat of her riding his upper leg.

Lowering his head, Merrick dragged his nose along the delicate skin of her neck so that he drowned in her scent. He clutched her harder to his body, sliding the tip of his tongue along the edge of her earlobe, stealing an ambrosia-laced sample of her.

For the want of a deeper taste, he cupped the back of her head, snarling her name, gliding his rough cheek along her silky one, trailing his mouth toward hers. The petal soft touch of her lips took his breath and he hovered for an instant, thickening more.

"*Holy Christ,*" his curse entered her mouth, and he nearly exhaled another as his entire body wrung tight with the mingling of their breaths. He'd have never believed the intensity, the tornado of sensation that ripped through a body when it held a potential mate.

Merrick plunged his tongue past Angelia's plump lips, desperate to ground himself, to lose himself, he didn't know. All he could understand was this urgency to possess her, to be possessed.

He played his tongue with hers, the raw taste of the woman carnal. Helplessly he licked for more, deepening the kiss as she melted against him.

* * * *

Holy Christ.

The rasp of Merrick's tortured curse attuned Angelia's body to his craving, and something flooded through her, burning and wringing her womb with a sweet ache.

She had never been kissed the way Merrick kissed her. Not where emotion flooded so ripe on a tongue, where hunger drove a mouth deeper, and desperation shed its latent power and consumed.

Angelia gripped the chimera's wet hair to root herself to him, her hips grinding helplessly against his thigh. She bit harder, stroking his tongue as he suckled, needing. A moan slid up her throat, and he gobbled it, his body growing rigid, trembling.

Receding?

Angelia resisted his withdrawal, wove her fingers deeper into his hair. "No."

But Merrick retreated from the devouring of her mouth. Pressing his forehead to hers, he nodded. He couldn't speak. Heck, he was barely breathing, so she knew she had to let him go. Eyes didn't lie, and Merrick's were deep and wild, as if the rage he harbored bubbled out of him like lava from a volcano.

No matter if she understood his reason or not, she still felt an expanding void from Merrick's withdrawal, a feeling of loss that threatened to engulf her.

From just one kiss.

One kiss and he had her. Just like that, she'd tossed aside the resolve she'd cultivated earlier, when she'd first laid eyes on him at the Triumvirate gathering.

She'd been entrusted to retrieve a priceless artifact. She had sworn to resurface with just one precious thing in her arms, not two. Her reputation as a scholar was at stake, her father had laid down a fortune for her safe return. This temptation for the chimera was a distraction from her quest.

Wasn't it? God help her, she didn't know for certain. She hadn't been able to cipher all the text she'd been working on before the Scriptum had been stolen. She couldn't remember what had been revealed to her—only bits and snatches. But she was certain the answer to her question lay within its illuminated pages. If only she hadn't fainted, maybe she could have stopped the thief.

Unless.

Unless, the Scriptum had meant to get stolen, and, therefore, meant for her to chase it.

Balls.

She needed that gilded manuscript. It contained her destiny and the answers to her innate attraction to the Kynd.

To Merrick, who shoved distance between them despite his initial claiming.

"Okay, then." *Hoo-wow.* Angelia flipped the heavy mass of her wet hair over her shoulders, she fiddled with the hem of her shirt, anything to not look at the rigid gargoyle braced off a few feet away from her.

She wanted more of his kiss. But she wouldn't look at him because she sensed he was barely clinging to what little control he had on himself. And, not to drop a pun, but his entire body had grown rock hard. He obviously needed what little he had.

Merrick was far more vulnerable than she'd imagined. Which galvanized her, making her feel somewhat powerful in her own right. She could protect him, too, as they traveled deeper into Hell.

Like they were a team, of sorts.

Maybe that was what the Scriptum had intended. The notion seated itself in her heart like it lived there. She couldn't ignore it. Not its rightness, its odd familiarity. That it might be meant for the chimera to be nestled in her heart emboldened her, enough so she found herself taking the initiative.

"Time's a-wasting, Kynd. Let's rock and roll." Angelia struck out for the Second Circle.

* * * *

As they hiked deeper into the darkening woods, Merrick felt the stroke of Angelia's gaze. He felt her smile, too, like it blazed from the inside out, warming his skin. The woman had no clue how she shined, utterly unaware she was his beacon as they traversed this dismal forest looming around them.

"I'm thinking the Scriptum is on its way to Lower Hell." She spoke low, as if there were eavesdroppers hiding within the blackened trees.

"Straight to where a thief would take it," he agreed, guiding her around a gnarled root tangling the path. He kept hold of her hand, savoring the rush of being in constant touch with another being.

"Do you think we'll catch him before he gets there?" Like she didn't notice he maintained contact.

Merrick glanced sideways at her, and she looked up, her eyes avid for their quest. He liked that. Too much. "Sorry to say, but I doubt it."

"I didn't think so. But you know what he looks like, right?"

Merrick nodded but kept walking until Angelia stopped, the weight of her body pulling him back so he had to quit walking, too. "And?"

"*And*," Merrick tugged her hand to get her moving again. "That's all I've got. I can't feel his soul, because he doesn't have one."

"Hold up." She halted again, making a *v* with her fingers. "Two things. He doesn't have a soul?"

"No. I don't let the soulless ones in, either, so I'm kicking myself in the ass here."

She giggled.

"I don't think giggling is allowed in Hell." Reluctantly he grinned, enjoying the sound of it.

"No, probably not."

Merrick watched her wrestle her mirth, subdue it so it shone only from her blue-black eyes.

He liked that shine a lot, too.

"You said *two* things," he reminded her. Like an idiot, because he knew the second thing would be about him directly.

"You *feel* souls?"

At least she didn't latch onto *how* he didn't let the soulless into Hell. "Yes. But trust me, it's no gift."

"I can imagine." She curled her other hand over his, as if to hold onto more of him.

God in Heaven, he loved the stroke of her palm across his rough knuckles. He struggled to keep his expression neutral. What would she think if he threw his face up to the sky with his eyes squeezed shut, as if in supplication?

He didn't want to know, in case it scared her and caused her to release his hand. So, he started them walking and kept talking. Curse him, but he wanted to delve, he was curious to know her.

"Can you imagine it, Angel? What do you think a soul should feel like?" He nudged her with his elbow to prod her. He was eager to know what she'd come up with, with all her education, her innate compassion.

She gazed up at him, her little teeth biting her lower lip as she thought about his question. "I bet the souls going into Hell are light, and not very warm."

"Hmm, that's very good. You're close."

"Yeah?" Her smile beamed like the rays of the sun, warming him to his bones.

"Yeah. The souls that pass are scraped thin, their sins chafing them raw. Some know it, and have a sense of their fate. Those are the ones who pass quietly." Merrick lost his grin and himself in the images of those souls who were hunched and cowed, their spirits beaten, their heads hung low. His rage simmered, threatening to suck him into its cyclonic spiral.

"And the others?" The glide of her voice stilled him. She leaned in, her tender touch anchoring him, as though she knew the feel and weight of her against him would temper his consuming anger.

Merrick gazed down with not a little wonder at this woman. He liked how golden her hair was, that there was a crooked part running haphazardly through the center of her crown, spilling highlights in its wake. Concentrating on that loosened his tongue, and the stranglehold of his ever-present ire.

In that moment, he felt his own soul release a bit of itself to her, trusting in her presence, in her inner strength she'd yet to plumb. Merrick squeezed her hand, tightening his fingers to mirror the pressure around his heart. He pushed onward.

"The others scream, Angel. They never fathomed the cost of the harm they were doing. They don't truly understand until it's too late." Merrick eased his grip when he realized how hard he was squishing Angelia's hand. Her fingers were ghost white from the loss of blood.

"Sorry."

She didn't say anything as she lifted his arm to duck in close, snuggling up to him as they walked.

God in heaven. He flexed his arm to hold her there, so she'd know he liked her bold move, that it had been the right thing to do, even though it peeled back one more layer of the stone that had thickened to keep his fury in check.

His Angel was softening him with her kindness.

A dangerous thing, actually, but he'd make damned sure not to unleash it on her. He lifted her over a sharp rock jutting out into the path, her weight nothing in his strong arms. They continued on as if he hefted her from harm's way every day, all day. *Familiar.*

"Thanks."

"No problem."

"Merrick?"

"Hmm?"

"Can I ask you another question?"

He nodded.

"Why did you agree to do this? Guide me into Hell, I mean. You could have said *no*. I don't think the Triumvirate could have forced you to do it."

No, they couldn't have. But that wasn't the explanation she was searching for. She wanted to know why he would do it for *her*. She was seeking reassurance, as much as he sought comfort in her touch.

"Well, Angel. Since we're baring our souls here." He winked at her, jesting to lighten the mood while they traversed through the blackened forest separating the Circles. He dared to give a little more of himself to her, even though a twinge of apprehension tickled his gut. What if his answer wedged her from him?

Shaking his head did nothing to ease his dread. It was one thing to secretly give himself over to her. But it came with a terrible cost, and already he grew afraid of losing her. He took the proverbial plunge. "I smelled you."

"What?" She grounded them both to a halt. Even in the deep shadows of the forest, he could see the blush blooming on her hornet-stung cheeks, could smell the very scent that had captivated him from the start.

He dabbed her nose with the tip of his finger, relieved to see her spark with modesty, not disgust. "I smelled you and I was intrigued. *Angry*, but curious, nonetheless."

"Seriously?"

He nodded, giving her a shy grin.

"Huh. I like that." She gave him a bashful grin, too. "It makes me feel special."

"You are that, Angel." Was she ever. And innocently beautiful, too. He craved more than just her touch—he wanted the intimacy that went with it. But, he knew better than to loosen his thoughts on that scenario. Thinking of himself physically cleaved to her, her twilight eyes drinking him in while his body was joined to hers, rendered his balls too tight. Goosebumps skittered across his ass.

"My turn for questions."

They resumed walking.

"All right."

"Can I braid your hair for you?" Not that he knew how, exactly. He just yearned to feel the golden softness of her tresses in his rough hands. If she denied him? He held his breath as he teetered on the edge of an uncertain and looming abyss.

* * * *

"Ah, yeah, sure. Right now?" Gads, his shoulder muscles bulged under his heavy leather coat, like he was doubtful but ready to demolish anything that dared trifle with him. The mix of his brawn and embarrassment spiraled straight from her heart to her mons. She tingled down there, while he stood in front of her, bravely anxious, his raw energy electrifying the air around them.

Merrick clenched his jaw, and twin baby's fists bunched on either side of it. His gray eyes stirred like mercury. "Why not? You haven't rested in a while," he growled, and she lost herself in the crawling of it along her skin.

Huh? Oh, yeah, he wanted to braid her hair immediately. *Catch up, idiot.* Besides, Mr. Gorgeous noticed something she didn't.

She hadn't rested for a while. Since she'd been higher than a rocket as Merrick held her close to him, she'd never noticed. She was too giddy with the rush of his wanting to touch her to pay attention to such trivial details.

Like a ewe in heat, she let him lead her off the path to a little clearing that opened up to reveal the crimson sky above them. Merrick shed his pack then squatted, resting his great weight on his spread knees, his long thighs burgeoning under the chocolate leather of his pants.

Angelia's insides squirmed, ruffling a heated flush across her skin. He wanted her to sit in the nest of his thick thighs so he could play with her hair. Did the chimera have any idea what a turn-on that was?

She cozied in before he could rethink his request.

And was immediately blanketed in the bulky warmth of him, in the scent of his leather clothes, in that wild, crystalline crispness she associated with his chimera.

Before her hands went AWOL to caress his muscular thighs, she bent her head and gathered up her hair, sectioning it into three heavy ropes. His upper legs flanked her peripheral vision and his wall of a chest hovered behind her.

Heavy heartbeats whaled against the air between them. Her own, or Merrick's?

Angelia licked her suddenly dry lips. "Here. You plait them, weave them back and forth, one through the other and the next, then back again."

A large hand tenderly cupped her scalp, stopping her breath. Then the chimera's fingers combed themselves into her hair, stroking her thoughts to her split ends, where they dropped unheeded.

One word shimmered across her mind. *Luxuriant.*

Merrick, the towering hulk of power and rage, was incongruously gentle.

Angelia surrendered to his ministrations, resting her arms on his legs like they were the armrests of an overstuffed chair. One she liked to curl up into when she read her hoarded romance novels.

She was going to melt into mush while he was nervously tender behind her. For once, she didn't let her self-consciousness ruin this moment for them. She basked instead, sensing Merrick needed this even more than she did.

He fought with himself, though she didn't quite know how she knew that. All she could understand in that moment was he didn't stop the slow, rhythmic sweeping of her locks, that he ran his palm across her hair more than he needed to just to braid it.

He was petting her.

Which made her feel coveted, cherished. Sure, her father and mother doted on her. They'd never been stingy with their affection for her. But, it was nothing like this. Merrick wasn't a being who dwelled within the walls of a loving home. He was the solitary, necessarily violent Guardian of the Archway to Hell.

And this simple need of his split her heart. She understood then a little of what it was to be Kynd, to be trapped and sentenced to an eternity of solitude.

She pressed her fingers into his leather-clad knees. Merrick's hands stilled.

"Angel." Her name was a guttural sigh squeezed from a strangled throat. Merrick's legs slid out from under her hands as he leaned over her, forcing her forward with his palm flattened across her back. She straddled the ground on her hands and knees, her new braid swinging down in front of her.

The chimera hovered over her, one muscled arm braced over her shoulder like a tree trunk while he, a giant above her, trembled.

* * * *

Burying his face under her braid, Merrick scraped his sharp teeth along the tender, thin flesh of Angelia's nape to stir up more of her intoxicating scent. He'd known better than to ask to touch her hair, had known how hard he would have to struggle to keep his animalistic longings in check. And yet, he'd needed to stroke her like he needed air to breathe.

Like he now needed to feel the plush of her body tucked beneath him, the silk of her skin in sacred contrast to his own rough, heavy mass.

Merrick ran his palm along her slender ribcage, tracing the narrow path of her waist to the flare of her hip, and then down the back of her long thigh. The pad of his thumb pressed as it glided along the clothed flesh of this soft female underneath him.

Great God in Heaven. He sucked in a staggering breath. No wonder humans sinned. No wonder they risked Hell for such exquisite pleasures. His erection burgeoned, heavy and crammed in his pants, and he pressed his groin to Angelia's bottom to relieve some of its throbbing ache.

The damned thing merely pined for more. Merrick found himself grinding his pelvis against his Angel's inviting rump, his fingers digging into her hips, desperate to assuage the pulsing of his cock while he nuzzled the cream of her neck.

She backed against him willingly, her spine curling like a beautiful cat, the honey-lavender scent of her rising with her heat.

Helplessly, he drew one hand from her robust hip to free himself. His engorged shaft felt hot against his palm, the searing silk of it burning like a brand. Merrick shoved himself backward, backpedaling until he could get his two feet beneath him. He stood heaving and sweating in the little clearing, his fingers spread like he needed to grab chunks of the entire world.

"Merrick?" She turned on her knees to face him, the buttons of her shirt undone low enough to reveal the fleshy melons of her small breasts. Her cheeks were flushed, her eyes nearly black.

"I'm sorry, Angel," he rasped. God, he panted like he'd just finished a hard fight to kill a ghoul, and all he'd done was—

Christ. There was nothing minor about what he caught himself doing.

"Merrick, it's okay." She comforted him. He'd come within a hair of desecrating her, and she sought to ease him? He didn't deserve her. How was that for a complete switch in attitude?

Merrick the chimera didn't deserve a human.

But Angelia wasn't just some human and he knew it as sure as he felt his swollen, singing cock.

"No." He shook his head hard. "No, it's not okay." He was base, vile to have touched her like that. He didn't like seeing her standing before him so uncertain, as if his retreat hurt her instead of made her feel better. She looked at him with confusion pooling in her darkened eyes.

Merrick reached for her, dropped his hand. Then he clapped both of his palms to his head as he blew out an exhale to get his frigging heart to settle down. Even his thick fangs had lengthened, for Christ's sake, as if in sympathy to his cock.

"Jesus. I'm a God damned train wreck."

She grinned a little, and his ramming heart steadied at the sight of it. She took a tentative step toward him.

Merrick faltered backward, maintaining their distance.

* * * *

Doesn't he want to get closer? Angelia shoved her insecurities aside to study the chimera, who looked like he was jacked to blow at the first snap of a twig.

Maybe he would, which was why he wanted the space.

Perhaps it was her lifetime of idolizing Kynd, but something niggled to set that reasoning off-kilter. She couldn't help feeling it was wrong for

Merrick to be alone right then, that it didn't seem normal for him to be standing there all by himself.

She needed to go to him, because it was the right thing to do, no matter if he spurned her advances. For him, she would push her self-doubts aside. He was Kynd, he needed touch to soothe him. And Angelia needed his touch right back, to strengthen her.

Two peas in a pod, they were. Who would have guessed?

Not giving herself time to change her mind, Angelia locked eyes with Merrick and marched up to him, her head tilting back the closer she got. His scent enveloped her, and she almost succumbed to the masculine allure of it, silently willing away the pulsing between her legs. She forced herself to stop within an arm's reach, and tentatively sought his fingers with the wiggling of her own.

The moment their fingers twined together, Merrick squeezed her hand and dropped his head with a jagged sigh. "Angel."

"Shush, chimera. It's all right. We just got a little carried away, that's all."

He didn't say anything, so she didn't know if he agreed or disagreed. That wasn't the point of her standing so close to him again. She was offering him relief, solace from his inner demons, and she would ignore the hot tremors emanating through her body. They would recede eventually, even though a part of her mourned the subsiding of those tingling shockwaves.

Tugging his hand, she felt like the captain of a large ship weighing anchor. "Come on. Let's get our packs. Maybe walking will do us both some good."

"I doubt that. This goddamned erection is killing me."

Angelia burst out laughing, dispersing the tension like a flurry of doves scattering upward toward the sky.

Merrick grinned, too, if a little reluctantly. She liked the sight of its uncertain tilt. It made him sexier, softening his features so he looked like the boy next door. Okay, not quite the typical boy next door. But then, Angelia had grown up with vampires, and they always had a dangerous edge to them.

"Come on, you baby. I promise it will go away if you stop thinking about it."

87

Merrick didn't budge. He yanked her back, his grin now teasing her as he drew her close, her chest bumping against his. "I don't think I like you knowing how a male's body parts work."

Yowza. Her nipples twisted like zealous schoolgirls with their hands reaching high, they were that desperate to make contact. "Jealous?"

Merrick's eyes slid to granite. "Maybe."

Her thoughts went haywire. He was serious. "I..." She what, didn't like it? She'd be a flaming liar if she said she didn't. "I think maybe..." Without dragging her gaze from the storming slate of Merrick's, she licked her lips. "I think maybe I like that." She was nothing if not articulate.

Merrick's gray eyes deepened, the pupils dilating as his fingers coiled tighter around hers.

"Angel," he growled, his lip lifting off a thick canine.

She didn't flinch, not when she could feel his heat, see the pleasure of her response ripple through him.

But then he blinked. *Hard.* And shook his head and shoulders, as if he were aligning his spine. Or maybe his wings. A few seconds passed before he spoke again.

"All right," Merrick ceded, his voice rough like he had to push it up his throat.

"All right," Angelia agreed. Although she wasn't sure what she was agreeing to. All she knew was that the chimera snatched up her hand again after letting it go to shoulder both of their packs, then led them back to the trail.

Chapter Seven

Darken wrung his fists around the handle of the scythe he still held, a memento to his centuries of trailing Death now that the Shade had departed without it. Now that the gargoyle had just abandoned his God-decreed post.

The weapon balanced beautifully in his rough hands. Like a wearisome companion, its mere presence was familiar to him. Because it was Darken who lifted then swung the scythe, severing the reluctant souls from their dying bodies.

The shrieks his cleaving wrought pierced his heart like the red-hot daggers they were. Until their numbers had grown too vast, too cumbersome, and Darken's heart, like his skin, grew too thick, as if the torment he incurred spread over him one layer of resentful soul at a time.

Standing in the quiet alley with Death's scythe, the gargoyle felt the rush of his impulsiveness expand inside him.

He was damned, which was nothing new. His fall had happened millennia ago, and since then, he'd done nothing but ensure that his divinely appointed fate would come to pass. Like so many other Kynd, Darken was well on his way to becoming Grotesque. One more swipe of the scythe wouldn't condemn him more.

If anything, it would free him, even if just for that crystalline moment of utter satisfaction, of knowing he touched kin, no matter how far away he was from Merrick. Darken would annihilate the vampire's threat to his brotherkynd with one, centuries' honed swing of his blade. Aro's over-long tour of the planet would end this night.

Stealing one last glimpse over his shoulder to watch Death fade into the ephemera, Darken felt the harsh edges of the physical realm scrape his thick skin, and he felt suddenly vulnerable, and terribly alone on this plane.

The mud beneath his bare feet squished between his toes, the queer sensation freezing him for a moment. The weight of his decision pressed on his bare shoulders as he wrung his grip on the wood handle. Renewing his resolve with every twist, Darken struck out after his quarry, his breaths puffing little plumes in the pre-dawn chill.

Every step increased his lust for this kill. His blood sluiced rhythmically, heating him so he sprung ever faster, his thick thigh muscles swallowing the distance to his prey. The stench of blood rode metallic and heavy on the wind.

The vampire was easy to track.

For once, Darken tingled with enthusiasm for the kill. His breaths came fast, easy, his body working fluidly. His lips stretched into a rare, fang-laced grin. He felt, suddenly, incongruously happy. Running after this new destiny filled him with inexpressible joy, even as the black gloom of condemnation pressed upon his muscular back.

Ignoring it was easy when the stench of his prey thickened. Darken knew he would pay dearly for his insubordination. He just wasn't sure how or when. Once he killed the vampire, what would happen then? Would God render him to stone instantly? Already his thoughts ran inward, assessing his body for the ways it moved.

Unhindered. Sinuous.

God was yet unaware, so he had time to annihilate the threat to his Kynd.

At the end of the alley, the vampire's scent congealed with that of the dead human, and went no further. Pivoting, Darken scanned the shadows. He tilted his head to better hear the panting as it curled into his ears. The breaths labored, then ceased, as if the vampire knew he was being followed and tried to hide in the recesses of the night by holding his breath.

As if he can. Kynd didn't need much light to see. He had been created to stand Witness—he didn't miss much. His fingers tightened around the shaft of the scythe.

"Aro." The vampire was pressed into a shadowed corner, trying to

90

be invisible. Killing the head of the Literati suddenly lost a bit of its charm. The vampire was a coward.

"Face your reward, leech." The copper-ish tang of fresh blood lay in the atmosphere like a miasma, the acrid bile of fear tainting it. Aro had fed so heavily the scent of his victim oozed from his pores.

Like it was day, Darken watched the vampire push himself away from the wall to face him, the demon's fangs glinting in the lowering moon. "That's your only weapon, huh?" A jesting mood settled on him, as if he were in the company of his Kynd, in the company of Merrick.

Which pleased him. If this was what it was to wreak vengeance against an enemy of his brethren, then he would do his damned best to avoid God and His punishments.

Darken grinned, returning the show of fang for fang. "Mine are nicer, don't you think? *Stronger.*" Even his body felt powerful, his adrenaline amping him up, making his huge muscles quiver with anticipation, like they were strung for the kill.

In a blink, Aro darted right, spinning to reel close in a blinding rush.

As if the vampire could move fast enough Darken wouldn't detect it. He was Kynd; his senses were keyed to the fractions of all movement, scent, sound. Laughing, he swung the scythe into Aro's path, the momentum of the vampire's attack severing his own head. The decapitation of the head of the Literati was steeped in irony, and Darken had always appreciated those odd quirks of Fate.

Aro's fanged face, when it finished rolling, gazed upward, the expression of surprise still frozen on his features. Seconds later, Darken faltered back to get away from the swirling dust that was now the dead vampire.

The lust for the kill ebbed with the last remnants of Aro particles swirling tenaciously on the pre-dawn breezes, as if the vampire, even in death, fought to remain on earth. Watching the motes eddy lulled him into a contemplative mood, relaxing his muscles. Killing was far more satisfying than severing souls. Though he couldn't help lament he hadn't dragged the vampire's death out a little longer.

In his haste, he hadn't gotten any answers. Aro's motivations had ceased to exist when his head took a tumble. Studying the kill site, Darken's eyes narrowed. In hindsight, he'd made a mistake in acting so impulsively.

He wouldn't let his regret linger. Not when he stood on Earth, freed from following Death's cloak like a burr, where his skin was becoming one great callous from his chafing misery.

Darken could find his answers elsewhere, and facing the Triumvirate Vampyres would be where he'd start. It was they, after all, who had hired Merrick for the doomed expedition into the nether reaches of Hell.

As far as Darken was concerned, the ruling Vampyres were likely just as guilty as the head of the Literati was. Except the human woman had been sacrificed, too.

Which was a piece of the puzzle that didn't fit with his accusations. Perhaps the Triumvirate was just as ignorant of Aro's plot as Merrick and the woman were. She was Anton's daughter. Surely, the Vampyre wouldn't sacrifice her for whatever devious plan was brewing.

Darken needed to figure this out, especially if his killing Aro hadn't eliminated the threat to his brotherkynd.

Renewing his grip on the scythe, he turned to go as he glanced up at the lightening sky. The glaring stars had lost their stark brilliance and were blinking out as the blanket of night faded to shades of gray. Soon, fingers of orange sun would spill across the horizon.

The gargoyle's thoughts turned to a more immediate problem.

He was Kynd, a Witness. He wasn't supposed to have interfered, at least not on the plane humans inhabited. It was one thing to sever souls under God's verdict, but Darken had breached His judgment and had slain a being of the Earth.

Surely, there would be consequences.

Darken rolled his massive shoulders and cracked his neck. Dawn arrived, and a dull, tangerine veneer spread upon the old boards lining the alleyway. It was then his suspicions physically manifested.

His heart began to burn as if frostbitten, and he rubbed his thick pectoral, trying to assuage some of the searing, hoping the chafe would warm it back up. Dread fell down hard into his stomach, even as his blood thickened and slogged through his veins.

The sun continued its ascent, and the gargoyle hurried to the eastern wall of the alley seeking shade, some respite from this frigid stiffening of his body.

God had found him.

Darken growled, his lip curling off his fangs as he clenched his fists in outrage against his God. Just for one damned day, he would have liked to have enjoyed his newfound freedom.

Now he understood Merrick's fear that the chimera would succumb to the allure of Hell. Darken had run his tongue along utter freedom, and had been filled with a joy he'd not felt for thousands of years.

God struck His punishing blow quickly, though.

Darken wiggled his fingers, which lifted and dropped with delayed reaction to his will.

The sun crested and bloomed across the land, casting long shadows upon the mud. He saw his own dark shape, weirdly stretched in shadow from the base of the board wall, and raised his hand to study the odd sensations creeping through it, throughout his entire body.

Stone.

The gargoyle was turning to stone. He had severed his ties with Death, defied God's eternal decree in order to protect his friend, and God's wrath was spearing down to render him Grotesque as punishment. Darken lifted his face to the sky and roared as his body betrayed his will and became immutable. His frozen visage was one of utter fury and terror.

* * * *

After clearing the woods, Merrick and Angelia found themselves hiking through vast acres of rockslides. The scree had settled haphazardly, forcing them to climb as much as step down, in order to make their way to the Second Circle.

In spite of not having to carry her own pack, Angelia felt like she was one breath away from hanging her tongue out like a tired dog. With all the up and down traversing, her legs were turning to jelly, and she wondered with each straining step upward if her hamstrings were going to lift her butt or finally go on strike.

Thank goodness she'd spent time away from her desk job conditioning her body. She prayed her physical training would muster her through, because there was nowhere to make camp on the rock-covered slope. Besides, it didn't look as if they'd be stopping soon. Merrick still moved as nimbly as when they'd started their descent into Hell. He was strong and the varied terrain didn't slow him one bit.

She slowed him.

He rarely let go of her hand while they picked their way across the stone-riddled landscape. The feel of his calloused palm against her skin constantly pulsed little thrills through her body as they hiked. It was probably what kept her going.

That, and the mere presence of him. Despite the barren environment, Angelia's eyes feasted.

On the man I'm with. Okay, so technically he wasn't a man. He was male. And what a specimen of the male physique he was. His clothes only concealed the skin, they couldn't mask the aura of power that surrounded him. His leather coat hugged his muscles like a chocolate coating.

A yummy, chocolate covered gargoyle, that is. Picturing it made her feel like she'd just stepped onto the set of a Tim Burton movie. *Oh, yeah. Come on Hallow-Easter!*

"You're tired, Angel."

"Hmm?" She dragged her eyes up to Merrick's face, now that he finally stopped. A thick wisp of hair came loose from her braid and clung to her brow, as if in dramatic representation of her fatigue.

She swiped at it, just as Merrick lifted her up to the top of the boulder nearest to them. He kept her steady by cupping her ribcage with his warm, sturdy hands.

He put her there so she could survey what still lay beneath and before them, so Angelia peeled her imaginings from the feel of Merrick's grip to assess their surroundings.

All she could see for thousands of yards was more scree that needed traversing. By goats. "Isn't this supposed to end at some point? Can't you just fly us out of here?"

The chimera let her go, turning his broad back to her to stare down the slope. She took his distraction to purview a closer tableau: the male right in front of her.

Man, he was cut like a god. Big, chiseled. Yet, his black hair was downy soft. She knew because she'd had her fingers threaded through it.

Remembering that shot a thrumming tingle straight to her core.

She resisted squirming around lest Merrick catch her doing so. Although, he didn't seem to be paying her much attention at the moment. As a matter of fact, he had yet to answer her question about flying them to the next Circle.

"Merrick?"

"I heard you." But, he didn't look at her. He held his gaze outward, as if he was contemplating the rest of the journey to the Second Ring.

Except he wasn't. She could tell, once she stopped drooling behind his back. Merrick's focus seemed inward, like the journey he was considering stretched for miles inside of him. Now that she was paying attention and not wallowing in her wanton thoughts or her fatigue, she felt his tension in the air around them as well, saw it in the hard line of his wide shoulders.

"You must be hungry." A comment out of the blue. An avoidance.

Fine. She would pick her battles and leave this one alone. If Merrick didn't want to shed his gargoyle shape, who was she to harp? If he didn't think it was a good idea to fly, then so be it. She could play evasion, too.

"I'm starving. What say you part with those packs so we can dig out something to eat?"

He shrugged the bags from his back then stepped off to perch on one of the larger boulders, resuming his study of the slope stretching endlessly below them.

He might as well have moved himself a million miles away.

* * * *

Can't you just fly us out of here?

No, he couldn't and that irritated the piss out of him. A closer look, it grinded on him so hard, he felt like his stone-rough skin was bleeding. How was that for a change? He couldn't make this descent into Lower Hell easier on his Angel, and he wanted to. With a yearning that pained him.

Shit.

Granted, when he took the job he hadn't wanted to make things easier, he hadn't thought twice about letting the human woman struggle as they navigated through the Circles. He'd wanted the human to suffer, just like he did every God damned day of his miserable, immortal existence.

But now?

Now, he wanted to take her back to the surface because he wanted her safe. She ought to forget the damned Scriptum and its secrets. If she wanted to know about gargoyles and chimerae, he'd tell her everything, for Christ's sake.

Because she'd wriggled under his thickening skin.

Merrick glanced over at Angelia, who crouched on the rock he'd left her on, emulating his stance as she, too, gazed down the barren hill. Their packs sat like forsaken lumps at the foot of the boulder, untouched. She wasn't eating and looked so God-awful forlorn sitting there, Merrick's heart squeezed with a familiar longing.

Even in his doleful state, he wanted to keep her company. Or maybe he did *because of* his mood. He wasn't sure. But he was certain of one thing: Together, they'd feel better.

God, what a stolen luxury to have her with him.

Merrick hopped off his rock to pick his way back to the woman perched on the boulder. "Hi." Why was he so blasted nervous?

She looked down at him, her pretty face still pocked with wasp stings. She had a few right on the bridge of her nose, like freckles, and they made her precious, beautiful.

"Mind if I join you?"

She scooted over to make room.

Merrick hopped up like the distance was nothing, like he didn't dare give her a second to change her mind. Because he was afraid she would. He coveted her touch, and the absence of it left him feeling bereft, like she was Kynd and he missed her.

He didn't think twice about nestling himself behind her, pulling her into his embrace, and resting his chin on the crown of her head. Merrick closed his eyes to breathe in the scent of her as she relaxed against him. "Better?"

She nodded.

Yeah, he had to agree, it was much better with her in his arms. Never mind that he couldn't spread his wings to get them closer to the Second Circle. For now, he could make the trip easier by doing what he was doing just then, by sharing the load and offering comfort where he could, without losing more of his soul.

Which is what would happen if he claimed his true form while he was in Hell. For centuries he hadn't cared that his soul grew thin as he succumbed to his building anger, as he brutalized his body in Hell to calm the fury raging like an inferno inside of him.

He had needed the outlet. Or so he'd thought at the time. Now, he knew the true cost of his temper. Every time he exploded into chimera while visiting Hell, Lucifer extracted portions of his soul, until Merrick had too little of it left.

One more outburst and his chimera was cooked.

So, *no*, he couldn't just fly them out of there. He had to save his last shot for getting them through the gates at the city of Dis, if they wound up having to go that far.

And it was looking as if they would.

* * * *

Angelia rubbed her cheek on Merrick's thick bicep as she snuggled deeper into him. She hoped it would remind him he was holding someone, bring his thoughts back around to the present. For all his warm bulk draped protectively around her, he seemed a thousand miles away.

It was like when her mother used to scratch her back when she was a little kid to help her fall asleep. Angelia would know when Marguerite's thoughts drifted because there was a withdrawal of energy from her fingertips, like they roved and traced patterns without the mind in the driver's seat.

Squirming her small back would lasso her mother's attention once again, and she would resume a more deliberate pattern of curly-cues on her daughter's bare skin. It was like that now with Merrick. Except when Angelia snuggled deeper against him, his arms automatically tightened, but he still seemed miles away.

She needed to take a more noticeable tack.

Turning in his arms so she could face him, she cupped her palms to his hard jaw.

Merrick lowered his eyes.

Slowly, she tilted her chin up, pressing his bottom lip between the two of hers. She suckled tenderly, before releasing him.

Locking her eyes on his, she repeated her brazen invitation.

The chimera's pupils expanded, swallowing the slate gray so all that remained was a steel, slivered ring. His muscles softened as he focused on her face, on her mouth.

Angelia pressed her fingertips a little harder to his skin, and tilted her head. This time she opened her mouth over his, slowly gliding her tongue past his parted lips until she found his.

They held their breaths, suspended in that audacious kiss, until she felt the curving of his entire body around hers, his arms pulling her closer.

As she dragged her lips away, she pinched the bottom of his between her teeth.

A low rumble caressed her ears as Merrick's nostrils flared and his slate eyes pinned her. He did not squeeze her any more than he had initially, like she was as delicate as flower petals and he didn't dare squish her. Gently, with aching hesitation, Merrick lowered his head, begging for another touch of her mouth to his.

Angelia gave, careful of the chimera, too, who seemed fragile in his trepidation, his uncertainty. He had never kissed a woman before her, in spite of that first intense kiss they'd shared the day before. She could tell he was inexperienced by his apprehension, in the way he followed her cues. She was teaching him how to kiss, and the novelty of it thrilled her.

Was Merrick a virgin?

The idea titillated her; she wanted more from this man of so much strength and weakness.

Never mind she kissed a chimera. She was connecting to the being within, and what form his body took mattered little just then.

Okay, she couldn't lie to herself. It mattered a lot, but it was taking a back seat. So long as it kept radiating this heat, this pent-up intensity. He was into her now, she'd brought him back to the present. And what a present it was.

Angelia yielded to the exploration of his mouth on hers, the soft suckling as he tasted, his jaw working beneath her fingertips. She closed her eyes to the sensation, tilting her head back so he could mine deeper, a bit more fervently. Still he was tender, careful with his sharp teeth.

"Angel." He sighed his breath into her as he pulled her even closer.

He drew his mouth away from hers, reluctantly, slow, then dabbed back in for one last taste of her bottom lip. He turned her away from him then, to wrap himself around her back as he nestled her into his leather-clad arms, between his powerful legs. Finally, he pressed his jaw to her crown as he had earlier, as if to seal her into his embrace, where she felt cocooned, sated with his kisses, his tender consideration.

Angelia's lids grew heavy, despite willing herself to stay awake to enjoy the tiny thrills pinging inside her. Perhaps, though, if she just closed her eyes, she could let her other senses play, could still savor this warm, inner vibration of feeling cherished.

Of self-assurance. She'd given something of herself, too, and it had been deemed worthy. Prized, even. She drifted into slumber while the chimera kept vigil, immovable in his post, like a loyal sentry.

* * * *

He knew she woke before she stirred. He felt it in the quickening bump of her heart, the scent of her growing heavier with the swelling beat of her pulse. Her vitality resonated beneath his skin, as if he were a violin and she the bow drawing across his strings.

As he had done in Limbo by the pond, he sent a quick prayer to his God, thanking Him for the interlude, the break from the burden of his rage. For a while, Merrick had known peace with his Angel curled up within his embrace.

Yet, he looked forward to her waking because he enjoyed her company, her easy manner, her kindness when he was not so forthcoming. He'd been withdrawn, had been wrestling with the curse that was his life and she'd gently tugged him back.

With a kiss, no less. She'd gazed up at him and joined her breath with his. The enchantment of which tightened his skin. In a good way. He'd been mesmerized, enthralled that sharing their breaths could be so intimate. Of course, he couldn't ignore it any more than he could overlook her waking now.

Her body tensed with a sleepy stretch, then relaxed into him. Her scent billowed, and Merrick once again resisted the urge to raise his face skyward in thanks. He consoled himself with the sight of her in his arms, instead.

"Hi." She repeated his greeting from before, her expression shy, doe-eyed.

Merrick couldn't help his grin. "Hi. You slept well?" She had, he knew, but he wanted to hear her say so and barely resisted wriggling with the joy he was feeling. *Dear God,* I'm *becoming a sap.* Maybe the old Vampyre was onto something.

"Yeah." She yawned, and her small body squirmed to stretch again. Merrick eased his hold so she could unfold her muscles without falling off the boulder.

"Man, I never thought sleeping on a rock could be so comfortable. No offense." She smiled, her embarrassment evident, lighting Merrick from the inside out.

"None taken." He stood up with her, making sure she was balanced and fully awake. An excuse, really, to keep touching her, but he could lie to himself all day about that, given the reward.

He shouldn't cling, no matter how reluctant he was to let her go. Regretting the emptiness of his hands, he hopped down, the small, flat stones chinking under his boots as he made contact with the ground. Merrick turned to hold his hand out for Angelia. To help her down, of course, not to cave to his urge to touch her again.

Oh, yes, he seriously could lie to himself all day.

"Thanks." She landed beside him, then headed for her pack as soon as he released her.

Waving two granola bars, she glanced over her shoulder at him. "Want one?"

Merrick felt a bit of weight press on the light mood. He hadn't eaten anything in a long time. He didn't have to and her offering of sustenance reminded him of who and what he was.

A Kynd destined for stone. *Soon.*

Merrick shook his head but watched as she ripped the wrapper off her bar with her little teeth and took a hefty bite, filling her cheeks as she chewed. He couldn't avert his eyes from the workings of her jaw.

Lord Almighty.

"Angel."

"Hmm?"

"Mind if I braid your hair again?"

She quit chewing, her beautiful eyes growing wide as a blush flowered across her face. "Ah, no." She downed a good chunk of her granola bar with a hard swallow. Obviously, she was recalling the last time he braided her hair.

"Just a braid. I promise." He'd follow through on that promise if it killed him. His arms felt empty. Hell, *he* felt empty and she was only standing several feet away. *And* he had just released her only moments before.

A fact he chose to overlook. He knew if he could get her close to him again, touch her golden hair, the void wouldn't seem anywhere near as big as it did just then. It also gave him the excuse to touch without seeming like a damned burdock. He needed to give her some space.

He knew humans. And he knew Kynd. They were nothing alike on that score.

Granted, they were nothing alike on a lot of things, but touching all the time was frowned upon in the human realm. So, he relied on the excuse to tidy her hair, even though the way it tousled unrestrained around her high cheekbones made him ache.

Angelia shrugged, like she weighed his promise and found it worthy. She grabbed her aluminum canister of water, another granola bar, and plunked down at his feet, facing away from him.

"Let her rip, chimera."

He chuckled. He liked her affability, her light spirit, even though he had to drive the toes of his boots into the stones to keep from leaping at her when she showed her backside to him.

Releasing his breath and his feet, Merrick crouched behind her, coveting the delicate curl of her ear, the sweep of her jawbone. He proceeded to untangle the plait he'd put in the day before, lest his mouth descend to the temptation.

Still, though, he lifted her hair to his nose, breathing in the honey-lavender smell of it. Even after a full day in Hell, it hadn't lost its essence. Beautiful. He caressed each section as he made his way toward her scalp, brushing his rough palms along her crown to capture the errant wisps.

Angelia leaned her head back, obviously enjoying his attentions.

"You have a nice touch. I could let you finger-comb my hair all day."

I could finger-comb your hair all day, he wanted to say, but remembered to restrict himself. He didn't want to give her any excuse to avoid him. Well, beyond the obvious, anyway. There were enough reasons on that list to make this simple act a frigging miracle.

"So, how much farther to the Second Circle? Another day? Half an hour?" Her voice took on a dreamy quality as she surrendered to his ministrations.

"More than half an hour, but less than a day."

"You're very cryptic, chimera. Got something a little more precise?"

Too soon. He was going to have to face Minos, the infallible Judge of Hell, and he was going to know Merrick entertained impure thoughts for the woman. Hell, the Beast was going to smell the lust all over him.

As he most likely would on Angelia.

A fiery burn sparked in his chest, similar to his lust for the kill, but far deeper, more potent than anything he'd experienced before. *Protect my Angel.* Minos wouldn't get within a hundred feet of her if Merrick could help it.

Except he was going to have to fight the great Beast without releasing the advantage of his wings, though he wasn't going to regret anything that had led them to this point, with him holding the woman's golden tresses in his hard hands.

He'd fought Minos before and won, he could do it again.

He would prefer to forget each victory had been when he was chimera, accessing the winged angel part of him, where the battles were won because Merrick had a nice edge over the brute strength of Minos.

"Merrick, you with me here?"

"Yeah, Angel. I'm with you. I just got a little sidetracked thinking about the journey ahead. It's going to get harder, you know."

A few moments of quietude lay between them before she spoke again. "I know about the Second Circle. About lust."

Merrick's hands stilled halfway through her braid.

"Do you think we'll get through without much trouble?" She was referring to the fact they barely kept themselves from the joys of the flesh. Which meant she was well aware of the problem they faced.

"Honestly, Angel?" Merrick resumed the work in his hands, hoping his heart would slog itself back into its natural rhythm. His rough knuckles bumped her back as he wound his way to the end of her braid.

She handed him the elastic to cinch it. "Give me the straight poop, chimera."

The straight poop. She was funny in a quirky kind of way, and it swept levity into the air around them despite their current topic of conversation. She was a blessing. A true angel.

"No. It's not going to be easy at all." He helped her to her feet, then let her go, with a Kynd's reluctance.

"I was afraid of that. Not regretful, mind you." She swung her braid like a saucy vixen. "We'll figure it out. Right?"

Merrick smiled a sharp-toothed grin back at her, the lethal reminder of what he was. "Right. Now hand me your pack before I change my mind and get us lost so we wind up back at the Archway."

"You wouldn't." She beamed, incredulous.

"I might."

She laughed, the sound bold and defiant considering where they were. Merrick almost forgot his worries. He shouldered their packs, and as soon as his hands were free, she slid her palm across his and closed her fingers around his knuckles.

It was as if God had forgotten about the Guardian to the Archway of Hell, and Merrick once again tasted the joy he had known during the Kynd's reign in Heaven.

"So, not to state the obvious…" Angelia glanced around them, her cheeks taking on a redder cast than what the sky perpetually colored them with. "But there aren't any trees around here, you know. No place where a girl could, ah, relieve herself?" She looked behind them as if the cover she searched for could have magically appeared with her wishing.

"Nope. But then, there isn't anyone around to watch you, is there."

* * * *

Angelia cuffed his arm. "Funny."

But he had a point. It wasn't as if the Devil watched from the cinnamon sky, his gigantic face spread across the clouds as he glared down, hoping to catch her taking a pee.

God, either. They both had better things to do. She hoped.

Merrick stopped and lifted her fingers to his lips like they were precious little piggies. "You squat, and I'll turn my back. How's that?"

"You're positively evil, you know that?"

"Yeah, I do. But at least I'm not going to look."

"Evil."

"Yep."

"You could keep walking and I'll catch up."

"No more time by yourself, Angel. We're not in Limbo anymore."

Like the wasteland they walked through wasn't an indication.

"So, we're close?"

"Go do your thing."

Her thing. Like it was a particular talent. She trotted a few paces away as Merrick turned his back to give her some privacy. And what a fine back he presented to her while she squatted on the shale. Wide at the shoulders and cut like a vee to narrow hips and a tight bum, with legs sturdy enough to make a mama right proud she'd birthed such a strapping boy.

God, did he have any idea how perfect he was? Men had cosmetic surgery to look that fine.

And he wanted *her*.

Stunning. But why look that gift horse in the mouth. She'd enjoy it while it lasted. Once they were back on the surface, their lives would resume. She'd go back to collecting dust, and Merrick would return to his particular Hell, the one that seemed to be giving him some peace now that he was actually in Hell.

Ironic, though no less sad. She worried what would become of him when this adventure was over. Especially now that she was getting to know him, and he was no longer some idol come to life off one of her old posters.

He was Kynd, and they were steeply layered, far beyond anything the literature had on them. So far, everything she'd read about gargoyles and chimerae was woefully misguiding. How could scholars have gotten it so wrong?

Angelia hitched her cargo pants up over her butt and buttoned them, briefly lamenting the lack of toilet paper. The next time the Triumvirate decided to send her on a little vacation, she was going to do the packing herself.

She trotted back to Merrick and took his hand again, because it just seemed the normal thing to do. And he didn't seem to mind. Which was a Kynd thing, wasn't it? Wanting to touch all the time? She wished she could remember what she'd read in the Scriptum.

She seemed to remember, before she bled all over it and passed out, that she was getting some pretty heady intel out of it. But what?

"All better?" Merrick led them down the scree-riddled slope, helping her up and down as he had the day before.

"Yes, no thanks to you."

"Hey, nobody saw you."

"Not the point."

The going wasn't so bad now that she was rested and fed, plus had Merrick for company. They moved along well, and Angelia could finally make out a tree line on the not so distant horizon.

"So, Angel. Tell me about your life in the world of the living."

Oh, God. If he knew the details, he'd think her utterly pathetic. She'd have to keep the description succinct, bare of the boring and pitiful details. The only thing missing from her useless existence was a collection of housecats.

"There's not much to tell," she hedged.

The chimera glanced sideways at her, an eyebrow raised in disbelief. He knew she was being evasive but she wouldn't spill. She had about five more days of Merrick's attentions. She would be losing him too soon as it was, no point in rushing the inevitable.

* * * *

"Seriously, there isn't." Her pretty brows lifted, as if to underscore the sincerity of her confession. "I live with vampires. My father's one of the Triumvirate. It's not like I go on a lot of dates."

Merrick felt his blood still in his veins at the mere hint of another male being interested in his Angel. He kept walking, hoping she didn't notice the jealousy shifting his muscles, making the hair on his nape thicken as his chimera stirred.

She was his. Period. And when she went back to the surface and left him behind? His empty stomach weighed heavy as a rock.

"Tell me about your home. Friends." Anything to get his mind off what was going to happen when she finally had that Scriptum in her hands. And have it she would, if he had to kill himself to make sure she succeeded. She hadn't had a lot of self-confidence when she'd started this little foray, and he'd do whatever he could to make sure she returned a hero, her ego stuffed full.

"Friends? A few, I suppose. But I'm weird, remember? I'm a human living with vampires, I don't exactly go unnoticed. And that's not a good thing."

Vampires. Merrick had killed his share. Gladly. They had no business trespassing into Hell. Neither did any Other dwelling topside, which was why he killed them before they could wreak havoc with their schemes.

Merrick crammed those lovely memories deep into his heart where they preferred to fester. "Angel, you're different. Not *weird*."

She sidled up close to hang off his arm, and batted her lashes. "Keep wooing me like that, Handsome, and I'll marry you before you can ask."

She was joking. Of course. Merrick forced a smile because that's what you did when someone was only kidding.

"But trust me," she went on, oblivious. "Sitting among cobwebs is a fine future for the likes of me. For two reasons."

She held up two fingers in front of her. "First, I'm only human."

So she was. He'd actually forgotten. "Why don't you leave? Go live with humans, then?"

She snorted, a very non-feminine pffft but he loved it. The sound distracted him from his desire to lay a permanent claim on her, from coiling his arm around her waist, stuffing her against his chest, and grunting, "Mine."

"You're kidding, right? I tried that. My father set me up in my own apartment and everything. Even Aro thought I should give it a try, that it would give me more insight. In Aro speak, that meant make me a better tool."

"And?"

She hesitated, then shrugged.

But he caught her reluctance. She didn't want to confess. Then decided to? Merrick stole a surreptitious breath as the thought flurried excitement through his chest, turning his rock heavy stomach into a vessel flitting with butterflies.

She was going to trust him with a confession. *Trust him.* The one who'd tormented her when they'd first met.

"*And* I was miserable. I couldn't cope. People are messed up, big time. Oh sure, I met a few nice ones, but all in all? Does the term *crabs in a barrel* mean anything to you?" She kept her eyes on the ground in front of her. "I high-tailed it back."

* * * *

Like a coward.

They finally made it to the tree line she'd been watching loom larger as they hiked. Merrick subtly pulled her closer as though he didn't want to frighten her with his intensifying awareness. It was his promise to protect her, nothing more. Surely, he wasn't trying to bolster her after her pathetic confession.

Not that she'd know now, when the timing of her confession and their reaching the forest couldn't have been worse. She already figured from this point on anything could happen, that he wouldn't have the advantage of seeing any danger coming from a distance.

They were entering another dark-as-a-pit forest, one with blackened trees that made the shadows even deeper, impenetrable. Their trunks were twisted, charred shapes that filled her with foreboding. Angelia snuggled even closer, glad for Merrick's possessiveness, for his compulsion to protect her. She'd sulk some other time.

"Secondly," she went on, hoping to keep them distracted as the woods swallowed them. Then spit them out onto a park of sorts. Angelia's next words clogged in her throat.

Merrick drew her behind him, shielding her. Around them, she could see great slabs of stones, like altars and monoliths, broken or leaning. The ruins dark and hulking under the merlot sky.

Mined up from some primordial place that washed shivers all over her skin, the chimera's voice rumbled out of his thick chest. "I'll have to take a rain check on hearing about that second thing. We've got company." Like he had to explain. If the bass of his snarl didn't alert her, she could see just fine what towered before them.

107

Minos. The Great Judge who stood between them and the Second Circle. The Beast of Hades, whose description warranted a capital letter *B*. Angelia's books had done nothing to prepare her for the sheer magnitude of dread his presence dredged from her soul.

"Holy shit," she muttered, her fingers clutching to the back of Merrick's leather jacket.

"Nothing holy about it, Angel." Merrick twisted his shoulders like a prizefighter, straightened his coat, and braced himself for Minos. Then he turned his face as the Beast erupted a fetid roar, the mist of it billowing its stench across the distance separating them.

* * * *

Merrick heard Angelia gag as she bent over, and waited for the splash that didn't come.

Good. She didn't retch. Minos would be highly insulted if she did. As it was, the Judge's temperament was volatile, and meeting up with him was a crapshoot every time. Merrick never knew, even before he'd met Angelia, if he'd be able to bluff his way through the gate or if he'd have to resort to physical violence.

It went either way, depending on the Beast's mood, or his own.

This time, however, Merrick wasn't looking forward to a physical fight, the release of his fury against a worthy opponent. Not when he needed to protect his Angel.

"Minos, my dear friend," Merrick let his fangs drop far enough for the threat to be evident, even as he spread his arms wide, to show he carried no weapon.

"I am not fooled by your clothing, chimera. Your posturing reveals nothing. And yet," he growled, the tenor of it deep as thunder. "It does not hide the human soul behind you."

Merrick's mane curled outward along his collar as he stepped forward, the emergence of his chimera automatic in the face of the direct threat to Angelia. A new development for a Kynd, and one which made harnessing his chimera all the harder. "She is no offering, Beast."

"Pity," Minos snarled, the flame of his red eyes ebbing then flaring anew. "I would have it, and let you pass."

"A tempting offer, but this soul is no gift for your court." Merrick buttoned his leather coat to his neck, hoping to keep his wings well fettered. If the Beast wanted to fight, he was ready to do it in his current form. He would be fighting without the advantage, but this time he had something worthwhile to fight for. He wouldn't lose.

He couldn't.

Cords of muscle bunched across Minos' shoulders, around his huge chest, giving the Beast the illusion of growth, like a cat who bristles its fur to appear larger. Not that Minos needed the boost. He was gargantuan and built solid, his center of gravity as secure as his position in Hell. He was a tough opponent even when Merrick wasn't constrained.

"I smell the lust, chimera. The woman's? For the likes of you?" Minos tipped his nine-foot staff. Lashing his whip-like tail, it curled uncannily around the second in a line of rings etched along the rod's length. "Or is it yours I sense?" The Beast's upper lip lifted in a distorted smile, and Merrick adjusted his stance.

Minos gurgled a menacing laugh. "If I am scenting the lust of a chimera, then I have lived my life." The smile disintegrated. "But, I know better. Kynd do not love, nor do they lust. I offer free passage to you yet again. The human soul stays here."

Merrick didn't budge. Damn Minos and his unerring judgment. The Beast reigned at the Second Circle where lustful souls resided for eternity. Of course, he would detect the frisson between himself and Angelia.

Angelia. She still held on to him. "Angel, I'm going to need you to stand over by that stone dais, all right."

Her grip tightened. "Not a snowball's chance in Hell, cowboy."

"What?" He did not just hear her say that. He was a little distracted, was all, what with Minos beginning to sidle for the better vantage point.

"You can't fight him, I don't think." Angelia grabbed his wrist.

"*You don't think?* Could you be a little surer about that, because he really wants to fight if I'm not willing to leave you here." Merrick didn't take his eyes off the Beast, even as the twin scents of honey and lavender curled into his head, the aroma growing thick because of the hard pumping of his Angel's heart.

Like he needed another impediment.

"Wait, give me a sec to remember."

"I don't exactly have a second, Angel. Move your ass to the dais and out of the way. *Now*."

Minos laid down his rod and wiped his drool with a knobby-knuckled hand—the give-away to his first charge. Merrick countered by moving left, distancing himself from Angelia since she wasn't budging. When the Beast charged, he didn't want her anywhere near them. The fight was never pretty, especially since Merrick usually got his ass kicked while he did his own kicking.

Not being able to use his wings was going to be a huge drawback. The leather he wore would hold up to Minos' attacks only so well and would do nothing to keep his bones from breaking.

He felt the tug of his coat as Angelia's clutching fingers lost their hold. Yet, still she didn't move toward the dais. She was daft. Had to be if she wasn't heading for safer ground at a time like this. Merrick turned his gaze a mere fraction to stab an angry glare at the woman, who apparently didn't have a lick of self-preservation in her fragile body.

"What do—?"

Minos charged, snuffing his curse. Merrick got his arms up to grab hold of bulging muscles just before the Beast pummeled him to the ground. The hit knocked his breath from his lungs, yet he didn't let go. He didn't dare. Not while he couldn't breathe, and lay helplessly stunned. So long as he kept a grip on the Beast, the thing wasn't going after Angelia.

A lame tactic, but it was all he could muster at the moment.

Minos' face loomed near, his putrid breath moistening Merrick's ear, obliterating any lingering scent of lavender. "You surprise me, chimera. I did not know Kynd chose sides."

Neither did Merrick, but maybe his rage had altered him on a fundamental level.

Which explained his lusting after Angelia. He'd have to examine the theory closer, perhaps when his head wasn't getting crushed between two talon tipped hands. Already, his own blood was streaming into his eyes.

"We don't," he bit out the lie, his denial, as the claws punctured deeper, piercing the bone of his skull like needles. Merrick grimaced, every muscle drawing tight. "But the woman must pass."

110

"Tsk. Such determination."

And pass, she will. His lungs working now, Merrick dragged his knee to his chest and thrust with all his might, shoving Minos backward, where he landed on his feet, his tail swishing.

Flipping to his feet as well, Merrick faced the Beast on equal footing, then leapt and spun, driving his heel into Minos' heavily muscled chest, sprawling him backward.

The guy was a frigging Weeble-Wobble: aaalmost down, but nope. The Judge bobbed right back up, ready for more. Just in time to reach up for Merrick's second roundhouse kick. Minos caught his booted ankle and heaved him away. In a blink, the chimera's lion claws descended, scraping four gaping wounds across the Beast's stomach, slowing his ride through the air.

Merrick heard an outraged roar trail off like a flaming comet as his body hurtled forward then smashed hard against a boulder. His body dropped to the ground like a dead horse: all heavy body with collapsing legs. Yet, he remembered to retract his three-inch claws before Lucifer grew the wiser.

Even a flash of his chimera could attract the Fallen One's attention. He needed to be more careful, couldn't let instinct ride him. Besides, Angelia had yet to see him in his full, God-given form. He'd likely scare her as Minos did.

Merrick crammed that problem down for later perusal. Just then, he still had a fight to win, even if his body was still numb from its abrupt contact with something more stone than he was.

A quick inspection of movable parts and he was ready to go. Getting vertical, he shook himself and tugged at the cuffs of his leather coat. Which were about as straightened and ready as he was.

* * * *

Angelia watched the fight, her fist pushed against her teeth to keep herself from screaming. Merrick could not win this, and the realization filled her with horror. As if in sympathy, the winds picked up a distressful moaning as they swirled around her legs, then grew to a higher pitch, more frenzied as they whipped and wailed around the entrance where the two men fought.

The gate to the Second Circle was opening, and from where Angelia stood, she could see burgundy clouds racing across the magenta sky. She could see, too, the Shades who were doomed because of lust.

Helen of Troy, Lancelot, Francesca. Souls who had feasted with carnal hunger.

But who had also loved.

Upon seeing the others, she remembered. The Scriptum's words rustling to life in her memory. They whispered to her heart and her mind. Resonating along a chord of truth, reminding her why she was right to refuse to stand upon the stone dais, away from the chimera.

She wasn't supposed to be apart from him. If she had done as Merrick ordered and removed herself to the dais, she wouldn't have seen the Shades hovering near the widening entrance.

Humming vibrated inside the stadium of her cranium. The celestial singing heard not by her ears, but between them, the songs comingling with her blood, branding their veracity to her body.

The souls she was seeing at the entrance did not belong there. Their punishments were unjust. For them, lust had merely been the prelude to keener passions, to deeper rooted emotions that had withstood the tortures of their crimes.

The entrance gaped wider and the hurricane winds slatted debris, carrying the cries of damned souls. *Condemned souls*, who kindled the tempest of fury in the chimera because he understood, yet could not bear the burden of witnessing so many lost.

Because he, too, harbored the same profound capacity to love.

The Scriptum, when she'd lost consciousness, had been singing this truth of the Kynd to her, and seeing the bowed heads of Francesca and Lancelot resurrected her memories.

Merrick wasn't supposed to battle Minos because this time, he would fight to the death. *Because this time*, the chimera would choose his side and not just bear witness as he and the Kynd had done for millennia.

Angelia's blood pooled to her feet, sucking her balance right out of her. Her vision swam as she reached out to steady herself, to withstand the onslaught of the hurricane winds of the Second Circle and the verity of the Scriptum coursing through her veins.

She swore to herself she would not faint as Dante had done or as she had done back in her cell at the Literati headquarters. She was more than just a human. She was a human loved by vampires. Maybe even loved by a chimera, if he followed the true path of his lust.

Angelia pushed against the wind as she struggled toward Merrick and Minos. She sickened to see how well matched they were. Both were wounded. Yet Merrick, who hadn't stripped his clothes to revert to his chimera, suffered the greater injuries. As it was, he was struggling to free his un-maned throat from the Beast's vice-like grip.

Minos was hunched over his victim, his back muscles rippling under the sheen of shed blood, his tail lashing behind him with ironic lust for the kill. Angelia scraped her sweating palms across the tops of her thighs.

She could do this.

For Merrick.

Rasping in a fortifying breath, she followed the arcing of Minos' switching tail like a cat watching a fly trapped against a window. Her head bobbled loose on her neck as she sighted in her target, then quick as that feline, she latched onto the swishing tail, yanking for all she was worth.

The Beast roared and bolted upright, releasing one hand from Merrick's throat as he twisted like a great lizard. Angelia flinched, but held her ground, holding her gaze steady on the Beast while her knees rattled together like castanets.

"Let the chimera go, please." Was that contrite voice *her*?

Minos cocked his head as he licked bloody froth from his lips. "You ask for this Kynd's life?" The Beast's cherry eyes flared, then cooled, as he regarded Angelia, his grip on Merrick not lessening.

"I do." She refused to lower her eyes from his searching. She'd appear the coward, and she couldn't afford that. Heck, Merrick was the one who couldn't afford it.

Minos grinned, his sharp teeth glinting red from the hurricane sky.

"It took you long enough."

Angelia blinked. *Long enough?* But he was right. Merrick had taken an awful beating while she was rediscovering the key to the great arbiter's gate. Angelia sucked air past the knot forming in her throat.

"You will release him." She clutched her hands into fists so he wouldn't see them trembling. She might be talking rationally, but her brain was firing like a trapped comet.

"I have waited a long time for this Coming, Angelia."

Her blood quit as her heart stopped. "How do you know my name?" She barely had breath in her lungs to push the question through her lips, let alone come up with her own reasons. She continued staring up at the great Minos.

"It is enough that I know." He removed his grip from Merrick's throat to rise to his full, imposing height. Angelia craned her neck back so she wouldn't lose eye contact. In her peripheral vision, she saw Merrick roll to his stomach and draw his knees under himself.

"Take your chimera, little angel, and guard him well. He is at a dangerous point in his long life. What is written can yet be undone."

"Figures." She offered up a rueful smile. Later, she would contemplate what his cryptic words meant. He knew something about the Scriptum, and if he did, then he had most likely let the soulless man pass. Or he'd slain him. Only one way to know. "Do they go to Lower Hell?"

Minos dipped his chin. "They travel swiftly. But give your chimera a chance to heal. You will need him more than you can fathom, Angelia."

That figured, too. Of course, she knew their passage wouldn't be simple or without its perils, but still. She didn't want to contemplate how bad it was going to get if she couldn't *fathom* it, as the Beast predicted.

Minos stepped away, lifting an impossibly long and muscled arm toward the entrance. "Go now through the gate and the Second Circle. Talk to no one as you pass, and keep your eyes to the ground, I warn you. Rest only when you reach the outer rim, before you enter the Third Circle. You will be safe in the flux. After that, be wary. You are not the only ones with seeking eyes."

Angelia stepped toward Merrick.

"One last thing, little angel."

Oh, man. This is where he retaliates for my pulling his tail. She would not let her bottom lip tremble. Instead, she gazed straight into his red eyes, which flared then ebbed to glowing embers.

"I will not relinquish my souls easily." With that pronouncement, he turned his back on her to make his way toward the gate, the wind curling behind him like an obedient dog on its master's heels, leaving Angelia to sway in the vacuum of his departure, his words pealing in her head like the gonging of great bells.

Her heart joined the terrifying symphony and pounded like thunder. *He won't give up his souls?* Like she was coming back to get them, to steal them away from him? Dear God, she would. Remembering what the Scriptum revealed, that's exactly what she would be doing.

With Merrick at her side? Perhaps. Or perhaps not. Minos' prediction that she'd need the chimera more than she could fathom swamped her with frantic questions.

But, she couldn't indulge. Not when her champion was coughing blood.

As soon as the Beast faded amongst the Shades of the Circle, she fell to her knees beside Merrick. Yet her hand hovered. Where to touch him that wouldn't hurt? She wanted to cry, he was so battered, but she locked her jaw and settled for smoothing his hair from his lacerated forehead.

He pushed her hand aside and rolled upright, staggering as he shuffled to his feet. Except for the bleeding of his wounds, he was as pale as the alabaster towers of the castle in Limbo.

His feet might have been unsteady but his slate eyes riveted on her, penetrating deep. "What did you offer him?"

* * * *

Pinning his stare on the woman kept him balanced. Otherwise, he was going to topple back into the dirt. Not just from his beating, either. With his blood cinched in his head from Minos' death grip, he hadn't heard their exchange. He knew Angelia had to have given the Beast *something*. Otherwise, why would he have released his victorious hold?

Why in Hell did the notion have to hurt more than his wounds? Yeah, his heart was kicking the inner wall of his chest like it wore booted stilettos, but it had more to do with his fear she'd done something irrevocable. Something *he* couldn't afford.

Another low rumble escaped him; he couldn't stop it. If she'd bargained herself for his life? Dread ran through him, sickening him. He had lost. He'd failed to protect her, had let Minos gain the upper hand in their battle, and his Angel had interfered.

To save him.

Whatever she offered, it was worthy enough for the Judge of Souls to let them pass, to remove his death grip from Merrick's neck. Which he now rubbed, erasing the vestiges of Minos' grasp, while he awaited Angelia's answer.

God strike him dead, but her rounded eyes would undo him.

"Nothing. I gave him nothing." Truth gleamed up at him as she shook her head. So did apprehension.

Of what? Better question: for who? Merrick grunted. Who was he to understand what had passed between the human soul and Minos. He had been hired to do a job, nothing more.

Which he'd failed at. Miserably. Not only had he not protected Anton's beloved daughter, the gem of the Literati, but he had most likely lost the very thing that had given him a little hope, even if their being together was temporary.

He felt the sting of his failure, but more than that, he felt the lash to his pride. His ego was bruised, right along with his body. As was his God damned heart. He believed she told him the truth. She'd given nothing to Minos, so why was she so uneasy?

Merrick drew in a jagged breath, his chest so tight it was hard to suck in air. His thoughts were circling like buzzards and he grew more frustrated by the second.

To rip his mind off his frigging emotions, Merrick grabbed their packs, and turned for the gate, now unguarded and parted open like the Red Sea and he was Moses. He halted the instant he realized his Angel didn't follow.

She remained standing where he'd been lying under Minos' lethal grip, where his soul had been thinning into nothingness as his chimera clawed to come out from under the leather. To save his ass, ironically.

And Angelia's. Yeah, but he wasn't in the mood for the rallying cheer of his conscience just then. Especially when he caught the full, unshielded expression of hurt on her beautiful, wasp-stung face.

Which loosened his knees, hitting him harder than anything Minos had dished out. God, he was a blackguard in so many ways. Growling at himself as he held his hand out for her, he wiggled his fingers to hurry her up.

"Come on, Angel. Before Minos' generosity runs out."

Her gaze dropped to his hand then lifted back to his face. For a stultifying moment, he didn't think she would take what he was offering.

Not that it was much.

But the longer she stared at his empty hand, the more vulnerable he felt. More so even than he did under the Beast's murderous grip, when his chimera had fought to surface.

God alive, wasn't she going to join him? His terror that she wouldn't stopped his breath, and he knew his fear flashed in his eyes before he could quell it. Yet, just as he lowered his hand, she stepped forward, slipping hers across his palm, the touch of it caressing his heart, hushing its frantic tap dancing.

Loving Christ, what was happening to him?

He didn't say a word as he closed his fingers tight around her hand to guide them through the Second Circle.

Chapter Eight

It was, surprisingly, the longest day in Darken's already very long life.

Poised as he was along the dilapidated fence of the alley, it was a miracle no humans passed by to see an intimately detailed, yet mysteriously placed Grotesque shrieking silently and perpetually toward the Heavens.

Darken had felt every damned second of his granite prison as the sun had traveled incrementally across the sky.

At first, when his body had turned to stone, he'd panicked. Even with more than two thousand years to grow used to the idea of the Kynd's inevitable doom, he hadn't been ready for it. His heart had thundered in the cave of his chest, the echo of it agonizing as it reverberated throughout his inert body. For hours, he'd suffered for his insubordination, his defiance, until he finally resigned himself to his premature fate and let his anger subside.

Not once did he regret the reason why he endured this current punishment. At least this time, he understood why God had meted out his justice. He had killed a vampire. Which wasn't the reason he was currently picnicking in a back alley amongst human garbage and other debris. The death of a vampire hardly warranted such extreme retribution.

No. Darken had been turned to stone because he was Kynd, and Kynd weren't supposed to make choices. It was why he'd been trailing Death and wielding a scythe for millennia—his particular sentence for not taking part in the Divine Schism.

He'd been punished eternally for *not* making a choice. So, as Darken saw it, choosing or not, either way he was screwed. At least by killing Aro, he might have saved the life of a brotherkynd. Although his current view could have been better.

If he was going to endure centuries poised in his granite prison, God could have at least waited to turn him to stone until *after* he'd left this decrepit alleyway. Who said the Almighty had no sense of humor?

Darken grinned within himself. He had to. His face certainly wasn't going to reflect the gradations of his emotions. What the world would see for the next few centuries was the moment Darken had raised his face to curse his God.

Shit. The irony didn't fail to amuse him, even if his future weighed heavier on him than the stone he was made of. He knew full well what his fury looked like. He was monstrous, his sharp teeth bared menacingly, his thick muscles bulging.

Grotesque. Frightening. A monster of intimate and imposing detail. Clutched in his clawed hand was Death's scythe, its razor edge parallel to the ground, as impotent as the creature holding it.

He'd laugh if he could. Show his God He hadn't won, that the punishment had been worth the sacrifice. With Aro dead, Merrick would resume his post at the Archway, his wings intact.

He hoped. Because, really, what else could Darken do? He'd made his choice, had struck his bargain with his fate and now found himself perched ineffectually in an obscure and forgotten back alley. He couldn't help the chimera anymore now if he wanted to.

Double shit. He wanted to spit but couldn't do that, either. All he could do was glare up at a frustratingly slow-changing sky and curse his Creator, while others were most likely carrying on with the plans the vampire had already set in motion.

The sun crept beyond Darken's immutable line of vision, but he felt its waning in the cooling of his granite skin. The clouds muted to dyed landscapes, the sky beyond them turning from shale to a deeper charcoal. A lone star spangled gloriously in his periphery. Another popped forth, then another, until their twinkling snatched his attention hither and thither.

S. C. Dane

Along with the stellar game came a tingling across his back. Darken's cells shivered, vibrating until he thought he'd combust.

The urge to stretch consumed him, and he yearned to shake the inertia from his muscles. His heart, once slogging, went ballistic, sluicing his blood like quicksilver to his limbs. Inhaling the breath he'd expelled hours before, Darken loosed the bellow that had been mushrooming in the cavern of his breast.

Glorious God! His jaw closed around it!

In a flash, he spun to scan his surroundings, to make sure no one had witnessed his transformation from stone. The scythe, still clutched in his fist, swiped a lethal arc. The claws of his toes punctured and shred the earth as he turned, ready to annihilate anyone unfortunate to be near enough to see.

He was alone. *Thank God.*

Darken smiled, and this time, he felt it spread across his face. He patted his fingertips across his features, relieved and stunned that they moved at all.

Yes, thank God. For once, in more than two thousand years, he meant it. He'd been granted a reprieve. He didn't waste time questioning it, either, because he didn't know how long it would last. Freedom was his—he'd be a ninny to question it.

Sticking around in this back alley was a bad idea, too. All day long he'd mulled over his decision to kill Aro. The one thing that had cropped up time and again was his haste in dispatching the vampire.

Darken needed answers, and now that his body was his once again, he intended to get them.

With a quick and final scan of his surroundings, he continued in the direction he'd been chasing the vampire the night before. Turning back the other way carried too many risks. There was a dead human back there, after all. Darken hadn't heard sirens or any other indication the body had been found, but why tempt his fate.

He escaped to the south, keeping tight to the shadows so he wouldn't be spotted. He walked the earthly plane now, and he was pretty savvy to the rules. Nudity was frowned upon. Darken wasn't human, he resembled one just enough to pass brief scrutiny. So, he needed clothing to blend in a little better, and he needed answers.

He knew exactly where he'd go, killing two proverbial birds in the process. Darken lit out for the Triumvirate's compound.

* * * *

Merrick didn't release Angelia during the entire journey through the realm of the Lustful. She remembered Minos' warning to keep her eyes on the ground. Neither did she speak to any of the Shades, even though she wouldn't have been able to anyway.

Merrick led a furious pace, sometimes pulling her close to shield her when debris, blown by the hurricane winds, hurtled toward them. The chimera never said a word, not even during the moments when he wrapped himself around her body to protect her. Once the danger passed, he unfolded himself from around her, kept his hold on her hand, and hiked onward.

Merrick didn't slow until the winds died down, and then finally ceased altogether.

"We'll rest on the other side of this esker." They were the first words he uttered since his battle with Minos. His fingers tightened around Angelia's hand as they climbed the ridge.

She let him pull her up the steep embankment to the thin plateau at the top. They'd been hiking for hours, and she didn't know how much longer she could keep going.

She didn't have a clue how Merrick kept up the pace. She could only see the wounds on his head and face, but she knew he nursed worse injuries under his leather clothing. She'd felt him flinch, then go rigid each time he held her close while the wind whipped dangerously around them.

At least, she hoped that was why he flinched when he pulled her close. Though she knew that wasn't the whole of it. He cringed with the idea of having to protect her at all.

She wouldn't kid herself. He'd gotten his butt kicked *badly* because of her. Angelia felt her familiar doubts creep in to gnaw at her recently gained self-confidence.

Logically she knew some of his stiffness came from emotional wounds. He wasn't happy with his near-defeat to Minos. Goodness, who would be? She still didn't understand why he didn't just shift into his truest form and go at the Beast as a full chimera. She highly doubted he'd have lost then.

He was scared I wouldn't take his hand.

True. She'd caught the flash of fear when she hesitated. He did want to hold her.

Maybe just to protect me as he promised.

She was going to kick doubt's butt someday, she really was.

Today was the day. She wasn't going to let Merrick's silence go unchallenged for long. Once they were settled, she was going to start prying, in spite of the barrier he'd erected.

She was concentrating so hard on keeping herself from falling face first down the side of the esker and chewing so earnestly on what she was going to say to Merrick, she ran into his halted backside before she could stop herself.

She hit him like a wall, her breath *oomphing* out of her. Merrick caught her before she could ricochet backward onto her fanny, and the concern flaring in his slate eyes slathered across her heart like a healing salve.

In that flash, she remembered he'd called her Angel when he'd held out his hand for her to enter the Second Circle. Okay, then. She could do this confrontation thing. She didn't think the chimera was mad at her, just himself, and Angelia felt the stirrings of anger in her breast.

Her consolation prize for being in Hell.

She liked it, too. There was something cleansing about getting your dander up. She just hoped she could keep the ability long after she was done with this mission. In the meantime, she'd use her newfound anger while she had it.

Well, she wouldn't yell at the poor guy, obviously, but she wouldn't be a candy ass like she usually was and back down.

I'll be nice.

One look at Merrick and she knew it was a promise she could keep.

* * * *

"We're here, at the edge of the Circles." Merrick released his Angel to shrug out of their packs and wanted to follow their descent to the ground. He was bone weary, muscle sore, and his head thumped like a hammer smashed it with every step he took.

He needed to lay down. Better still, he needed to shed his gargoyle form and retreat into his chimera so he would heal faster. Which he couldn't do.

Merrick cursed under his breath as he watched Angelia busy herself with digging into her pack to set up camp. Her movements were slow, heavy, when usually she moved like a dancer, graceful and light.

Self-reproach weighed heavier than a sack of concrete.

Merrick knew he should say something; explain his silence, especially since his conscience nagged him to do so. Every time he'd held her close, that honey-lavender scent of hers would entwine itself around his heart, squeezing it until he thought the damned thing would quit beating.

Every time, his words jammed themselves in his throat in a disorganized mess. He didn't know where to begin, or how, and he knew the longer he went without saying anything to Angelia, the worse she felt.

He saw it in her withdrawal, felt her uncertainty in the resistance of her body against his. Which only lodged his words deeper, made it more difficult for him to confess his cowardice, his wounded pride that he had failed her.

All because he hadn't dared embrace the chimera within him to defeat Minos, because he didn't have the courage to live without his soul.

Self-pity be damned. He couldn't stand watching her struggle a minute longer. Merrick drew up behind Angelia and reached down to help her take her sleeping bag from her pack.

"I can get it."

He stiffened, ready to guard his wounded ego. The tender touch to his forearm mirrored the soft caress of her voice. She hadn't snapped at him. He was the one getting defensive.

"You should be sitting down somewhere, whether you sleep or not." She was being considerate in the face of his temper tantrum?

God, he didn't deserve this kindness. He didn't take her advice, but stood watching her tired grace as she readied her bed, unzipping her sleeping bag so when she spread it out it was twice its size.

He thought her utterly lovely, given that she remained full of compassion, even after their march through the Second Circle. He had been relentless, driving them as hard as the inner war he waged against himself, and she didn't get angry with him, or petulant.

He felt like a damned cad, and wrestled too many conflicting emotions when she took his wrist in her hand. "Come on. Sit with me."

"Angelia," he protested, leaning against her hold for a moment, resisting her before surrendering to the gentle pleading in her blue-black eyes. She meant to comfort him while he healed, and it made him feel worse for being such a wretch. He hadn't even stopped so she could drink some water and she'd never complained, not once.

"I can perch myself halfway back up the esker." He jacked his thumb over his shoulder. "I can watch out from there, see more."

Angelia shook her head. "No, you'll rest with me. Don't make me beg." She said it flippantly, but he saw the dip in her self-confidence in the way she averted her eyes.

"You're trusting the advice of Minos," he asserted, even as he lowered his battered body to the comfort of Angelia's sleeping bag. Her scent fluffed around him as the bag flattened under his weight, and Merrick shut his eyes to enjoy it. The honey-lavender intensified as she knelt over him.

"I am. So far, his advice has served us well. I'll bank on the rest of it." She brushed a lock of his hair away from the crusting cut on his forehead. His entire body trembled with the ecstasy of it. In spite of him, she held sway, didn't stop being kind.

Just as he would have done had their roles been reversed, had she been the one laying on the ground with a head wound. Merrick sighed as his spirit yielded to her soft touches. Her fingers tugged at the buttons of his jacket, and he gripped them to halt her progress. "I'm fine, Angel."

"I know, but let me see. I'll rest better knowing you're not bleeding to death under there."

The corner of his mouth lifted in a wry grin. "No chance of that. I'm stone, remember?"

"You are not. At least, not yet anyway. Let me see."

Her hands tugged gently at his shoulders, and he leaned forward to help her get his coat off him, then settled back against the rock.

"Are you sure you don't moonlight as a male model?"

Merrick scoffed but kept his eyes shut. It made his head feel better. Just like Angelia's teasing stroked his wounded pride, soothing his heart.

"I mean, pardon the pun, but you're cut. *Chiseled*. One of Michelangelo's carvings."

Merrick grinned outright then opened his eyes to the most beautiful thing he'd ever seen: Angelia straddling his legs and peering down at him, her twilight eyes shining with compassion and hunger, brimming with humor. It was a heady concoction that hit him hard.

"Yeah, well, I've posed for the old man a time or two." He couldn't resist her. The woman charmed him.

She slapped the air and cocked her chin, playing coy. "Aw, c'mon, now." She beamed, mischief filling her eyes, casting a new shine to the blue, brightening it.

Merrick lost himself in the mercurial shifting of her irises. He sat enthralled, transfixed, so all he could do was gaze and forget he had a very battered body.

Then her weight lifted, and he let his gaze follow her as she got up to retrieve the first aid kit. Keeping his attention riveted on her, he watched her grab a smaller sack along with the kit then return. He kept studying her as she retook her position over his legs.

Would he ever get enough? He doubted it. They only had a few more days together—an eternity wouldn't be long enough to watch her.

Merrick sniffed. "What's in the other bag?"

"Dinner. Such as it is." She rummaged until she pulled out an apple, set it on his groin, dug back in, and hauled out a bag of mixed nuts and dried fruit. "Man, didn't they pack a roasted turkey, a leg of lamb? I'm starving here, I could use more than twigs and bark to eat." She took a hearty bite of apple, and then held it out for Merrick to take a chomp.

What the Hell? He stabbed his sharp teeth into the side she wasn't holding.

Angelia set the apple aside as she readied the first aid kit. "Okay, this might sting a bit," she spoke around her full cheeks.

Dear God, she was gorgeous, and didn't even know it. Merrick held up his hand to stop her. "I'm fine, seriously. In a few hours, you'll never know I had the shit pounded out of me."

His words doused her humor, sobering her. She swallowed her bite of apple as she traced a thick bruise blooming on his ribs. Her long lashes feathered her high cheekbones as she followed the path of her fingers, her lips parting on a sigh. "I'm sorry. I should have done something sooner. I should have remembered what I've read, and then you wouldn't have gotten hurt defending me."

"I didn't exactly do much defending." His confession came out easily now that she loosened the tension threatening to rend them apart. Thank God, he'd had the presence of mind to physically hold onto her, to not let her go while they'd weathered the trip through the Second Circle.

"Yeah, you did. Look at yourself—you fought like a hero. You bought me the time I needed to remember." She was studying the wad of gauze she picked up so as not to look at him. "I'm sorry it came at such a cost."

"Angel, don't." He couldn't bear to see her guilt, not when it wasn't hers to feel. "You did the best you could under the circumstances." He meant it, too. Minos was intimidating to the dead, let alone the living. Thinking about how she'd courageously faced the Beast sent his pride soaring for her, instead of limping wounded for himself.

Merrick didn't know many souls, living or dead, who would stand up to the Beast, let alone pull his tail.

"We're both doing our best, don't you think? I mean, we made it here, didn't we?" Angelia smirked with just a hint of uncertainty, and Merrick found himself reaching to run his scabbed knuckles along her wind burned cheek.

"Yes, we did." She was a temptress, a sorceress who enticed him to open himself entirely to her charms. She was sharing his burden and it should have bothered him.

Instead, Merrick felt lighter, encouraged to reveal more as he stared up into her darkening eyes. The bandage forgotten, his Angel held his hand to her face and pushed her soft cheek against his rough skin. She pressed moist kisses to the gashes on his knuckles then buried her nose in his palm.

Merrick grew thick and heavy, so that he had to adjust himself. His chimera shifted within him, stretching to feel Angelia's touch as well.

"So good," he rasped, as he thickened everywhere, as though he

126

grew too much for his gargoyle's skin.

* * * *

Angelia felt the moment of Merrick's surrender, saw the easing of his muscles, the smoothing of the strong lines of his face. She could smell the earth on his palm, the copper tang of blood from his knuckles, and that other she associated with the chimera, the crystalline scent, his maleness.

Leaning in for a kiss, she bit gently onto Merrick's bottom lip, caressing it with her tongue, then drew back to watch him.

Because of his wounds, he was more handsome. Not out of pity, but because he'd gotten them for her. He knew what he would face when he'd stood between her and Minos, and he hadn't backed down.

Nor had he fought with everything he had, and she planned to get to the bottom of that. Even if she'd have to brave his wrath. For all his holding onto her, he could easily lose the hold on himself, on his rage.

"Tell me…" Angelia leaned in for another taste of his lips. "Why you didn't let your chimera out to protect yourself."

Merrick's whole body went rigid beneath her, his latent strength engulfing her, making her feel suddenly fragile. He cupped the mitt of his hand to her nape to return her bite then held her so her face was mere inches from his. The pinch of his teeth still throbbed upon her lower lip.

"It costs me my soul." His claws poked her skin. "I don't have much left to spare. I've squandered it." He swore to God then, the oath riding a forced exhale as he released her, and she knew it was because he'd just revealed his greatest weakness.

She wasn't some ninny. She understood what his confession meant. "Merrick." She didn't know what to say in the face of such a damning revelation. The man hardly had a soul. She felt the sting behind her eyes as her jaw went tight.

I am not going to cry. She wasn't. Any more than she'd let her fears control her. She was done with that. If the chimera had the faith in her to confess something so dear to him, she wouldn't let him down. She'd be brave for him. That she could do, instead of bawling her heart out at the unfairness of the chimera's lost soul.

The other thing she could do? Comfort him, plain and simple. He was Kynd, he'd respond to it, even if reluctantly. She knew that much and was learning more the deeper she went into Hell.

Since the confrontation with Minos, she was fast realizing that part of the Scriptum was already *inside* of her, resonating its truths if she just had the courage to listen. She didn't need eyes and ears. She needed a spine.

For Merrick, and for herself, she'd stiffen it.

Angelia's hands drifted over the heat of Merrick's flat, broad chest. His nipples were pebbles scraping her palms. When he inhaled a jagged breath, she glanced up into slate eyes deeper than any canyon.

Her body gushed as if it overflowed. She giggled like she was drunk on champagne and put her mouth fully to his, sweeping her tongue along the ridge of his, suckling to draw him closer, deeper.

Between her thighs, she felt him thicken, and Merrick's strength was no longer dormant. The hand at her nape clutched her tighter and his other gripped the back of her thigh. His hips lifted to push his cock to her heating core, and her panties dampened as she wetted for him.

She yielded readily, matching his aggression as she took hold of his chest, the tips of her fingers digging into his rough skin.

"Angel," he groaned into her mouth then pulled back. "I'm telling you my soul is thin. I'm one shift away from being Grotesque."

She forced him quiet with a sweep of her tongue against his. She didn't care, because it wouldn't happen. He wasn't Grotesque. None of the Kynd were.

No? She knew exactly where her conviction on that point came from. The Scriptum. At its heart lay the secret to preventing those horrible fates. She was getting closer to it, she felt it. As sure as she felt the chimera's passion well up over them both, engulfing them.

Even so, Merrick gripped her shoulders, drawing her back so she'd look at him. "Angelia," he snarled. "See me for what I am. Do not do this to yourself."

His lips were cut into a hard, thin line across his sharp teeth, his fangs lengthening. Around his neck, she saw his black hair grow thick like a lion's mane.

She wove her fingers into the silk of it. "Do what, chimera, kiss you? Take pleasure from what you give to me?" She taunted him with seduction, refusing to match his rising frustration, or let her fear for him get the better of her.

"Human," he snarled again. "I am not like you." He squeezed her shoulders harder, resisting her taunt.

"No, but then that's not the point." Since he was holding her upper arms in place, she walked her fingers up his bare and chiseled stomach.

"Not the point?" His words choked out from a strangled throat, the sound of it emboldening her. Like unrepentant soldiers, her fingers tiptoed straight to his pebbly nipples and pinched. "Angelia!" he croaked.

She liked the desperate sound of that, too.

"That bite of apple is the first thing I've eaten in months, maybe a year." He got up onto his knees but still cradled her in his strong arms. God, he was so big compared to her, his muscles hard and thick. His skin hot. "I'm losing here, Angel, don't you get it? I've seen enough."

His frustration toppled toward desperation, she felt it in his grip, how it no longer shoved her away, but clutched at her. She should have been scared of him. He barely contained the rage that ripped like a cyclone through him.

She could feel that, too, could see it in the hardening sheen of his eyes. Yet she ignored it, heeding instead the delicious twisting of her womb, the throbbing between her legs that he invoked, that Merrick the chimera awakened in her.

"But you haven't seen it all," she teased.

* * * *

He watched stupefied as her fingers went to the buttons on her shirt and loosened them, revealing her bra and the crescent moons of her breasts curving above the delicate lace. The whole while her fingers danced down her front, her pupils expanded and her lips plumped. Angelia ran her tongue across her bottom lip, wetting it and Merrick swallowed, his eyes dipping again for another peek at her lingerie.

"Mother Mary," he breathed. How many naked breasts had he seen on the Shades passing beneath the Archway, how many demons flaunting themselves, uninhibited, through the millennia?

Yet Merrick had never seen this. He had never seen a human woman look at him the way Angelia did, with wanton hunger glimmering in her black eyes. He could savage her and regret it later. Hell, his erection was singing for it, crushing itself as it thickened with blood. He wanted to tear the leather from his legs, to free himself from the pain.

Instead, he rubbed the rough pads of his fingertips across the silk of Angelia's willowy stomach, tracing the line of her abdomen to the waist of her pants. She trembled beneath his touch, her nipples sprung so tight they puckered the satin of her bra.

Merrick sniffed and shot his gaze upward to his Angel's face. She moistened for him, he smelled her rising heat, the dew gathering between her thighs, and so help him, he couldn't resist the feel of her. He wanted more.

She gave by arching her back to press her breasts toward him, as if she ached to feel the rough cut of his palms cupping her. Virgin that he was, he understood her yearning. He bent to take the breast in his mouth, lapping his tongue along its underside to lift it to freedom. He pinched her rosebud nipple with his sharp teeth and quickly laved to assuage the bite.

She moaned, her head falling back as she arched deeper, thrusting her breasts to the wonders of his mouth.

Blood singing in his veins, he flattened her back to the sleeping bag and dragged his nose along her sternum, where it caught on satin. With a growl, he bit away the hindrance and buried his face into the silk of her warm valley, pressing her freed breasts to his cheeks as he cupped them in his hands.

He could devour her! Lave her raw with his tongue! Her scent overwhelmed him, and his hips rocked helplessly, seeking her, intensifying his erection so it throbbed.

Her arms coiled around his head, clasping him harder to her breasts, until Merrick thought he'd go mad with the burying. His mouth yanked urgently on her nipples, milking more of her scent from her core. His cock uncurled to peek its dripping head from the waist of his pants, riding hot against his stomach.

Mercy. He groaned as his Angel's thighs spread, her palms rubbing the muscles of his back, her nails digging furrows across his shoulders. She gripped them hard in her abandon, and even as her hips rocked in their seeking, he winced, gasping a quick breath. Ignoring the pain of his battered body, he sought the force of this female, sliding his tongue along hers.

Angelia pulled her mouth away but held Merrick's face in her hands as she gazed up at him, her eyes shining, her cheeks flushed. She pressed her forehead to his damp brow, and he felt the wave of their passion flatten out, dropping them both back to the ground.

To Hell's solid ground.

He took a deep breath to get a hold on himself. Jesus, they would have done something she would have regretted if she hadn't stopped them. He should be grateful. Instead his frustration crushed back in on him.

Merrick lifted a hip to ease the pressure of his cock, and to push the damned thing back into the confines of his pants.

His Angel's dark eyes followed then returned to his face, ignoring how close he'd come to violating her. "How hurt are you?"

He shrugged. "It's nothing."

"You're practically made of rock and you winced. It is not nothing."

"Now you admit I'm half stone." He teased her because he didn't like the pinching of the skin between her brows. It made her look too serious, too worried, and she shouldn't be worried about him.

"Don't kid about this, please, Merrick. You're hurt worse than you let on." Her eyes scanned his chest, his shoulders. She sat up to peer around behind him, assessing the bruises flowering like lichen on his skin.

"Is anything broken?" She twisted the last button of her shirt into place, closing off his view.

Merrick shrugged again, and leaned against the boulder. Angelia re-straddled his legs. Instinctively, he cupped her butt to hold her. He wasn't ready for her to pull away, even if their exploring of each other had done a one-eighty. The Kynd in him still wanted to feel some part of his angel touching him, even if he'd almost despoiled her.

"Where does it hurt?"

So much for the passion sweeping her away beyond rational thought. One flinch from him and she'd gone all Mother Hen. He didn't want her to worry, even though he could feel her concern flowing through him in soft, comforting strokes.

"Honestly?"

She nodded.

"Everywhere."

* * * *

"Merrick." His name came out of her mouth like a scold, she couldn't help it. How could he not tell her how badly he was injured? Yeah, she'd watched the fight. She saw Minos throw him against a rock wall, jump and land on him, choke him.

But still. He had broken bones and he'd never let on? Jesus, he really was made of stone. At least when it came to his stubborn willpower. "We've been hiking through Hell for hours." She traced the cut on his forehead with her fingertip, pinching her bottom lip between her teeth.

"Tell me about it." He smirked, hoping to tease her again.

"It's not funny, Merrick." Not at all. It was her fault he suffered. *Again.* No wonder Minos had given her the advice he had. He'd known how beat up Merrick was, that he would need time to heal.

What else had the Beast said to her? Oh yeah. She should take her chimera and guard him well because he was at a dangerous point in his long life. That was the advice Minos had imparted and had she heeded it?

No. She'd seduced her chimera instead of guarding him. And Merrick had gone so far as to confess the thinning of his soul, his turning into a true Grotesque, where he'd be trapped in stone until he crumbled. *Dear God.*

"Please don't cry, Angel."

Angelia turned her face away, her nose itching with unshed tears.

"Come here. Sit with me." Merrick slid her off his legs to snuggle her under his arm. She folded against him like a second skin, as if she'd been created to fit in just that spot. He kissed the top of her head as he had before, when he'd cradled her on the boulder.

She felt his breath on her hair. "Let me tell you a little something about Kynd and maybe then you won't cry. Okay?"

He picked up the apple, chomped a good bite and handed it over to her. "Here—like popcorn with a movie. Pretend it's a drumstick."

She scoffed but felt a reluctant grin surface. Angelia took the apple he offered, salvaged the bag of trail mix, and wriggled back in under the chimera's arm, like a lizard to a warm rock. "Okay, start."

Merrick cleared his throat and Angelia felt it rumble up her side. "Once upon a time—"

"Stop it. This isn't a fairy tale."

"All right. In a galaxy far, far—"

"Funny. I think I know the part about the chimerae and gargoyles. You guys were once beings of Heaven, right? But then didn't take sides between God and Lucifer, so the Old Geezer cast you to Earth."

"I couldn't have said it better myself." Merrick took another bite of the apple Angelia offered then handed it back. "You eat the rest. The twigs and bark, too. I'm all set."

She resisted the impulse to thrust the apple back at him. *Two bites?* But then if what he said was true, two bites was more than he'd eaten in a whole year. A sobering thought.

"So," Merrick continued, "we're on Earth as the Witnesses God intended us to be. The end."

"Not buying it. You've missed a couple of thousand years in between. Besides, you have fighting skills that make Chuck Norris look like a mime. It kind of leaves your story wanting, you know?"

She looked up from under his arm, taking time to appreciate the lines of his bruised throat, the dip and bob of his Adam's apple as he swallowed, the strong cut of his jaw, his collarbone. He was beautiful, definitely a creature of Heaven.

"What else is there?" He glanced down over his cheekbones.

"Oh, I don't know. How about telling me if there are womenkynd, children, pets with wings, that sort of thing. And why don't you guys ever try righting the wrongs against you? Why don't you let the world know you're not grotesque beasts? Want me to keep going, because I've got a million questions."

"A million, huh?"

Angelia nodded and grinned up at him. Yep, she had at least that many. A lot of them pertaining to Merrick personally, but she figured she'd better hold off on picking his brain for those. Better to stay in the safe zone for now. She wouldn't forget again that he was healing, that he needed to stay quiet for a while.

"For starters, we don't have womenkynd and don't usually keep pets, even those with wings. Most of us do eat but we're vegetarians."

"That's why we don't have a leg of lamb in our rations. I should have known it was something like that."

Merrick chuckled then let it trail off. He grew quiet, the atmosphere around them growing still. She put her hand to his chest, where she could feel his heart thumping strong but steady, as if it were becalmed. Under her palm, she felt him take a deep breath. "Another fact about Kynd not many know is that we are very connected to each other. We don't like being alone."

"I thought you said you were going to tell me something that wouldn't make me cry."

"Yeah, well, I'm getting to that part. Quit interrupting." Merrick tucked her closer, as if savoring the press of her body against his, as though she were Kynd and he gained strength just by holding her.

As she considered his legs stretched out in front of him, Angelia could see how people could overlook the Kynd's sensitivity. His limbs were long, thick, and *powerful*, just like the rest of him. Sensitive? Not a word the average person would pick to describe a gargoyle, or a chimera.

Apparently, he didn't notice her savoring his body because the chimera kept talking. "It was part of God's punishment that we be separated, assigned abhorrent tasks around the world, at various posts in all the realms."

"That seems cruel." It also meant Merrick could never leave the Archway for long, that he would never have a life with her, no matter how badly she might want it.

"*Seems,* huh? It is, Angel. We Kynd may not choose sides, but we are very loyal to one another. The pain each one of us feels is collective. In Heaven, we shared our burdens of witnessing, making the onus of such a duty endurable. Here on Earth, we don't have that, except in pieces, when we leave our posts to visit other Kynd."

"Like when Darken came for you." She remembered how buoyant and affable Merrick had been with the gargoyle, how easily they'd touched each other, embraced. It surprised her then, but now it saddened her. Merrick and Darken came together to share more than a greeting. They touched out of necessity, both of them sharing their woes, commiserating silently.

"Yes. It's also why you never see just one stone Grotesque perched on a building. In our drawn out deaths we seek the final comfort of being together, God be damned. We flock to bear witness to the passing of a beautiful soul driven too far and to shoulder our burdens together, as we had done in Heaven. Buildings are the Kynd's version of human cemeteries; they are our final resting places."

Angelia lay quiet under Merrick's arm as she stroked a fingertip along his bruised side. His skin felt thin, yet unfathomably thick at the same time. Like stone. He wasn't exaggerating about his giving up, but it made her wonder about his warning to Darken. Why would Merrick choose to stay in Hell rather than join his loved ones at a final resting place?

Someday, but not this one, she'd have to ask him. For now, it was enough that while he was with her he fought the urge to give in, making his sacrifice all the more incredible. He had faced the Beast knowing he'd have to endure the agony of broken bones. *For my sake.*

Angelia's tears slipped from her lashes and dribbled down her cheeks.

For her, he willingly suffered and would continue to do so. Because they were going deeper into Hell, where things were only going to get worse. Minos' warning scraped her stomach hollow. Merrick *was* at a critical point, and he was clutching to the last scrap of his soul to keep her safe while they traversed the Circles in search of the Scriptum.

He also sought her touch, as if she gave him some measure of comfort the way his Kynd did. That she could give him something in return filled some of the emptiness in her. She could help Merrick, in her way, and it made her feel special when she'd spent her whole life feeling painfully ordinary in a world of spectacular beings.

* * * *

"Are you okay, Angel?" He felt the sudden blush of her heating body against his side, but shifted a bit to peer down at her, to make sure with his own eyes that she was. He saw the glistening tears on her soft cheeks but in spite of them, she wore the hint of a smile on her lips.

Merrick's heart skipped a regular beat then resumed its usual thumping. He pulled the sleeping bag up around her, sealing in her warmth. She snuggled deeper, draping an arm across his stomach to hold him close to her.

In that moment, Merrick felt as close to Heaven as he had so many centuries ago, before he'd been cast out. He felt the weight of his burden lift to become bearable for a time. At least for as long as this stolen moment would last. He would take it. He needed to heal to keep this precious soul beside him safe.

A wry grin twisted his lips as he thought back a few days, to when he'd accepted this job. He'd figured he wouldn't care if he released his chimera. What was the loss of his wings when measured against the weight of his rage, when gauged with the relief of succumbing to it?

Yet somehow, the human woman had managed to get inside of him, to take hold of his willpower. How easily she made him forget his pain, even the fury that had been his constant companion for centuries.

She fed his starving spirit so that he fought harder against the attraction to lose himself in this Godforsaken place. She fed more than his spirit, too. For the first time in months, he'd eaten something. He was surprised by how good the apple had tasted. He'd forgotten the joy of eating, the explosion of texture and flavor that filled the mouth with every bite.

It was another gift Angelia imparted without realizing it.

His Angel. So young, yet so wise beyond her years. She was as fundamentally sound as any true angel he knew—pure of heart, her compassion seemingly boundless. And his for the time being, if he would accept the gift of herself she wanted to give him.

For now.

He was lying to himself and knew it. There would be no temporary connection to this human woman for him. Already he felt the twining of her soul around his, the healing of his body, of his heart.

When this job was over, when she returned to the safety of the surface with the Scriptum in her arms, he would miss her as much as he missed his Kynd. Probably more.

That was later, though. Right then, he would appreciate the reprieve he'd been gifted. Merrick pulled Angelia onto his lap where she could curl up on his stomach and chest. He needed to feel more of her, needed the weight and warmth of her body, as if he was a rock on a wintry brae basking in the rays of the sun.

For the first time in centuries, he allowed his chimera to rest, and his soul to heal.

Chapter Nine

Standing outside the Triumvirate mansion looking in, Darken harbored second thoughts about approaching the Vampyre father, Anton. He needed clothing, yes, but not so badly he would interrupt the scene playing out in the family room he looked in on.

The Vampyre sat at an enormous wooden desk, pouring over some thick tome beneath a circle of butterscotch illumination, while his life-mate lounged on an overstuffed sofa nearby, nursing their boy child.

The lad was curled up at his mother's side, his mouth locked onto the vein of her inner elbow. She had her free arm draped around him, finger-combing locks of his golden hair as he fed. An expression of maternal bliss quirked the corners of the mother's lips into an unconscious smile.

Beautiful. Darken's clawed hand reached for the glass then withdrew. Better not to touch, to soil the tranquility he was witnessing. For seeing his fingers reminded him of what he was.

Grotesque. Not just because he'd been turned to stone. He was a hideous creature, a reaper of souls. Every one he'd severed had altered him, disgracing his once pure soul. His beauty of form had become gruesome over the millennia. He knew that. He'd seen the cemeteries of his fallen Kynd, their anguished faces twisted ghoulishly as they clung to building ledges.

Just as his had been when the rising sun had turned him to stone. He had shrieked his wrath toward a pitiless God, and like his brethren, would have spent the next several hundred years viewed by human eyes as the furious gargoyle he was.

He'd bared his claws and fangs to threaten his Creator. An impotent warning, but he'd meant every betrayed intention in his Kynd soul. Even though God had granted him a reprieve, proving He wasn't so merciless after all.

Darken would be smart not to squander it, which he'd be doing if he entered this home. Why spend precious time consoling a frightened child and reassuring him he was no monster when that was exactly what he was? Clothing could be found anywhere.

And the help he needed? Would not be found here, either. Even with Merrick gone from the Archway, Darken doubted Kharon would let the Vampyre pass. What he needed was the help of his fellow Kynd, if he could convince them to betray their allotted fates to embrace another.

With no guarantee they wouldn't be punished severely for doing so. A shiver rippled across Darken's thick skin, reminding him he had only hours before dawn rendered him useless once again. Which didn't leave much time.

Anton needed to know his human daughter was in peril. As was the Literati. While he'd been stone, Darken had had plenty of time to ponder the value of such an institution. Too many treasured relics remained in its care to lay unprotected. With Aro dismembered, quite literally, there would need to be someone to replace him.

His hand once again reached for the windowpane. Before he tapped a single claw, silver eyes locked onto his, penetrating the glass as if it weren't a barrier between the gargoyle and the Vampyre. Anton muttered something to his life-mate, for she bundled up their boy with an affectionate kiss to his cherub cheek and brought him to his father.

Who bent to place his own kiss on a beloved child as the mother turned toward the window where Darken hovered. Her eyes scanned the area, so he knew neither she nor the child had seen him, yet he stepped back anyway.

Just in case.

If he could shield the lad, as his father obviously intended, the quicker this exchange would happen. Anton motioned him toward the French doors as soon as his family left the room then stepped back cautiously, as if the monster did indeed approach. Silver eyes glistened as the Vampyre tensed for a fight, even though he'd not get one.

"Kynd." A stiff nod to acknowledge the guest, nothing more.

"You are Anton, Vampyre of the Triumvirate. Father to the human woman."

The caution gave way to anger, the promise of it stark in those glittering eyes, the set of his marble jaw. Darken was well aware of the power the Vampyre possessed. He'd fight ruthlessly, especially for a daughter.

The gargoyle would win, though. The Kynd weren't reviled without instinct playing its part. They were maligned out of fear, he well knew that.

Anton waited, every molecule poised, his fangs sliding beyond his bottom lip.

Another few seconds, and Darken would be proving his physical superiority.

"She's with Merrick. Safe for now, I hope."

"But?" One word, laden with the promise of retribution.

"I have killed the head of your Literati for treachery." The confession was met with surprise, then suspicion. As he expected it would be. Darken softened his shoulders in a vain attempt at a non-threatening posture. He didn't need Anton thinking he'd come to slay him as well.

"Aro is dead?"

"I severed his head with my scythe." Which he'd left at the window he'd been peering through. He was scary enough without the weapon adding to it. "He spoke of betrayal. He was behind the theft of the Scriptum."

As a former Witness, the gargoyle heard the hiss and everything it implied. The Vampyre was furious but not surprised.

"Then you did right, gargoyle. But my daughter?" He reached to touch. An unconscious gesture, yet Darken caught himself straining toward it, then stiffened as he took a step back.

He'd never been touched by any but Kynd. Yet, his reasons for flinching went far deeper than that. Thoughts best laid to rest while he dealt with the problem facing him.

Anton rubbed his thumb across his empty fingertips as he dropped his arm.

"I'm going in for Merrick. Your daughter will be all right." He hoped.

The Vampyre didn't look convinced, either.

"We'll keep her safe if that's how we find her." He could promise nothing else. But Merrick had sworn his oath to keep the woman from harm, so Darken would do what he could to honor that. If Merrick had already lost his wings and his soul? He'd deal with that when and *if* the time came.

"I'm going with you." Darken saw the intent in the subtle squaring of the Vampyre's shoulders.

"No. Kharon will not let you pass. And I won't be alone. There are brethren who will join me." He hoped for that, too. Darken would be asking his brothers to blaspheme their God with no guarantee of the punishment their rebellion might incur. They could all be permanently turned to stone, and not just because their Maker decreed it so.

He would be asking them to choose sides. A revolution counter to the blood of Kynd, and Darken still didn't fully understand if his becoming Grotesque during daylight hours was the cost of having chosen, of taking sides.

Would his brotherkynd make such a trade?

"Who are these *brethren*? My God, I don't even know your name, and you're recruiting others." Anton's hands fisted, as if he held himself in check. Given the present circumstances, Darken thought it quite a feat the man hadn't yet attacked, had *invited* him into his home.

The gargoyle managed a smile, which probably looked like a sneer to the Vampyre. Not reassuring, but hell, it was all he had. "More Kynd." His voice, used so little, scraped deep wounds in the air around them, but Darken pressed on. "Old friends from the time before." Before they'd been scattered throughout the different realms.

"Of course." Anton acknowledged the sacrifice with a brief nod, deferring to the potential strength of such a gathering. His fists uncoiled, and he reached once more for the gargoyle who trespassed into his beautiful home. This time to ask for his visitor's hand. A gesture of trust.

Darken gazed at the outstretched palm, his heart fluttering like it had little butterflies in it. The Vampyre would hear it, of course. Except that was what trust was about, wasn't it? Putting faith in another who could one day be your enemy. Who could use your weaknesses against you.

As Kynd, trusting an outsider wasn't done. But he had little choice. Besides, these were different times, and two thousand years of torture had a way of reshaping one's idea of things. He reached across the distance, bridging entire worlds with a single gesture.

"I am Darken," he said, clasping his rough hand around the Vampyre's, engulfing it. Within his grasp, he felt the father's titanium strength of centuries. Neither could he help but see the power in those level, silver eyes.

"Thank you, Darken, for *everything.*" Anton squeezed his hand when he said *everything.*

The man was glad he'd slain a fellow vampire? Then he realized. The vile creature called Aro had been out to harm his daughter. Of course the Vampyre father would see the other dead, and gratefully so.

He had yet to release Darken's hand. "I understand your sacrifice."

As Kynd, Darken saw much others missed and his eyes narrowed to scrutinizing slits.

Anton did not mistake the cost. "Tell me what you need and I will give it. *Anything,*" he hissed.

"Clothing. If I'm to traipse this plane, I must blend as best I can."

The Vampyre's lips twisted into a small, yet droll smile. "Yes, of course. But camouflaging yourself? Good luck with that."

He finds humor at a time like this? It was something the gargoyle could appreciate.

"Something large. But no sheet."

Fangs emerged when Anton grinned. "No toga. Right. I'll see what we can scrape up." He stepped off to leave then caught himself. "Do you need a phone? A Vampyre escort to locate your brethren?" He meant did he want Anton to teleport him through the different realms.

"No. The ones I call are close to me in spirit. They will hear my plea." *Now, if only they'll answer it.* But Darken didn't say that. He knew the Vampyre worried enough about his daughter, and would insist on going with him if the others didn't join him to save Merrick.

"I just need a little privacy to do this." He nudged his chin at the door. "Mind?"

"I'll get your clothing." Anton exited without a look back and without a flinch of hesitation. Yet, the man was no lackey. His desire to help his daughter simply overrode his pride.

Love is what makes this house beautiful. Darken's chest tightened, squeezing his ribs so it was an effort to breathe. He stood too close to the sacrosanct of family, the root-like bonds working under his thickening skin, making him feel too vulnerable. Like those tendrils were peeling back scabs better left intact.

Better to think on something else before he bled out all his emotions on the Vampyre's beloved home. Darken might be a monster, but he knew that wasn't how you paid someone back for their faith.

Like a benediction, he concentrated on the brotherkynd who had been closest to his heart before the Schism. Not counting Merrick, there were four of them he could call. As with the Guardian of the Archway, Darken had seen each Kynd briefly during his travels to reap souls. All of them were close to surrendering, making him wonder what he was taking on if they responded to his appeal.

How emotionally damaged had their repugnant tasks rendered them?

There was only one way to know. Shutting his eyes to envision each of them, he sent his telepathic plea out into the Nether regions. He imagined it gently circling outward, like concentric ripples from a dropped stone in a becalmed lake.

What returned was a single tidal wave of one resounding answer: *Yes!*

It slammed into him so hard he realized the lemon scent in his nostrils was floor polish. Too stunned to do much else, Darken gaped up at the ceiling, his hands clutched tight to his head as if shards of his skull would dirty the drapes.

They come! Every damned one of them would come.

A grating sound chortled beyond the grasp of his lungs. Laughter? Darken bit down on it. Then let the sound bubble forth again, amazed by its effervescence. Without letting go of his head, he sat up, resting his elbows on his bare knees. Fizzing rumbles tickled up his chest.

My brotherkynd are coming. This time, with the shackles of their various duties removed, they would be free to touch, to share. To be

Kynd.

Or not. A sobering thought, one that dried his newfound joy in his throat. Yes, his brethren would help him find Merrick and the woman.

But would the four be so far gone they would need their own saving?

* * * *

Angelia awakened slowly. She felt utterly cozy wrapped up tight in the chimera's embrace, and was unwilling to abandon the spot too soon. Nor did she want to stir, afraid she would disturb the man who still held her even though he slept.

Because Merrick was sleeping, and the truth of it flushed her full with relief and with so much pride, she could feel the swelling of her heart.

The chimera trusted her enough to drop his inherent watchfulness.

She hoped that was why he'd fallen asleep, anyway. A skinny strand of doubt made her think he did it solely for practical purpose. He had, after all, gotten the living snot beat out of him by Minos. If sleeping helped to heal him then he was doing what he had to.

She chose to ignore the insidious needling of her thoughts because Merrick still held her. He had readjusted his position so she was curled up into him, his arms, legs, and body curved over and around her, protecting her even while he slept. Surely, she was more than just the job to him.

He'd confessed his greatest weakness to her, which had to count for something.

Her first impression of Merrick, when he had deigned to stuff his seething self into the Triumvirate's gallery with the rest of them, was that he didn't like anyone, tolerating those around him out of sheer necessity.

The chimera had blatantly disregarded the authority of the Vampyres, who made up the powerful, ruling Triumvirate, for goodness sake. Forget the Literati. Merrick hadn't even bothered to veil his contempt for Aro and the ghouls. *Or for me.*

But that was then. Now, she couldn't help but feel privileged he would reveal his vulnerability to her, that he had told her secrets of the

Kynd. He had no guarantee she wouldn't spill her guts to her boss, yet he had entrusted her with the knowledge anyway.

Did he feel the pull between them as she did? For her, at least, the attraction went way beyond the physical.

Well, she was enjoying the physical, too, and blushed as she thought about how she lay herself wide open for Merrick to take as he'd wanted. She was a virgin, for Pete's sake, she knew nothing of lovemaking. Yet, her body knew the ancient code stamped into her DNA, it acted of its own wanton volition.

Merrick had definitely reacted. Her blush returned as she recalled how he'd instinctively pumped his hips against her spread thighs, his tongue lashing her breasts, his mouth sucking so hard upon her nipples, she'd felt her clitoris throb and her womb drip cream. Her brain had gone on hiatus, returning only when her lover involuntarily winced, revealing how much pain he was in.

She could smell him now, wrapped up as he was in the sleeping bag with her. That crystalline scent she associated with the chimera permeating her well-being better than the aroma of freshly baked brownies.

Angelia rubbed her nose against Merrick's chest, surreptitiously breathing in the heady male scent of him. He smelled like the earth— deep, powerful, steadfast. She had to bite down on her tongue before it licked his bare chest. She was dying to know if he tasted like he smelled. His skin was like stone, after all, so her curiosity niggled.

"Go ahead. You can tell me what you think."

Angelia stiffened, practically falling out of the muscled arms holding her close, yet she couldn't ignore the bass rumble of his voice across her skin. "I didn't know you were awake." Her embarrassed smile beaming like a darned neon sign flashing *Guilt*.

"So I guessed." Merrick's slate eyes were bright, his black hair a little tousled, as if the curly ends strained riotously to be stroked by her fingers. She fisted her hand to wrangle the traitorous thing before it caressed those curly-cues.

"Hi," he said, rubbing his forehead to hers, as if to nudge her embarrassment toward affection.

"Hi." She grinned like a silly girl, her heart dancing like an ecstatic

Snoopy. "Are you feeling better?"

Merrick nodded and closed his eyes again as he took a deep breath, as if he were scenting her the way she'd just done to him.

"Hmm, nice," he purred.

He was. He'd drawn in the smell of her, and she should have been self-conscious about that, given she hadn't showered for a few days. Instead, she felt a delicate wringing and squirmed her hips to ease it.

She felt coveted as Merrick drew her up tighter.

The singing from the Scriptum coiled like warm mist around her spine, filling her head, so she heard the celestial choir *inside* of her ears, feeling its truth as much as she heard it. What the Scriptum imparted hugged her as surely as the mighty arms holding her.

The chimera. He needed her. *Her.* Angelia Delacroix. The orphan raised by vampires.

Angelia's eyes snapped wide as her heart and her brain finally synchronized the Scriptum's decoded message.

"It's me," she blurted, stiffening in Merrick's arms as she kicked her feet so she could stand up. She had to stand. Her body had just been electrocuted with stunning information and it needed to do something.

Merrick rose with her. Yet Angelia kept hold of the grounding force of him, encircling his wrist with her fingers in case he let her go completely. She cast a startled glance up at the man standing with her, at the Kynd who readily stayed because they both needed him to.

"It's *me*, Merrick. The Scriptum wrote about me."

* * * *

Merrick watched the range of emotions play across Angelia's face. Disbelief. Denial. Wondrous awe in the face of the truth. She was electric with it, like the energy oozed out of her skin, making it shine. Making *her* shine. Like a frigging angel.

Holy Hell. She wasn't really, was she?

"Merrick?" Now she looked frightened. The downward turn of her pretty lips, the very ones he adored tasting, struck him hard and fast like a blow to the gut, so that he stepped back to keep his balance.

She couldn't be a real angel. Yet, how could she not be? She was so blasted pure, compassionate. Understanding. Like she *empathized*, not

146

sympathized. Which was an angel's trait, was it not?

It was the reason why the Fallen One had argued with his God. Why Angelia hadn't been able to stand the crush of living among so many humans.

Merrick groaned.

"Merrick?" Angelia took a hesitant step toward him.

Christ. He stuck both hands in his hair and took a deep breath. "Sorry, Angel, it's just—" What could he say? *I won't touch you again because I think you're a real angel?*

Which was bullshit, and he knew it. He didn't have the strength *not* to touch her now that he had already done so. As it was, he fought everything within him that made him Kynd not to reach out for her, to give her comfort when she seemed so desperately to need it.

Exhaling, he managed to say, "It's okay." Which was a lie. He was sorry, but it wasn't okay. Not for him, anyway. Not anymore. His stolen days of relief had just been smashed like the delicate things they were.

So ironic the truth, if that's what Angelia's revelation was. For here they stood on the cusp of the Third Circle, where the Gluttonous were mired. Which was where Merrick belonged. He wasn't supposed to have peace. He and the Kynd were being punished.

And Merrick thought he'd found a brief reprieve? He'd thought Angelia was like Kynd?

Idiot. He'd almost ruined her with his greed. No wonder Minos had let him pass through the Second Circle. He didn't belong there. It was Kerberos Merrick would have to contend with.

The three-headed dog who guarded the Gluttonous. Granted, he wasn't a dog, but a fellow chimera. A fact that didn't give Merrick a free pass. Kerberos had his assignment and would have to obey his divine orders by not permitting his brotherkynd passage to the next Circle.

"Turn around, Angel." His nickname for her scraped up through his throat like a strand of barbed wire.

"What?"

"Turn around." Merrick didn't wait for her to do it herself, but spun her around so she faced away from him. He pushed her braid up over her shoulder, indulging the caress of it on his knuckles.

So Jesus-ly soft. Her hair, tousled within the plait of her braid, was like a rope of silk. He fought not to bury his face against her neck, where the smell of her lingered warm and inviting, where delicate tendrils of spun gold curled to hug her nape.

* * * *

Merrick stood rigid behind her, his fingers digging into her shoulders. She felt his tension, the rigid line of his body.

"What?" Fear crept up her spine, she couldn't help it. Merrick's sudden shift in attitude scared her. He seemed barely contained in his skin, and she knew she was the cause of it.

What she'd blurted about the Scriptum had pulled the pin out of his hand grenade. He had yet to let go of the handle, but still. He stood behind her like a bomb, holding her ruthlessly.

"Take off your shirt." His words ground out of his mouth, and Angelia knew he pushed them through his clenched jaw, passed his sharp teeth.

"If this is your idea of foreplay…" She tried to tease, even though fear churned in her belly and made her palms clammy. Merrick wasn't in a kidding mood. Far from it. He was downright dangerous. As lethal as he'd been when she'd first laid eyes on him.

He growled. Then reached around her to fist the front of her blouse. With a swift yank, he sent the buttons scattering. Merrick crumpled the fabric of the shirt in his fingers, gripping the front closed, the tendons in his forearm bulging under his skin.

Angelia felt him suck in a hard breath and hold it, felt him brush his forehead along the crown of her head. As if he didn't quite dare to touch her. As if he struggled not to.

Her heart pounded against his fist. She didn't breathe. Not until she felt his fingers pinch the shoulders of her shirt and carefully slide the garment down her arms, exposing her back. He was looking for something. In his current mood, he certainly wasn't checking her out to make love to her. Far from it.

What the dickens had set him off like this? Oh yeah. She'd blurted the Scriptum had been written about her, or something along those lines.

Truth. She couldn't deny it, not when the words tattooed themselves to her blood, singing their wisdom into her head. But why should that upset him? If anything, she thought Merrick would be glad she was remembering what she'd read. It could help them the deeper into Hell they had to go.

They could use the help. Now that Merrick was trying to keep the last of his soul, every advantage they gained would make it easier for him to keep his wings safely tucked away.

Instead, he stripped her to the waist. As if he thought the pages of the book were written across the skin of her back. She felt the heat of his gaze burning along her bared skin. Shame scorched her cheeks, instead of the lust she'd felt earlier, and she curled her forearms over her naked breasts. Hiding them, trying in vain to cover her rising humiliation.

Mortification from what? Her nudity in front of the chimera, who bared his *soul* to her, threadbare as it was?

No. She was being a coward in the face of Merrick's *fear*. Not his rage.

If she'd take a second to stop wallowing in her insecurities, she'd see his reaction for what it was. Something about what she had exclaimed *frightened* him. Enough so the tenuous hold he had on his fury slipped. Nothing more.

Angelia lowered her arms, and straightened her spine.

* * * *

She didn't turn to face him when he pushed away from her, but stood with her slender back bared to him, the unmarred cream of it an accusation. He'd ravaged her. Stripped her of more than her clothes, he knew, his grinding teeth the only barrier between his rage and the woman before him.

He'd almost lost it. That he could be so far gone not to know when he was in the presence of the Divine? The possibility unmoored him.

Yet, she bore no marks. No trace along the alabaster skin of her back where her wings would be if she had them. He knew what it was he looked for, had seen it countless times those thousands of years ago when he was still graced by his Maker.

An angel bore evidence of its wings when they were hidden. Just as he did.

Merrick crouched, driving his strong fingers into the soil as a roar mushroomed from his chest to suffocate him. The chimera struggled for release, to unbind the fury that choked him, that would render him Grotesque.

The touch of fingers to his shoulder startled him, and Merrick surged backward, drawing away from the offer of comfort.

"No," he snarled, disgusted with himself that he could shame the beautiful creature before him. And *she* who offered to ease *him*. "Stay away." He tore the words from his squished heart, even as he wrested for scraps of control.

"Do not touch me, Angelia." *Angelia*. Not *his* Angel.

She withdrew her hand.

"Merrick, I'm—"

"Don't. Don't say it." He couldn't bear it. He wasn't holding himself tight enough to hear her apology. Like it was her fault he'd panicked and had ripped her clothing from her sacred body. Because sacred it was, whether she was angel or not.

Merrick still wasn't sure the absence of the marks along her back was proof she wasn't Divine. He saw her glow, for Christ's sake. Even now, standing there looking at him, she was too innocent, too damned empathic, the pain she felt for him shimmering in those dark eyes. She stood mere feet from him, her shirt hanging forgotten at her waist, as if his distress outstripped hers.

Holy loving God, wasn't the fact he'd been condemned to guard Hell punishment enough? Now, he was the Creator's plaything? To be taunted and teased by a creature quite likely sent from Heaven itself?

And what of her? Unknowing of her fate, of her role in this twisted quest to retrieve an ancient tome with her name engraved upon its pages? She was as much a puppet as he was.

It was too much. Almost.

Merrick dug into himself just a little bit deeper. When he thought he'd already mined the bottom of his resolve, he scratched up a bit more for her sake.

"I'm the one…" Merrick fisted his hair, then dropped his arms when the gesture reminded him of fisting Angelia's shirt. He reached for the buttons on his leather coat instead, sliding the heavy garment from his shoulders.

* * * *

He's offering me his jacket?

Angelia watched Merrick struggle to harness the rage seeping away from his control. She saw the line of his jaw grow hard as the granite of his expressive eyes, witnessed the thickening and lengthening of his raven black hair. A lion's mane.

Part of Merrick's chimera was lion. It was his mane pushing forth, enveloping and perhaps embracing the man. She didn't know if that was what it was doing because she still didn't know what other creature— besides the gargoyle and the lion—had been woven together to form him. She never actually *saw* him in his one, true form.

Though she knew distress when she witnessed it. She knew shame, too, intimately. And the chimera, in spite of his fury, exuded both.

He offered her his coat to cover herself, the tendons in his bare shoulder flexing as he held it out for her.

"Please." He would not look her in the eye, but turned his chin as she accepted his peace offering.

Yet, before she held its weight in her own hands, she withdrew. Perversely, she wanted him to know he'd hurt her, that she wasn't some pushover who would easily forgive him for what he'd done. He'd been right to tell her not to apologize. This wasn't her fault, and the notion of it stiffened her spine with a little starch, made her readjust her shoulders.

Merrick watched her from the corner of his eye.

Angelia waited. She would see him do more than offer his coat if he was going to act all contrite for almost releasing his chimera. For almost losing his soul. She wouldn't forgive him for that, no matter how intense or monstrous the fury within him boiled. He was worth picking a fight over.

Well, she wouldn't exactly fight him—the stick in the hornet's nest and all that.

"Take the coat to cover yourself," he growled without looking straight at her.

"Not yet," she dared, curling her fingers into her palms to steady the trembling of her hands. "First, let me touch you." Oh, but she'd be brazen while she was here in Hell. Like the place gave her license to step

151

beyond her usual timidity.

Merrick's jaw ticked as he ground his sharp teeth together.

"Let me touch you," she repeated, not because she knew he hadn't heard her, but because she wanted him to know she was adamant about it. He needed it as much as she did, and she'd be darned if she'd let him torture himself with another minute of deprivation. He'd long endured enough of that.

Whatever he'd gleaned from her outburst concerning the Scriptum, he was going to have to get over it. At least on her watch, anyway.

Fascinated, she watched as he turned away from her, the inner war he waged rippling through his powerful body. Thick muscles twisted, rolling across his ribs as his breathing deepened and quickened, as though he ran.

Angelia risked closing the distance between them. She wrapped her arms around his waist and pressed her cheek to his broad back, the knobs of his spine surfacing as he sucked in a jagged breath. No other part of him moved, and she hovered with her offer of comfort for one heartbeat... two...three...four. They grew louder in her head, harder on her sternum.

Finally, Merrick's fingers curled around hers, the beat of her heart suspending as she wondered if he would pluck her hand away, or draw it tighter to him. As he exhaled, Merrick softened against her, pressing her fist into his taut stomach.

"You kill me," he groaned, his head hanging.

"You make me feel alive," she rejoined, without even thinking of the words she spoke. Yet, they were true. It was because of him she discovered parts of herself she didn't know existed. He made her feel like the woman she should be.

Angelia kissed the bottom edge of one of the scars on the chimera's upper back, then kissed its twin on the opposite side of his spine. Where his wings were hidden.

* * * *

He straightened when he felt the moist heat of her lips, spun around to cup her head in his hands, to hold her still. Like a coward, he kept his eyes shut against her audacious gaze.

"Angeli—"

Her fingers found his lips and squished them shut.

"*Angel*, chimera. I'm your Angel."

She had no idea. She didn't have a clue how close she just might be to that being the case. With her arms around him, so triumphant, so gloriously indignant, he let the humor of the irony spin its golden thread through him.

The mirth quelled his fury as surely as the woman's arms resurrected him.

Then her moist mouth suckled his nipple, and Merrick's knees loosened. He locked his legs as his eyes flew open. The sensation of her little teeth scraping? Rioted through his body, an electrical impulse unlike anything he'd ever felt before. It was like his nipples were linked to his groin, so that the milking of her mouth tightened his balls until they ached.

Merrick's hips rocked sensually as he palmed the back of Angelia's head, encouraging her as he succumbed to the exquisite pleasure of her mouth on his body. She took command, her fingers tracing the length of his back, down to his ass, where she stopped to squeeze, wringing a moan from his throat.

Crooking a finger under her jaw, Merrick tilted her face to take her mouth with his, plunging his tongue for the taste of her, to join himself intimately with this woman who dared grab his rage and shake it.

To shake him into mindfulness. Into awareness of himself. Of who and what he was.

Right. Ever so gently, he removed himself, sliding her bottom lip between his sharp teeth as he withdrew. He couldn't do this to her, not if she might be what he suspected. If she was angel by some incredible chance and didn't know it, he wouldn't be the one to stain her with his earthly cravings.

"Put on my coat, Angel. Cover yourself."

Embarrassment clouded her shining eyes. For the briefest of moments, but he saw it.

Merrick lifted her with one arm, pulling her up to his mouth, taking it hard, earnestly. He held nothing back of his hunger for her. He would not let his Angel feel she wasn't coveted, even if he couldn't have her the way he wanted to.

Flesh of my flesh.

In her ear, he rasped, "Tell me more of what the Scriptum says to you." Because he was a bleeding sadist to heap another torture on himself and would come straight back to Hell when she was safely back on the surface.

He would have to. Merrick was back to teetering on the brink between choosing stone over charred, mutilated wings.

He loosened his hold, easing her to the ground. But he didn't let go of her; she had asked not to stand alone. He knew why she demanded he let her touch him, he wasn't ignorant of what she was trying to do for him.

He would let her. For now.

Angelia looked up, her lips plump and bruised from his kiss. Then her tongue slid the length of her bottom lip, dragging his gaze along with it. Her lips curled ever so slightly, as though she tasted him lingering upon her mouth. *The cat who licked the cream.*

Fisting his leather coat, he thrust it between them. As soothing as she was, he didn't trust his animalistic drive to claim her.

She hesitated. "This will leave—"

My back wide open for my wings to burst forth? He hardened his expression to cut her off. Yeah, he knew that, but his coat would protect her soft skin. A far better use, in his opinion.

Reluctantly, she reached for it and slid her arms through its heavy sleeves. "Fine."

The damned thing swallowed her. Yet, she clutched either side of the collar and drove her nose into its cavernous folds. Smelling him. *Good God.* He pressed his claws into his palms to keep from touching her.

"Well, are you going to share what happened or keep it all to yourself?" *Just talk.* He needed the distraction from seeing her enveloped in what he thought of as his second skin. Even if his questions threatened to blow the cover off his fury. He'd walked that razor's edge for centuries, he could keep doing it for her sake.

To keep his body sidetracked, he began to pack up their makeshift camp, unzipping the sleeping bags from one another. Merrick breathed through his mouth so he wouldn't smell her scent wafting around where they'd slept.

It slid over his tongue, instead, so he tasted her. *Christ*, there was no escaping her. It was like his entire body was finely tuned to the female's frequency.

Not helping yourself, chimera. No, he wasn't. Thinking she was as finely tuned to him only amped up the crawling of his skin. He wanted her desperately.

He would do well to start thinking it was the *angel* half of her, which sensed the nuances in his emotions, before he lost his resolve to keep her pure, before he shredded their sleeping bags. His claws were already doing damage to the slippery nylon.

She ignored his inner conflicts and bed-mauling by digging into their rations for a canister of water. "Yeah, I just don't quite know how to explain it."

Merrick dragged his gaze from her crouching body, tried not stoking the pleasure of seeing her dwarfed in his jacket. Because, he dutifully reminded himself, he had... *Torn. Her shirt. Off.*

"Start from the beginning. What came back to you?" He was such a sucker. But his curiosity was for his Angel's sake, to help her, so he'd endure.

"Right. Okay, you know the Scriptum was stolen." Angelia took a swig from the canister. "Well, before it was taken, I was sitting at my bench decoding it." She lowered the canteen and pointed her finger. "Fascinating stuff *about you*, Merrick."

He opted for casual, while his insides picked up a low roaring. "Me personally? Or Kynd in general?"

"Kynd in general, at first, I think."

Merrick quit rolling the sleeping bag. "At first?"

"Yeah, well, that's the part I'm missing." She frowned. "Not the only part, actually, but I was reading..." She trailed off, shrugging.

Merrick waited, clutching the balled up sleeping bags like they were life jackets.

"The reading had reached a finer point, narrowing down to specifics. But that was when the singing started—"

"The singing?"

155

"Yeah, like a choir. It was so beautiful, and *huge*—like I could see it in front of me it was so big." She shook her head, spreading her arms before her. "No, not big. *Vast*. Consuming."

"And then what?" Despite himself, Merrick felt drawn to Angelia's telling.

"And then I passed out."

Involuntarily, his upper lip curled off a canine in a silent snarl. He crammed the bags into their packs. "Your story is as bad as mine. What was it singing before you fainted?"

"I don't know exactly. Truth, I suppose?"

"Truth? The Scriptum was singing Truth?"

"I know, it sounds dumb, but that's how it felt. Like I was hearing some great truth."

"And just now? What did it say to you a few minutes ago?"

"Well, that..." Delicate pools of blush colored her cheeks. "That's the weird part. I mean, why is an ancient text singing my name? I'm not like you or Anton. I haven't been around for thousands of years."

Merrick had his suspicions, but for now he'd keep them to himself. No point in upsetting her. He didn't think she was going to calmly accept her angel status. Really, who would? Merrick knew what it was to be angel. It was one of the elements of his chimera. Hence, the loss of his wings, not just his soul, if he surrendered to his rage and shifted into his true form while being in Hell.

Shouldering both their packs, Merrick held his hand out for Angelia to take. He eyed her appreciatively as she reached for him, liking the look of his leather coat draped around her, loving that she so easily stuck her hand out for him to take.

She appeared so delicate and small beneath the garment's soft, scuffed bulk. But she looked safe there, too, and Merrick definitely liked the sight of that. An illusion, considering where they were traveling, but he'd take it just the same.

Right then, he'd take anything that helped.

Chapter Ten

For being Hell, Angelia thought the landscape between the Second and Third Circles was surprisingly easy to traverse. She knew she and Merrick traveled deeper into the belly of the beast, yet this part seemed incongruously *flat*.

The sky above remained stretched like a red goblet above them, as if it reflected all the blood that had been spilled and sacrificed to this subterranean region. With that in mind, Angelia didn't let her guard down, even though she wasn't tripping over gnarled roots or sharp rocks.

Just because the footing was easier, didn't mean other things would be.

She hadn't forgotten Minos' warning about keeping a wary eye out for others looking for the Scriptum. Someone had dared to steal the codex from the Literati and had brought it to this realm for a reason. There would be others who coveted the information encoded within its pages.

Maybe there were some here capable of deciphering the text. The idea didn't exactly add the kind of excitement she was looking for in her great adventure. If there were others, then they were already one step ahead of her—they knew *why* the Scriptum was valuable. Which meant they most likely had more than an inkling of the power it contained and planned to use it.

The fact it had *spoken* her name to her? She squeezed Merrick's hand, grateful that the chimera had agreed to guide her and to keep her safe. She could be stolen just as easily as the Scriptum had been. Seriously, if she was the key, then Aro's insistence she follow the book started to look a little suspicious.

Like he was trying to get rid of her. Not that she could blame the vampire. She wasn't exactly a crucial member of the Literati team. She was the dust-buster in the cleaning closet—little jobs and seldom used.

God, do I really think of myself that way?

Angelia gazed up at Merrick, who still encircled his warm fingers around hers, just as he'd been doing since their near trampling in the Vestibule. She knew now his reasons went beyond duty. He wasn't merely keeping her safe because he'd struck a bargain with her father.

Uh-uh. The chimera *liked* her. *Wanted* her, in fact, and Angelia's whole body grew hot, her labia twitching with electrical spasms. She studied the ground as she grinned indulgently, savoring how her body reacted to the mere thought of the ways Merrick's attentions transported her.

Yeah, she needed to get off that delectable train of thought and get back to thinking about the danger she and Merrick were getting themselves into. They were headed for another Circle, and if Dante had been right, this one wasn't going to be pretty.

It was going to be disgusting, if she remembered her literature correctly. The Third Circle contained the Gluttonous, those who were doomed for an eternity to abide slashing rain, sleet, and bitter snows, all the while enduring the torments of Cerberus, the three-headed dog.

To Angelia, it seemed like a horrific punishment for those who, in life, had been over-indulgent. As if in sympathy, goose bumps erupted, shooting the fine hairs on her forearms erect. She rubbed her free hand up and down her arm as she scrunched her shoulders.

"So, we're not far from the Third Circle, right? Any chance you can feed Cerberus slime like Virgil did, so he'll let us pass?"

* * * *

"Kerberos."

"Huh?" Angelia wrinkled her brow, and Merrick felt his rage subside a little more. The pressure of her fingers entwined with his going a long way toward keeping him steady, provided he didn't think about who or what, she might truly be.

"Kerberos. With a *K*. The three-headed dog, as he's been described, isn't a *dog* at all—he's Kynd. Chimera to be exact."

"Get out!" Angelia halted in her tracks, her blue-black eyes alive with fascination. "You're kidding, right?"

Her surprise made him feel like he'd given her a big gift. Which he supposed he had. Not many knew Kerberos' true identity. But then her smile faded, as did the sheen that had lit her face. Yeah, he knew exactly where her thoughts were going.

"Angel." But what could he say to reassure her? Kerberos' immortal life was as full of despair as the rest of the Kynd's were. And his Angel *felt* it. "He copes like the rest of us."

"Don't sugar-coat it, please. He suffers like the rest of you."

So he did. Which was the only consolation to getting mired in the Third Circle as the Glutton he was, getting to hang out with another Kynd when he wasn't writhing in fetid waste. Except.

He had every intention of circling the Circle. Of avoiding Kerberos if he could. He didn't want to fight his brotherkynd and he'd have to in order to keep searching for the Scriptum. In order to keep Angelia safe.

He couldn't get caught in the Circle where he belonged. He had other plans for where he'd wind up. Merrick picked up the thread of conversation he'd dropped. "He does suffer, but—"

"But?" She challenged him, stopping to toss her golden braid over her shoulder. His eyes involuntarily followed its arc.

"All right. There is no *but*. He hurts like the rest of us and can't do anything about it." Merrick envisioned himself physically pressing his rage down, which threatened to spill if he thought too closely about his brethren's unfair lot.

Angelia squeezed his hand, and resumed walking, pulling him right along with her. "I wonder if that's part of the puzzle with the Scriptum." She glanced up at him from under long lashes. "I mean, if it mentions me specifically and the Kynd, maybe I'm supposed to *do* something, you know. Maybe I'm supposed to help you guys somehow."

Merrick almost scoffed but swallowed it when he saw how the idea galvanized her. "I don't think God has any intention of releasing us from our punishments." *Do I?* Merrick gnashed his sharp teeth hard on that line of thinking.

He didn't need some golden strand of optimism to enter his heart, because something as powerful as hope could crack what little control he had on himself.

"Why not? Why can't it be Fate bringing us together for this journey into Hell?"

"Because—" Yet, he really didn't have a good argument against his Angel's theory.

"*Because?* That's your big reason?" She feigned supreme shock, teasing him.

Merrick's lips quirked to fight his grin. She had him as hard and true as any Kynd would have, and he was taken with her. Attached to her.

"*Because* you know I might be right. Although, something bothers me about it." She grew quiet as they trudged along, studying the ground, stepping around soft areas where the slime was beginning to form. They neared the Third Circle.

Merrick didn't like the slump in her humor. He bumped her with his elbow. "What bothers you, Angel?"

She offered him an apologetic smile, as if what she might say would seem as preposterous as dolphins blowing up balloons. But he didn't miss the hurt shadowing her features. He didn't miss much of anything, actually. "I think Aro is trying to get rid of me."

Merrick's spine went rigid as his mane itched to surface. "Oh, yeah? Why would you think such a thing?" If it was true, then when Merrick got Angelia back safely to Anton, he was going to tear Aro's arms off his body and eat them while the vampire watched.

"I'm not exactly a prized member of the Literati, Merrick, even for being the only human on their team. This Scriptum job is the first time I've ever been allowed to handle something important. And look, I blew that, too."

"You didn't *blow* anything, Angel. Especially if your theory has any merit. You're supposed to be here, right?" *With me*, he would love to believe, but couldn't.

The earth under their feet grew soft and squishy, and Merrick tucked Angelia up tight against him. One misstep from this point on, and the bog would have their boots.

* * * *

160

Merrick lifted her effortlessly, as if she weighed nothing more than a crumb. Which was about how she was feeling the more she considered the possibility that the head of the Literati was hoping she wouldn't come back from her excursion into Hell. If it hadn't been for Merrick, Angelia would have been trampled before she'd even gotten through Hell's door.

Thank God for the chimera.

The gratitude returned Angelia's thoughts to the idea of Fate bringing her and Merrick together to search for the Scriptum. There were stranger things in this world, she knew.

Aro, she suspected, was banking on the chimera's contempt for humans, and most likely figured Merrick wouldn't try very hard to keep her alive. Did the vampire know how close Merrick was to losing it altogether? It was a disturbing thought, and a fierce, protective wave had Angelia's body seeking even closer contact with the man who already had his arm around her.

Forget the treacherous footing. The real threat wasn't coming from under their feet.

"Merrick, what if Aro wants us both gone?" She hated the quaver in her voice, when inside she began to seethe.

"Then I would say he underestimated his opponents." He didn't even flinch, or so much as blink. Obviously, he wasn't the least bit intimidated by the vampire.

"There are dangerous things here," she protested, as the image of his bruised and battered body loomed in her frontal lobe.

"In case it escaped you, Angel, I'm one of them." He wasn't joking. When he glanced down at her, his jaw muscles bunched.

True, Minos might have given him a thumping but Merrick had been holding back. And that worried her. She didn't want him feeling that sense of failure again. She would protect him as diligently as he did her. She would not lose her chimera to Hell.

My chimera.

Angelia liked the ring of it, relished the warmth spreading throughout her body. What the heck, she could dream, couldn't she? Once this was over, she knew, they'd have to part ways. Merrick would have to return to his post as Guardian to the Archway and she'd have to

161

go back to her—*what?*

Not her usual life, that was for sure. Besides, Fate might have something else in mind, and Angelia's heart quickened the more she thought about it. This was her adventure. This was what she'd been searching for when she'd signed on to the Literati. And she had a chimera to share it with. Who wanted to share it with her.

Again, thank you, God.

She was so blessedly pleased and so tuned for her adventure, she readily felt the despair lurking in the air long before they neared the gate to the Third Circle.

"Oh, this is awful."

Merrick squeezed her tight before removing his arm from around her and taking her hand. He gave her a reassuring smile. Which melted her heart. She planted her feet in the mucky ground and leaned up to steal a kiss in spite of the atmosphere of utter ruin and misery around them.

The second he realized what she wanted, Merrick's mouth claimed hers, his tongue lashing as he sucked. He tilted his head to command more of her, squeezing her against the hot skin of his chest. Her body melted to his as her fingers curled into his hair.

She felt him shudder against her, and an instant later he withdrew as if an invisible wedge had been jimmied between them. They were both breathing hard, and Merrick's granite eyes were deep, unfathomable.

He dropped to one knee, and with shaking fingers started to button her coat like her mother used to do when she was a little kid.

"Cut it out." She giggled, his flavor still riding her tongue while tiny tremors slid along her thigh muscles. "What are you doing?" She tried pushing his hands away.

"Making sure you're covered. There will be snow, hail, and rain once we cross the threshold, or had you forgotten?"

As if on cue, a great wailing arose around them and Angelia paled, their stolen moment of lust cowering away like a scolded dog. "I hadn't forgotten."

"I know." He dabbed his fingertip to the end of her nose, reminding her of the wasp stings on the bridge of it. The reality of Hell rolled back in like a cold fog.

"But, what about you?" Merrick didn't have a coat to protect him, to keep him warm and dry.

"I'll be fine." He tugged the collar up to her ears, as if for good measure. "Ready?"

She nodded.

"Okay, then. Here goes nothing." He winked at her, and she beamed in spite of her fear.

Merrick took her hand again, leading them toward the divide, where their boots sunk into the slime as they slid down the narrow path. The wailing became a great crescendo without cease, and her chimera tilted his head against the assault to his sensitive hearing.

Angelia's fingers tightened around his.

Too soon, they reached an ocean of Shades mired in their own filth. They lay supine, their contorted faces lashed by the freezing rain, their mouths open as they swallowed slime like the Gluttons they were.

Their bodies roiled under and drowned, then squirmed and twisted so their faces were exposed anew, their mouths opening in endless wails, only to swallow, to drown all over again, and then resurface.

"Oh, God, I'm going to be sick." She turned her back to the Hell in front of her and vomited. Shades writhed toward her, unable to stop themselves from consuming what she'd deposited at her feet. She screamed as she scrambled backward, her feet slipping in the slick mud.

Strong arms caught her, the body surrounding her steadfast and warm. Merrick scooped her fully into both arms, his large hand folding over her face to shield her eyes.

"Oh, God," she muttered again.

Merrick said nothing, but his jaw was clenched so hard she saw the tendons bulging.

This was Gluttony. Holy loving sacrament, this went beyond disgusting. It was repellent, repugnant.

"Hold on, Angel."

So she did. Behind them, the despondent howl of Kerberos coiled itself through the wails of the damned. Merrick pulled Angelia closer and bent his head against the sleet, the ruin, and the absolute despair.

* * * *

Darken was picking himself up from the floor just as Anton came back into the den.

Despite the resounding roar still echoing from his brotherkynd's answer, he didn't miss the little vampire boy, who was hugging himself to his father's leg. His cherub face alternated from peering curiously at the gargoyle, to burying shyly into the fabric of his da's pants.

Never mind his sore head, Darken thought his heart would squeeze through his ribs and plop onto the rug. The Vampyre brought his flesh and blood in close proximity to the Grotesque, an act of faith that nearly crippled Darken with its overwhelming message of trust.

Gaping like a lost straggler at a desert oasis, somehow he found his tongue. "The lad. He's wondrous. He has a name?"

With a firm, yet gentle nudge, Anton shuffled the boy forward. "This is Emilio." He smiled down at his son. "Go on, say hello."

Darken squatted to be at the boy's level. "My name is Darken. Do you know what I am?" He didn't move, afraid he'd scare the little man, who was bravely shuffling closer, with one hand still clasped to his father's fingers. The lad's thumb was jammed into his mouth, his burgundy eyes round as saucers, yet inquisitive, as he nodded.

The mother entered silently, leaning her shoulder against the threshold, her arms folded.

"You're Kynd," the boy said around his thumb.

Something warm unfolded in Darken's chest and spread throughout him. He smiled, careful not to show his teeth, although the lad would be no stranger to fangs. The gargoyle glanced up at the father, who shrugged.

"His sister is a fan. And we teach tolerance in this home."

Darken could only nod as his throat cinched tight. Then, like a playful kitten, Emilio dashed forward, tagged the gargoyle's knee, and scurried back to hide once more behind his father's leg, where he peered out to see what the Kynd would do.

A woman's laughter cascaded into the room as Anton's life-mate abandoned her post at the door to scoop the giggling boy into her arms. "You're trouble, and it's time for your bath." She dabbed his nose, and Emilio buried his face into his mother's shoulder.

Her sable eyes danced with warmth and merriment as she reached a hand in greeting. Darken straightened to stand. "I'm Marguerite. It's nice to meet you…"

"Darken." For a brief moment, he stared at her outstretched palm, stunned that she, like Anton, wanted to touch him. They weren't Kynd, yet still they sought contact.

And shared their blood-child.

Without warning, he was suddenly swamped by the hellish shrieks of the souls he'd reaped. Overwhelmed, he felt his knees shake, his roped muscles tense.

"Take Emilio, Marguerite," Anton ordered, stepping between his family and the unstable gargoyle.

Darken held up his hand, giving his head a single, hard shake. "Wait." He wouldn't hurt them for the world, surely they knew that. No matter how his memories haunted him, he would never unleash himself on the innocent. Would he?

Holy God, I don't know. He dropped his hand, defeated by his uncertainty. Was he ruined, then? Worse than Grotesque, who were at least rendered harmless while their fury and their grief consumed them? "Take the lad. Go," he growled, his jaw clenched tight to stifle the roar building in his broad chest.

Loving Christ, he wouldn't scream. He just couldn't. Not with the boy so close. Darken staggered back as he forced air in and out of his squeezing lungs.

Anton followed. "Kynd, let me…"

"No. Stay where you are." Another sharp shake of his head sloshed his brain against his skull but did nothing to help him dislodge the reminders of his past. Regrettably, he'd seen the lad's saucer-like eyes riding above his mother's shoulder as she'd sped him from the room.

Away from the murderous gargoyle.

"I'm sorry." Darken kept his own eyes trained on the rug beneath his clawed toes. He was beginning to muster some of his control, banishing his twisted memories to the background. "I'm not accustomed…to dwelling among the living." He looked up in time to see the Vampyre offer an understanding nod.

"You aided the Reapers then?"

Suspicion hovered over Darken like a bank of cold fog, and he narrowed his eyes as if to peer through it.

"I saw the scythe in your hand before you entered. Thank you for leaving it at the door." Anton's smile was friendly, tolerant. He was ignoring the gargoyle's distrust.

"Yet, you brought your boy—" His words clogged in his throat. The Vampyre had introduced his son, fully suspecting what the Kynd had been doing for too many centuries.

"I did. I also entrusted my daughter to the care of your brother."

The reminder had the calming effect Anton was most likely striving toward. Darken shuddered, releasing the tension in his muscles.

He had come to the Vampyre's home in the name of doing something honorable. Beast he may be, but he was still salvageable to some degree. Merrick, however, wouldn't be, and the longer Darken took coming to grips with walking amongst the living, the more likely it was that his brotherkynd was slipping deeper toward the temptations of Hell.

"I will do my best to bring her out." He would, too. Along with the rest of his brethren, no matter what shape they were in when they all went into Hell to rescue Merrick. Courageous enough to flout God's punishment, they deserved the chance to avert their granite destinies.

"I know." Anton held out the clothes as he approached. "Here, these should come close to fitting. As for the others, they will come here?"

Darken nodded.

A glance toward the den's door was the only clue to Anton's unease. Then he offered the same understanding smile that had earlier softened the silver of his strange eyes.

"They won't harm—" Darken protested, despite the uncertainty of what shape his brotherkynd would be in.

"I know that, too. As does Marguerite, who has no doubt already explained it to Emilio." Anton laid the clothes on a brocaded chair. "What will they need? I should, perhaps, call the rest of the Triumvirate."

Again, Darken nodded. The Vampyre's generosity astounded him. Even though he was the first he turned to for help, he hadn't expected such acceptance. But then, the Vampyre was a leader of his people. No small feat, given who his people were. Keeping a blood-hungered population at peace with other species was beyond admirable.

It bordered on impossible.

Yet, Anton, Kristov, and Godrick had succeeded. For the most part. Aro had been an anomaly, a criminal in this new world of tenuous peace between the Others. The Literati played an important role in keeping that peace.

"We will leave as soon we can." Darken grew anxious, afraid that already he wasted too much time in finding Merrick. He leaned into the comforting touch of the Vampyre's hand upon his shoulder.

"Get dressed, Kynd, and I'll call the others, apprise them of the situation while your friends arrive. Meanwhile, I'll see what clothing I can dig up for your brothers."

"If they'll need it," he admitted. "There are two chimera." As if that explained everything.

To Anton's credit, the Vampyre didn't flinch. He winked. "Then I'll find clothing for two gargoyles and a couple of sheets for the others."

He's joking? A pig-pile of Kynd couldn't have eased Darken better, and he lay his rough palm over Anton's hand. "I can't thank you enough for what you're doing for us, for my brotherkynd. I hope we can repay your kindness soon."

"As do I, Darken. Just bring my little girl home, all right? I don't care if—" His fears locked the words in his throat, and he took a deep breath, his eyes flashing like twin moonbeams on the blade of a sword.

"We'll bring her back no matter what state any of us are in. I promise you that. Now, go make contact with the rest of your Triumvirate. I feel my brethren nearing." He was hearing them, too. Roars like freight trains were expanding in his head, threatening to split his skull.

Unchaining them, Darken well knew, also unleashed their pent-up rage. Whether that wrath could be brought under control remained to be seen.

He wouldn't risk having Anton around. The tempers of the Kynd were too volatile, too fragile. The sight of a Vampyre might unhinge what little control some of them mustered. Hard enough two of his friends were gargoyle, but he was tied emotionally to two chimera, as well. What form they arrived in would be telling.

He didn't want to harm the one ally the Kynd had in this new life they dared to grasp. Especially since he wasn't sure how long God's reprieve would last. Aside from that, if the rising sun ignited the curse of the Grotesque and rendered them all to stone for twelve hours, he and his brotherkynd would need a safe and private place to wait it out.

Somewhere far from the curious and destructive habits of human beings.

Darken squeezed his eyes shut, as if doing so would keep his head from exploding. Then the air around him rippled, contracted, and shimmered. Drakus, Kronos, Kallen, and Urick popped into the spacious den. The roars that had been deafening him ceased abruptly.

Four pairs of anguished eyes scanned the room, and then each other.

Darken witnessed something he had not seen in more than two thousand years: his brethren together. Wild and unpredictable, scarred and haunted.

To him, they were beautiful. His arms instinctively spread wide to encompass them, and he stood before his brotherkynd utterly stripped of prejudice. He didn't care what wounds they brought with them. Together they would heal. Together they would triumph. *If* the four he had called to his side retained any essence of being Kynd.

He let his tears wash down his rough cheeks as he waited for them to touch him.

Terrified that they wouldn't.

* * * *

They'd traveled for hours before Merrick finally relented and put Angelia down. She tried not to look at the writhing bodies consuming their own slime over and over, but no matter where she averted her eyes, she saw them.

So many it sickened her. She felt no humor in the irony of their revolting fates, either. Especially when she felt the sting of the icy rain and snow on her face.

Poor Merrick. He'd given her his coat, refusing to take it back even when his skin bloomed red and raw from exposure. The only places on him not getting pelted were his legs and where their packs protected his back.

He walked hunched over as he bore the brunt of the storms, keeping Angelia behind him now that he wasn't holding her. She hated every minute of the hours passing. Hated seeing the chimera endure in the face of the biting rain. Skin made of stone, her eye. When they were safely out of this weather, she was going to give him an earful.

It took a long while, and by the time the swirling snow and lashing sleet abated, she was too pooped to do much beyond collapse right where Merrick deemed would be a good place to rest for a minute.

A minute. Like that would rejuvenate her.

She was even too tired to ask why they hadn't gone to visit Kerberos, even if it was just to ask if the soulless man had passed through his Circle. She had her suspicions, so she wouldn't push. Merrick had pledged to help her find the Scriptum, to keep her safe. If he thought they needed to hurry through that hellhole and miss saying hi to another Kynd, then she wasn't going to question it.

She trusted him. And she was dog tired. She'd kill for a cup of hot tea. Or a hot meal. Surprising, given how grossed out she'd been by the sight of the Shades churning in their own filth. Plunking her butt on a rock, Angelia savored the relief of taking the weight off her feet like she'd just kicked back in a Lazy-Boy.

Except, she didn't feel as at ease as she should, not when she was looking at Merrick and his frostbitten skin. He was crouched and digging through his pack, his broad back arching a springy curve down to his waistline. As if he felt her gaze, he turned, an apple poised on his fingertips.

Oh, Adam, you deviant deliverer of sin.

"Hungry?"

She was, only not for the fruit. She wanted the man. Like a lustful Eve, she wriggled her hips around the sensuous tingling of her lady parts.

Above them, the sky burned crimson and maroon, clouds the color of dried blood skimmed past, casting a devilish tint to his already reddened skin. Which matched the expression he wore. Gone was his tender care. Merrick's eyes had turned sheer slate, his mouth a feral slash.

* * * *

169

Merrick's nostrils flared as he lifted his chin to catch his Angel's scent. He couldn't unpin her from his fierce glare, not when the smell of her pierced him to the ground he crouched on. She wanted him. Despite the fact he'd run like a coward from facing his brotherkynd.

He wouldn't beat himself up about it. He'd done what he had to for his Angel. Right this second, it looked like he'd get his reward. His cock thought so. It filled, hugging and riding the inside of his thigh. Merrick rose, his nose absorbing as much of the woman before him as his eyes did.

Now he wanted to touch, to taste, to feel the heat of her mouth on his.

The apple dropped to his booted feet, and in one stride, he accomplished what his body commanded. He girded his Angel and lifted her, pulling her mouth tantalizing close to his.

She gazed up at him, her eyes growing black and shiny as obsidian, her breath warm. Not shy in the least, she claimed his mouth with a hard pull and sweep of her tongue.

Merrick groaned, his knees buckling and boring into the ground. Yet, the woman in his arms remained snug against him, her arms clutched around his neck. He lowered her slowly to the ground, his hips already pumping, his erection sprung and seeking as he lost himself in the heat of her mouth.

Somewhere in his mind, he knew he shouldn't be doing this. But his warning bells had been stripped from their ropes, his tenuous control obliterated as her scent enveloped him. Clamping his mouth to her tender neck, he stroked his tongue along the soft skin, sliding a dizzying path down her sternum, his coat flayed to each side of her exposed breasts.

For a brief flash he wondered, couldn't recall unfastening any buttons so she lay un-trussed and opened beneath him. When had he done that? Had she?

No matter. His mouth crushed down on a creamy breast, his breath steaming the supple skin, pricking her nipple tight, a heady contrast to the plump fullness of the rest of her.

His pelvis instinctively pushed against and dragged the length of her long thigh as she arched into him, pressing herself up to him, her moan the rasping strike of a match. Merrick's hands freed her hips, shoving the obstructing cloth out of his way. He pinched her nipple with his teeth, traced his tongue to her bellybutton, his palm cupping her springy coils, her dew moistening his fingers.

Her thighs spread as if to encourage him, and Merrick rode another surge of lust as his muscles tensed with the burning of his blood. With a growl, he wedged his broad shoulders between her legs and took her core, his tongue darting, tasting so deep she undulated her hips around his devouring mouth.

He wanted to weep at the taste of her!

Feverish, he barely felt her hands fisting his hair, until the sensual rhythm of her hips grinded harder against his mouth, her body begging him to lap and suckle more. Moaning, he dug his toes into the ground as his fingers bit into the flesh of her thighs, tugging her glistening core tighter to his face.

As she tossed her head and pinned his shoulders between her knees, he ruthlessly gorged on her, refusing to stop even when her muscles clenched on his tongue as she rode wave after wave of orgasm. His throbbing cock thickened painfully, demanding its own pleasure.

Merrick hesitated, drawing back to absorb the abandon of the woman beneath him.

She took his breath.

Beauty lay beneath him, between his arms. Transported, tousled, unafraid—of *him*, who could give her this abandon. Merrick's breath stuttered in his chest as his heart grew over-large, crushing itself in his tightening chest.

Her scent was in him, clinging to his lips, curling into his head, his guts. His skin rippled in a delicious shiver as heat enveloped him. Like the coat, somehow his leather pants had come undone, and the head of his striving cock bobbed between them. Merrick nestled it against the hot, wet folds between his Angel's thighs.

One brutal thrust and he would have his desire; he would know what it was to be sated.

She would be flesh of his flesh.

Still he hesitated.

She lay before him, innocent. Pure in spite of what he'd done to her because her heart remained so. He understood she finally saw all of him

171

as he'd intentionally bared himself to her; he'd let her look at the utter ruin of his soul.

To scare her, maybe. Frighten her away from the trail he'd ardently led her down. He wanted her so intensely it hurt, far more than the stiffening of his cells. The hardening of his cock burned him at the site and deep within.

He thought it had seared his regard right out of his brains. His damnation would have been worth every milking clench of her hot, slick muscles. But…

My Angel.

He could not surrender to this scorching fever, to this ache and yearning, any more than he could succumb to his full rage. So he retreated. And hated himself all the more for it.

Merrick thrust himself to his feet and roared.

* * * *

Angelia curled her legs under her and sat up, pulling the leather coat up to cover herself. She resisted clapping her hands to her ears. Instead, she squeezed her eyes shut against the swamping wave of the chimera's tortured bellow. She heard him panting and looked up at him.

Merrick stood with his legs braced apart, his great hands spread, his fingers clawed. His muscles stood rigidly pronounced from his trembling bones, and his wide chest heaved with each of his ragged breaths. He would not look at her.

She could feel his regret waft from him. She felt his indecisiveness as if he pined to touch her, to comfort her, yet couldn't. If this was the cost to the banished Kynd, Angelia would have none of it. Her insecurities be damned. God be damned. She may not remember all the details from the Scriptum, but she knew the Kynd weren't doomed to endure this kind of torture until they all turned to stone.

Merrick and the others had hope.

She just needed to get her hands on that dang book, and realized in that moment her reasons for finding it were not the ones she'd entered Hell with. The Scriptum was no longer an object she needed to recover to prove her worth. She needed to rescue that book to replace the torment Merrick and his Kynd felt now, to replace it with…touch.

Maybe even...*love*.

She leapt to her feet and flung herself at Merrick, uncaring how pathetically needy it might seem. The only judge of that stood like a tortured beast in front of her. There was no way the Kynd in him would resent her instinct to touch and soothe.

* * * *

Merrick clasped her to him like a drowning man, and sank to his knees so more of his body could touch hers. This time the need was different. This time his soul demanded first attention, as if it recognized that without it they were all condemned.

So close his chimera came to quivering its release. So near Merrick came to losing his wings. All for the ecstasy of bonding, heart and soul, to another. To one a little like himself. For he no longer doubted her veins ran thick with an angel's blood. It was there in the purity shining from those blue-black eyes.

He was a rotting mess of conflicting emotions. His gratitude for Angelia sparring with his regret for having laid eyes on her in the first place. She saved him, but it was going to ruin him. Was this paradox Merrick's version of Hell?

No matter. She was in his arms. The Kynd in him would savor the feel of her like the life-generating nectar it was. Even as he teetered precariously, Merrick nuzzled his face in the warmth of her nape, dragging in the quelling scent of honey-lavender as her braid curved along his cheek.

He eased his grip on her, realizing that he was almost crushing her in his desperation for solace. She squeezed herself to him tighter when his arms loosened. Such a pair. Merrick pulled his face from heaven and swept errant wisps from Angelia's brow and temples.

"Such a pair," he repeated aloud, giving her an embarrassed grin. She had seen him stripped bare, and he'd not done that for more than two thousand years. Never to that degree. So, here he was in Hell offering himself, asking his Angel to share her abundant soul with his ruined one.

"Chimera, you would join yourself to a human?"

She taunted him, her eyes shimmering playfully, hiding what lay beneath.

* * * *

Angelia knew the instant he recognized her façade for what it was. She joked about his offer, though it floored her, stripped her heart bare. If he rescinded, he'd wound her.

"No. But, you aren't human. Not all anyway. And I would have you if you'd let it be so."

She let go of the breath caught in her throat. "Yes." She heard the quaver in her voice and wished her tone had been as strong as the surging of her heart just then.

The chimera would have her. It was, for her, a lifelong fantasy come true. "But I am human, so if you've delusions…" she protested, in spite of her grasping. Really, their declaring a bond was only temporary. He'd have to leave her the moment he returned her to the surface with the Scriptum.

"I've no delusions, Angel. Besides…" Merrick paused and stood, lifting her with him as if she weighed but a feather. "Despite your refusal to the contrary, you and I have more in common than you think." He procured the apple on his fingertips as he had earlier and waved it in front of her. When he'd snagged it, she couldn't guess. Merrick was like a frickin' magician: skills with a touch of flair.

She took it from him, her stomach growling as the smell of its autumn goodness reached her nose. "Yeah, we both growl." She bit into the apple.

"No. We're both a little angel."

She almost laughed, then saw his face. He wasn't kidding. The apple sat unchewed in her cheeks.

"When you get righteous, you emanate. You have an aura. A halo, if you'll allow me to use the proper term."

This would be funny if he didn't look so serious.

"No one's ever said anything about it." She couldn't be glib as she looked up at Merrick, his black bangs curling around his strong face. Maybe nobody had said anything because she'd never taken a stand before. Not for herself, not for anyone.

Not until she'd met Merrick.

He pried the apple from her fingers and took a bite, his sharp teeth slicing through the skin like razors. While he chewed, he watched her, as though her thoughts played out on her face.

"Okay, so we say I'm an angel—"

"Which you are. Partly."

She shook her head. "So, I'm an angel, *partly*. You are, too? You're saying one of the creatures that makes up your chimera is angel?"

"Yep. Angel, lion, and gargoyle. Still want me?" He sounded flippant, but she saw the shadows of uncertainty and doubt cloud his slate eyes.

"Of course. Do you still want me?"

"Like I said, Angel, we're quite a pair."

"Yeah." She liked the idea a lot. *A pair*. Merrick, the Guardian of Hell's Archway, a true chimera, had declared it so. If only it would last.

The apple was demolished in the face of their appetites. Merrick put Angelia on her feet then buttoned his coat up to her chin, like a doting caretaker. Yet, the bite of his teeth to her lower lip was far removed from anything paternal. As was the sheen of his granite eyes.

"Thank you, Angel," he said as he leaned in to suck her lower lip between his, then swipe his tongue for a fleeting taste of her.

"Thank *you*, chimera." She meant it with all her heart. So what if he thought her part angel. She'd take whatever had changed his mind about her. She'd take the gift of him, lock, stock and barrel, so long as their adventure in Hell lasted.

Chapter Eleven

The Fourth Circle offered nothing more horrid than what Angelia had faced in the Third, provided she ignore the Shades wrestling in ceaseless combat with each other. At least she and Merrick weren't being pelted by freezing rain and snow as they slogged their way through the marshes lining the banks of the river Styx. Which Angelia remembered to be the Fifth Circle.

They were making great progress. *Emotionally, too,* she thought, her grin spreading across her cheeks, her heart squeezing her breath. She wanted to giggle, she was so dang happy. This was her adventure and it had blossomed into a love story. A little like the Indiana Jones movies, after all.

Who knew a body could skip in Hell?

* * * *

Merrick grinned down at her, amused.

"You seem content, Angel."

"I am." She beamed up at him, causing Merrick's skin to grow tight. God, she was a stolen treasure. One he'd keep as long as he could. Less than three days he had with her. They loomed like three days of paradise, provided the rest of the trip went this easy. He knew it wouldn't, but just then, walking in the glow of his Angel's gladness, he let hope steal its warm fingers into his heart.

She sidled up closer to him as brackish water oozed up over their boots. "We're getting close to the river, huh? Is the boatman Kynd, too?"

"No. You can be sure he's not going to be pleased to see us standing on the banks waiting for him." Merrick wouldn't fight him, though. Long ago, they'd come to the understanding that trading hits got Merrick nowhere.

He half-snorted aloud thinking about the many times he'd come unleashed to do some serious ass-kicking, to release some of his pent-up rage. Yet, no matter how many times he'd beaten the boatman physically, mentally the guy wouldn't budge.

He had a will stronger than iron.

The chimera couldn't even put his hands over the boatman's and force him to push them across the slimy river Styx to the city Dis. The pole pusher himself turned eely, like the slime, so Merrick couldn't get a grip on him to force him to do anything.

Frustration. That's what the chimera met each time on the banks of the river Styx. Which was probably the point. The souls of the Wrathful and Slothful dwelled in this area, so was it any wonder nothing was accomplished?

"What's funny?"

"Hmm?" Merrick glanced down, marveling at Angelia's curious beauty, the healing scabs on her cheeks, where the little wounds made her all the more precious to him. "Oh, I was reminiscing. I used to come here to fight the boatman to take me across."

"Fight him? Why would you have to fight him?"

"Just wait, you'll see."

"Did it work?"

"Not even once." Merrick's mirth ebbed as he thought of the many times he'd taken himself across to Dis.

He'd flown. For no good reason other than to take the edge off, to help him endure his task at the Archway. He'd been so wrathful himself, like the Shades on the riverbank, that he'd foregone the comforting company of Kharon and Kerberos. Instead, he had doled out layer upon layer of his soul.

"What the crap?" Angelia squealed and halted, her knees lifting like a prancing horse. "Ewww, holy crap, crap, crap." She sidestepped, practically crawling up Merrick's back to get away from the sinewy hand she'd stepped on. He immediately swung her up in his arms before leaping back a few yards.

177

"Wrathful Shades," he reminded her.

"*In* the gall-darn swamp?" Angelia craned her neck to look down. Below them, bodies gripped fistfuls of loose skin and tore it from flesh. Over and over.

"It's...*disgusting.*" She paled as though her stomach executed a sickening roll. "Oh, man."

Merrick retreated farther up the marshy bank, away from the undulating swamp, to give her a moment to recover.

"Are you all right?" He peered down into her ashen face, his fear for her smacking his heart around in his chest, spiking his pulse, shrinking his skin.

"Yeah. Just give me a second, okay." Her knees curled to her chest when Merrick went to set her down. Angelia shot him a sheepish grin then stretched her long legs, and tentatively placed each booted foot back onto the bog beneath them.

"Sorry about that. It wigged me out. I wasn't expecting it."

"No problem." He didn't let go of her, but pulled her close so her back curved along the front of him. Merrick lowered his head to nuzzle her nape. His whole body warmed, his pulse still wild from Angelia's outburst.

"I'll carry you to where Phlegyas will pick us up." He'd carry her the entire way to Lower Hell if she'd let him.

"Phlegyas," Angelia repeated as she glanced down at the Shades rending their flesh from each other, where the torn pieces regenerated, only to be stripped time and again. It was a silent massacre and unrelenting. "So, Dante had this right?"

"Much of it, *yes.*" Except the most important part, where these Shades could free themselves from their personal torments if they released their sins. Merrick had yet to witness a single Shade come back through the Archway.

"And the City of Dis?"

"Worse than he described."

"Because he and Virgil passed it by. They went through the gate but didn't go inside its walls like you have."

Merrick kept them balanced as the writhing bodies he treaded across continued their shredding of each other, undeterred and unaware of the trespass. They were too engrossed in their sins to notice otherwise. Whenever a body Merrick stepped on lowered, he counterbalanced, keeping his Angel safely above the turmoil.

"No, they kept walking, as we will do." He'd been there, he knew what awaited them, and he'd keep Angelia as far from the city as he possibly could.

"But what if the soulless man is there?" She clasped her two hands around his neck as he dipped and bobbed precariously, the body he stepped on having risen to consume another. Angelia buried her face against his bare chest, and Merrick felt a shiver course through her.

"I wish I'd killed him like all the others."

Angelia pulled her face from his chest, her expression inquisitive, not dark with judgment.

Merrick readjusted his grip on her. What could he say just then? He couldn't offer excuses, not when he had long ago surrendered himself to his fate. He was the Guardian—it was his duty to prevent the passing of those who did not belong in Hell. He did his job very well. And every killing, like the spreading of his wings in Hades, had shaved off pieces of his Kynd soul.

"You couldn't have known." Angelia's voice threaded musically into his ears, the reverberation of it like a caress.

"No, but I should have." Even now he couldn't fully acknowledge his regret. Letting the soulless man pass put him here, with his Angel in his arms. Selfish, yes, but he deserved some reprieve, didn't he?

She let his admission slide. "Merrick?"

His answer was a quick look down at her before returning is attention to the precarious footing beneath them.

"We'll have to go into Dis to look for the thief."

"Not a snowball's chance, Angel."

She struggled in his arms, wanting to stand on her own two feet when she argued with him. Merrick squashed the grin threatening to erupt. He loved her brass, he truly did. He loved, too, how it was something newly unlocked and that she had found it with him. It made him feel all the more connected to her because he had witnessed her unveiling, the discovery of herself.

"You really want me to put you down?" His grin escaped his

control. He knew the corner of his lip lifted to reveal the tip of a fang.

Angelia quit struggling. "Funny, chimera. Just quit dawdling and get us to the river."

* * * *

She regretted her order the second they arrived and gazed, disgusted, from one bank to the other. "This is not a river." Uh-uh. It was a cesspool, an enormous lagoon of sludge with an unctuous sheen like blood reflecting the sky above. Angelia stared, trying to process its enormity, its sheer malevolence.

This is no river, she repeated internally. It was a septic tank rife with Slothful Shades, the gas bubbles blooming to the surface giving them away with gurgles and plops.

Underneath that sea of slime were thousands upon thousands of souls. She would not be sick. No, God, she couldn't. But the sight of the Styx only compounded the weight of the misery she'd been trying to process since traversing that sickening marsh.

It was going to be too much. It was the straw on the camel's back, the one hotdog too many.

Angelia clamped her hand to her mouth, even as her gaze continued to sweep over the scene in front of her. Her hand sought the empty air around her then found her chimera. She gripped tight to his fingers, crushing them in hers.

He said nothing, just stood there beside her offering silent comfort while she dug a little deeper to find the means to cope.

"Dis cannot be worse," she moaned.

"It only gets worse, Angel."

She heard the edge in his warning. He wouldn't paint a false picture of what yet lay before them. She knew if she couldn't hack it, he'd race her back to the surface. All she would have to do was tilt her chin and he'd be gone with her, returning her to safety.

She knew how much it bothered him to have her here. For different reasons from when they'd started and that truth steeled her, stiffening her resolve so that with a great swallow, her stomach settled and her shoulders squared.

She was not the same woman who had sat meekly awaiting her

sentence in the Triumvirate's gallery. "All right. Light that frigging torch and get that bastard boatman over here."

Merrick's appreciation rumbled, his laughter scraping through the stench, making it bearable.

Yeah, she could absolutely do this.

"Merrick, you said you couldn't fight the boatman, right?"

"I did."

"So, forcing him doesn't work. What else did you try?"

"Nothing, Angel. I was a little too self-absorbed for nuance."

He'd spread his wings to cross, she knew that, but it wasn't an option anymore. A setback, but not one they couldn't overcome.

"Fair enough. Light that signal, please."

"You have an idea." It wasn't a question. He eyed her close, as if guessing her thoughts. Maybe he did. As Kynd, he would be eerily observant. Which should have been a little unnerving, she supposed, but she found she liked how clued in to her he was.

As though he found in her what he was looking for, Merrick rolled his shoulders then hefted the six-foot torch from its iron stanchion and shinnied the thirty feet up the side of the towering lighthouse. The beacon flared, and Merrick dropped to the ground with ease, returning the torch to its iron fitting.

When he was finished, he turned to catch her scrutinizing him just as he'd been doing to her before he'd gone to light the beacon. Gads, he was magnificent to watch. His power was raw, the leonine grace evident in his every move. He'd climbed a thirty-foot height like it was nothing, even though his thick muscles bulged and slid under his skin with the effort.

Angelia knew exactly how they were going to get across that river, and she was going to enjoy every toe-curling second of it.

"Are you going to share that idea or just stand there appreciating the goods," he teased.

Angelia lowered her lashes demurely. "How long before the boatman comes?" She slid her tongue across her lower lip. Merrick's gaze dragged itself along with it as he shrugged his answer.

Angelia's lips twitched as she stepped closer to Merrick, her hips reaching for him along with her hands. "Come here, then." She curled her fingers between the leather of his pants and his chiseled stomach, hitching him closer so she could run her inner thigh along the outer length of his muscular leg.

Merrick hardened all over, his gaze hungry. Angelia turned her chin up, took his mouth with hers, and ran her tongue along his sharp teeth, teasing him to bite deeper. With a snarl, he squeezed her butt and lifted her so her body pressed hard to his groin. He fisted her braid, pulling her head back so he could deepen his kiss.

"Holy Christ, Angel," he gasped, as his tongue blazed a path to her neck, where it traced circles in the warm hollow of her shoulder. His fangs scraped her skin, dragging a moan from her throat.

She let her weight drop back, unafraid in the chimera's strong grasp, his leather coat she wore falling to either side of her, as if unpeeling her body for the taking.

Merrick's mouth clamped onto her melon breast. He suckled her sprung nipple, pinched it in his teeth then suckled more, lifting Angelia in a wave of coiling pleasure. The scrape of wood on the shore alerted her to the boatman's arrival, and Merrick turned, his fangs sliding forth as he growled a jealous warning toward Phlegyas.

Angelia cupped his cheek, turning his face away from the intruder, and begged his attention with her mouth, her tongue gliding through the reverberations of Merrick's uncontrolled snarls.

His rumblings threaded through her body, across her skin, and she fully wetted for him, her core wringing with need, her folds throbbing as they thickened with her heating blood. She clutched at the waistline of Merrick's leather pants and hauled him toward her as she stepped backward for the raft, toward Phlegyas, who moved aside as if transfixed.

The pair toppled into the boat, and Angelia's mouth latched onto Merrick's as he enfolded her to him, protecting her back from hitting the bottom of the skiff. Unheeding to their means of transportation, Angelia wrapped her legs around Merrick's hips, her heels digging in to ride her chimera as her pelvis rolled helplessly upward, her body arching, aching to be filled.

Merrick cupped her to him then ripped his mouth from hers as he lashed a fearful snarl at the boatman, his entire body rigid, his threat dangerously clear. Angelia once again pressed her palm to his cheek, turning his head to her, where she reclaimed his mouth, dragging her tongue along his lengthening fangs.

Trembling, Merrick gathered her fully to him and retreated to the bow of the boat, as far as he could get away from Phlegyas, who rhythmically poled, stabbing the sludge and thrusting, stabbing again and thrusting, skimming the boat along to the other shore, toward the city Dis, his face hidden in his shroud.

"You are a diabolical woman, Angel," Merrick growled against the sensitive skin behind her ear.

"Yes, don't stop." She was breathless as she swiped her tongue from his Adam's apple to his lower lip. "We're almost there." Her hips undulated upward; she didn't want to stop. She didn't care if someone witnessed Merrick's taking of her, just so long as he satisfied this breath-stealing pleasure building inside of her, lifting her, sensitizing her to his every molecule.

* * * *

Merrick gripped her harder, his muscles tight, his skin hot. Pressing his forehead to Angelia's, he sucked in a ragged breath.

"Not here, Angel. Someplace other than here," he begged, barely maintaining what bit of control he had. His cock was damned near singing. And the smell of the woman. So help him, he would spear himself so deep into her he'd crush his balls. Over and over. Right there in the bow of the boat as they sailed across acres of sludge. In front of Phlegyas.

Merrick didn't have too many romantic notions, but he was pretty sure this place was far down at the bottom of the list of places to claim a woman's maidenhead. As it was, he was ready to chuck his resolve like the paltry thing it had turned into. He wanted his Angel so bad he could taste her. Holy Christ, could he taste her. The scent of her lay heavy on his tongue, filling him with an irrational lust until his head buzzed with it.

Phlegyas, hovering near and utterly enrapt, helped to rein him in. Merrick wanted to puncture the bastard's eyes out of his skeletal head; he wanted to sink his fangs into that scrawny neck to shake the voyeur to

S. C. Dane

his death. No one had a right to look at his Angel—not when she lay open for him alone.

"Merrick?" Her voice was a melody flying in serpentines through the enraged buzzing in his head. "Merrick."

He gripped her tighter as his every cell cued into her, while his eyes remained riveted on the intruder. He barely registered the scraping of the boat on the opposite shore, even though his whole body rocked as the prow bumped solid earth.

"Come on, chimera. Move that sexy butt of yours."

He felt her tugging against him as he bore his challenging glare into Phlegyas, his throat thick with his fury that the boatman would dare look at his mate.

"Merrick, let's go." Angelia gave a hard yank, jostling his attention. Reluctantly, he let her lead him off the boat.

"We did it." His Angel's voice rippled with excitement, with the thrill of success, drawing his full attention only after the threat of the boatman was removed.

He'd been holding her to him so desperately, his claws were embedded in the thick leather of the coat she wore. He forced a grin, and knew that he showed her a mouthful of elongated fangs.

Merrick plucked his talons out of the leather.

* * * *

Angelia watched, fascinated, as the impenetrable granite of Merrick's eyes deepened to a soft shale, then stroked the length of her with a visual caress. Warming beneath his gaze, she molded her body against his, needing to feel more than just his gray eyes on her.

Only moments ago, the chimera had been wrath barely chained, promising annihilation to the boatman should the guy take one step toward her. She was Merrick's coveted prize and that had sexy written all over it.

Stupid of her? Uh-uh. In her world, a male who would guard what he considered his was a valuable asset. Even if that male was chimera, a creature dangerous and volatile enough to command the respect of the ancient Triumvirate and Phlegyas, whatever grim thing he was.

She understood that look in those shale eyes. Feral Merrick might

184

be, but he wouldn't harm her no matter how enraged he was. Angelia couldn't help rubbing herself against him as if she were a big cat, too.

For a spellbinding moment, Merrick sniffed the air to catch her scent. Then he crushed her against himself, his big hand palming her butt, his fingers digging into her ample flesh, as if he clung to her.

"Don't ever do that again." He cursed on a sigh, his breath fanning across her nape, tickling the loosened strands of her hair, fevering her skin.

"It worked, didn't it?" She was unrepentant, crammed full with pleasure.

Until the shrieks, rending the very air around them, cut straight to her brain. She curled in on herself, her hands clasped tight to her ears as the man holding her set her gently to the ground. Eyes watering, she shot a frightened look at Merrick, who straddled her protectively, his chin tilted as if he bore the shrieks like they were pelting sleet.

She watched him fill his lungs, his chest expanding magnificently, the thick muscles pulling on his ribcage. He bellowed an answering roar, slicing the screams so abruptly the air became a vacuum with the loss of sound. Merrick roared again, his sharp teeth bared as every muscle of his body strained against his bones.

Angelia turned her gaze toward Dis. Hundreds of monstrous angels, those who had sided with Lucifer, were glaring down from the towering gate and outer wall, their faces distorted with silenced fury.

Lowering her hands from her head, Angelia didn't care if they shook. Why bother when the rest of her still teetered like she'd been shoving her entire strength against an invisible door and it had suddenly opened.

"Holy Moses, what in God's name was that all about?" Her voice sounded distant, muffled and cavernous, like she'd borrowed Darth Vader's helmet.

"A challenge. They're a little pissed the Kynd weren't cast down to share the same fate." Merrick shrugged like it was no big deal, but she could tell there was more.

"And," she fished.

"*And...*" The chimera glared back up at the furious faces blazing down at them from the high wall. "They're especially pissed at me. I'm part angel, so by rights, they think I should be trapped right along with them."

"But you didn't—"

"No, I didn't stand against God. I stood with Kynd."

Angelia might have been momentarily deafened, but she was able to catch his defensive tone. Although his soul was compromised, the chimera was proud to be Kynd.

"You've fought these things?" She shuddered as dread rippled through her. How in blazes had he survived it?

"Yeah." He rolled his shoulders again, nonchalant like.

"*Yeah*? Like it's no big deal? Merrick, those things are hideous. And there are so many. Why would you do such a dangerous thing?"

His answer was to stand there watching her, wary. Muscles tense and his gray eyes turning slate hard. "You're upset, Angel."

"Dang right I'm upset." She gawked back up to the top of the enormous gate, which was their only way into the Sixth Circle. "How in God's name are we supposed to get through that alive?" She knew her jaw hung open, but there were flipping angels lining the length of that limestone wall as far as her eyes could see.

Merrick moved so she could stand up. "Well, Angel, this is where we test the amount of angel you've got flowing in your blood. God willing, they won't come near you."

"*God willing?*" She was incredulous. Surely Merrick wasn't going to gamble his suspicions with their lives. "You're one-third angel, chimera, and they attacked you. What makes you think they're not going to bother me?"

He shrugged again. "A hunch."

She threw him a sardonic glare. "*A hunch?* I could use something a little more reassuring than that."

"Open the gate." He jutted his strong chin toward the twenty-foot height of the double doors.

"Merrick, I don't think this is a good idea." She wasn't a chicken. At least, not anymore. What was causing her to hesitate was the thickening of the chimera's mane. He was readying for a fight, just in case his hunch proved wrong.

* * * *

Anton stood in his den, breathless in the face of what he witnessed. In all his centuries of living, he'd never seen anything so painful, yet so bursting with anxious...*hope*. Along with pent-up fury. The four Kynd, who had shimmered into existence on this earthly plane, trembled with it. They were like fragile vessels of nitroglycerin. One wrong bump and all hell was going to erupt.

In the middle of his home.

Nor would it be pretty, if anyone survived to tally the aftermath. Anton wasn't even sure he'd have a house standing if one of them lost the tenuous control they were trying to wield. They were impressive. And downright bloodcurdling.

There wasn't much on this planet or the other realms that could unnerve the ancient Vampyre, but this gathering did.

Not one of the Kynd seemed stable enough to grasp control, let alone keep it for any length of time. These creatures shivered menace— with the blatant ability to deliver death swiftly and horrifically.

He'd allowed this gathering to take place while his life-mate and son were in the same house? With only thin wooden walls separating them from potential disaster? *Sacré,* he needed his head examined.

He felt he could handle interacting with one Kynd at a time, for the most part. But as a group? These creatures were *huge*. Built with strength and innate weapons meant to decimate anything they tackled.

Yet, they were Witnesses. Which meant they didn't miss a damned thing—an exceptional skill lending them the advantage when their bodies didn't. The gargoyles were bad enough with their thick muscles and claws that could tear flesh from bone like it was over-cooked chicken.

But the chimerae? What had God been thinking? What had *he* been thinking? He'd sent his precious Angelia off to Hell with one of them, believing Merrick would keep her safe. Yes, he needed his goddamned head looked at.

Anton couldn't tell half of what made these creatures what they were. Part human, a third...dragon? If not for his iron control, a wretched moan would have escaped his throat. He'd entrusted his beloved daughter to the care of a chimera. Anton only just kept his hands from clutching his head in an abysmal display of regret.

No. He wouldn't succumb to his fear. He hadn't allowed such a thing for centuries. Instead, he laid his trust upon his instincts, and his own blade-honed watchfulness. He studied the Kynd standing before him. Especially Darken, who remained with his massive arms sprawled, his countenance one of dread.

Though his eyes, the Vampyre noticed, gave him away.

They glimmered with an expectant sheen, the gray soft as fog, yet so much warmer.

Inviting. He was inviting his brethren to move inside of his arms so he could hold them.

The four newcomers watched Darken furtively, unsure of his open arms, as though they didn't quite know what he was doing with them. They stole surreptitious glances between themselves, and one gargoyle dropped to dig his clawed hands into the floor, raking deep grooves into the wood as he grounded himself, his unleashed roar stretching the muscles of his ribcage, bulging the tendons of his neck.

Still, Darken didn't drop his arms. His invitation remained.

The chimera who looked to be part dragon, whipped his tail, the tri-horns at the tip end of it slashing the sofa cushions like they were as substantial as soap bubbles. He circled Darken, a low rumbling whine leaking from his spikey throat. He slid in close enough to graze his shoulder against the welcoming gargoyle, and before Anton's eyes, the beast shimmered and coalesced into something else, something closely resembling Darken.

It was all the Vampyre could do not to gasp. In the place of the dragon creature, stood a tall and heavily muscled *human*. The only thing giving away the fact he wasn't quite what he appeared to be, was the presence of a tattoo spreading down his bare back.

The bottom of that permanent stain narrowed into a tail, which coiled the circumference of the man's hips and spiraled around the length of his right leg, stopping at the ankle. The tip depicted the very horns that had only moments before decimated Anton's couch.

The remainder of the artwork spread upwards and across the man's shoulders, where the rust trailed down his left arm, the talons of the dragon encircling the human wrist in intricate detail. The head of the tattoo ran up his neck, lining the male's jaw and cheek.

Definitely dragon. For they'd been doubly cursed by the fae and bore the mark for all to see, should the chimera try hiding what he was by walking in another form.

The man reached a shaking hand out to the gargoyle. "Brotherkynd…" His words, consumed within a scratchy growl, trailed away as his hand convulsed to make a fist.

Without hesitation, Darken reached for him. With that one touch, a chain reaction was set off. As if magnetized, the other three inched inevitably forward, swallowing the space between them until five Kynd were collected in a loose, yet definite cluster.

Mary, mother of God. Anton had never seen such a thing.

Every face wore an expression of rapture.

No. The Vampyre shook his head. Not rapture. Something deeper.

Brotherkynd. Not just a descriptive word. Watching them touch— furtive, uncertain after so many centuries, yet compelled—Anton knew he'd been entrusted with a gift beyond measure. Darken was letting him witness the secret of Kynd. Their essential, and extremely necessary craving to be together.

Of its own volition, Anton's hand went to his heart, as if to still its erratic plunging as blood tears pooled along his lower eyelids, threatening to spill. His daughter would be all right. No matter how brutal these Kynd appeared to be, underneath their savage exteriors beat gentle hearts. Moreover, one had sworn to keep his Angelia safe.

Anton had not mistaken what he'd seen when Merrick had faced the Triumvirate. Even if the safety of his daughter was secondary to the deal the chimera had struck with the Vampyre, Merrick of the Kynd would make certain he delivered sanctuary for his brethren.

For these creatures gathered in his den looked as if nothing could stand between them. Not even God's Word. A proven fact, given there were five Kynd standing together in his house. An unprecedented anomaly since the Schism. God only knew what He would hand down as punishment for their insubordination.

The bastards were brave; Anton would give them that. He'd also give them any help he and the other members of the Triumvirate could.

As though cued, Godrick and Kristov materialized on either side of him.

"My eyes deceive me," Godrick hissed between his fangs, his golden eyes riveted to the tableau in front of him.

Anton raised a finger to his lips then grabbed the other two Triumvirates at the elbow to teleport them to another part of the house.

Godrick's curses erupted the second their feet hit the carpet. "What in Hell is going on here? Those were gargoyles down there and a chimera! And who knows what that human-looking thing was doing there." The Vampyre's lips were pursed so tight they peeled back from his fangs. "What have you done, Anton!"

"I'm afraid I must agree with Godrick. What were you thinking to call these creatures together?" Usually the voice of reason, Kristov's alarm reminded Anton that the gathering downstairs could get forced apart. And not by the Triumvirate.

God Himself just might have something to say about it.

"You've far over-stepped this time, Anton. It was one thing to force us to accept that human babe as yours. But this?" Godrick pointed a sharp nailed finger at the floor, as if the Kynd were right beneath his feet, not on the other side of the house. "This galls like nothing else. Our truce among the other realms is tenuous, at best. And yet you sanction a gathering of the Kynd in your living room? You are a fool! A madman, Vampyre!"

Anton bristled. "Do you think I've not weighed the possibilities of what that group represents?" he seethed. "It's why I called you here. I am well aware how much of a threat they are. I know full well how the Others will take to learning of a Kynd reunion. I know my history. But if you think, that as one-third of the great Triumvirate, I would turn a gargoyle away in his hour of need then you are sorely mistaken. We are the Triumvirate!"

Anton knotted his fist as if in triumph; he and Godrick shared the briefest of embarrassed grins.

Relaxing his arm, Anton went on with a steadier breath, his demeanor a trifle calmer. "It is we who withhold judgment until the entire truth is known. My God, Vampyre, they defied their Creator to amass. There is something more far-reaching going on here than belligerent Kynd."

His declaration hung heavy upon the silent swathe it cut through the room. Anton looked from one Vampyre to the other. "My dearest friends. *Think*. Now is not the time for our fears to do our deciding for us.

"The gargoyle, Darken, came to me not only to confess his killing of the head of the Literati, but because he understood what that meant." His eyes cast back and forth between his fellow Vampyres. "Darken *knew* the implications of his actions. These Kynd, banished they might be, but let us not forget they are Witnesses. They see and know more than any of us combined! If Darken killed Aro because of the vampire's treachery, then there is more at stake here than any of us imagined. We'd be smart to heed the gargoyle's warning."

"By standing strong with the Kynd?" Godrick looked mildly stupefied, with a dash of pissed.

Much to Anton's relief, Kristov interjected, buffering the other Vampyre's exasperation. "Anton's right. We would be fools to ignore the greater implications. However, Godrick raises compelling points to consider. The Kynd are cursed, Anton. If we side with them?"

Anton didn't need to hear their unspoken questions; he saw them plainly enough in their wary eyes. Kristov made a valid and undeniable point, too. The Kynd *were* cursed. Ancient rumor had it they'd refused to choose between God and the rebellious Lucifer, and God had punished them for seeing the right existing on both sides of the argument.

Much like the Triumvirate did in their dealings with the Others. How could Anton, in good conscience, find fault in their failure to favor one right over the other? Yet, the Kynd had been punished cruelly. A truth which rankled the Vampyre.

Was his outrage over such an injustice not the very reason he'd stepped up with Godrick and Kristov to form an alliance against such tyranny?

"We owe them our protection."

"*Our protection?* Anton, they have disobeyed *God*, for Heaven's sake!" As if the Omnipotent One was, at this very moment, sharpening his lightning bolts.

Anton was stoical. "Yet, here they are. I'm sure they are acutely aware of what they have done. Dearest Godrick, *they have chosen*. In the thousands of years they have traipsed these realms, the Kynd have finally chosen! Come what may they have done so, and I will do everything in my power to help them."

Godrick deflated onto a nearby chair, ceding the argument, his hand cupped to his brow. The Vampyre had lost his self-righteous steam as Anton's rationale prevailed. Nevertheless, gloating had never been in Anton's nature. He raised his eyes to Kristov, who merely nodded. Anton saw no resignation, only the machinations of a diabolically concise mind. Kristov was already formulating the plans, weighing their every implication.

Anton pulled him back to the present. "They are going into Hell to retrieve their brother." No point including Angelia's rescue, it went without saying. "Aro has initiated some plot by orchestrating the theft of the Scriptum. Hopefully, it will come back in the Kynd's possession."

"We can't ask them to attempt its retrieval if Merrick and your daughter were unsuccessful." A surprising statement. Kristov showed compassion toward others, although his heart was gone. Lost when his life-mate was murdered centuries ago.

The Vampyre compensated for its absence by analyzing then responding in the proper manner so others wouldn't know he felt nothing. After centuries of honing the skill, few could tell the difference. It was a secret neither Anton nor Godrick would betray. The proof being that neither had, not even under torture.

Anton placed his hand on his old friend's shoulder. "No, Kristov, we could not. As you could plainly see for yourself, the Kynd have enough to contend with right now."

"If they have a future here on this earth?"

For the first time since the other Vampyres arrived, Anton grinned fully. "Then we'd do well to align ourselves with them, wouldn't you say?"

A spark flashed in Kristov's eyes, but it was Godrick who answered as he rose from his chair with a dismissive flip of his hand. "As usual, Anton's optimism prevails." A quirk of a smile twisted the Vampyre's lips. "Of course, we should ally ourselves to a cursed species. We'd be fools not to."

"Funny, but I'm glad you're with us on this, Godrick."

"I am. *Reluctantly.* But I will be the first to say *I told you so.*"

"We'd expect nothing less." Anton's heart swelled. The Triumvirate stood strong; his friends stood strong with him. He clasped a hand to Godrick's shoulder, as well. The three heads leaned close together, a triad that was near indomitable.

"All right. So we tell the Kynd they have our support."

"With provisions."

"Yes, there will be a limit to how far we'll go in our help," Anton ceded, even as he knew his gratitude to the Kynd would have him turning his cheek to offenses he'd otherwise punish. It had the potential to weaken the Triumvirate, yet the Vampyre could do little else. If Darken got his daughter out of this mess alive then Anton owed these creatures his very life.

Godrick's lids narrowed over his golden eyes. "We'll be watching you, Vampyre."

Of course, he knew where Anton's thoughts traveled, as did Kristov. The Vampyres had been through their own kinds of Hell together. There wasn't much they didn't know about each other.

"So," Kristov interjected. "I think we've given that group downstairs enough time to catch up."

It would take years for them to *catch up*. It would also take more than a group huddle to repair the damage done to the Kynd, and a time-sensitive mission loomed.

With a thought, the Triumvirate reconvened in Anton's den.

* * * *

"I can't do this," Angelia admitted, turning defiantly to Merrick, even as she felt the weight of hundreds of furious eyes boring down on her shoulder blades. "We need to talk about this. Plan it better or something."

Merrick shook his head, a small smile creeping along his sensuous lips. "Angel, unlocking that gate and going through it is the only way to get into Lower Hell. Are you so ready to give up the quest now?"

Yes, she realized, her heart hammering against her chest, her throat constricting with her tears. The fact she cried angered her, which only made her throat tighten more. She wasn't a crybaby, and she sure wasn't crying over losing the Scriptum. Not when she compared it to the chimera standing in front of her.

As though sensing the cost of her stubborn resolve, Merrick snatched her to him in a flash of motion, his muscular arms encasing her as he brushed his cheek against the top of her head, his heat enveloping her like a security blanket.

Her body softened to mold to his, her cheek pressing to the warmth of his slab chest, her fingers curling through his thickened mane. "It's not worth it, Merrick. Those things up there will tear you apart. If they don't, it's only because you'll fight them as your chimera. I won't risk that, Merrick. I won't."

She wouldn't sacrifice him for a book, no matter how valuable the words within its pages were. So what if the thing opened for her and her alone. Granted, it had been filling her with truths about Kynd, but there was one standing right in front of her. She could ask him anything she wanted to know, and he would confide in her.

She wouldn't trade such faith for a book. Not in a million years. Nor would she sacrifice Merrick's soul for her own self-confidence. Screw Aro and his petty opinions.

Strong arms pulled her tighter. "Angel," Merrick's voice rumbled like a caress across her skin, lulling her so she almost wasn't paying attention to his words, just their comforting intimations. "I will go," he murmured. "The Scriptum is worth it to me."

* * * *

At first, she didn't react. She remained snuggled and pliant against him, like bliss delivered in a silken package. A moment later, Angelia looked up, her surprise evident in the widening of her hypnotic, twilight eyes.

Merrick offered her a rueful smile. "It's worth it to me," he repeated as he gazed down, struggling not to lose himself in the frightened depths of his Angel's pupils. "That book, I'm betting, holds things neither of us knows." His grin turned teasing, curving up on one side. "Well, you probably know, you just have to remember. But," he was quick to interject, "even if it doesn't, I made a deal. I plan to keep it."

He had bargained for a beautiful place on which the Kynd could rest eternally. A magnificent structure overlooking a park where the goodness in humans tended to come forth. Where they picnicked, played with their dogs, and kissed on park benches.

Finer emotions on display than what most Kynd had been enduring since their banishment. The Grotesques deserved the reprieve in their final stages of immovable stone. Though that wasn't the true reason Merrick challenged the woman in his arms.

He had faith in her, in her raw purity. She didn't, which was why she wanted to turn back. Conflicting emotions warred within him. Merrick felt as if his body and soul were being wrung by merciless hands. He would take her to the surface in a heartbeat, because she asked him to. He wanted her safe, his deal with Anton be damned.

Almost.

He sensed they were close, the Scriptum within their grasp. All his Angel had to do was cross this threshold and seize it. Once she did, she'd complete her quest, and return triumphant.

Return with self-confidence, with her eyes shining bright and her head held high. The fact he would also provide a glorious resting place for his Kynd went hand in hand with his Angel's success. A nice bargain, after all.

Provided he kept her safe. Yes, the angels were outraged, but they wouldn't touch her. If anything, he would bet she would protect him through this gauntlet. If she had the courage.

He knew she did. She didn't. Which was why he pushed.

If they retreated to the surface, she would lose what self-respect she'd gained during their journey through Hell, and he couldn't stand that. He didn't want to see her shoulders slumped, her head bowed like the Shades who passed beneath the Archway. Not his Angel.

"Merrick, it's just a book. I won't trade it for you."

His beloved angel trembled with her fear for him. It hollowed him out, made his knees weak. "You won't be trading me for anything," Merrick leaned down to taste her bottom lip as he swallowed the sting of his lie. "You will keep me safe."

He wouldn't tell her he had every intention of staying. Of giving up his wings if it came to that. He was going to have to give them up, anyway. Sooner or later. Trading them for Angelia was a far better bargain than losing them to his rage.

"Keep *you* safe?" She was incredulous, her eyes shining, her long lashes outlining them dramatically, sucking him away from his darker thoughts. Merrick resisted the urge to kiss them.

* * * *

"You're crazy," Angelia turned back around to gawk up toward the top of the gate. Some of the angels had dispersed, most were still hovering, their fury emanating so strongly it fused with the blood red of the sky above them.

Merrick was nuts, just as she accused him of being. There was no way in Hell, pardon her pun, she was going to protect him from a small army.

Angelia's mind frantically returned to what she knew of Dante's passage into the Sixth Circle. The knowledge there gave her little hope.

One of God's Angels had come down to blaze their safe path. Even Virgil, Dante's stalwart guide, had trembled and paled, and he'd been working under the protection of the Big Man Himself.

What was Merrick thinking to believe they could walk through those gates unmolested?

"So, what you're thinking is that combined we make up two-thirds of an Angel?" She was kidding, of course, but Merrick cloaked himself around her back and pulled her to him.

She heard and felt the intake of his breath, his arms squeezing her a little tighter as he did so. "No, Angel, I'm not thinking that at all. You will keep me safe so I won't have to unfurl my wings." He delivered his nugget of faith and sealed it with a kiss pressed solidly to her temple.

Her body relaxed into the one holding her. She was caving. Darn him. She realized in that physical moment she believed him, trusted him with every fiber of her being. Just the feel of him touching her body filled her with strength.

If he had faith in her, then just maybe it was justified.

Heck, he'd been here before. He knew what to expect, she didn't. Angelia turned into Merrick's embrace so she could breathe in the warm crystalline scent of the man who held her, her cheek flush against the thick planes of his chest.

Her tongue slid out to trace his nipple with wet spirals, and as it puckered, she pinched it with her teeth. Across the crown of her head, she felt him draw in his breath and his hand slide down the length of her back. He cupped her butt to grind his growing cock against her.

She aroused him easily, as if he was always only a moment away from wanting her. Angelia felt herself moisten as a building heat radiated within her, answering the call to the tenderness of her chimera's tautly controlled hug.

He could savage her, yet he touched and held her with a gentleness that belied his physical strength, his intensity. She felt it in the rock hard stiffening of his muscles, even as he drew her carefully close.

Angelia raised her face for a kiss. She would have him. Before they risked their lives to cross the threshold into the Sixth Circle, before those monstrous angels descended to tear them apart, she would know the glory of merging with her chimera.

She would know Merrick inside of her, feel his beautiful body joined with hers, filling her. She didn't care if hundreds of furious eyes blazed down upon their union. Nothing mattered except this chimera who had already given so much to her already.

Angelia dragged her palm along the steel of Merrick's outer thigh and cupped the bulge pressing against leather. She gripped then released to finger open the buttons, to free his shaft, the head of it already poking beyond the waistband of his pants, riding his taut stomach. Merrick's hand encircled her neck, his thumb tilting her chin upward so he could take her mouth.

His growling filled her, rumbling an excited path straight down the front of her as his attentions grew earnest, his mouth hot. She tasted him; every slide of her tongue, every panting breath brought him into her, so that she knew his flavor.

She wanted more. Angelia went to her knees, trailing kisses and laving her tongue along his unique skin, which seemed softer to her, as if it yielded to her attentions, warming as his blood flushed through his veins. She dug her fingers into his hips, ran her cheek along his jumping cock. Even as Merrick groaned, his pelvis swiveled, mimicking its instinctual urge to grind inside of her.

S. C. Dane

Licking her lips, Angelia took him in her mouth until his bulbous head bumped the back of her throat, and she began milking his shaft, sucking in her cheeks, flicking her tongue with alternating long, wide swipes along its satin hardness.

* * * *

He yelled. His fingers fisted her hair. His knees unhinged. Yet, still his hips rocked helplessly, as if his body commanded its pleasure. Merrick's brain fizzed, and his eyes rolled back. The exquisite pleasure! His balls squeezed tight, forcing him to lock his knees so he wouldn't collapse. He fought the primitive urge to pump harder, faster into her mouth.

Dear God, he didn't want to hurt her, but she was ripping him into a thousand, brilliant, star-like pieces. Her mouth burned wet and hot around his shaft, her tongue a slippery, fiery brand exciting him beyond anything he'd ever known.

Then her soft hand cupped his hardened sac and Merrick's legs gave way, his Angel's mouth sliding off him, the cooler air startling. It was all he could do not to thrust his cock back into the heat of that glorious mouth.

Her hands cupped his head, turning it so that the mouth he'd desperately struggled not to fill with his thumping cock found his and he tasted himself upon her tongue. Snarling like a crude beast, he nudged her back to the ground, his lips never separating from hers as he hovered his weight over her slender, inviting body. The pleasure exploded like a bomb inside of him, expanding to consume every inch of him.

He trembled from the blast of it, even as he slid a tentative caress down her narrow ribcage, along her little waist, across her hipbone, his palm growing warmer the closer he got to her core. The flare of her heat maddening him.

Panting, afraid, Merrick yanked himself away from this terrible passion and crouched between his Angel's feet, her bent knees kissing his elbows. "Holy living Christ, Angel." He scraped his fingers across his scalp, leaving his hands lodged in his hair. "I'm going to hurt you."

Her lips curled into an amused smile, her eyes shining hot, her cheeks flushed. "It's supposed to be like that."

198

"No," he denied. How could a body withstand it? How did a heart not shatter? Merrick gazed down on his Angel laying wide open before him, and he knew in that moment his heart wasn't supposed to bear it.

It was meant to fracture, so the acceptance of the woman who took him could encapsulate it within the safety of her own breast. She would own it, *own him*, and the pain of surrender would be the most joyous, excruciating thing that had ever happened to him.

Merrick returned to hover above his Angel and gaze down upon her face, into those burning eyes that watched him so closely, so warily, like a wild doe.

To say he loved her? Trifling. Tiny words uttered in the face of something so vast, so titanic. He pressed his lips to hers, as if he dared to kiss a butterfly's wings. Afraid they would crumble and with them his heart.

If she did not love him back? Merrick squeezed his lids shut against the agonizing thought. *No matter.* He would adore her, anyway. She owned him now. Whatever happened beyond this moment, he would be hers. Even when she left him to return to her own world, his heart would go with her.

The chimera traced his finger the length of her thin collarbone. She was a fragile flower, yet a thousand times more resilient. The incongruity of it rocked him, and he cupped his lips upon her taut-nippled breast to anchor himself. He felt the caress of her fingers trace down his temple, along his jaw, and he could weep with the utter tenderness of that touch to his rough skin.

* * * *

With her nipple drawn into his sucking mouth, Merrick gazed up at her. Angelia couldn't mistake the look in those shale eyes any more than she could mistake the humming in her head. Both were beautiful, both were captivating. She opened her heart to the messages from both.

The humming was familiar, subdued and soft as a rose's petals as it swirled inside her head, filling her not with words so much as feeling for the creature in her arms, whom she held with more than just her hands.

He had given himself to her.

She felt his giving as a physical entity, as though the chimera curled

199

himself up small to fit inside her skin, filling her entire being so she no longer seemed a single individual, but larger somehow. *More.* She forced her lungs to breathe around the fullness.

The choir rejoiced in her head, unfolding her heart as if it were made of many layers, peeling it open gently. The singing filled her as Merrick was doing. As each layer opened, her body and her skin felt as if they were expanding exponentially, and she grew fiery with a blazing desire to keep her chimera safe at any cost.

Chapter Twelve

Jesus, we've been gone twenty minutes at the most! In that time, it looked as if Hell had decided to come looking for Darken and his crew, not the other way around.

"My house!" Around Anton's feet lay pieces of his broken furniture, torn floorboards. *Blood.* The smell of it hit him like a wet rag to the face. "Christ Almighty, what happened?" Easily, the Vampyre traced its source, he didn't even have to move his feet to find it. Darken was a bleeding mess, the scent of him splashed all over the second chimera, the one who now stood on two legs in partial gargoyle form, his *bear* claws dripping Darken's blood onto the shredded carpet.

"Sacré, gargoyle. What the fuck?" Mystery solved, at least. The second chimera was part ursine.

"Your family is unhurt." Darken tensed, his massive shoulders growing as his muscles bunched in a defensive posture.

Anton dismissed the threat. "Screw the reassurances, Kynd, I already know that. What the hell happened *here*?" He already knew the answer to that, too, had anticipated such a thing would occur when the others arrived in his home. They weren't wrapped tight and one of them had come unwound.

The fact that Darken defended his attacker came as no surprise, either. Anton expected nothing less from the Kynd. What bothered him was the gargoyle had been harmed. Protecting *his* life-mate and child, no doubt. Could the damned man endear himself just a smidgen more? Already Anton owed him a debt he could ill afford.

The other Kynd gathered behind Darken, a knot of pissed-off

nobody wanted to see untied. The Vampyre held up his hand, his pulse jacking. "Kristov, Godrick. *Go.*"

"Never," Godrick swore, his fangs stretching beyond his bottom lip.

"I'll be fine. Just go!"

Kristov stepped closer to Godrick. Never let it be said the Triumvirate weren't their own kind of brotherhood. Anton appreciated that the Vampyres had his back, but in this case, it was like thrashing a bleeding wound around in shark-infested waters.

"Please, I'll be all right." He didn't need to see them pulverized, not when this was a mess of his own making. Besides, for now it was just one room damaged, he didn't need his entire house demolished, as would most assuredly happen if he didn't get things under control. The Vampyres would teleport while they fought, disorienting their opponents. A tricky and very effective weapon, but one that would spread the battle scene all through Anton's home.

Godrick jabbed a finger at the group poised in front of them, his eyes flashing like gold coins. "Hurt him, miscreants, and you'll wish you'd never left your miserable posts."

"Vampyre! Enough already! Just go." *Jesus.* As if these Kynd needed prompting to unleash themselves. Anton put both hands up like he was shushing an angry lion. Or bear, as the case turned out to be.

Godrick and Kristov vanished behind him. He felt their absence instantly, as though their leaving left a vacuum along his spine. Which was good, because he didn't dare take his eyes off the creatures in front of him.

"All right? Just everybody calm down. No one's getting hurt here." He hoped, anyway. Looking at Darken didn't exactly stuff him with reassurances. "Are you okay, Darken?" He enunciated slowly, so none of them got the wrong idea. He was concerned, not accusing.

"Aye, I'm fine. We're just a little tense, is all." He swiped at the blood dripping from his chin.

Anton nodded in lieu of the joke he wanted to mutter about understatements. "Is everyone else okay?" He scanned the lethal troupe collected in his wrecked den. God have mercy, seriously. Damaged goods, every cursed one of them. And they were going to Hell to retrieve one of their own?

The chimera who was dripping blood from his fingertips took a step forward, his head lowered over stone eyes that pierced Anton to his core. "We are sorry," he growled, so gutturally he could barely be understood. The chimera cleared his throat and tried speaking again. "It has been too long."

This was, apparently, a ripe time to be dropping the term *understatement.* Too long? How about two thousand years' worth of too long. But Anton wasn't one of the ruling Triumvirate because he didn't keep his head. Or his tongue. "It's only a room. Full of items easily replaced. However, if any of you feel this is too much..." He waved his arm to encompass their surroundings, his meaning going well beyond the walls of his house. "We have a place you can stay until you feel better able to process all of this."

"No, we're leaving soon."

Anton was struck suddenly by their vulnerability. They weren't ready for Hell, even though they were naturally well armed for such an excursion. Nobody could look at them and think they couldn't tear the surface off the earth. Not together, as they were. But it wasn't their physical prowess in question. It was their mental stability he had concerns about. Behind every stone-colored eye the Vampyre looked into loomed a haunted and wounded soul.

"We worry, Anton. Our brother grows more vulnerable with every passing day. We cannot lose him." Darken clutched another gargoyle's hand, who in turn clasped another, who latched onto another until the Kynd were once again knotted tight to each other.

Anton found himself nodding his head. "You will be careful for yourselves, too, I trust?"

Darken's lips slid into a small, yet knowing grin. "Aye, Vampyre. We will take care. But, *when* we return—"

"You will have a secure home to return to, I promise you." At the moment he had no idea where. Nevertheless, he would deliver on his oath. The gargoyle grasped Anton's open, outstretched palm. He shook it once but held onto it, his slate eyes searching as Anton felt a wave of power ripple through him, not unlike a low electric current.

Darken's grin spread wide as Anton's gaze flitted to the others, who watched him expectantly, too.

"My God," he stuttered, knowing his silver eyes were wide with a child's awe.

"No. Kynd."

Kynd. The wattage of energy they generated as a group was another secret kept through the millennia. For having lived as long as he had, Anton realized he knew next to nothing about them, only a bit more than what had been common knowledge, or to be more precise, the *myths* surrounding them. He also realized why they'd been maligned, relegated to the annals of lore, to near obscurity.

Kynd were dangerous on a level the ancient Vampyre had never perceived.

Dear God in Heaven, what has Aro wrought? Implications to ponder later, for just then a snap cracked so sharp Anton winced then stared at a man with a dragon's wings unfurled behind his back, his rust colored tail sweeping deadly arcs behind him.

He folded the bear chimera against him, time-steeped hatred burning from his slate eyes as he gently cupped his hand to the other Kynd's head, tucking him to his breast. Another snap of his wings, and the two dematerialized.

In a blur, Anton felt the removal of Darken's hand from his, and the others vanished, leaving him to stand alone. The only evidence the Kynd had been there was Death's scythe leaning against the outside wall of Anton's home.

* * * *

God Almighty, he needed to touch more of her, he needed to join himself to her like he'd never done with Kynd. As linked as he was to his brethren, what mastered him now burned far stronger than any bonding he'd ever known.

"Come, *please.*" He begged. Curse and bless his God, he begged to be physically joined to this Angel. As he rose to his feet, the relief that she joined him weakened his knees, yet oddly fortified him. A bizarre juxtaposition of emotion that made him quake.

Looking up at him, her enchanting eyes missed nothing of his turmoil. He knew it by the tilt of her head, the slide of her tongue across her bottom lip. He couldn't rip his attention off the tip of that tongue.

"Merrick."

He gave one, sharp shake to his skull. He was rendered stupid, just by the wanting of her. "Come." It was all he could say, but his body knew what it needed and he acted. Without releasing her, he drew her away from the gates, away from the impotent glare of Lucifer's angels. He wanted privacy for what he would do, so he led her farther down the shore of the river Styx, careful to keep them high enough above the banks to avoid the churning Shades as they perpetuated their own kind of hell.

He didn't want his Angel to have to bear seeing such a thing again. Her pain was his, and the dawning of that truth played on his senses, too. It both awed and scared the shit out of him, yet he'd have it no other way. He dropped their packs near a fallen log, where the bend in the river shielded them from the jealous stares of the angels at the gate.

He unfurled their sleeping bags and began zipping them together. Angelia remained curiously silent, watching him without interrupting. Her quiet attention made him feel eerily coveted, yet disconcertedly alone, as though his own self-confidence grew shaky.

What if she didn't want what he was about to offer?

Against his will, his eyes shot to where she was standing, an amused grin barely tugging her wonderful lips. Her expression was enigmatic, her pupils blown so her eyes were full black. Merrick spread the bags and held his calloused hand out for her, where it hung empty, suspended in the air untouched.

Before his defeat could swamp him, he saw her reach for the clasp of her pants then slide them down her thighs. She stopped just as she exposed a silky triangle of red. Her panties.

A growl rolled up thick from his chest. His mouth watered so he had to swallow against it. Again, she'd rendered him deliriously confused. His leather jacket fell around her booted feet, and Merrick's hand went to his mouth, a helpless gesture to calm the sharpening of his fangs. His cock kicked, excited.

He stretched out his hand again. "Lay with me."

Before he lost it. *It* meaning *everything*. His body was queerly fizzing, shaking. His cauldron of rage had spilled or had expanded so his anger no longer bubbled menacingly, he couldn't tell which. All he could

S. C. Dane

tell was that he wanted this woman who stood glorious before him, offering herself to the stone wreck standing on a square of nylon in Hell.

He was leveled, razed.

Seeing the want rise behind her eyes, her smooth flesh growing bumpy with an electric need he saw shudder through her, made him feel like the Kynd he remembered himself to be. Even much more than that.

Merrick went to her, pulling her the last few steps to their makeshift bed, which he'd spread out to protect her precious body from the soil of this place when he lay her down. He nestled her gently to her wingless back, stretching the length of his body over hers, his weight supported on one arm. With his thick legs lodged between hers, he tenderly dragged his fingertips down the softness of her belly.

"So beautiful." She gazed at him, and he felt his soul drowning in those blue-black pools. Gladly, he surrendered it, as paltry as it was. For once, the price was worthy, for this one moment with his Angel. For he knew, once they crossed into the Sixth Circle, they'd have the Scriptum and she would be lost to him forever.

"Merrick." Her voice pulled him back to the moment, and he pressed his cheek into the hand she raised to caress his temple. "Kiss me."

She didn't ask twice. Merrick lowered his face to brush his lips over hers, ran his tongue along the ridge of her bottom teeth, their dull surfaces exciting him. He stabbed his tongue deeper, gauging her desire by the hungry strokes of her tongue to his, the working of her jaw as she craved and sought more of him.

He caved, offering everything of himself in that kiss, yet careful not to harm her with the brutal lust that rose in him like a living beast. Merrick drew back, gazing into the hungry depths of Angelia's eyes. She would take everything and give back so much more. Did she even realize the imbalance in the sharing of their souls?

No matter, he supposed. They would soon be separated. He'd enjoy what he could, while he could, and hoped to give what he got. At least, physically.

He sat back to kneel between his Angel's bent legs, reverently undoing the laces of her boots. Her naked feet were so delicate in his big hands, and soft. Merrick caressed his palms across the insteps to enjoy

206

their tenderness. He rubbed his nose into the cleft behind her ankle bone, where the scent of her leaked out to madden him. It seemed no matter where he touched her, her scent beckoned, taunting its invitation.

Suppressing a pleasured growl, he curled his fingers into the waist of her pants and finished what she'd started, peeling the outer layer down her milky white thighs so he could touch.

As soon as her legs were free, she clasped her ankles around his waist, forcing him toward her. He resisted so he could feast on the full length of her stretched nearly naked before him, his attention riveted to the silky, red triangle and the skinny string of lace curving across her hip bone.

Just above, her narrow waist arced inward, her belly a full and tender cushion, softening the lines. Unable to resist, Merrick pressed his face into it like a pillow and drank in her scent. His erection, too engorged, straightened beyond his buttons. He wanted her desperately, though he would take the time to savor, to memorize every detail. To keep his hands from rushing, he dug his claws into the bedding, unheeding to the rip of fabric.

He let his regard sweep the delicate line of her ribcage, the ridges of bone lifting and dipping with his Angel's shallow breaths, her breasts jiggling. She raised her arm to hide her full breasts, and Merrick halted her with a touch.

"No." He swept his gaze to her face, where her cheeks were dusted with a faint blush. "So beautiful," he repeated, and watched, delighted beyond enduring as her lids lowered, hooding her eyes. She was pleased with his compliment.

He could lavish her with a thousand more, just to see that expression on her face.

Virgin to lovemaking he might be, but he was at heart a Witness. Without effort, he learned what pleasured her. Well, not so effortlessly. Pleasing her heightened his wanting. With a snarl, he released the buttons from his leather pants, freeing his shaft so it sprung heavy and rigid between them, the head of it dripping a clear fluid.

Angelia wetted her lips. Merrick felt the pull of his hips for that mouth, so she'd claim him as she'd done earlier. *God, not this time.* He wanted to last so he could learn all of her and knew he wouldn't if he let that mouth anywhere near his cock. Still, he felt his pride stir that she would want him like that.

He cupped one of her breasts, rejoiced in the way it filled his calloused palm, the nipple puckering for his mouth. He skimmed his sharp teeth across the velvet of the soft mound.

"Tell me, Angel, of your first memory." Merrick licked hard, bobbing her breast, catching the ruddy and jostled nipple with his fangs.

She arched, pushing herself deeper into his mouth. "M-my first memory?"

"Mm-hmm." He had a mouthful.

She wasn't Kynd, but she quickly figured out his game and ran her shin along his leather-clad balls. Merrick fell still as his skin erupted in a fine shivering.

"Do that again." His command was a mixture of groan and whine.

That enigmatic grin reappeared and she did not do as he begged. "My first memory was of being in my room, back when my mother had it decorated for a little girl. Frilly pink shams, stuffed animals." Her smile slipped. "Merrick, I don't want to." She retraced the path of her shinbone, rubbing a reverse trail down his balls.

A shuddering moan escaped his throat as he burrowed his nose behind her ear. "Yes," he whispered. "I want to know you."

There was a little pause before she sighed. "I was sad, sitting on my bed with my mangled gargoyle dolly."

Merrick pulled his face out of her hair. "Your what?"

The faint rose of a blush returned to her cheeks. "My gargoyle doll. I don't remember when my parents gave him to me, but I kept him with me. Everywhere I went that poor doll got dragged along."

"To Hell and back, eh?"

She giggled and his heart soared. She'd left her sadness behind for a moment. Still, he wanted to know the things that made her unhappy, to know all of her. Selfish, but the details would be the things he would draw on once he was damned. "Be glad I've grown up. My dolly loved to dress up for tea parties."

The humor exploded inside of him, filling him with light, stuffing him so his skin felt tight. Merrick did not hide his smile but laughed deeply, savoring the rumble of it. And the warmth of this woman's body against his. He rolled them over, so she lay on top of him. "Remove my leggings."

She quirked an eyebrow, still embroiled in their playful lovemaking. "Please."

"That's better." He didn't miss the twist of her grin as she moved to settle herself between his legs. As soon as his legs were free, she draped her body across his, her panties a silken caress as she grinded her hips. His cock stuck out straight between them, twitching its joy, demanding a harder touch.

Angelia complied, reaching down between them to fist his cock and rub it. Up and down, up and down the gorged, thin skin of his shaft. Merrick drove his heels into the ground as he bucked in her hand.

"That's—" All he could bite out as he clenched his jaw, his claws once again shredding the sleeping bag, his hips rocking to her riding grip.

"That night, in my room," Angelia continued, as though she didn't have a writhing chimera at the mercy of her sliding hand, "I'd just come home from my first night of school. Crying because I wasn't like the others."

"No, you're not," he squelched out.

The pumping of her hand slowed as she delved deeper into her memory. "My mother, Marguerite, tried consoling me. But we both knew, deep down, I didn't belong with those other kids, and I never would."

Merrick released the sleeping bag and held this soft woman to him as he rolled on top of her. Resting the bulk of his weight on his elbows, he brushed a wisp of her hair from her forehead and looked deep into those twilight eyes, where he saw himself reflected in that trusting gaze. All the while her hand still gripped his shaft, anchoring him to her as he slowly pushed and dragged himself through her fist.

"Because you belong with me." He kissed her harder than he intended to, his need getting the better of him. She did belong to him. No matter when they parted, she would always have what was left of his soul tucked away, safely inside of her. They wouldn't be together physically, but by God, they'd be together where it mattered, belonging to each other.

209

Merrick put his fangs to the silk of her panties and yanked. They gave with a snap, and the scent of her need billowed forth as if he released a cork from a bottle. Nostrils flaring, he drove his face into the springy curls, flicking his tongue at the hard nub where her coiling hair curly-cued together, an invitation to her core.

"So good," he moaned, swallowing the liquid taste of her. So help him, if he kept this up he wouldn't last. His cock was so swollen it pained him, yet he remained latched to his woman by his mouth, struggling with his twin desires to consume her and to be consumed. He wanted in her, but couldn't stop his tongue from stirring her scent. The wetter she got, the more fevered she became, her fingers clasping his hair as she jutted her hips rhythmically, seeking a more forceful touch to her most intimate part.

God, he loved that look of abandon upon her face. Seeing her back arched, her head thrashing, hearing her mewling cries, excited him. He stabbed his tongue deeper, his large hands grasping her bucking hips as she yelled out, pushing her body harder to his mouth as her juices slid down his throat. *Mine.* He was crazy with the sight of her, her essence wet upon his lips and chin, the flavor of her. No, he could not share her, not even with other Kynd. She was his alone.

Whether it had been the centuries without his brethren that made him so selfish, he couldn't know and didn't care. All he knew was that for him, she let her soul fly as he plundered her with his mouth and he would not share her. He would selfishly cling to her, claim her as his own.

"Angel," he rasped, barely able to breathe with these overwhelming and painful needs swamping his senses. "I want—" His words tumbled away in a fierce snarl. Merrick shook his head, pleading silently and earnestly for this woman to understand him.

* * * *

I want.

Angelia gazed down over her stomach, between her bent knees, where Merrick stared up at her, his ferocity like lava in his molten eyes, consuming him. His muscles bulged and trembled, his fingers digging into the ample flesh of her butt, her inner thighs chafed from his attentions.

I want. She knew what he wanted, how it reduced him, distilling him like the boiling down of herbs to extract their pure essence. In that stark moment, he was as base as he'd ever been.

She would strip him further, mercilessly. For she wanted, too. Somewhere when he'd been devouring her with his mouth to her core, feasting ravenously as his tongue flicked her higher, to where her skin caught fire and thinned so it no longer contained her and she burst forth, flowing her release all over his face, he had unlocked her. She'd let herself go, safe in his hands, and still he drank of her, pushing for more as though he'd never get his fill of her. So, yes! She gloried in his helplessness, just as moments before he had gloried in hers.

Shamelessly, Angelia squirmed, straightening her legs. For a brief second she caught the flash of despair in Merrick's gaze, as though he misunderstood her wriggling to free herself. Her heart seized painfully, catching her breath in her throat.

No. She reached for him out of reflex, her body reacting before her brain could catch up. Without even thinking about it, she wanted him. *All of him.* Not just that physical part but the kernel within him that had sparked true fear at the thought of her spurning him.

He gave her power with his surrender, and Angelia felt it curl through her like smoke, expanding across her muscles into her every cell. Although her body had never welcomed another before Merrick's, her heels carved paths down the backs of his long thighs and hooked at his knees, pulling him toward her until she felt the weight of his erection bump against the heat of her wet lips.

As if aware of the gift, Merrick hovered above her, his huge body straining, blanketing her bare skin with his warmth. The balled muscles of his shoulder flexed as he reached between her thighs, two of his fingers working her for a slicker passage for his entrance. She felt his fingers recede, then the bulbous head of his cock when he penetrated. Her body stretched then closed around him as he slid himself deeper.

Merrick's jaw clamped as he shivered. "*So tight*," he groaned as he drew back before forging a few inches deeper. Methodically, he repeated his exploration, a jewel of sweat dragging a thin line down his chest and dripping to hers. With a twist of his broad shoulders, he lowered to lick her neck, his hot breath trailing tentative kisses.

"Angel." Her name was a plea, a prayer, as he worked himself deeper. His size filled her, so she had to spread her thighs to make room for him, her body giving, accepting. Every plunge lifted her incrementally higher, quickened her breathing until she panted and cried out with every thrust, tried desperately to lock her hands to his strong back, the muscles of it twisting, growing slick as his pleasure mounted. He pushed her higher and she clutched as pure desire ignited her.

She thought his tongue thrilled her? Dearest God in Heaven, she was joined with this man, forged in a way that transcended the fullness of him within her. He was *inside* of her, beyond the physical. Every pumping thrust shot her higher, and he right along with her. He growled helplessly with every gasping breath as he plunged harder, quicker. Angelia thrust back to drive him deeper, until the velvet of his cock grew so hot, and she grew so slick she wet his sac as it smacked again and again against her crease.

Incrementally, he'd built a fire in her, fanning it with every glide, with every stroke of his rough palms on her sensitive skin until it roared under her fevered skin, and clamped tight her throat so every push of air from her lungs was a wanton chant, a hoarse cry. She exploded, just as hot jets of seed speared through her. They yelled together, his bellow a rumbling and complimentary tenor to her soprano cries. Yet even in their throes, his muscles were locked to hold her with care.

Panting, Angelia stared up at the red sky overhead, stunned, as Merrick buried his face into the sweaty tangle of her hair, his fingers curling and fisting it as his hips continued the sated, rhythmic wringing of the last of his seed.

"Holy Christ, Angel." His breath fanned hot across her nape, trapped in the knot of her hair. At some point, her braid had worked loose, and she felt him wrap it around his fist, as if he needed to anchor himself.

Maybe the tough chimera did. She hadn't been alone during that blast-off into the stratosphere. Uh-uh. Merrick had been catapulted right along with her. He was still wrecked, heaving on top of her.

Pride and tenderness swamped her in that moment and she drew her chimera to her with a tightening hug, wrapping and locking her legs around his slowing hips to hold him to her. For all his strength, he was

212

precious. *Fragile.* She'd seen it in his wary eyes, felt it as though her heart had been physically rent open to receive him.

As the realization struck her, a tear coursed down her temple, to her ear. Merrick had not just had sex with her. He'd given her his love.

They'd made love. Which explained his wanting to know her earliest memory, his delving into her past. How in God's name was she going to leave him at the Archway?

Angelia closed her eyes against the pain of it. But in doing so, she didn't see the man approach, his hands resting familiar on the knives sheathed at both hips.

* * * *

Fascinated by what must surely be a gift from the Fates, the soulless man crept from the shadows along the riverbank of the Styx. *Impossible!* Yet, there she was. The same plain woman he'd withheld from carving, who had been lying unconscious on the floor when he'd stolen the Scriptum from the Literati. Now, here she was, as though it was destined she be made beautiful by his knives.

Why not render her into something more than ordinary? He'd delivered the relic, had received the four angel feathers, which were wrapped safe in his pack, as proof of the book's delivery. The only thing left for him to do was return to the surface to receive his payment.

For that, he could barely wait, even after the horrors he'd witnessed during his descent into this abyss. Had he been a regular man, one not destined for greater things, he would never have survived this mind-warping trip.

Hell existed. The Sisters and Father Martin had been right.

Vampires were real, too. He'd been hired by one. It was how he'd learned Hell really was a place most people should fear. Once the vampire had his feathers, Aro would bestow his gift of eternal life upon him. No matter that he would forever need blood for sustenance. He spilt enough. Drinking it would simply be an added flair to his artistic touch.

Oh, the Fates favored him. Easily he'd navigated through Hell, as if he'd been destined for the gift of immortality, as though it was his birthright and the Universe knew it. For certainly, he'd thought he would never get through the gate. He'd thought he would have to fight the lion creature with the black, feathered wings poised at the Archway.

It was then, for the second time in his life, he had been afraid.

Yet, as he'd neared, the beast had remained perched on the stone wall watching, but not moving. Its eyes were like mirrors, reflecting his skulking image back at him. The glare had been brutally cold, yet searing with a rage that could mow him down like a blade of grass if the creature decided to stop him.

Even in the clutches of the vampire, he hadn't felt that kind of terror overtake him.

The fear prickling cold sweat across his skin had been far different from that which he'd felt as a small boy at St. Augustine's, when he had been trapped among hundreds of other children without parents, living at the mercy of those around him.

The children knew instinctively there was something off about him. At every turn, they either shunned him, or piled on more injuries to his already bruised skin. The Sisters had tried to protect him in their way, but even they sensed something off-putting about him and had shuffled him around, averse to spending more time around the odd boy than they had to.

By his teens, the soulless man had learned why. He *was* different from those around him. He'd learned this by watching, by comparing his thoughts to how others behaved and reacted.

The people around him cared about things and he simply did not. Nothing stirred him, outside of his earlier fear. Where others sighed, the young man's heart remained unmoved.

Until he'd been allowed into the big kitchen, where he'd discovered the fundamental beauty of blades. Knives contained a brilliance all their own. They were tools that took something mundane and rendered it to something else entirely.

For the first time in his life, he had felt an emotion that wasn't fear. His heart romped wild in his chest, making him sweat as he covetously watched the cook slash away at a head of cabbage, his eyes flickering with every rapid chop of the blade. Knives belonged in his hands, and as though his destiny gifted him with his discovery, he had palmed a knife from the counter, effortlessly slipping it up his sleeve undetected.

It wasn't cabbages he was meant to transform. He knew that, felt the knife's power humming through his blood the farther he got from the kitchen, the closer he got to the other children.

Nevertheless, years under the heavy hands of the Sisters had taught him restraint. He had been meticulously careful, the reward for which had led him up to this moment, where he stood outside the towering walls of a fortified city, with four angel feathers in his pack and a promise of immortality. With a blank canvas before him.

Blank it was, even as he heard the woman's lustful cries, saw her blonde hair spilled and knotted in a loosening braid, uncaring of the world around her as she clutched at the muscled man thrusting into her.

The soulless man watched their carnal act, more fascinated with the man, who could rut with something so plain when he himself was so exceptional. The scars on his back were magnificent—twin arcs undulating in symphony with his thick muscles. Every deep breath the man took he growled, a sound so guttural as to be inhuman. Those twin scars on the man's shoulder blades stretched with every expansion of the man's heaving chest.

Beautiful. How much more so when his knife would make its lethal swipe across the man's throat. A pity to have to kill him, but he was a threat, and would interfere with his true work: the blank canvas before him. He could carve her at his leisure, take his time etching intricate patterns into her bland skin. He was in Hell, after all, who was there to stop him?

The soulless man edged closer, his fingertips caressing his sheathed knives. A well-placed stab through the ribs at the man's back would bring his head up, exposing the vulnerable neck. A perfect one-two maneuver, when a killer was as quick as he was. The soulless man crept closer, confident in his abilities.

The plain woman's eyes were now closed, the man spent and sated on top of her, the bulk of his impressive weight resting on his elbows, his face driven deep into the woman's nape. He could smell their heat, the man's seed.

With a forceful and carefully aimed thrust, he jabbed the knife he held in his right hand through the space of the man's heaving ribs, mere inches from one of those pretty scars. Arching his left arm, he readied the lethal swing for the instant when the man would jerk his head up.

The man did not react predictably to a knife stabbed into his back. Instead, he went rigid, instantaneously curling himself protectively around the woman and snagging out his left arm. Vise-like, the hand clamped around the soulless man's swinging wrist with freakish accuracy, crushing to splinter bone. The knife dropped from his useless fingers, the agony flaring white in his eyes, blinding him. Through his own shrieks, a deafening roar battered his eardrums.

Like a nightmare, his vision flashed images of fangs, movement of bulk too quick, and then crimson bloomed in his eyes as he felt the wrench of his shoulder and the sickening tug and tear of flesh, like paper.

His severed arm arced in grotesque flight toward the riverbank. He shrieked and shrieked, his terror manifest as his brain snapped through the flashing images, registering the brutal cold and the searing heat of a rage that could mow him down like a blade of grass.

The creature at the Archway. The soulless man's frantic and last thought as his knees folded, and he crumpled to the red-tinged dirt.

* * * *

Balling his hand into a fist, Merrick jack-hammered a punch against the dead man's skull, cracking it so the face fell back into the dirt disfigured, the cheek and jaw bone skewed, one lifeless eye popping free of its crushed socket.

He knew the man was dead but he couldn't stop the eruption of his fury. It spewed out of him, shaking his muscles as he struggled to claw it back in, to shove the lid down on it. In spite of the slicing blade wedged deep into his lung, he roared. Merrick turned toward Dis and roared again, the resounding echo battering off the high walls.

He reached behind him for the hilt of the blade, but couldn't get his hands on it. He circled, struggling to at least flick the fucking thing with his fingers, anything to dislodge it. But, it had been well placed, its position intentionally out of reach no matter which arm he grabbed with, no matter if he sought to grasp it from over his shoulders, or under his arms. The pain in his right dorsal muscle screeched through his whole body as his wings, sympathetic to his rage, fluttered to stretch.

No matter, the more the knife evaded his attempts to pull it free, the more his fury expanded, burning his skin, his hands losing the power to

216

grip as they morphed into paws with razor blade claws. He panted, fumbled at his pants gathered around his boots as he struggled to free himself from their God-awful constricting.

"Merrick."

He spun to face that glorious voice and grew queerly still.

His Angel stood at the edge of the sleeping bags, where only moments before he'd been joined to her. She was still naked, clothed only in her creamy skin, cloaked in the scent of their lovemaking.

She raised her hand, palm up, as though asking him to place his in hers. "Come to me."

Merrick stuck his malformed hands up in front of him, the outline of his fingers still visible at the back of his paws, the claws sharp and curled. He spoke through thick and elongated fangs, his words slurring. "Angel, no." He couldn't suppress his rage. His chimera battered at his bones to come forth.

"Come to me, Merrick," she commanded again.

His body responded by taking a hesitant step. But Merrick willed himself to stop, and shook his head, feeling the heft of his thickening mane curl along his neck. He felt the length of the knife in his muscle, inside of his lung. It had nicked his folded wing, infuriating him; he didn't dare go to the woman who asked him to come to her.

Except she wasn't merely commanding him, as much as compelling him. His feet itched to move toward her, his skin tingled, and not with his emerging fur. A calm was settling upon him the longer he remained still and watched her.

She stood tall, curvaceous, and radiant, her eyes an iridescent black, shining with...*fury?*

Curious, Merrick fell into those eyes, enamored by the whipping fire of sympathy and hatred he saw in their obsidian depths. His Angel was furious, and it radiated from her in an ever-widening aura, caressing his skin with its power.

By the time he obeyed his body's yearning, the hand that reached for his Angel was merely that—his hand. The lethal claws and thick pads of his paws had receded. She made that happen, he knew. The attack by the soulless man had severed what little control he had, and he had annihilated the scum with nearly every ounce of his anger. But not quite all of it. The rest of his rage seethed outward after, too monstrous for him to get a handle on.

Yet, Angelia stood before his burgeoning chimera, siphoning his fury, calming it like a zephyr wind caressing a storming sea. Awed by her, Merrick dropped to his knees, terrified she would change her mind and shun him.

She had seen him unhinged, at the mercy of his rage. There'd been no coherent thought, no strategic plan of attack. He'd erupted, and his Angel stood in the face of it, absorbing his anger as if it were her own. It became her own. He saw it in those gleaming black eyes, their depths colossal, consuming.

The moment his knees buckled to the earth, Merrick pushed his forehead into Angelia's bare stomach, his heart lurching madly as her arms encircled his head, and she leaned forward to bury her nose in his hair.

Her breath was warm, her arms soft, yet solid. The scent of their lovemaking enveloped him, her scent gloriously entwined with his own, her arousal still fresh. He embraced her hips, clutching her closer, driving his face harder against her stomach.

The knife sliced deeper with the stretching and contracting of his back muscles, the long blade burning as it scraped bone. He winced and gasped, but grasped his mate tighter still. Her giggles trickled across his skin, tickling his belly so it flipped in a giddy wash of pleasure.

"Merrick, you're going to crush me." He heard the smile in her scolding.

For the life of him, he didn't want to let go. She was his epicenter, the calm within his storm. A refuge he'd never known, not even during the ages when the Kynd were still in God's Grace.

She cupped his jaw in her hands and drew his face upward so she could look down upon him. Her smile beamed beatific, yet he caught the flash of fear before it settled behind their mesmerizing shine.

"We need to get that knife out of your back."

She worried it would kill him? Merrick let his own smile creep outward from his heart. "I'll live, Angel. Just yank it out fast, the same way it went in."

She nodded as she stared down at him, but her doubt resurfaced. "It will hurt."

"More so than it did going in."

Her smile faltered. "Will it kill you?"

"No," he said, picking up her fallen grin. "I'm pretty hard to kill. But I'm going to cough some blood until the wound closes."

"You've had this happen before."

Yes, he had, but not while he lay cock deep in the woman he loved, completely enrapt so nothing else existed around him. Not even danger. "Fuck, Angel, I'm sorry."

Her feathery little brows actually furrowed. "Whatever for?"

* * * *

Why was he sorry, when he was the one kneeling at her feet with a knife sticking out of his back? The one who should be sorry and couldn't be now, was the one-armed man lying crumpled and dead in the dirt. He'd got off easy, the bastard.

Angelia felt like she was the one who could have smashed her fist into his disgusting face. And she wouldn't have stopped after just one swing. She'd have *whaled* on that motherfucker for hurting Merrick. For hurting the man she loved with every speck of her being.

They'd made love, were basking in the baptismal beauty of it. She'd been glorying in the feel of Merrick *planted* inside of her. She'd felt like she was a part of him, inextricably joined.

Bonded. Yes, their physical joining had been so much more than sex. Although, that had been out of this world. They'd both been catapulted to the stars. The weight of Merrick, as he lay spent on top of her? That was the icing, the scrumptious chocolate glaze of dessert she could spend a lifetime reveling in.

So tender he'd been with her, even though she'd felt him tremble with his terrible wanting.

He'd watched her so closely, for every pleasure-seeking nuance her body revealed, and he'd given as he'd abstained. Until he couldn't hold back any longer, and then she'd seen him crack.

No. Merrick had shattered and had trusted her to keep him whole.

When that knife went through him and his fury exploded, unleashing his chimera in the one place he couldn't afford to do so, Angelia ruptured. Never had she felt such a surging of emotions. Entwined with her love were the raw energies of hatred and anger, coalesced into righteous retribution. She'd flipped to her feet, never giving a thought to her nudity, and watched transfixed and triumphantly satisfied as Merrick wreaked his damage.

He was horrifying. Diabolically quick, preternaturally strong. Utterly magnificent. She'd reveled in his capacity for carnage, was silently encouraging him, like a rabid spectator at a UFC match, as though Merrick was an extension of herself and she gloried in their swift justice. Until his gargoyle body receded behind emerging fur and his hands fisted, his palms growing thick as they morphed into paws.

Then her righteous anger did a curious thing, though she was too enrapt in the moment to question it. Instead, she let the strange twinning have its due. Her love for Merrick unfurled like a tidal wave inside of her, rolling thick and heavy out of her skin, not swamping her fury but embracing it, so the two beamed out of her as a singular force.

Without thinking, she reached out for her beautiful chimera to rein him in. He would not sacrifice his soul over such a paltry being as that which lay bleeding out at their feet. He would come to her and she would assuage his fury, would coil it back. He didn't possess the ability, but forged with him as she was, she did.

And she had. Without a hangover, too, like she was equipped to handle monstrous outpourings of energy. *The angel?* Maybe Merrick knew what the heck he was talking about. Except, at the moment, she wasn't feeling particularly pious. Her lover had a knife sticking out of his back and he needed her to pull it out, in spite of the pain it was going to cause him.

She wavered, her stomach suddenly too empty, like the bottom had dropped out of it. She felt queasy and hollow.

"Now you're getting squeamish on me?"

She looked down at Merrick's lopsided grin. He was teasing her, even though moments before, he'd been on the brink of losing the last of his soul.

She'd done that, too, she realized, given him back his control. Keeping that in mind helped to dry out her clammy skin. Yes, she would get that God-awful knife out of his back. She just couldn't think about it while she was doing it.

Angelia twirled her fingers in a circle. "All right. Turn around. And no whining. This is going to be hard enough as it is." At least she sounded brave.

Merrick turned his back to her, bending on one knee while he drove his strong fingers into the ground. "Just do it quick."

As she neared, she saw how slick his back was with sweat. The blood from the wound sluiced down in a skinny rivulet. More would drain as soon as she removed the blade, causing her anger to rise up inside her, coating her tongue with an odd, metallic flavor. She reached out to touch the hilt with her shaking fingers.

Just as they skimmed the brass knob, Merrick turned. "Just grab it and yank, all right?"

"Gah! Yes, I know." She balled her fists at her sides then stared once again at Merrick's wounded back as he faced away from her, her fear for him enmeshing itself to her anger.

She reached for the knife once more, just as Merrick twisted around again, as if he wanted to say something more.

"Jesus Christ! Would you cut that out? I'm trying to help you here."

He smiled up at her, his slate eyes shining with mischief. "You said *Jesus Christ.* You only swear when you get righteous."

"I'm going to do more than swear if you don't cut it out."

"Yeah? What are you going to do?"

"Rip *your* arm off and beat you with it." The sparkle in his eyes vanished as if it had never been there and she instantly regretted her threat. She hadn't thought he'd be so sensitive about the killing, but she should have known. Hadn't he been telling her all along he didn't like being the Guardian? "Merrick, I'm sorry."

She couldn't read his face. He had turned away from her, baring his back so she could remove the knife.

"Just grab the damned thing and yank, Angel."

Straddling him to brace herself, she closed her palm around the hilt. The knife was lodged firmly, and moved stiffly in her hand as Merrick inhaled shallow breaths.

"If you hadn't killed him, I would have tried." She gritted her teeth.

"Are you trying to make me feel better?" He glanced over his shoulder.

"Yeah." Angelia got a better grip, her stomach turning hollow again. She could feel the life, his strength, skewered on the end of that blade. "Turn around. I can't have you watching me while I do this."

Merrick wriggled his hips, nestling himself between her legs, so she rode him like he was a small horse. His sweat-slicked skin warmed her, lodging her as firmly as the bulk of his body did. She felt better, having his weight pressed against her inner thighs, and even though they were in the middle of this awful moment, she enjoyed the smooth feel of his skin against hers.

"On the count of three."

Merrick nodded.

"One. Two." Yanking the knife, she simultaneously gripped with her thighs and would have toppled backward if her legs hadn't been latched so hard to the man beneath her. She'd used too much force, the knife slipping from the flesh far easier than she'd expected. She tossed the horrid blade away with a disgusted flick of her arm.

Blood bubbled out of the wound. Merrick coughed. "Christ, I thought we were doing this on three." He spit a wad of red mucous onto the rust-colored earth.

Angelia watched it puddle like a bubbly quarter before it disappeared into the ground, leaving a small dark patch behind. More blood streamed down his back, curving a crimson trail down his buttocks, and when he coughed again, a glob spurted from the open wound. His knees gave way and he bent over, dragging air into his sputtering lungs.

Oh, God. Her chimera was dying. Okay, so he was immortal. But it didn't mean he wouldn't come horribly close to death before his body recovered. A two-hundred-pound weight settled on her chest. he found it hard to breathe right. Seeing Merrick incapacitated was scaring the crap out of her. She had to *do* something.

Angelia grabbed her forgotten cargo pants, wadded them up like a rag, and crammed them against the slice in his back, effectively stemming the flow of blood and sealing the hole that was letting the air escape his lungs. His relief was obvious. The healthy color blooming back into his skin, chasing away the bluish gray.

"Thanks." Merrick kept his head bowed, but she could see that his breaths came easier, more regular.

"No problem. Anytime."

"Anytime, eh?" He shook his head. "Not if I can help it."

"So, that was the soulless man, wasn't it?"

"Yeah." He spit again, clearing his mouth of the blood.

"He deserved what he got. Heck, if you weren't going to kill him, I would have. For what he did to you." She felt her cheeks flush and was glad she stood behind him so he couldn't see how her confession embarrassed her. She loved him so much, but the feeling was raw, too new. She felt too exposed, her heart swollen and delicate.

Merrick's fingers curled around her ankle. "Angel."

She'd thought to hide her emotions? Silly her. She was in love with a chimera. One of the Kynd. God's Witnesses, who missed nothing. Well, almost nothing. Merrick hadn't seen the soulless man coming, but then neither had she. They'd both been too caught up in the sacrament of their joining.

And joined they were. She couldn't deny the outpouring she'd felt from Merrick. He had filled her with more than his body. She'd held his soul. Still did. All she had to do was forget her insecurities, and she felt the strength of her chimera inside of her. Felt his weakness, too.

The hand he reached out to touch her ankle with telegraphed his own rawness. He needed her like she did him.

Hell went blurry as Angelia swiped her free hand across her eyes.

* * * *

His Angel was crying. He could smell her tears, feel the warming of her skin. All because he'd gotten hurt. Maybe it went against everything he'd hated for millennia, but loving her was right.

He'd not misplaced his heart. She really would have tried killing the soulless man because he'd hurt him. Would have sacrificed her own life doing it, too. The truth of which scared him witless, but was oddly comforting.

Merrick thought he had been nurturing his Angel's courage all this time? He was an idiot, if he thought that. The opposite was true; he understood that now. All along, she was the one fostering his, building an inner strength within him that hadn't existed before. He had so much to learn from his Angel.

"Our man had a bag with him. Let's see what he left us." When he stood, she rose with him, still holding pressure to his wound.

He was glad she did, because his legs felt like cooked pasta, his head too light for his body. Leaning against her for a second brought his equilibrium back. Ironic? No. *The way it should be.*

Merrick held onto his Angel a little longer than he had to.

"I'm okay now." He lifted his arms as he turned, then lowered them to pull her close. The wound stretched and pained him but he didn't feel his life draining out of it any longer. Instead, he felt his whole being wrapped up in his arms, and he rubbed his face against his Angel's hair, smelling that honey-lavender scent of hers that wouldn't quit. If anything, it grew more intoxicating, having melded itself inextricably with his own.

He would make love to her a billion more times if he could. How had he and his brotherkynd missed this divine, yet secular, miracle? A moot point now. The Kynd were doomed, and this wonder of a woman would be returning to the surface where she belonged.

Merrick reluctantly extricated himself from their embrace to retrieve the soulless man's bag. He didn't need to heft it to know the Scriptum wasn't in it. Nor was he surprised to find the carefully wrapped feathers from one of Lucifer's angels.

"Proof." He handed the four feathers to Angelia.

"Proof? Of what?" She looked up at him, perplexed, strands of her hair wisping around her face.

"My guess is he traded the Scriptum for them and needed evidence that he had."

"Which means there is someone above waiting for them."

"Aro," they said in unison.

"The bastard." Angelia clutched the feathers tighter, her knuckles paling.

"He didn't want one of us to come back." Or both. The vampire's scheme had yet to reveal its truths, beyond the obvious. But this complicated matters. And flushed Merrick's plan down the proverbial toilet.

Danger awaited Angelia when she returned to the surface. Death awaited her behind the walls of Dis. It wasn't a matter of getting the Scriptum from some soulless human anymore. The fallen angels had it. They wouldn't let it go without something of equal value in trade.

He'd volunteer himself in a heartbeat. Except who would keep his Angel safe on the surface? Yes, Anton and the Triumvirate were formidable, but this was about the Kynd. There was something far more powerful at work here. Another hunch, but this one sat cold and heavy in his gut.

"Still want the Scriptum?"

"More so than ever." When she gazed up at him, her determination sparked like flint in her blue-black eyes. "He manipulated us, Merrick. I have to know why. If there's something in that book I missed—"

"Shh. You hear that?" Merrick cocked an ear toward the river. Was that..."Darken?" The gargoyle was on the other side of the Styx, and he wasn't alone. Impossible. Merrick's senses were playing tricks. Had to be. Because the arrival of his brethren would be a fucking miracle.

The Kynd weren't accorded His graces. Yet, he couldn't deny the bits of conversation floating from the far bank, and his heart sped up the more he listened.

Grinning, Merrick gazed like a struck fool at his Angel. "God, I wish you could hear this. Come with me." Placing his hand on her bare hip to guide her toward the river stopped him cold. He turned them so his back faced the riverbank, obscuring her from view. "Let's get you dressed." He didn't wait for her answer. He pushed her ahead of him, using his body like a shield as he glanced over his shoulder.

Kynd were coming in numbers, and damned if he wasn't as eager for it as he had been just a second ago. If he could quit thinking of his Angel bare-assed, her beautiful body on full display, he might be able to enjoy the novelty of something he'd not experienced in ages.

He only just stopped himself from swaddling her in the sleeping bags.

You're being unreasonable. Yeah, maybe he was, but he still wanted his mate clothed when his brothers arrived. With a speed belying the fact he sported a hole through his back, he shook out her bloody pants and started helping her get into them.

"Chimera, what the crap are...*oomph*! Would you cut that out? I can dress myself." All he could do was nod, urging her to hurry it up then.

No sooner was she fastening her pants, he was draping his leather coat across her shoulders and buttoning the front of it shut, all the way to her chin. He glanced nervously toward the river, grateful it was his coat covering her, that she was wrapped in more of his scent.

Giggles began to bubble out of her, and she was smiling when she looked up at him, her feathery brows furrowed. "All right. Something's up. You're acting ridiculous. What is it I'm supposed to be hearing?"

She was clothed, well covered up, so Merrick finally felt like he could drop his guard. A bit. He hauled on his pants but left his feet bare, just in case shit went wrong in a hurry. "It's my brethren, Angel. Darken is with *others*." His excitement was tempered by anxiety as he took her hands in his. Surely, God would punish this insurrection.

She didn't say anything as he steered them toward the bank of the river, but she did lean into him once they got there. Merrick wrapped his arms around her, resting his chin on her head. "Five of them. See?" He squeezed her closer, uneasy. Had Darken called their old group?

Dear God, if he had, what kind of shape would they be in?

"You think my eyesight's that good? I can barely see the other bank."

"At the base of the lighthouse." He pointed over her shoulder. "Darken's insulting the boatman's skimpy raft. He says they'll all sink before they reach the other side." His humor rolled back in like a white cloud on a summer's day. Squinting, he tried to see who the others were with the gargoyle.

"There!" He grabbed Angelia's shoulders, glad for something to hold onto in order to still his shaking. "It's Drakus. Christ Almighty, it's the dragon. And he's carrying...a bear."

"You're taking drugs."

He snorted as he thought about what he'd just said. "Funny. But, no. It's Drakus carrying Urick. They've sent Phlegyas and his empty boat packing." As the dragon neared, Merrick pulled Angelia away from the riverbank, placing himself between her and the nearing chimerae.

Drakus was a creature even Merrick didn't want to tangle with. But if the damned Kynd was unhinged, he wouldn't hesitate to protect his mate. He'd have to access the angel part of him, but so help him, he'd do it for her sake.

Caught between growling a threat and trembling with anticipation, he awaited their arrival, watching them get bigger the closer they got.

"Wow." His Angel could see them just fine now. "It's a freakin' *dragon.*"

"Yep." The question was how in God's name did he get here, and why?

"You guys are just full of surprises."

Hopefully good ones, in this case. Merrick pushed Angelia behind him without letting go of her. Drakus landed with a *whomp*, his huge skin wings kicking up dust. Urick tumbled, coating his furry bulk with red earth. The second the grizzly's paws were beneath him he began tearing up ground with his front claws as he lunged at the dragon, roaring his disgust at the unceremonious landing.

Shit.

Drakus swung his spiked tail. But instead of swatting the bear like a nuisance, the dragon wrapped Urick to him, pulling his brotherkynd close. His reptilian muscles bulged as though he warred with his instincts, but he didn't retaliate. They were in better shape than Merrick thought. Or so it looked.

"Angel, stay here. Please, whatever happens, just stay put."

Chapter Thirteen

Like she was leaving. Or maybe he didn't want her straying too far in case he needed her to rein him in again. She didn't trust the tenuous control of either chimera, hers included. There was no mistaking the wild roll and flash of the newcomers' eyes.

And Merrick? His dark mane was sprouting. It didn't take a road map to see where he was going.

Just keep your flippin' wings in, chimera. She watched him closely, alert for the first sign of feathers. So far, he was doing all right, giving her a fabulous show of his well-muscled back, his broad shoulders and narrow hips hugged in dark-chocolate leather. Merrick's long, thick legs strode confidently, his muscled ass sitting atop of them like...*buns.* Yummy buns that had her itching to hold her hands in the air to pretend to squeeze them.

Heck, she was already sloughing off the trauma of Merrick's stabbing. But she didn't lose her wariness. She would guard Merrick, just as he did her. The angel part of him was not allowed to visit his brothers, no matter how long it had been since he'd seen them. Besides, she didn't like that the other two hadn't shed their lethal forms.

Or maybe these were the least lethal forms they had? Her life had grown a little crazy when the least dangerous thing she could see was a grizzly bear. The truth of which had her blood buzzing in her veins, like the jolts she felt from the Scriptum.

Which is farther away than it ever was.

True. And all she had to show for it were four dingy angel feathers.

An earsplitting snap rent the air as the dragon, Drakus, soared upward then back toward the others on the opposite shore. Ten minutes later, she was witnessing a reunion more than two thousand years in the making.

In their gargoyle forms, Kynd were knotted together, their faces rapt when they weren't freaking out. They trembled and roared, and gripped so hard to the ground or each other, she was sure some bones were broken.

Yet none of them let go of each other. Not even Merrick, who kept glancing over at her, his expression dumbfounded, yet earnest. He didn't want her to leave. He didn't want her anywhere near that barely controlled throng, either.

She stood on the outskirts with her face soaking wet from her raining tears. Happy? Euphoric. Her heart hurt watching them. All her years of adoring creatures she thought legendary, rather than Grotesque? She was raking in a jackpot that annihilated the sadness of every hour she'd spent alone daydreaming about them. Now she understood she'd been preparing.

The Scriptum had been the key. Merrick the door. And the rest of these Kynd?

Man, she couldn't wait to see what else her future held. Still feeling that inner hum, she wanted to jump into the fray. She wanted to share their joy. Merrick's stern and frequent glances kept her feet planted. She *was not* to come near.

Fine. But she could pout. Yeah, she could, if she still wasn't so fricking glad for them.

Finally, they seemed to be petering out, their grips on one another a bit less on the white-knuckled side. As they separated, she saw the blood. Dripping from wounds already healing. She was going to have to ask Merrick about that. Did Kynd heal faster when they gathered like that? If so, it was a secret their enemies didn't need to know. Another reason to get that book back.

Her book. Not the Literati's. It belonged to her, Merrick, and their brotherkynd.

So bold! *Their* brotherkynd, like she was one of them? Angelia held her breath, waiting for her doubts to smack her like they always used to.

In a heady flash of insight, she understood Merrick wouldn't drop her like a piece of cat crap. Not even now, when he was reunited with other Kynd. Instead, she felt thickened, heavier, as if the chimera's love was a physical weight within her, strengthening her like stone.

Standing by herself, but never again alone, Angelia nursed a well-deserved, indulgent grin.

Why were the others now standing alone, minus the smiles? In fact, aside from Merrick, the rest of the gargoyles looked malevolently ill, like they sickened themselves with their own savagery. Okay. So they could heal each other physically, but not emotionally? What was up with that? They'd just been a tangled embodiment of bliss. What the heck happened?

Without a thought, she headed for the group as it dispersed, each Kynd claiming a boulder, a hillock, or the plain, red ground. *Away* from each other. There was no mistaking the don't-come-another-fucking-step-closer looks they gave each other. And her.

She halted in her tracks. No way was she going to test if their threats were serious. This adventure aside, Angelia had a pretty healthy sense of self-preservation.

"Merrick?"

He was stepping back slow, inching toward her without taking his attention off the others. Not easy, given how far they'd spread out. She saw his claws extend, his back muscles ripple.

"I'll come to you. Stay right there." Without having to look at his face, she knew his fangs were out. She heard the slur when he said *stay*.

No problem. So long as everyone honored each other's need for space, everyone seemed to be able to keep himself under wraps. To a degree. Angelia looked where Merrick focused most of his attention. On Drakus. Who wasn't a gargoyle, she realized, eyeing him closer now that he remained aloof and alone. He was human, and half of his body was covered with an elaborate dragon tattoo. Even his face.

Whoever etched that onto his skin didn't want some innocent mistaking the human's true identity—that was obvious. The poor bastard. Who would get close to him unless it was another Kynd? And God had made sure even his brethren didn't. No wonder he was beyond pissed, that his cheese had slipped off his cracker. Intuitively, she found her body leaning toward the dragon chimera.

"Don't you dare."

Merrick. Angelia gazed over at her chimera, and straight into hard, granite eyes.

"Take another step toward Drakus, Angel, and it's most likely going to be your last. Come to me," he growled. He held his palm, now thick like a lion's paw, out for her.

"Christ," she swore on an exhale. She was surrounded by so much fury she felt it on her skin. Yet, her haven lay in that hand-paw. Merrick wouldn't have offered it if he didn't have a good grip on himself. She trusted that implicitly.

As soon as his heat engulfed her hand, he drew her tight against him, wrapping her hard in his arms as he backed away to claim their own space. His heart hammered against her back, giving away just how tenuous things were. The Kynd might be ecstatic to be reunited, but they were seriously effed-up.

She'd been ready to *help* Drakus? How in Hell did she think she was going to pull that off?

The answer to that resided in the quiet humming still vibrating inside her skull. Man, she needed to get her hands on that Scriptum. Not so easy now that a mere human didn't have it. And now she had *six* men who needed just as much help as they were offering.

Without warning, Merrick flipped her off her feet, cradling her as he squatted. A quick glance around told a lot about her odds of getting that book back. Her chimera nestled them where they could see the other five, who in turn could see them.

Separated they might be, but the Kynd had formed an all-encompassing circle. Angelia would not be leaving Hell empty handed.

Not if the Kynd could help it.

* * * *

Dearest God, he loved the feel of his mate in his arms, even after the reunion he'd had with his brethren. *Especially after the reunion I've had with my brothers.* He felt incomparably safe with his Angel, his soul securely nestled within hers. All the turbulent emotion he'd been embroiled in with his brothers soothed away the longer he held her.

So, when she sleepily muttered their desperate need to find the

Scriptum now that five Kynd had risked their fates, he understood her urgency. He really did.

The arrival of his brethren had solved his dilemma. He could trade himself for the Scriptum, just as he'd earlier planned. The solution tore him to pieces but he couldn't quit now. Nor could he let his brothers behind those walls. He needed them, as messed up as they were, to protect his Angel when he wouldn't be around to do it.

"You look a million miles away, chimera." His Angel awakened, her raspy voice curling through him like tendrils of steam.

Merrick brought her closer, burying his face into her neck, inhaling the irresistible scent of her. If only he was a million miles away, with her safe in his grasp. "Yeah," he stroked her cheek with his. "I was thinking on our situation."

"Yeah?"

He nodded, stirring lavender. "This isn't good, even with your being part angel. It's going to get dangerous."

"Worse than what we were going to face before?" Her cheeks paled, but he felt her supple, little body square up, her adorable chin jutting ever so slightly. "So be it. Whatever they throw at us, we can handle."

He wished he could believe her, but he knew better. Maybe someday, years down the road, Darken would find the humor in this irony, in what Merrick intended to do. He had finally found something worth living for and now his life was coming to an end.

Maybe by that time, too, his Angel would have found a way to forgive him for his deceit. For he had no intention of telling her his plans. She'd never agree to them. As it was, the other Kynd were none too happy about what he intended to do. It was the main reason their control had slipped. To have found their brother, only to let him go?

They would honor his sacrifice, even if they didn't fully understand it. Angelia must survive, along with the Scriptum. They would keep both safe because he asked it of them.

"Still have the feathers?" His attention redirected itself to her lips, to where she nibbled at the bottom one. *Ah God.* He so wanted to taste that mouth, could smell her willingness to let him.

Instead, he got to his feet, gently setting the woman he held down on hers.

"I'll take these." He held up the feathers, showing her. "To trade for the Scriptum. As soon as that book is in your hands, you run for the others. I'll be right behind you. All right?"

She pouted, like she was upset she wouldn't be kicking some angel ass. It made him want to scrap this whole plan and squeeze her close for the rest of her life. Precious thing that she was to him.

"Ready?" No point in putting off the inevitable, or giving her time to argue. He kissed her fingers and led them toward the great entrance, his seething brothers closing the circle, getting themselves ready to stop his Angel from coming back in after him. To keep themselves from doing the same.

* * * *

"Shouldn't we pack up our things, Merrick?" Angelia craned her neck to look at their belongings. Her cheeks flushed at the sight of the rumpled sleeping bags. There were torn hillocks where Merrick had fisted his claws into the fabric.

"We'll get them on the way back." He tugged her hand, his fingers gripping tight to hers as he headed for the gates.

The angels glared down, eerily silent. Without having to look, she knew the Kynd were glaring right back up at them. *Reinforcements, you crummy bastards, if you so much as lay a finger on my chimera.* "Do you think they know we're coming in?"

Merrick gazed upward, his jaw set. She could see the muscles of it bunching under his ear.

"They know." He stood aside, letting go of her fingers long enough for her to grasp the knob and crank it. The giant door fell open, groaning like an ancient tree toppling the length of its leviathan height.

Beyond, Angelia could see the sheer walls of Dis, like it was yet another fortress to surmount in order to gain entry. *Or to escape.* The great city was nothing like she'd imagined. It was worse. When she'd been picturing it, she hadn't been able to feel its hostility.

Hatred reigned supreme, and skirting it heavily was a thick sense of doom, like a physical wall, one she couldn't push through. Angelia backpedaled into Merrick's bulk as he stood tall and strong behind her.

She leaned into him as his arms wrapped around her, pulling her snug against him. "You'll be okay, my angel," he whispered, his breath soft in her ear. "Never forget who you are."

Who I am? Good lord, I'm a chicken-shit. Nothing about Hell she'd already experienced prepared her for this. It was as if all the anger, the treachery, and spilled blood of Hell stewed in this one spot, converging to squash her once she opened the gateway.

She was just a human. She wasn't meant to bear this horrid pall. No wonder Virgil quaked. Eternal death, with its crushing despair, birthed itself over and over in this place, filling every crevice, every cranny and cracked surface, and every pore of her body until she was caked with it.

"Remember," a growl tickled her ear. "These gates opened only for you, *Angel.*"

Yeah, they did. She was going through them with her man, even if she couldn't breathe. As his snarl faded, another low rumble gained momentum in her head, billowing and expanding like a white cloud in her skull, along her spine. Her skin tingled with the sensation as the reverberation lifted in pitch, resonating higher.

The Scriptum.

Angelia shut her eyes, letting its truth fill her and push away the shroud of hatred, which had tried its evil best to devour her. Instead, she felt fortified, strong from the inside out. The singing reached its pitch and plateaued, humming wondrously in the back of her head, a comforting accompaniment to the muscular arms girdling her waist.

She realized in that moment how the two were perfectly harmonized within her. Her chimera and the Scriptum. Taking a deep breath, she straightened, leaving the support of Merrick behind to stand on her own.

She no sooner relished the starch in her spine when the angels descended. Swarms of them teemed, their wings flapping thunderously, churning the fetid air, heating it until it was suffocating. Their shrieks rent the air, as though the angels tried to deafen her. Merrick's hands gripped her shoulders as he hovered protectively, his warning growls scraping reassuringly up her back, and he hissed like a great cat toward the blotted out sky, his long fangs bared.

"Stop it!" Angelia spread her arms like a conductor, her gaze imperious.

Instantly, the cacophony ended, leaving a vacuum, one which left her feeling a bit deaf. Capitalizing on the stunned silence, she stepped into the midst of the grounded angels, ignoring the murderous, inhuman glares of the ones who remained hovering along the wall. "I want the one who holds my Scriptum."

No angel moved, not even the flutter of a single wing. The silence gnawed at her newfound will. Angelia kicked it off like a wrapper stuck to her shoe. She didn't dare succumb to her insecurities. Not here. Not now.

"Three seconds. I'll give you three seconds to give me what I want." She was never any good at granting the full count and she grinned, even as her thoughts touched on when she'd removed the knife from her chimera's back.

"One."

Merrick remained silent, allowing her to orchestrate the show. She stole a glance back at him, wishing he weren't so terribly far away. Despite being only several feet from her, he looked so alone standing there, his chiseled body rigid, his slate eyes wary. His fingers were pointed with his lion's claws, his black mane curling across the width of each of his thick shoulders, merging just below his Adam's apple.

He stood like a sculpted, pagan god, his strong body magnificent, like chiseled marble. Angelia's swelling heart kicked against her sternum, demanding room. Here she was confronting bad-ass angels, and she was lusting after the man promising to lock himself into battle with the legions that threatened her. God, what a turn-on.

"I have your precious book." It was a voice meant to scrape paint from the walls.

Angelia cringed inwardly, her attention diverted from her living art. What she looked at instead was the antithesis of beauty. This being had wings and fangs but neither inspired her with wanting.

Instead, it filled her with sorrowful dread. Once, this creature had been beautiful. His features still were. But they were lacking, as if death and its decomposition had eaten away at him from the inside, never touching the outer shell, except to leave it an empty husk. It took every ounce of fortitude she could muster to look the thing in its flat eyes. It blinked like a bird, like a vulture sitting on the bleached bones of a horse carcass.

Merrick stepped between them, holding up the four feathers. With his back to her, she could no longer see the set of his jaw, but she could see his determination in the stiffening of his broad shoulders. He leaned toward the angel, whispering something in Latin. She heard *trade*, recognized *peace* and *Kynd*.

Behind her, she could hear the rustling of a million feathers as wings shifted. An evil sneer spread across the angel's cruel face. His eerie eyes flickered, as though a third eyelid passed over the iris.

"Deal, chimera." Like magic, the Scriptum appeared at its feet, and the angel kicked it across the dirt toward Merrick.

Without wasting a moment, Merrick picked it up and put the book into her arms, double-checking she held it tight. He locked his granite eyes upon her. For all the world, he looked as though he wanted to devour her in a kiss.

Angelia leaned forward on her toes, expecting it.

Merrick hissed instead. "Run," he commanded, his eyes blazing the length of her before shoving her backward. "Run!"

She took off like her feet were on fire. Only realizing after the monolithic doors dragged shut behind her, and the Kynd closed in like a protective wall, that Merrick had still been holding the feathers when he'd thrust the Scriptum at her and had ordered her to run.

No wonder he'd been gazing at her with all the hunger of his heart. He was never going to see her again. Merrick hadn't traded the feathers, she realized, as panic flooded coherent thought, and strong arms reached to hold her before she could spin around and run back for the doors.

"No, God. No, no, no, no…" she wailed. "Merrick, no! *He traded himself!*" she screamed, even knowing the other Kynd were well aware of it.

She shoved against the bodies blocking her, seeking Darken's face, until a brilliant blast of white light exploded within her head, blinding her, stripping her skin so she had no form. She careened with no sense of up and down, no sense of the others, just that she was falling, or soaring.

Then she knew nothing at all.

* * * *

Cold permeated one side of her body, which, Angelia realized as she

236

blinked at a table's legs, was because she lay on flagstones, her body curled around something biting into the skin of her cramped fingers. Her memories crashed down on her, as though the rafters of a skyscraper collapsed, raining tons of debris to bury her.

She heard someone wailing, a winding misery that shivered across her skin, then realized it was her. She was moaning like a survivor of a train wreck who still lay on the ground amongst the debris.

Her body felt like it had survived a train wreck. The pain was enormous. A cold sweat broke out across her back; Angelia rolled to her knees, ready to vomit. The rough stone bit into her kneecaps but felt soothingly cool to her palms. Her braid, now a ratted knot, dropped over one cheek, halving her vision.

She swallowed rapidly, forcing down the saliva washing her molars.

Mustn't puke. Although why not escaped her, other than it seemed like a sign of weakness. And for all her misery, her will wouldn't let her seem feeble. Even though her insides were heaving and her heart felt like road-kill—baked sere and irreparably flattened.

Merrick was gone, sacrificing himself for God knew what. The Scriptum? Wasn't worth it. Not in a million centuries. Not when weighed against the nobility of the man she loved. Who loved her back with a tenderness…

Oh, God! Angelia sat back on her shins, clutching the book to her breast as her tears tracked unheeded down her face. Merrick had been so careful of her, as though she were precious. Yet, he'd pushed her, seeing a determination she hadn't known existed until he'd coaxed it out, nourished it.

Again, for what? For her to confront an angel and demand her property back? Resentment bloomed, then ebbed before it took root. No. That wasn't how it had been at all. Merrick had seen her for who she truly was and hadn't given her an inch to act otherwise.

He'd helped her find the courage to be herself. While he threw himself away.

She couldn't muster her resentment for that thought, either, because it wasn't true. His sacrifice hadn't been for nothing. Yes, the Scriptum was now in her hands, safe on the surface for the moment, but that wasn't his only reason for surrendering.

He'd saved his brothers by doing it. The Kynd would be safe now that she had their secrets in her care. Her entire body grew stiff, as implacable as her will. She would not let her chimera's sacrifice be for nothing. She would strive to keep the vulnerable Kynd safe.

For Merrick.

Angelia's eyes burned with tears, but she refused to let more of them fall. In honor of her lover, she would not. Instead, she roused herself to her feet, taking courage from the steadfast stone of the floor, and took her bearings.

Something, or someone, had zapped her back to her office, to the exact same spot she'd passed out in when the Scriptum had been stolen. The Kynd? Doubtful. For one, they didn't know this to be the origin. Second, they were spread around the room looking as wrecked as she felt. Darken lay unconscious, his arms and legs sprawled as if he'd been carelessly flung by a giant god.

Perhaps he had. Her resolve twisted into resentment. How dare He, when the Kynd fought so hard just to function.

She looked around the room at the others. They were strewn just as haphazardly, their magnificent bodies twisted akimbo, cementing her certainty of their innocence. Merrick's brethren had had no part in directing this fuck-show.

With crushing awe, she realized God had done this, that her chimera's fate had been divinely sealed. Heavenly creatures they might have once been, but there was nothing in the Kynd's power to overturn the ordained if He did not wish it so. The proof of that was in their scattered bodies, of their removal from one plane to another as though they'd been flicked like fleas.

Besides, Merrick hadn't wanted her interference. He had locked eyes with her, conveying everything in that unflinching stare. She was not to interfere with his choice, or she'd ruin everything. His sacrifice would mean nothing.

Angelia crumpled to the floor and waited for her new brothers to regain consciousness.

Chapter Fourteen

Three weeks later…

Merrick lay on his bruised side, turning over his thoughts in his mind, fondling his memories of his Angel like the precious things they were. He recalled with utter clarity the wasp stings on her little nose, the silk of her hair in his rough hands.

Three tresses, lapped over each…

So on, and so on, down the length of her back until he'd formed a golden braid. He closed his eyes to breathe in her scent, could almost conjure it in his fantasy. In his memories, he leaned in close to her nape, skimming his hand along her shoulder. Then as dreams will do, he found himself inexplicably stretched on top of her nude body, with her gazing up at him, so trusting.

Even in his dank prison, his cock stretched to painful life, and Merrick fisted himself as he retreated once again into his memories, to his Angel spread open, inviting him. She reached for him, her soft skin a caress against his as she explored every inch of him, tracing her fingers over the ridges of his muscles.

As he slid his shaft across the crisp hairs of her heat, she rolled her hips to meet him, a smile curling upon her lips. *So beautiful.* Ever so gently, he ran his rough fingertips along her temple, smoothing away stray wisps of her hair as he lowered his lips to hers.

Inhaling deep, he dragged in the honey-lavender scent of his Angel, the warmth of her breath.

I love you, she whispered, her knees parting and her silken inner thighs caressing his thrusting hips as he sought her core with his swollen crown. So hot. Dripping in her need for him, she writhed as he fumbled, sliding passed her slick, tulip folds. Frustrated, he growled, lifted his hips and plunged again, slipping and grinding, but unable to penetrate.

His cock grew engorged, heavy, and painful. Anger welled, stiffening his body so his thrusts were those of a beast, brutal in his desperation. Still he could not find her, could not be flesh of her flesh. Always she faded away.

"Angelia!" he bellowed, pushing his battered face into the red dirt, as his hand pumped furiously along his cock. Merrick curled around himself, breathless, disgusted, unspent. Groaning, he rolled to his back and hissed, re-curling to his side, drawing his knees under himself to sit up. The daily beatings he received were nothing compared to the agony of his severed wings, their nubs splintered and oozing blood.

Merrick scrubbed his hand over his face, unmindful of the cuts as he escaped once again into his precious memories. Recalling with utter clarity the wasp stings on her little nose, the silk of her hair in his rough hands.

Three tresses, lapped over each... His Hell. The cost of his sacrifice. The repetition of his memories interrupted by the beatings from the angels.

"Merrick."

His hand lingered over his eyes as he drew in a heavy breath. Her scent. He could almost conjure it. He leaned in close to her nape, skimming his hand along her shoulder. Then as dreams will do, he found himself inexplicably stretched on top...

"Merrick, it is me. *Alielle.*"

"Angel?" Had she come for him when he'd willed her not to?

"No, but close."

No, not my Angel. Though the voice was beautiful.

"Open your eyes to me, Kynd."

His Angelia vanished from beneath him and Merrick raised his swollen lids to view his knees, his throbbing shaft erect against his stomach—the price of his lust and his greed. He would suffer for both without regret. Yet, still he wept.

"Oh, chimera, how far you have fallen."

The rustling of wings stilled him, and his body tensed, his bleeding nubs flailing as if to spread their missing wings. His lion's tail pushed from his spine, forcing Merrick to lean forward to his hands and knees.

Battle. Lucifer's angels were near.

"Quiet, Kynd. It is just me, Alielle. The others are not here. They will not come." Such a soothing voice, speaking truth.

Merrick settled back, raising his eyes to his visitor for the first time. Immediately he squeezed his lids shut against the light, having been too long shut in the darkness.

"Here, now. Try again." The warmth of the light ebbed, but not from the voice.

Merrick raised his face, cautiously cracking open his puffy eyes. "You," scraped from his raw throat, and he swallowed to soothe it. *Alielle.* One of God's treasured Archangels.

"Aye, chimera. As I said it was."

"Why have you come?" He lay back down on his side, drawing his knees to his chest.

"To remove you from this...*place*."

"I will not return to that wall. I'll stay right here if it's all the same to you."

"Ah, so it is true." The Angel cocked his head, peering closer. The corner of Merrick's lip lifted in a snarl until Alielle drew back. "You suffer much, Kynd."

Merrick didn't respond to the observation. Of course, he suffered. He'd *been* suffering for more than two thousand years, right along with the rest of the Kynd.

"But this is too much." Alielle tilted his head once more. "All for love? It seems a steep price to pay." He reached to touch the chimera's back.

Merrick winced. "Worth it."

"You would do this again?"

"Over and over, Alielle."

"I do not understand."

"Didn't expect you to. Now go, you're cramping my alone time."

"Not until I finish what I have come to do."

"Suit yourself."

241

S. C. Dane

"Are you not even interested in why I am here?"

Sighing, Merrick sat back up since the Archangel wasn't going to leave him alone. "No, I am not interested in why you are here."

"I have a message from the Big Guy aloft."

"Oh, yeah? I have one for him, too."

"That is hardly the attitude to take when He offers you freedom."

Careful not to pull on the skin of his back too much, Merrick sat up straighter.

"I thought that might get your attention."

"What are the conditions?"

"So suspicious."

"*Alielle*. The conditions." There would be strings attached to this offer of freedom, the chimera knew that only too well. Anything God did had its objectives.

"In exchange for your return to the Chosen One—"

"Wait." Lifting his hand engaged his back muscles, and Merrick bit down on an involuntary gasp. Grinding his teeth, he asked, "The Chosen One? Angelia?"

"In this case, yes. Angelia Delacroix is your Chosen One."

"*My* chosen one. As in there are others?" He knew there was something special about her. But others? Were there more women in the worlds fated for the Kynd?

"Precisely. For as many Kynd as there are, there is a Chosen. A life-mate who shows them the true meaning of love."

As his Angel had done for him. Although he rotted, tortured in this prison of Dis, his heart and soul were not here. They were safe, residing within his beautiful human woman. He had circumvented his fate, tricked his God. Or had he? Alielle was here, after all, explaining to him about the Chosen Ones.

"The soulless thief? Our easy passage through Hell?"

"Orchestrated. To a degree."

Figured. Merrick's old rage swelled, then evaporated. *My fate isn't so bad.* But if he could be returned to his Angel? If he could help the Kynd find their life-mates, convince them such a thing existed? Free them from their granite fates.

For the first time in weeks, his heart rammed crazy in his breast.

242

Hope.

Suspicion dogged its heels, and Merrick rose unsteady to his feet. *Throttle Alielle for what they've done.* Wouldn't that make a pleasant gift to God—retribution for the millennia of suffering his Kynd had endured. They had not chosen sides, so God had sought to teach them a lesson.

Begrudgingly, Merrick conceded a hand well played. The centuries had been worth it now he had his Angel. "What do I have to do?"

"Help your brethren find the word of God."

"The Scriptum? It's in my Angel's hands already. You know that."

"No, not the Scriptum. The word of God, as you know, is everywhere. In everything."

"So, I'm supposed to help my brothers find something we don't know we're looking for?" God and His mysterious objectives. *I should go to the source and throttle Him, instead.* Alielle's sad gaze weakened his knees. Merrick sat back down, defeated.

"The relic is not as important as the quest itself, Kynd. You know this now. You understand the value of true sacrifice. *Of true love.*"

So he did. Would his brotherkynd avoid their stone deaths if they could learn the same?

Now that we are ruined. Who would want such damaged goods, especially when all God's creatures were conditioned to despise the Grotesques?

"It is a tall order, I know." Alielle's compassion washed over Merrick, squeezing his bruised muscles so he trembled.

He fisted his clawed hands to quiet his shivering body. Yet, the truth in Alielle's words flooded him with hope. His Angel had seen beyond his stiffening skin, beyond the rage. Because she was Chosen. *One of thousands.*

It could be done. He was living proof it could. Though if he went to her, would she still want him? She was on the surface now, returned to her life, her cherished family. Would there be room in it for him?

Merrick stared down on himself, assessing the damage. He wasn't even a whole chimera any more. His wings had been mutilated. *He* was mutilated. There'd been too many deaths at his hands. Killings he'd become proud of, even while his skin hardened and his soul thinned into nothing. He would be a burden, a liability. There would be retribution sought from those avenging the thousands he'd killed as Guardian.

He would put his Angel in harm's way being at her side. *Talk about damaged goods.*

Confusion warred. At once, his heart soared with the joy of being reunited with his Angel, while it plummeted with dread. "What if she…" His cinching throat strangled his words. She would not accept him as her life-mate, not when his mere presence would endanger her, her loved ones. Not when he had betrayed her.

"Rejects you?" Alielle leaned back. "Do not look so fierce, chimera. Your fears are no different from any of those who love with all their might."

"It's possible." He had abused her trust in him. At least, if he remained a prisoner in Dis, she could not give him back his heart, return his soul. It had taken him centuries to feel whole once more. He coveted the feeling and wasn't eager to lose it, no matter what was happening to his body now.

"Yes, she could spurn you. But how will you know if you do not give her the chance to prove her love as you have done?"

"You're a pain in the ass, Alielle. Always were."

"You are wasting time best spent with your Chosen One."

"If she'll have me." In Hell, at least, he had his memories, where his Angel would always love him in return, no matter what he had done or had done to her.

"If she will have you," the Angel echoed.

* * * *

The orchestra thrummed too loud, the myriad faces too distorted as they leaned toward her, offering Angelia their congratulations. Liaison to the Kynd? How extraordinary! What an honor! So difficult, when one of them stands accused of murdering Aro. But of course, you're up to the task, darling!

Blabbity, blah, blah.

Swirlings of expensive silks, stiffly ironed tuxedoes. A veritable sea of Others. Vampire, ghoul, fae. Every representative of every realm in attendance, curious to meet this ambassador to the Kynd, the woman who survived Hell, only to come back burdened with the Grotesques.

Willingly.

Anton Delacroix's human daughter, who *lived with* the Grotesques. The horror! The shame of it! If she caught one whisper of that ilk in her own ears, she was going to go ape-shit crazy, designer dress be damned.

Mere human she might be, but she wasn't harmless. Nor was she an imbecile. The only reason behind the huge attendance was curiosity. Everyone wanted to see a Grotesque. They had been asking her all night how they were, veiling their inquisitiveness behind concern, when what they really wanted to know was *where* the mysterious creatures were.

"Miss Delacroix! What a coup from such a meek one as yourself! A true wolf in sheep's clothing."

Spinning on her high heels, Angelia gripped tight to her champagne flute before she whoopsied it all over the faeline sliding toward her on legs too long and lethal. For the men, at least.

"Gistelle, so nice to see you." One more lie tonight and Angelia might just get to meet Kharon the Ferryman, after all. The faeline had worked as one of Aro's key operatives and had lorded her eminence over those relegated to the dusty chambers. Those like Angelia. "You put your credit cards down long enough to attend my party. How thoughtful."

Painted lips pursed then spread into a pasted smile. "Yes, well."

Angelia pressed the manicured fingers offered to her, slathering on her own fake smile. *Must do this.*

"Tell me, Angelia, are these Kynd as hideous as the rumors say? Or do they come with fringe benefits?" The faeline hoisted one eyebrow, her innuendo clear. As was her revulsion.

Angelia felt her cheeks bloom hot. Like a fool, the faeline interpreted her high color for embarrassment.

Gistelle plowed on, oblivious, sharpening her claws. "A terrible pity what happened. We will miss Aro tremendously. He was the life's blood of our elite, little band." Even sipping from a glass, the faeline could bite.

"Yes, well," Angelia mocked, her smile hardening. "It's hard to lead when your head's *missing*." She'd have loved to have seen the expression on the vampire's face when Darken's scythe had slipped across his pretentious shoulders.

S. C. Dane

Ignoring present company, she scanned the crowd, taking note of those attending her "celebration." *She* wasn't celebrating and had only agreed to attend this charade because the Triumvirate insisted, reminding her of the importance of such gatherings.

"It is your chance to do inventory," her father had said. "To take stock of those who fall under suspicion." He should know. How many of these parties had he and his family attended during her short lifetime? Too many.

Nevertheless, here she was, carrying on the tradition.

The spacious ballroom was crammed. Minus the Kynd, who were not ready for public anything. They were still reeling from their unexpected expulsion from Hell. Darken seemed the better recovered of all of them, but that wasn't saying a heck of a lot. It was like comparing dog shit to horse shit. Which one would you really want to step in?

Angelia cast heartfelt thoughts out to them, careful to keep the mental vibrations shielded from the mind readers in the room. She surreptitiously eyed the ghouls by the bar.

There was a human attending her party, his arm jealously clutched by a feline shifter. A tricky match, but not an impossible one.

Tears stung her eyes as her thoughts returned to her chimera, who had never once hurt her, not even when their bodies were joined and he'd discovered the transcendent joys of a woman's flesh.

When we'd bonded.

Her hand reached out involuntarily, as if he'd be there like he'd always been. As though he was now within reach. A smooth palm caressed her grasping fingers.

"Chickie, the party is winding down." *Her father.* Stepping in close behind her, her pillar whenever she needed one.

She resisted leaning against him. *Because he isn't Merrick.* She tightened her fingers, bussed a kiss to his cheek. "Thanks, Papa." As always, he knew her feelings, was there to comfort her as best he could. She smiled up at him. "Where is Mom?"

He tossed his head, indicating the corner where she'd last seen Kristov. "She's gone to effect a rescue." A gorgeous nymph was practically dry humping the Vampyre's hip as she threw her head back to laugh at something he'd said. Poor guy. He looked like he wanted to

246

teleport through the floor. Or twist the woman's head from her shoulders.

Strange. Angelia thought he'd relish the attention from such a beauty. Come to think on it, she'd never seen Kristov flirting at any of these parties. "A rescue, huh?"

He took her question as rhetorical and didn't answer her. "It would not be unseemly for you to excuse yourself, Chickie. *A busy day tomorrow* is always a good alibi."

She smiled up at her father. "You would know."

He nodded, grinning like a co-conspirator.

She wouldn't be lying. She did have a full day scheduled. The most important item on her list was visiting Drakus, who had taken up her father's offer of sanctuary with the Triumvirate. Of all the Kynd who'd voluntarily left their posts to help Merrick, the dragon was the most damaged.

She didn't know what in God's name he'd endured to be worse off than the others, but it was no matter. Like the rest of the Kynd, she would not abandon him. Drakus had risked his life for her chimera; she would do anything she could to help him recover.

It didn't help that God continued to mete out His punishment in the form of stone. The five brothers became immovable at dawn, frozen in granite, looking like the Grotesques the rest of the world knew them to be.

So unfair. And so far, the only information the Scriptum yielded about that was finding the word of God. Whatever the hell that meant. They should be researching Bibles? She'd assigned three ghouls to look into it, in case the key happened to be in any of the ancient Biblical texts the Literati already possessed. Under the pretext of something else entirely, of course.

Meanwhile, the rest of the brotherkynd living with her at the Triumvirate safe house were working at getting a grip on their new lives. They'd retreated to separate rooms, coming together only at night when their fluid bodies returned to them.

Maybe they wanted their privacy, but she visited with each of them during the day anyway. So far, not one of them complained about her invading their space, so she took their silence as acceptance. Besides, she needed the contact. Her heart was killing her, and being with the Kynd relieved some of the ache. Perhaps they understood it was the only thing keeping her together, too.

"…a good evening, Gistelle."

Huh? Angelia looked around to see her father dismissing the faeline. Good grief, this night couldn't end soon enough. She wasn't ready for this kind of social interaction any more than Darken and the others.

"Thanks, Papa." She kissed his cheek then surrendered to the flashing tug of teleportation.

She stood alone in the foyer of the safe house, her father's kiss still warm on her cheek.

* * * *

For a damned Kynd, the waiting was killing him. How late was his Angel going to stay out, anyway? Worry and unease itched his skin as he fretted on the edge of an overstuffed chair pulled a bit too close to the cold fireplace. His mate could get burned, an ember could spark, singeing her. At this very minute, some lecherous nymph could be moving in on her.

Merrick sank his claws into the chintz of the armrest.

His fear was flinging his thoughts all over the Christ-less place. He would wait for her in her suite, where they could have their privacy. *In case she spurns me.* Holy Hell. Her scent saturated this room. He smelled the others, too, knew they were close, that they resided in this cavernous dwelling with his Angel. They had survived to return with her and remained. As they'd sworn they would.

They'd seen her aura, had been attracted to it like moths. The brotherkynd would keep her safe for their own reasons.

The click of the door had him surging to his feet, his thoughts quickening to the fore, the skin across his back screaming in protest at his haste. At least the nubs had quit bleeding. God, he should have cleaned himself up first, instead of letting Alielle rush him here.

He saw her shadow in the crack under the door just before a vee of golden light fanned across the room. His Angel slipped into the room, backlit from the lamps in the corridor. Merrick remained in darkness, rapidly inventorying everything about her. The tired slump of her lovely shoulders, the soft tread of her shoeless feet upon the carpet.

"Welcome home, Angel," he rasped, with barely enough air in his lungs to say anything. He'd never felt so horrifyingly unsure in all his life. She would reject him. She'd be furious. She'd cut him out of her life sharper and cleaner than an Archangel's blazing sword.

"Merrick?" Her shoes hung from her fingers as she peered into the darkness. She let them drop as she reached for the switch on the wall.

"Don't. Keep it dark, please." There had been no offer of a miracle healing for him. God meant for him to feel every bruise, cut, and broken bone. He was a fucking wreck and didn't want his Angel to see it. Didn't want to frighten her more than he was already.

"Why?"

He heard her uncertainty and didn't think it was possible to hate himself more. Apparently, he'd discovered a new low. He was a piece of shit for putting that tone back in her voice. His legs grew wobbly and his knees gave out, forcing him to perch on the edge of the chair like a coward, his hand gripping the shredded armrest to steady himself.

Oh, she wasn't powerless. She leveled a damned chimera, a creature feared for good reason.

"I'm ah…the light hurts my eyes." *Coward.*

She tiptoed toward him, sinking to her knees before him. A groan squelched up his throat, and he clamped it off, digging his claws back into the chintz to root himself before he snatched her up in a bone-crushing hug.

Despite his swollen eyes, he easily saw her muted features in the pale moonlight suffusing the room. She was trying to see him in the darkness, her twilight eyes searching.

So, so beautiful. He palmed his chest where sharp pains stabbed and squeezed his heart. "Angel, I'm sorry."

"For?" She would force him to confess his sins against her, as it should be. He offered her less than nothing by being here, his presence merely putting her in danger. He would apologize and leave.

No. He would say he was sorry and give her the option. It was likely it wasn't his confession she was fishing for, that she genuinely didn't know why he was apologizing. Admitting Alielle was right burned what little pride he had, but his Angel deserved the right to prove her love, too.

Her fingers brushed his knee, jolting his attention directly onto her, where he focused fiercely, riveted by her singular touch. "Merrick? You've nothing to apologize for." She inched closer. Still on her knees, she inserted herself between his bare, filthy legs. With all his might, he kept himself from recoiling lest she take it wrong.

"*I have everything to apologize for*," he snarled.

She was not cowed. Instead, she rose and leaned across him, snicking on the lamp beside them. Merrick flinched, but forced himself to take the hand she offered, noting her delicate tapered fingers, her ivory skin. She assessed him, too, her eyes lightly passing over every inch of his body, intently scrutinizing.

"Come." She tugged gently, and led him toward her bathroom. Without releasing her hold, she drew water for a bath. She positioned him to face it as she moved behind him, running her fingertips along his blood encrusted back. There were tears in her voice when she said, "You lost them." She meant his wings. He had cried for their loss, as well, even though it had been his choice.

"They were torn off the moment the gates closed." He would have nightmares about it, if he ever learned to sleep.

Behind him, he heard the slip of silk and a soft rustle as her dress slipped to the tiles at their feet. He didn't dare think she'd shed her clothing for him. That would be a fall from a height he would not survive if it were not true. Still, he couldn't quiet the fluttering in his chest, couldn't stop his shaking hands.

Without a word, he followed her into the tub, submerging himself between her legs, his ugly nubs glaring at her as he stared at the brass fixtures where warm water still streamed. Gently, she cupped the water over his shoulders, down his back, the pool they sat in growing red and murky brown.

"A shower might be better." He twisted to see her.

"A shower would hurt." Her eyes teased, but there was a grim set to her pretty mouth. With her fingers on his head, she turned him to face front again, and resumed her ministrations.

"That feels good." He meant the cascading of the warm water over his skin, the sense of her naked body near his. For once, his insistent cock lay quiet, floating soft and apparently content between his legs.

Merrick, too, felt contentment steal through him, so his body felt heavy. Like a fine song, the water dribbled, his Angel's hands caressing away the filth. So tender she touched him, his bruises. Even the raw wounds at his back lost their stinging agony, and he slipped deeper under her spell as she worked her own miracle of healing upon him.

Alielle, the sneaky bastard. Had the Archangel healed Merrick, the chimera would not have learned the bliss of a lover's tender touch. He would not have seen the soft shimmer of her eyes, felt the butterfly kisses of her lips to his various cuts and scrapes as she paid tribute to his sacrifice and what it had cost him.

A gentle nudge had him standing, the water sluicing down his clean muscles. She wrapped him in a thick towel, her eyes and hands enjoying his body as she daubed him dry.

"Angel, I—

"Quiet, chimera. There is nothing to say." She led him back to the other room, tugging him toward a bed so soft, it dipped ridiculously as she knelt upon it. "Lay with me."

It was as if she returned him to heaven. Merrick gave a slow shake of his head, even as he laid down with her. No, it was not like heaven at all. This was better. As though she had done so a million times before, she slid her body to fit her back against his stomach and they lay melded together, fitted as though of the same flesh. Merrick buried his nose in her hair, vaguely fearful this would be another of his memories and he would awaken in Hell's prison.

His last thought before sleep overtook him? *My Angel has forgiven me.*

* * * *

She woke feeling heavy, pushed deep into her soft mattress, warm as a kitten in cashmere. Content as that feline while fingers stroked the length of her arm. Up and down, up and down, in a mesmerizing rhythm.

Merrick.

He had been returned to her. No explanation, no warning. It was a gift she wouldn't question. It was enough to have him draped around her, his body firm and whole against her, protecting her.

Well, not fully whole. He had lost his wings.

But not his soul. That was in her keeping. She'd have let no stint in Hell strip him of it, no matter how angry she'd been with him at first. As the days had passed into weeks, and she saw the incremental changes in Darken and the others, she understood why Merrick had done what he had. His sacrifice had been as much for them as for her.

He hadn't told her of his plan because she would have tried to stop him, and they all would have wound up prisoners in Dis. Merrick had given himself so those he cared for would live free. He was so noble, so much more than the wrathful chimera she'd met at the Triumvirate's headquarters.

Angelia squirmed deeper, nestling her bottom against Merrick's thick erection. *So, it works.* She had wondered about that as she'd cleaned him, but he was so near to drifting off, she'd worried he'd fall asleep in her tub.

Merrick had slept.

She realized, too, he'd done so through the night and it was now morning. Light streamed in around the edges of the heavy drapes, and unlike the others, her chimera's skin was still soft and warm, he wasn't immobilized in stone.

The only rigid thing about him was his cock, which he glided between her legs with a subtle rocking of his hips. She felt herself dampen, her inner thighs heat up as they grew slick, and Merrick's shaft slipped easier. From behind, he rumbled some strangled mix of growl and moan as his arms tightened around her. She turned to face him, careful not to hurt him as she twisted over, then snuggled herself back over his erection.

"You're not stone, and it's daylight."

"Should I be?" She saw his curiosity, his concern.

"I don't know. It happens to the others every dawn."

The concern flared vengeful, the gray of his irises flattening hard then fluctuating back to their previous shale depths. "God thinks I've paid my dues." His hips picked up their slow rocking again as he cradled her head in his hands. Caressing her temples with his thumbs, he stared into her eyes, as though looking beyond the pupils and into her.

She felt skewered on the length of that penetrating gaze and couldn't pull her eyes away. He loved her. Though he forced her to see him, too, daring her to love him back despite what she saw in him now. Just because he'd been freed from the Kynd's curse, didn't mean he was done with it.

Unflinching, she took in the bruising around his eyes, which was already fading to yellow and brown. The whites of them were clotted red where blood vessels had burst. He'd been blinded for a while; there was too much trauma to the flesh for it not to be so. She also saw deeper than the wounds, saw how none of the pain mattered. He'd remained untouched because he had already given away the most important part of himself.

The bulb of his cock poked into her folds, and he held his breath, his heart pounding hard enough to seemingly pulse the air between them. He awaited her permission, until she shifted her hips and lifted her knee. On a growling sigh, he effortlessly rolled her onto her back, his muscular legs spreading hers. Careful not to hurt her, he braced his arms at her sides, his broad shoulders bunching to hold his weight, stirring hints of his lion, the latent power of the big cat sliding beneath his skin.

Twisting a bit, Merrick lowered his face to her ear. She felt his breath rush along her temple as he whispered, *"Angel."*

Shutting her eyes against the surging of her own heart, she bit her tongue down on her cry. Then felt the probing of his fingers alongside his cockhead, the trembling of his arm against her shoulder, and she opened her eyes to catch him watching her keenly, his granite eyes locked on hers, spearing her with an intimacy that melded with the long, forceful thrust of him driving himself into her.

"Flesh of my flesh," he rasped. For the fierce potency of his claim, his eyes belied his longing, his fear, as though she could even now refuse him.

"Heart of my heart," she answered, her hands cupping his ass to pull him deeper, her knees falling to the sides to accommodate his sheer size. She locked her ankles at his waist as his hips picked up rhythm, until he thrust helplessly, igniting a flame between her legs, through her core.

Still he did not break his intimate gaze. He drove her higher, building pleasure as they maintained that intense eye contact. "Soul of my soul," he growled, claiming her, his own pleasure revealed in the clenching of his jaw, the desperate thrusting of his body as he begged for more, demanded it, his wanton snarls growing urgent.

"Yes!" she cried, bearing his weight, acknowledging the import of it all, of what it meant to be connected to him. The strength, the loss, pain, and the joy of a shared future. "Bone of my bone, chimera."

Let nothing tear it asunder.

About the Author

S.C. Dane currently lives in Wyoming on a working cattle ranch. When she's not riding horses on the range, she's immersed in her second passion: writing. She loves traveling, too, and isn't sure what adventures her next move will find for her. You can get to know a little more about the author on her website *paranormalromancebyscdane.com*.

Other Works by the Author at Melange Books, LLC

Luna Chronicles, Book 1, Luna
Luna Chronicles, Book 2, Grane
Luna Chronicles, Book 3, Kenrickey

www.ingramcontent.com/pod-product-compliance
Lightning Source LLC
Chambersburg PA
CBHW050501260626
47157CB00004B/1135